The Rocket Scientist

A Dr. Julie McCray Novel, Volume 1

Arthur Geis

Published by Geis Media Enterprises, 2026.

This is a work of fiction. Similarities to real people, places, or events are entirely coincidental.

THE ROCKET SCIENTIST

First edition. January 17, 2026.

ISBN: 979-8994559307

Written by Arthur Geis.

Table of Contents

For Leah and Sharon

Chapter One: Curiosity 2

Mission Control, Jet Propulsion Laboratory

November 2032

Julie hustled into the Jet Propulsion Lab's (JPL) Mission Control Center, knowing she had to find them soon, especially now with Earth hurling toward chaos. The room full of engineers and scientists buzzed with anticipation as she took her position in front of the wall-sized monitor, soon to be teeming with images of the Martian morning. As Director of Mars Programs, Dr. Julie McCray commanded NASA's most heralded project, finding life on Mars. However, for the past two weeks, her SUV-sized rover, Curiosity 2, had failed to discover the elusive microbes she knew flourished beneath the planet's rocky surface.

From their consoles, the staff couldn't see the worry lines etched on Julie's face. Her manicured nails dug into her side as she prepared to announce today's tasking. Taking a deep breath, she turned to brief her team.

"Good morning, everyone. Sol 13." She smiled, taking in each face as she spoke. "Our search quadrant today is Grid 35, mid-Gale Crater, the heart of the ancient lakebed. Our AI analytics predict an 87 percent probability of finding organics there. This is our best chance." Then she pointed to her mission director. "Wake up my boy, Franklin. Let's make it happen."

"Transmitting instructions now, Director," said the twenty-nine-year-old scientist. He wore a T-shirt stamped with *Colonize Mars* in tall white letters.

Julie checked her watch. She knew in seven minutes C-2's antenna would receive her instructions, and the rover would shift from stand-by into active mode. Its bionic eyes would snap open and scan the orange-tinted terrain of the Martian dawn. Sensors would activate and provide positional data to the navigation computer, preparing it for its journey down the steep grade of Mt. Sharp.

Julie mingled with her staff until C-2's images flooded JPL's main screen. A hush fell over the room. Julie turned transfixed, watching the rover kick up puffs of regolith. "What an amazing sight," she whispered to herself, stroking her late father's gold necklace. But her fascination was short-lived. An email from NASA HQ came overnight, needing her immediate attention.

Trudging her way up the aisle, Julie leaned over Franklin's cubicle. "Let's hope our sensor adjustments do it this time. I *know* they're in Grid 35." Her shoulders dropped, and she whispered, "HQ's demanding another budget revision."

Franklin's eyes darted up at her. "Not again."

Julie grimaced, seeing his apprehension. "I'll keep us whole, Franklin. But we need to find them." She gave him a weary smile. "Call me when C-2 gets the sample. I'm counting on you."

"Will do, boss." He gave Julie an enthusiastic thumbs-up. "Today's the day."

Julie's eyes lingered on the Martian vistas before stepping out of Mission Control, her blonde ponytail swaying behind her as she veered toward her office.

***

It was late afternoon when Julie received Franklin's call that the rover was in position to take the sample. Julie rushed into Mission Control and stood behind her mission director. The main screen showed C-2's wheels locked, ready to exhume the next sample. Then its telescopic arm slowly rose from inside its body, rotated, and extended down to the Martian surface. Its high-speed drill began spinning, creating a mini-blast zone of pulverized rock.

"How are we doing, Franklin?" asked Julie.

"I have green lights across the board, and sensors indicate a high concentration of methane."

Julie refocused on the screen. The drill mechanism raised the soil sample from below and inserted it into the chromatograph-mass spectrometer, scrutinizing it for the DNA of microbial life. When the scan finished, C-2 raised its high-frequency antenna and shot the findings back to the JPL.

"Analysis is on its way, Director. Seven minutes and we'll know."

"I hate this waiting. I'm going to check with our astrobiologist, make sure she's ready. Be right back."

Minutes later, Franklin's voice came over Julie's headset.

"Computer's decoding now," Franklin said. "Just another minute."

Julie came up the aisle, her heart thumping with hope. She turned and stared at the Martian image, waiting for the results. Then she heard Franklin gasp.

"No! Dammit. It's another duster."

The words pierced Julie like icy daggers. Dropping her head, she fought the crushing disappointment. *What am I doing wrong?* Groans from the staff echoed throughout the room. Before she could respond, Franklin leaned back and whispered so the rest couldn't hear. "Director, only a few prime sites remain. What should we do?"

Staring at the rover's image on the screen, Julie folded her arms across her chest, her methodical brain assessing the situation. "I know the methane sensor's right. Search criteria must be off. I'll do a mission review tonight and see what we need to recalibrate."

Julie released her focus from the Martian images. "Move C-2 over to Grid 36 for me. I'm heading home." She gave his shoulder a quick squeeze. "Thanks for your help today. See you tomorrow."

Walking across the lobby, Julie activated the car app on her phone. The usual red alert flashed across her screen: 'Warning! Heat index 117.' She tapped the max air button and continued to her office. After responding to several emails, she packed her briefcase for the night's analysis and waited for her car's interior to become habitable. When the app signaled 75 degrees, she strapped on her government-issued breathing mask and steeled herself for the harsh conditions as she stepped out into the sweltering parking lot.

The acrid smell of gray, polluted air filled her nostrils. Waves of heat rising from the baked asphalt penetrated the soles of her running shoes. By the time Julie reached her EV Subaru wagon, sweat streamed down her back, creating dark streaks on her blue cotton shirt. Unplugging the car from the charging station, Julie climbed inside. She leaned toward the vent, letting the micro-filtered cool air blast across her face. Refreshed, she switched on the motor. The radio news blared through the car's speakers. She paused to listen.

"President Martha Jennings and the leaders of the 'Top Nine' polluting countries agreed to the Climate Initiative today, an emergency plan to slash Earth's accelerating temperature propelled by several major volcanic eruptions over the ..."

An incoming call silenced the announcer. The ID displayed Michael Boxman. Julie's stomach tightened, anticipating the NASA Administrator's inquiry. "Hello, Doctor Boxman, it's...

"What's today's report, Dr. McCray? Find'em yet?"

"Not yet, but Curiosity's performing great. I know we'll..."

"Look, I know you're doing your best, but there's no way to sugarcoat this. Jennings wanted your budget for her Climate Initiative, but I bought you a little time."

"President Jennings? I thought you were calling about my budget submission. I didn't cut any ..."

"That too. I'm closing out the Jupiter mission instead."

Julie's eyebrows lifted. "Great. Thank you, but why the reprieve?"

"You're my brightest astrophysicist, and NASA needs a win. I need a win. Your Mars mission is our best chance. So, find those microbes. I can't hold her off for long." Click.

Julie stared at the JPL letters above the entrance, feeling both relief and urgency from Boxman's call. She glanced at the briefcase containing her computer, knowing the solution lie inside if only she could unlock it. Then her thoughts shifted to Boxman's budget move. He recognized her talents and fast-tracked her up the ranks, passing those with more seniority. But she knew Earth's climate crisis made funding space exploration unpopular, and Boxman needed a success to hold off the politicians. *He wants me to save NASA.*

She leaned back against the headrest, her damp shirt clinging to her skin. She thought about the bureaucratic and technical hurdles she had overcome, and finally, after six years, her rover was exploring Mars. But now, President Jennings wanted to snatch her historic mission. Glancing in the rearview mirror, she gave herself a determined stare. *Got to figure this out.* Then she put the gearshift into drive and spun out of the parking lot.

***

Julie unlocked the door to her one-bedroom condo. Waiting for her on the entranceway rug was Gizmo, her orange and white Persian cat. His soft purring and welcoming meow eased the tension she carried from the day's disappointing search. She scooped him up and smiled as his scratchy tongue scraped against her cheek. "Hi, buddy. Let's go into the kitchen. I need an emergency wine." Walking past her bare walls, she set her computer on the counter and poured a small glass of buttery chardonnay. She took a long, savoring drink, grabbed a ready-made meal from the refrigerator, and slid it into the microwave.

After a quick water-saving shower, Julie strolled back into the kitchen, feeling refreshed, her damp hair hanging limp on her shoulders. She fed Gizmo, and when the microwave chimed, she placed the steaming pasta on the counter beside her laptop. Stabbing her fork into her mindless meal, Julie booted up her computer with renewed determination.

She believed the search criteria led her rover to the wrong locations. Engaging her mission's AI analytics, Julie arranged a series of trials, manipulating key variable combinations collected from C-2's thirteen days of exploring. Gizmo hopped up on the counter and snuggled next to the computer. Julie petted him, took the last sip of her wine, and began her experiment. Over an hour later, her analytics revealed no new clues. She rubbed her neck and stretched, not wanting to give in to the frustration.

"I'm getting nowhere, Giz. No matter what variables I manipulate, the program spits out the same search criteria." She closed her laptop. "Going to be another long night, but right now, my brain needs a break." She brewed some tea and retreated to the soft leather sectional in the living room, perforated with Gizmo's claw marks. He trotted behind and climbed into Julie's lap. "Let's watch *The Martian*. That always cheers me up." She stretched her legs on the ottoman and selected it from her movie library.

Julie eased into the plush cushions and sipped her lavender brew, its fragrant aroma soothing her. "C-2's performing well. He's dependable, just like you," she said, stroking Giz's head.

Minutes into the movie, Julie laughed, giving her a brief respite from her Mars dilemma. "Look, here's where he blows himself up. He forgot about the oxygen he exhaled and ... Wait." She put Gizmo aside and paced around the living room, her heart racing with newfound hope. "Oxygen, of course ... Think ..." After another two laps, she stopped and slapped her thigh. "It's the subsurface ice particles." Chest heaving, Julie grabbed her phone and called Dr. Marge Jamison, her number two, supervising the night shift.

When she answered, Julie gasped, "I know how to find 'em, Marge. It's the chlorates. Pair them with the methane. Where there's both is where we'll dig."

"But Julie, C-2 doesn't have the instrumentation."

"I know. That's why we missed it. Program the Mars Reconnaissance Orbiter and have it scan the Gale Crater."

"Ya know, *two* of us could bang this out a lot faster."

Julie grinned. "I'm on my way. Call in Franklin, too."

Chapter Two: Realignment

Julie rushed to the JPL, where over the next hour, she and Marge reconfigured the MRO and sent instructions for the satellite to scan Grid 36. When the MRO beamed back the chlorate locations, their search program recalculated new coordinates, and Franklin transmitted them to the rover. Fifteen minutes later, Julie's mouth turned dry as sandpaper as she watched C-2 journey to the nearby extraction site and retrieve the new sample.

Franklin leaned back in his chair. "Hey, while we're waiting, fill me in. What's the deal with the chlorates? I'm not much of a chem head."

"Sure," said Julie. "Concentrations of salts, particularly chlorates, mix with other minerals, creating a chemical reaction generating heat. This liquefies the subsurface ice particles, and the resulting brine is similar to ocean water."

"Cool," said Franklin. "Why didn't we figure this out before?"

"Instrumentation limits on C-2. Thought the methane sensor would be enough," said Julie. "My mistake."

"The chlorate variable is brilliant," said Marge. "How'd you come up with it?"

"In *The Martian*, when Watney ...."

Marge and Franklin burst out laughing. "Watching it again?" teased Marge.

Julie shrugged. "He's inspirational. Never gives up." She motioned for Marge to step to the back row. Julie slipped her hands into her jeans pockets and leaned in close.

"The chlorates have got to be it," she whispered, her voice tense.

Marge's forehead wrinkled. "You're not convinced? What's going on?"

Julie stared at her feet. "Boxman told me if we don't find the microbes soon, President Jennings will grab our funds." Then she locked eyes with her colleague. "The President, Marge. If I'm wrong, it's mission over. And our dreams along with it."

She grasped Julie's elbow. "Look, if this sample comes up negative, we'll analyze the data, and you'll come up with the right answer. Like always."

A weak smile crossed Julie's face. "Thanks. Appreciate the ..."

Franklin turned and waved. "Director, analysis is loading. Time to find out." Julie swallowed hard as she and Marge hustled in behind him. "Please," murmured Julie, her voice barely above a whisper. Marge put her arm around her. They both stood like statues, watching the data flood onto Franklin's screen.

He spun around, eyes wide and yelled, "We've got them! We've got organics!"

Julie pumped her fists. "Yes! Finally!" Satisfaction raced up her spine like a warm soothing salve. She grinned at Marge and said, "Franklin, put the results on the main monitor. Everyone needs to see this."

She bolted to the front of the control room. Three distinct bacterial DNA patterns exploded onto the giant screen, proving Julie's theory. Joyful tears flooded her eyes, and she gazed upward. "Thanks, Dad. You always believed in me."

The night staff leaped to their feet, yelling and embracing each other. Watching them revel in the moment, a wave of joy swelled inside Julie. When the pandemonium subsided, she raised her fist and boomed, "We did it! We're the first to find life outside Earth. Thank you all so much. It's a great day for science. Wow, I can hardly breathe."

Her staff cheered her again as Julie put her hand on her chest. Grinning, she held up her hand to quiet them. "Thank you. We're now on communication lockdown until NASA tells us how they want to handle the announcement. Everyone got it?" Her team mumbled acknowledgment. "Good. Franklin and Marge, I need to see you in my office. We'll be back in a few."

The three scientists gathered around Julie's conference table, all sporting radiant smiles. "We just made history," beamed Julie. "And I couldn't have done it without you. Thank you." She opened her office fridge and pulled out a bottle of Schramsberg. "I've been saving this for the day we proved Mars is a living planet." Julie poured three glasses, the bubbly foam spilling over the sides.

"Six long years! Here's to us," toasted Julie. They clinked their glasses and took a sip.

"I have something to say, too," said Marge, leaning in and raising her glass.

"Julie, with all the cuts, I don't know how you convinced Boxman to approve the exploration phase, but we wouldn't be here without you fighting for our mission." They clinked and sipped again.

"Comes from my dad." Julie touched her cross, her voice softening. "He told me never to stop chasing my dreams." Her lips quivered. "He's a part of this moment too."

Marge raised her glass again. "Here's to your dad."

After finishing their drinks, Julie said, "Thanks, Marge. That was nice." Then her tone became serious. "Okay, back to work. Franklin, secure the DNA data. Only Marge and I can have access. Then, identify the next sample sites. We'll start there with the morning shift."

"On it, boss," said Franklin, and he spun out of the room. Julie pushed up from the table. "Time to tell Boxman. Can't wait to hear his reaction." She hovered over the phone with Marge next to her.

"Damn, McCray. What is it? It's four AM."

"We found life on Mars, Dr. Boxman," gushed Julie.

"What? Did you say... Hold it. You have absolute proof?

Julie gave Marge a knowing look. "Yes, Dr. Boxman. It's definitive."

"Thank God. Congratulations, Dr. McCray. I knew you could do it. Now, lockdown communication and retrieve more samples. We'll need robust findings no one can dispute. Then we'll tell the world. It's the greatest discovery in NASA history. The publicity will get us the funding we need. Call me when you have them. Again, great work." He hung up.

"Wow. That felt awesome," said Julie, grinning at Marge. "Let's write the press release." The two scientists dove into their task, wordsmithing back and forth when Julie's office door flung open, and an intern barged in.

"Dr. McCray," she wheezed. "Franklin said come quick. There's big trouble."

Julie rushed into Mission Control. The red warning lights flashed. She glanced at the main screen on her way to see Franklin, and her heart sank. 'Loss of Signal' scrolled across the blank screen.

"What happened?" asked Julie, reaching his workstation.

Franklin sat frozen-like, staring at his computer. He looked up at Julie, his voice trembling. "C-2 stopped functioning. I initiated an emergency reboot. But ..." He winced, shaking his head. "Curiosity's dead."

Chapter Three: Deception

Same Time, CIA headquarters, Langley, VA

Strolling into his office, CJ Jackson, Deputy Director of Special Projects, set his morning coffee on the desk, straightened his six-foot frame to attention, and saluted the small-framed picture of two grinning Army soldiers dressed in combat uniforms. "Morning men. Let's get to it."

Clicking on his computer, he reviewed the overnight intel summary, pleased to see progress on his most recent assignment. But before he could finish, a Level Three emergency message shot across his screen. The warning came from NSA's Senior Analyst, Layla Burton. CJ's stomach knotted. He swept his hand through his wavy brown hair and whispered his mantra, "That was then, this is now," as he contacted the analyst.

Burton's image popped up on his wall monitor. Sitting on a silver metal chair inside a featureless conference room, Layla tapped her blue computer stylus on the tabletop like a hard rock drummer. Her long red hair, streaked with vibrant green accents, framed her face and the tips of her lightning bolt tattoos peeked out from under her sleeves. Layla's wired eyes greeted him.

"What's the emergency, Ms. Burton? You look like you're on your third Red Bull."

She pushed up her lime-colored glasses. "Another spike in cyber-attacks targeting NASA's personnel," she said, her words clipped. "A thousand files been hit."

CJ's brown eyes grew wide. "You confirmed the source?"

"Chinese. Ministry of State Security. Like before. Probed travel history and salary."

"Dammit. Her again." CJ shifted in his seat. "Searching for informants. What's your plan?"

"We've flooded NASA with thousands of fake employees to throw them off. We're investigating the compromised records. We'll check their bank accounts, credit card spending, the usual. I'll let you know if someone pops up."

CJ nodded. "Good. I'll coordinate with Beijing Station." Then he leaned back in his chair. "Saw your JPL summary in the overnight brief. Nice work with McCray."

"Yep, the Mars lady. Everything's secure."

"The Chinese know she's searching for life up there." CJ paused and stroked his chin with his thumb and index finger. "We'll need to protect her now. Is it ready, Ms. Burton?"

Determined green eyes flashed back at him. "I'm on it. Package's in place. Effective tonight."

CJ waved his hand, and Layla's image vanished. Looking out his office window, he knew the devious Minister of State Security, Liu Wang, was behind the NASA hack. Reaching into his pocket, he grasped his amethyst worry stone, feeling its cool, reassuring surface against his palm. The intrusion was too obvious for a person as sophisticated as Wang. *What's she really after?*

***

Mission Control

JPL, Pasadena, CA

Julie's fingernails dug into her palms, glaring at Mission Control's lifeless screen with its fatal 'Loss of Signal' message. *I can't believe this is happening.* Marching to the front, Julie turned and directed her staff.

"Listen up. I need answers." Julie pointed as she spoke. "Marge, call Innovative Science and get them working. Franklin, get your team to examine C-2's activities right before we lost contact." Julie planted her hands on her hips. "I want to know what happened in less than sixty. Let's move."

Shuffling back into her office, Julie loomed over the phone. She punched in the first four digits then stopped, putting the phone back in its cradle. Julie sat rubbing her temples when her eyes landed on the framed picture resting on her desk. She was ten, hugging a small white telescope with her dad smiling behind her. "Well, dad, this'll be fun."

"Dammit," growled Boxman after hearing Julie's report. "If you managed your subcontractors better, your equipment wouldn't fail."

Julie didn't respond, not rising to the bait of getting into a pointless argument. Silence hung between them until Boxman sighed into the phone. "We can't communicate our success with only one data point. They'd laugh me out of the room." Another sigh. "What about Innovative Science?"

"Marge is organizing them. I know we can figure this out and get the samples, but I wanted you to hear about the situation right away."

"I appreciate that, Doctor." He stopped, and his tone shifted. "Listen, the political pressure is enormous. If the failure turns out to be a management screw-up, they'll look for someone to fire. That'll be you, and NASA's funding will dry up as a consequence. Get it fixed."

The phone clicked off as Franklin and Marge charged into the room. Julie's grimace vanished from her face a second too late.

"Boxman?" Marge asked.

Julie nodded. "I told him."

"What'd he say?"

Julie waved her hand. "Not worth getting into. Any news?"

"Yeah, it's bad," said Marge with a steady voice. "Innovative's preliminary analysis indicates a critical malfunction, an unrecoverable one. Their full team's on the way in."

Julie frowned. "What's the basis for their conclusion?"

"They said they've only seen something like this when the communication module receives a power surge, which fries the components."

"Franklin?" Julie asked.

He shook his head. "We did detect a high-energy signal right before we lost contact. It hit shortly after Curiosity transmitted the DNA analysis. Could've been a gamma-ray burst. Rare, but it would be enough to toast the transmitter."

"Doesn't make sense." Julie stared at the floor, her mind racing to identify the cause. She looked up at Franklin. "Have your team dissect each command and response. That's the place to start."

He picked up his tablet and rushed out, but Marge stayed, closing the office door. "Okay, vent. You look like you're going to explode."

Julie's face flushed. "An energy burst? Are you fucking kidding me? C-2 was performing perfectly. Now, I'm supposed to believe a one-in-a-million gamma-ray event knocked us out right when we discovered proof of life?"

"What else, Jules? Not like you to lose your cool."

Julie gave Marge a quick glance then lowered her gaze. "It's Boxman. Told me if this is our fault, he'd have to fire me."

"What? He's the one who backed you for Director."

"Said he's under political pressure. The volcanoes have everyone panicked." Then Julie paused. "Okay, bitch session's over. Let's get some coffee and make a recovery plan."

In the cafeteria, Julie and Marge moved toward the coffee station behind other JPL employees. Minutes later, they huddled together at a secluded table, steam rising from their dark brews. They deliberated back and forth before agreeing on a collaborative approach for Innovative Science and the staff to discover the cause of the failure. Then Julie became quiet, turning her empty cup back and forth in her hand.

"Talk to me, Julie." Marge reached over and held her hand, their black and white fingers intertwined.

"When I caught Bill with that other woman, I felt blindsided, never saw it coming." Julie gazed down at the table, her voice becoming a whisper. "Today, when C-2 stopped transmitting, I felt betrayed all over again." She looked away, her lips quivering. "Silly, I know. It's only a machine."

Marge squeezed her colleague's hand. "I remember," she said in a soothing voice. "We'll find a way to fix this."

A gritty smile creased Julie's face. "Yes, we will. Now, go home to your little girl. I'll stay with Franklin and get our plan implemented."

"Okay, boss. See you tomorrow." She patted Julie's shoulder as she walked away.

With a refilled mug in hand, Julie walked back to her office. She stopped and surveyed the wall behind her desk. Pictures of past JPL directors shaking hands with presidents, commemorative mission plaques, and astonishing images of the solar system were on full display. She smiled. Two of them came from her missions.

Then Boxman's threat reemerged. Her gaze drifted to the nameplate displayed on her desk, 'Dr. Julie McCray, Director.' *What a steep price I paid to earn that.* Pride and determination rippled up her spine. She grasped her gold cross. "I'm not getting axed just when I found life on another planet."

Chapter Four: Mission Planning

CIA Headquarters, Langley, Virginia

DCI Locke's Office, Same Day

CJ entered Director Phil Locke's office to update his boss on the latest Mars findings. Locke was on the phone. "Finishing up a call," he whispered and pointed for CJ to sit at the conference table.

CJ strolled past the interior glass wall overlooking the courtyard, sixty feet below. His role in the agency was to research and triage new threats or opportunities to determine if they warranted becoming a formal mission for the Operations Division to pursue. The point of their meeting was to determine if the CIA should recommend a mission based on Dr. Julie McCray's discovery.

Pulling up a chair at the polished oak table, he glanced at the plaque on Phil's desk displaying Benjamin Franklin's famous quote: "Three people can keep a secret if two of them are dead." He smirked and thought how difficult it would be to keep the sensitive Mars information from leaking if an ops mission resulted from his brief. Soon Phil joined him, and CJ gave him a one-minute concise summary of his analysis.

Phil asked, "We control the DNA information?"

CJ sat at attention, his back straight. "It's still in JPL's system, but Layla has access and locked it down. Can't be moved or copied."

"Good. What's your assessment of these lifeforms?"

CJ checked the notes on his tablet. "Our AI unit analyzed JPL's Mars data. These organisms thrive in a carbon-dioxide atmosphere, enduring extreme temperatures while being bombarded by solar radiation. The study concluded the DNA could lead to significant breakthroughs, especially in agriculture and climate change management.

"Any downside?"

CJ nodded. "One AI scenario indicated, with a 63% probability, sections of the Martian DNA chain could be combined with other bacterial DNA, creating a highly infectious and deadly organism. Enemies could inoculate themselves against it and blackmail anyone who wants to live or eliminate those they don't want around."

Phil's eyebrows shot up. "And because the biology's not from Earth, we couldn't detect it until it was too late."

"Exactly. Know of any experts with the right clearances to sort this out?"

"Yeah, Emil Grunhart, the Nobel Prize winner. If it's a go, he'll do it. I'll brief Jennings. Advise her to hold off on the JPL cuts until we can organize the project plan with Defense and NSA. Next, any active threats?"

CJ checked his phone. "Yes. Layla tracked another Chinese intrusion into NASA personnel files. Wang's outfit. It's a Level Three."

Phil grimaced. "Damn, she's a pain in the ass. What up with this?"

"Beijing Station says Wang's getting pressure from their generals to establish China's moon base. She needs information on livable habitats. Since NASA has the best one, their analysis is she's searching for informants." CJ looked down at his notes. "Last thing. I put a surveillance package on McCray."

"Little much isn't it?"

CJ leaned forward with his palms open. "Look, if this project's a go, she *is* the only one who can take us to Mars. Don't you want to know who she's bringing home and what her patterns are? Can't parade a liability in front of the President."

Phil waved his hand. "Your call. Let's move on. What about the meeting?"

"Let's do Friday after Thanksgiving. Less conspicuous. Everyone'll be distracted by the holiday. Who should be there?"

"Scott, the Admiral, Space Command, and Boxman. I'll get them. You bring in McCray."

CJ tilted his head. "Wait. Who's the project lead I hand this off to?"

Phil pointed his finger at CJ. "No one. You'll be running it."

CJ's eyes widened. "Me? I don't do ops. Come on, Phil. The risk profile's way up. These scientists have no clue how to keep secrets. They even have conferences with the Chinese and the Russians."

Phil put his elbows on the table, and spoke in a quiet voice. "CJ, you were the one who discovered how the money flowed into Middle East terrorist networks, allowing us to shut them down. You're a hero."

"But then, I could scrutinize every detail and ensure our intel was accurate. I didn't have the pressure of making decisions in real time."

Phil pointed his finger at CJ. "I need you to run this mission. If Jennings gives us the green light, we'll call it Project Magellan."

A bead of sweat trickled down CJ's back. He flashed back to the terrible decision he made in Iraq costing two men their lives. He glared at Phil. "If the Chinese or Russians get a sniff, you know they'll sabotage the shit out of us."

"It's why Defense and NSA are involved. Handle it. Lewis says you're ready."

Phil stood, signaling the meeting had ended. CJ left and pulled out his worry stone, stroking it as he hustled down the hall to his office. When he reached his desk, he called his CIA therapist, Dr. Rita Lewis, and scheduled a session.

***

Julie McCray's Meeting Room, JPL

Thirty-six hours later

Picking the last of her vegetable fried rice from the take-out container, Julie tossed the empty carton into the wastebasket, brimming with two days' worth of food delivery remnants. Depleted coffee cups and energy drinks lie scattered among stacks of computer printouts. Marge and Franklin slumped across from her.

"Marge, what's our status?"

She frowned and shook her head. "We've tried to reboot on every viable frequency, but the rover still doesn't respond. Nothing works."

Julie's eyes shifted to her Mission Director. "Franklin, anything new from Innovative?"

He shook his head and mumbled. "Only the energy burst theory."

Julie's eyes narrowed into slits. "This makes no sense. We've found no technical reason why my boy shut down up there."

Marge tapped the printouts with her finger. "We've been through them over and over. C-2's in the Gale Crater, and we can't talk to it."

Julie stared straight ahead, her jaws clenched tight. Franklin raised his eyebrows and glanced at Marge, who gave him a warning look not to interrupt. Without another word, she stepped back from the table, slung her backpack over her shoulder, and stomped out.

"Wow. She's taking this hard," Franklin said after the door slammed shut.

Marge leaned back in her chair and sighed. "She's a perfectionist, right? Blames herself if anything goes wrong. After two days, we find no evidence why C-2 shut down, except for this improbable burst theory, which she doesn't accept. She's frustrated as hell."

Chapter Five: New Information

Wiley and Wiley Investments, New York

When the phone rang, Fitzgerald Wiley, president of Wiley and Wiley Investments, checked the caller ID and rolled his eyes.

"It's Jerry Aldridge," he said to his granddaughter and fund manager, Emily Woodson, sitting opposite him as he switched the call to speaker.

"Hello, Jerry."

"Hey, Fitz. I'm calling to thank you again for your generous donation to President Jennings' last campaign. And we were glad to appoint your son-in-law, Dr. Boxman, as NASA Administrator, like you wanted."

Fitz drummed his fingers on the desk and gave his granddaughter a knowing look. "How much this time, Jerry?"

"We're gearing up for her reelection run. Can I put you down for another five million?"

"No. Timing's not right for us."

"I see. Well, we're also soliciting funds for Vice President Martin Atkins. He's very influential in the car and banking industries. We're helping ..."

Emily's face perked up, but Fitz frowned. "I see. You're raising funds for his presidential campaign, even though it's years away, so he doesn't run against Jennings and fuck up the primaries."

"Perceptive as always, Fitz. It's how politics ..."

"No thanks, Jerry. We've worked with Atkins in the past, but those aren't strong investment areas for us now." Fitz hung up and leaned back in his chair.

"The lesson here, dear granddaughter," he said, pointing his finger at Emily, "always donate money for a specific favor. Make it a transaction. Get something concrete in return."

"Thanks, Grandfather." Emily smiled and said, "Are we done?" Fitz nodded and gave her a dismissive wave. Hurrying down the hall to her office, she thought, *Does he think I'm an idiot?* When she reached her desk, she called back the president's campaign manager. He picked up on the second ring.

"Mr. Aldridge, this is Emily Woodson from Wiley and Wiley. I listened in on your call with Fitz. I have a party who may be interested in supporting Mr. Atkins. However, this would have to be confidential. My grandfather mustn't know. This a problem?"

"What's on your mind?"

Sitting back in her chair, Emily answered, "That's a conversation I'll have with Mr. Atkins. May we proceed?" Emily listened for a moment then confirmed, "Monday. Noon. The Continental. Got it." She smiled and punched the meeting logistics into her smartphone.

***

Wednesday before Thanksgiving

Director Locke's Office, CIA Headquarters

"What were the results of the McCray surveillance?" Phil asked, his elbows resting on the desk. CJ fidgeted in his seat and opened his electronic folder.

"Lives alone. Her phone calls are mostly to a few friends and her brother, Gary. Moves between work, gym, and home. Rarely goes out. Has a cat. No apparent vices or vulnerabilities. Went through a difficult divorce, but he's out of the picture. No significant boyfriend or girlfriend. No one-night stands during the surveillance period. Work record's impressive. Been fast-tracked by NASA and has lived up to it. Very dedicated, works almost non-stop."

"Sounds like you."

CJ glanced up from his notes. "Work can be a refuge."

Phil stared at CJ. "You comfortable with her?"

"Yeah. She's clean."

Phil's shoulders relaxed. "Good. The meeting's set for Friday, 5 PM. Bring her in."

CJ stood, ready to leave when Phil raised his hand. "Hold on. I checked with Dr. Lewis again, you know, to make sure. Still gave me the green light."

CJ sprouted a grim smile. "I'm glad you coordinate with her. I appreciate that." He took in the American flag standing behind his boss. "I just don't want to let you down."

"Dr. Lewis believes the mission will help you progress." Then he paused. "How are the flashbacks?"

"Better, thanks." CJ slipped his hands into his pockets and grasped his worry stone. "Because of that faulty decision in Afghanistan, I hesitate. Wait for certainty. It's a vulnerability. You sure?"

"I trust you, CJ."

He met Phil's gaze. "Thanks, means a lot."

Phil stood and moved behind his desk chair. "I talked to the Admiral. Convinced him to assign Burton. She'll give you some real firepower. Take away a lot of the fog."

"Yeah. She's good."

"Okay, we're set. Bring in McCray. See you Friday."

When CJ reached his office, he retrieved Burton's NSA's personnel file and reviewed her qualifications. When the screen flashed TS/SI/G/TK, his shoulders eased with relief. Top Secret clearance with Special Intelligence meant she had access to the control system for information about surveillance sources and methods. The Gamma certification allowed her to see intercepted communications, and Talent Keyhole covered secrets about spy satellites and surveillance from above.

His hand rubbed across his forehead, knowing the senior analyst had access to a vast array of intelligence. With Wang snooping around, he knew he would need it.

***

Mr. Blue logged into the anonymous part of the internet known as the Dark Web and stared at the blinking white cursor, waiting for the conversation to begin.

Mr. Green: *Did you capture the DNA?*

Mr. Blue: *An unknown energy burst disrupted the transmission. Was it you?*

Mr. Green: *Not us. She won't be pleased. Think about another way.*

Mr. Blue: *Might not be possible. But in the meantime, I can get you the plans for the habitat structure for your moon mission. Interested?*

Mr. Green: *Hold. I'll check.*

Half an hour crept by before the reply came.

Mr. Green: *She approved it. 10 million for the plans. Contact me here. One week. She still wants the DNA. Figure it out.*

When Mr. Green clicked off, Mr. Blue smiled and poured himself a glass of twenty-five-year-old scotch. He leaned back and took a congratulatory swallow, savoring its smooth, peaty flavor. Spinning his chair around, he gazed into the ornate mirror on the wall. He raised his glass and toasted his success.

"Once I get the money, I'll be gone, and the DNA won't be my problem."

Chapter Six: Building the Team

Friday Morning After Thanksgiving

Julie's Condo

Julie made her way into the kitchen with Gizmo trotting close behind. She put a few spoonfuls of wet cat food into his dish and made herself a turkey sandwich using the leftovers from yesterday's Thanksgiving meal she shared with Lisa, a friend who lived in the condo across the hall. Pouring coffee into her NASA travel mug, she checked her watch.

"Okay Giz, I'm off. Have to beat the Black Friday shoppers. See you tonight."

Hustling to her car, Julie began the short drive to the JPL. On the way, she saw long lines of masked people outside the mall, waiting in the dark for the doors to open. She shook her head and wondered why anyone would stand for hours in polluted air when they could shop online. After crawling past the congested parking lot entrance, she pressed the accelerator and sped through the empty Pasadena streets.

Pulling into her space in the JPL parking lot, Julie donned her mask and headed to the front door. She took two steps and froze. Right above the horizon, she spotted Mars blinking at her through the swirling, thick clouds. Her mind flashed to the image of her rover, last seen stranded in the rugged terrain of Grid 36. *What happened to you up there?* Then, with a heavy sigh, she peeled her eyes away and trudged into the building.

Her running shoes squeaked on the polished floor as she navigated through the maze of empty cubicles and walked down the hall to her office. She unlocked the door and stepped in when the phone rang. She rushed to answer it and placed the call on speaker.

"Good morning, Dr. McCray. I'm CJ Jackson, Deputy Director, CIA. A car is out front to take you to the airport for a meeting here in DC. We'll need your presence for two days. Clothes and accommodations will be provided. This is a matter of national security."

Julie frowned. "CIA? National security? I don't ..."

"I know this is sudden, but you must come to DC."

Julie's right foot tapped on the floor. "Excuse me, Director, I'm not going anywhere until I know what this is all about."

"Dr. McCray, we'll explain everything when you get here."

"The CIA has no authority over the JPL, so you can explain it to me right now." Julie snapped, her face turning crimson. She folded her arms and waited. Silence ticked by. "I've no time for this, Director." She reached for the button to end the conversation when CJ responded.

"Dr. McCray, no gamma-ray burst disabled your Curiosity rover. When you get here, we'll tell you all about it."

Julie gasped, her heart pounded. For weeks, she had agonized over every detail of the mission, finding no answers. How could he possibly know? She glared at the phone, her eyes narrowed.

"Tell me what you know, right now." Her voice trembled, barely controlling her anger at the deception.

"I'm sorry, this isn't a secure line. But your boss, Dr. Boxman, will be here. You should be, too, don't you think?"

Julie muted the call and loomed over the phone. *Dammit, I have to know what happened,* she thought. Boxman will be there. Maybe this is okay. She pushed the speaker button again and said, "I don't like this, Mr. Jackson. I'll come, but you have a lot to explain." She ended the call before he could reply.

After Lisa agreed to cat sit, Julie grabbed her computer and headed to the front door. As she stepped outside, she looked up at the array of security cameras attached to the exterior of the building. *That's how Jackson knew I was here.* Seconds later, a black town car glided up the driveway, and a tall man with a military bearing stepped out. He opened the rear door.

"Dr. McCray, I'm Agent Roberts. Director Jackson sent me. Please make yourself comfortable."

Julie settled inside. She crossed her arms and stared straight ahead through the front windshield. Roberts glanced at her through the rear-view mirror.

"Ready, Dr. McCray?"

"You bet I am."

***

Julie landed at Joint Base Andrews after a fast, cross-country flight on an unmarked private jet. The thick brown air turned the late afternoon sun into a shrouded orange ball as it dipped into the horizon. The plane taxied to a secluded hangar, where a blue government-issued sedan waited for her.

"How long until we get there?"

"'Bout thirty minutes, Dr. McCray."

On the way, she gazed out the window, analyzing her situation. Jackson admitted he knew the cause of C-2's malfunction. How? And why drag me out here at the last minute? Seems unplanned. He said Boxman would attend but who else? The CIA and the JPL didn't work together. She tapped her fingers on the armrest. Did the CIA hijack my mission?

"Comfortable?" asked the driver, interrupting her thoughts.

"Yes, thanks."

Julie looked down and winced. The day after Thanksgiving was a JPL holiday, so she dressed casual, wearing a blue NASA sweatshirt, jeans, and pink Nike running shoes. *Won't make much of an impression in this,* she thought. Reaching for her makeup kit, she refreshed her lipstick, brushed her unwashed hair, and pulled it into a ponytail.

Feeling as prepared as she could be given the circumstances, she turned to look outside and observed her worried reflection in the car's window. This situation was far from the predictable way government agencies acted. She wondered what other surprises she would encounter in the hours ahead.

When the driver pulled up to the main building, she turned and pointed. "Go straight through those doors. Director Jackson will be waiting for you."

Entering the lobby, a man, about six feet tall, mid-forties, and dressed in a gray suit and yellow tie, waved and approached Julie. Having never worked with a spy, she wasn't sure what to expect. She thought he looked more like an accountant than James Bond.

A staff member, walking behind Jackson, stumbled, and the stack of files he carried crashed to the floor. The startling bang reverberated in the cavernous reception hall. CJ spun around, his eyes wide open, scanning the area. *Seems jumpy*, thought Julie. When he saw the scattered files, the tension lines in his face retreated. He straightened his jacket and continued toward Julie.

"Dr. McCray, I'm CJ Jackson." He shook her hand and gave her a visitor's badge. "You'll need to be escorted at all times. Come with me, the others are waiting."

How about a simple, 'Hello, thanks for coming? Sorry for jerking you around,' she thought, clipping on her badge. She followed a few steps behind CJ and scoped out the place. They passed over the large CIA seal inserted in the floor and approached the Memorial Wall displaying rows of black unmarked stars next to a large marble stairway. She stopped while CJ climbed the steps.

"Excuse me, Director," said Julie. "The black stars?"

CJ turned and faced the memorial. "Thank you for asking. Each star represents a CIA agent who gave his or her life in the service of the United States."

"And no names because they were spies?"

"Right. If our enemies knew their names, they would have known how deeply we penetrated their organizations. But the families know. Come now, Dr. McCray, we're late."

They marched up the wide staircase. When Julie's foot hit the top, her heartbeat quickened. She had hoped CJ would have commented on the meeting attendees and given her reassurance about C-2. Julie glanced at her faded jeans, swallowed hard, and strode into the windowless wood-paneled chamber.

Halogen lights from above pierced the darkened room, illuminating a polished wooden conference table with eight matching chairs per side. Switched-off monitors hung on the walls like dark looming eyes. The American flag stood in front. Three military officers in crisp dress uniforms with gleaming stars on their shoulders stood as Julie joined them. Michael Boxman, in a brown suit and tie, stood apart from them. *How's the military involved with our Mars...* A booming voice interrupted her thoughts.

"Dr. McCray, welcome. I'm General Richard Scott, Chair of the Joint Chiefs." He walked over and shook her hand. "This is General Avery, Air Force Space Command. Next to him is Admiral Garza, head of the National Security Agency. And of course, you know Dr. Boxman."

Julie shot him a look, and he gave her a questioning expression. *He didn't know about this meeting either.*

"Thank you for joining us on such short notice," continued the General. "We thought this would be a good time to bring you in without raising too much attention. Please have a seat."

Probably would've dragged me out if I didn't. Julie sat across from the two officers as General Scott went to the head of the table. CJ stayed at the other end.

"Dr. McCray and Dr. Boxman," General Scott said. "Under certain circumstances, NASA comes under the jurisdiction of the military. Congress inserted this clause so the expertise of NASA and its key laboratories, like the JPL, can assist us in times of need. This is one of those times." The General paused, letting those facts sink in.

"Before each of you is the presidential order outlining Project Magellan. We'll ask President Jennings to approve it after your review. It's classified Top Secret requiring you to sign the National Security Letter of Intent before we can reveal the project's details.

Julie picked up the letter and began to read. The General continued, "If you refuse to sign, which is your right, your positions with JPL and NASA will be terminated on the grounds of national security."

Julie stiffened. *Terminated?* She put the letter down and focused her attention on him.

"Any deviation from national security protocols will put you in a deep dark place for a very long time." The General paused, his steely gaze sending a chill up Julie's spine. "However, if President Jennings approves it, an expanded Mars program will be funded and your positions secured. This is all the information I can share with you at this time."

Blood pounded in Julie's ears, processing her new situation. "Hold it, General. First, you drag me all the way out here, in my jeans and sweats, stewing four hours on a plane, under the pretext of finding out what happened to my Mars rover, which you could've told me over the phone. And now, I need to sign a piece of paper, or I lose my job? Am I in Russia? What the hell is going on?"

"Expanded funding?" interrupted Boxman. "I'll be glad to sign." He scribbled his name on the form and sat back in his seat with a self-assured smile.

Rolling her eyes, Julie studied the paper in front of her. *This is all happening so fast.* She felt the gaze of the five men waiting for her response. Looking up, she scanned their faces, finally locking eyes with the General.

"I want to make sure I understand," she said, pointing at the document. "If I sign this, our Mars program might be fully funded, and I'll keep my job. However, there are rules I need to follow, or I go to jail, but you won't tell me what they are until I sign. And, if I don't sign, I'll automatically lose my job. Do I have this right?"

"Exactly right, Dr. McCray."

I don't trust these guys, but at least Boxman's here. Julie touched her cross and planted her elbows on the table. She spoke in a calm but firm voice.

"I joined NASA to add to our knowledge of the solar system, not to be a part of some military-spy program, or whatever this is. And I *especially* don't appreciate being blackmailed into a job I already have."

She paused and pointed her pen at General Scott. "But no one is going to take away my Mars program." She scribbled her name and pushed the document across the table. She folded her arms across her chest. "Let's get on with it."

"You made a good decision, Dr. McCray," said Scott. "Your country needs you, and now you'll know why. CJ, lead us from here."

CJ stood and addressed Julie. "Dr. McCray, the day you called Dr. Boxman confirming Curiosity's discovery, the CIA, in conjunction with the NSA, beamed a signal into your rover's receiver, resulting in an apparent catastrophic failure."

Relief flooded through her, then she eyed Boxman. "See, not my fault."

He shrugged. "I'm finding out about this the same time you are, Dr. McCray."

Glad he wasn't in on it, she thought. She turned to face NSA's Admiral Garza. "Why'd you do it?"

"Because the bacteria's DNA could be incompatible with Earth's lifeforms. If a terrorist organization or an enemy got a hold of it, they could develop a catastrophic bioweapon. The DNA information needed maximum security, more than NASA can provide."

He pointed to CJ. "Go on, tell her the rest."

"We want you to go to Mars and return the microbes to a safe place on Earth for thorough study. Our mission needs to be secret so others won't attempt to capture what might be the most valuable commodity on the planet. I'll share our plan in a moment, but any questions so far?"

Boxman shook his head no.

Julie tilted her head. "You have a plan? I'm not being difficult, Director, but it seems to me when the plan is put together by people with no expertise in planetary exploration, it's not a very smart way to go."

"We're all aware of our limitations, Doctor," General Scott said. "We're simply defining the scope of work. You'll have a chance to challenge and improve on everything we discuss today. Let's continue, you'll see."

CJ shifted his stance. "We've adhered to much of NASA's strategic plan to avoid raising any new alarms with the space community, especially the Chinese. With the public's attention focused on the Climate Initiative, we can accomplish our mission in public view, obscuring our real purpose."

"Wait a minute," Julie said. "You said C-2 had an apparent catastrophic failure. What did you mean?"

"Your rover isn't dead, Dr. McCray," said CJ, reassuring her. "We embedded a shutdown code in the high-energy signal we sent to make the rover's transmitter appear disabled. We can reactivate C-2 whenever you're ready."

Her jaw dropped. "But how did you know how to shut it down? The transmission code in C-2's software is secret."

CJ raised an eyebrow. "Well, we *are* spies."

"You mean you deceived us," Boxman interjected.

Finally, he said something, thought Julie. Not much of a wingman.

"Yes, Dr. Boxman, but let's not digress. Project Magellan has two main parts. First, we'll land a decoy rover in the South Polar region to act as a diversion. At the same time, we'll secretly place a return rocket in the Gale Crater to bring back the Martian bacteria.

"In the second part of the mission, we'll land your astrobots with their HAB laboratory structure in the Gale Crater, capture the microbes, and return them to Earth. We'll study them at our Level Three lab in Area 51. Comments on the scope?"

Julie raised her eyebrows. "Yeah well, it sounds about right, but we don't have enough time to fabricate the HAB, program the astrobots, and build the MAV to meet the looming launch window. You'll have to wait another two years before the planets will be close enough before we can liftoff."

CJ shook his head, picking up two bulging information packets. "With black box status, you won't need to go out to bid or have the normal oversight meetings, saving a lot of time. We'd like you and Dr. Boxman to examine the plan tonight and tell us how to meet the launch window. We'll finalize it tomorrow morning. When the President returns next week, General Scott, you and I will brief her and get her decision."

Boxman stiffened in his seat, and his jaws clenched. He frowned at CJ when he handed him the thick mission portfolio, plopping it on the table.

Space Command's General Avery leaned forward and pointed at the packet. "Dr. McCray, I've included the technical specs of our laser pulse propulsion system. It'll get you to Mars much faster. We're available to help if you want."

"I've heard about your work, General," said Julie. "It's impressive. I look forward to reviewing the details."

CJ put his hands on the table. "Meeting's over. Thanks for coming. Dr. McCray, Dr. Boxman, we have accommodations here in the building, with a full wardrobe and twenty-four-hour room service. Agents are waiting outside to escort you."

Everyone stood and moved toward the door. Julie hung back, waiting to speak with CJ alone. She noticed Boxman left the portfolio on the table and pulled CJ aside. After whispering in his ear, the red-faced Boxman stomped out the door. *Guess it's up to me,* thought Julie. Soon she and CJ were the only two remaining.

"Director Jackson, I have a question."

CJ turned to face her. "Go ahead."

"What's the probability of Project Magellan being approved?"

CJ slid his hand in his pocket and grasped his worry stone. "Hard to say. Jennings is grabbing all the funds she can for the Climate Initiative, but General Scott's in favor of our project, and she listens to him."

"Sounds like a long shot." Julie shook her head. "Okay, let's assume this goes through. Are you the one in charge?"

"General Scott is the Program Executive Officer. I'm the project manager. You report to me."

That's what I thought. "Have you ever worked in space before? No, of course not." She shook her head. "Discovering life on another planet, the most historic discovery of our space program, is my doing, and I don't want some amateur project team micro-managing our mission, screwing it all up. Clear where I'm coming from?"

CJ's eyes flared.

"What I'm not is an amateur in the security of this nation. I'm trusting you to do the space part secretly, something you've never done before either."

CJ looked up at the ceiling and exhaled. "Look, I know this is sudden," he said in a calm voice. "Eight hours ago, you didn't know I existed, and now we're taking over your mission. I'd be pissed too. But you and I need to figure out how to work together because we're both on unfamiliar ground. I won't intrude on the space part if you don't try to be a national security expert. Can we start there?"

"Project expertise aside, Director, I don't like being jerked around. You deceived me for weeks, making all of us at JPL believe six years of painstaking effort had gone out the window. And now, you want to work together as if nothing happened? I have a lot to consider tonight, but my take from this meeting is you need me a lot more than I need you. How about we start *there*?"

Julie spun on her toes, and headed to her room, leaving CJ standing in her wake.

***

One Hour Later

Boxman's Office, NASA Headquarters

Michael Boxman poured himself a scotch. The golden-brown liquid glistened as it flowed over the ice cubes. He put his feet up on the corner of his polished mahogany desk and took a sip. He gazed up at the picture of his swearing-in ceremony, a gift from Barbara, his wonderful wife. He stood next to the President, beaming, as she proclaimed his outstanding qualifications. *Proudest day of my life.*

Then Jackson's insult during the meeting flooded his mind. He has the nerve not to invite me to the President's meeting. And in front of McCray? Wouldn't even be on Mars without me. His face reddened while his fingers strangled the whiskey glass.

He downed his drink in one gulp and slammed the glass on his desk. "Fuck Jackson," he snarled and made the call. "Pull the car around and bring the pilots back. I'm going to New York after all."

Chapter Seven: Seeds of Disruption

Next Morning

CIA Headquarters

After breakfast in her room, Julie opened the closet and leafed through the outfits, all crisp and pressed. She chose a silky white blouse, a blue skirt, a tailored jacket, and a pair of comfortable, matching pumps. She noticed the clothes were all her size, but her thoughts were focused on the mission, her recommendations, and how yesterday's conversation with CJ would carry over into today. Grabbing the Magellan portfolio, she opened the door, and the guard stationed outside escorted her to the meeting room.

CJ sat alone at the conference table, drinking coffee. He looked up. "Good morning, Dr. McCray. How was your evening?"

"I stayed up reading. Where is everyone?"

CJ put down his cup and leaned back in his chair. "The generals left the planning details to us. Boxman got pissed off at the end of the meeting. You might have seen that. Went back to New York and said to leave the planning to you. Seemed like a way to avoid blame if things go wrong. Sound like him?"

Walking over to the table, Julie put down her laptop across from CJ. "Yeah, but you didn't invite him to present the project to the President. He's touchy about those things."

"They told me not to." CJ pointed to the credenza against the wall. "Coffee's over there. Grab a cup and let's get started."

After retrieving her coffee, Julie pulled up the mission notes on her computer.

"What revisions do you have?" asked CJ, his voice calm and businesslike.

Hmm. So far, he seems okay, thought Julie.

"To meet our launch window, we'll send our mockup C-2 to the South Pole as the decoy. It'll shave months off our mission timeline. Adapting our existing HAB design for the astrobots and training them to use our core drilling machine is doable.

"Marge Jamison, my Deputy Director, must know all about this. Can't do it without her." She glanced at CJ to gauge his reaction, but his face appeared neutral. Julie returned to her notes. "We have a launch vehicle already in production and a used SpaceX one from the scrubbed Jupiter mission. Without going out to bid, we can build and prepare the Mars Ascent Vehicle. Those are the positives. But we have two challenges to overcome."

Sitting erect, CJ's fingers were ready to type Julie's observations into his laptop. "What are they?"

"The first is travel time. The positioning of Mars and Earth will be ideal in four months. We'll be 34 million miles away, but only have a three-week span to launch both rockets. Then the planets move away from each other toward opposite sides of the sun."

CJ's nose wrinkled. "Ah, I think you should explain the basics to me before we go much further, Doctor."

Julie took a sip of her coffee. *At least he's not pretending to know this stuff.* "Sure. A day on Mars is 24 hours, 39 minutes. We call it a sol. Mars orbits the sun in an elliptical pattern every 687 Earth days. Because Earth's closer to the sun, we're orbiting almost twice as fast."

"What about the launch window you mentioned?"

She grabbed his coffee cup and raised it. "Your cup is Earth, mine is Mars." Moving the cups, she explained, "Earth approaches Mars from behind then races past it. We're closest to Mars about every 26 months. Right now, Earth is approaching Mars. We have until March 25, 2033, to take advantage of this."

"Got it. Can't be late."

"But wait. For our mission to be successful, we need to launch the Mars Ascent Vehicle and the C-2 decoy first. This will give us another ten days to program the astrobots and adapt the HAB. The MAV needs to launch from Mars by March 25 to minimize its travel time back here. This means we'll only have a few sols to find the living microbes. Timing's tight."

Worry lines creased CJ's forehead. "What's your solution?"

Julie's index finger tapped the Magellan portfolio. "It's General Avery's space sail technology, using ground-based laser pulse beams as the propellant. However, JPL's never used it. We'll need their lead engineer to show us how to adapt the sail to our spacecraft and sync the lasers from their Lawrence Livermore Lab to our rocket after launch."

"I'll arrange it," said CJ, typing in her instructions. "What's the second?"

"The astrobots. Our contractor is behind schedule."

His eyes shot over to her. "Implications?"

"Their role is crucial. The two astrobots power up the HAB, position the core drilling machine, run the analysis equipment on the soil samples, and load the living microbes into the MAV. Right now, they can barely walk."

"That's serious. Can you fix it?"

Julie frowned. "Not sure the current team can. We're giving them one more try. If not, we'll need their top project engineer."

CJ again typed in notes. "Not much margin for error."

"Yes. It's what I meant by needing a highly experienced project team. One slip-up will ruin the mission."

CJ glanced at her. "You implied something a little different, Doctor, but let's move on. Contact me about the engineer if you need to make the change."

Didn't get away with that one. "I will."

She inched forward in her chair and turned her computer around, allowing CJ to see the screen. "I've put together a high-level budget for all this."

As Julie explained her numbers, she noticed he listened in earnest and didn't try to control the conversation. *Maybe he will let me run the space part.* By late morning, they agreed on the mission scope, resources required, and which vendors to use.

CJ closed his computer and smiled. "Nice job, Doctor." Then his face turned serious. "We'll need to route the Magellan project through the NSA and isolate it from NASA to keep the information secure."

Julie sat back in her chair. "Will NASA HQ have access?"

"No." CJ shot her a look. "Only vital personnel. Need to compartmentalize information whenever we can."

"Well, I like less bureaucrats. How do I involve Marge Jamison?"

Walking over to the table, CJ refilled his coffee. "President Jennings returns from her Top Nine climate meeting in a few days. We're on her schedule, and if she approves, I'll come out to read Dr. Jamison in."

"Okay." Julie closed her tablet. *Still one stiff dude,* she thought.

"One last thing." CJ sipped his coffee. "The DNA pattern. We're going to start its analysis."

"Already working on it. I have one of our astrobiologists..."

CJ held up his hand. "Emil Grunhart's going to do it."

Julie's eyes widened. "The Nobel Prize winner?"

"He's worked with us in the past." CJ checked his watch. "Layla Burton, from the NSA, is waiting outside to review several security matters. Give her the DNA information. She'll handle it. See you at the meeting."

***

Saturday Afternoon, 5 PM

When Julie returned from Washington, she picked up Gizmo from Lisa's and carried him into the kitchen. "I missed you, buddy. I'm a little stiff from the plane ride. I need a shower to loosen up." She put food in his dish and headed into her bedroom. After a hot, steamy rinse, Julie made a cup of tea and sat on the couch while Gizmo nuzzled next to her. Turning on her phone, Julie stared at her brother's five unanswered calls she had ignored during her trip. She swallowed hard and made the FaceTime call.

"Hey sis, missed you over Thanksgiving. Didn't you get my calls?"

Julie gripped the cup in her hand, knowing she had to keep her whereabouts secret. "Sorry, Gary. I was buried in work." She took a sip of tea. "Besides, Thanksgiving at Mom's is tough. Part of the reason I stayed here. No offense."

Gary cleared his throat. "I know, Jules. I remember when you came alone. Told us you caught Bill with another woman, and you were staying with Marge."

"I cried the whole time. Ruined everyone's holiday." Julie's voice quivered. "Shit, Gary, why are you going over this?"

"Because it's time for you to get on with your life. I know you're lonely. It's not healthy and you deserve to be happy."

She stared at the brown liquid and whispered, "Bill's betrayal devastated me. I don't think I can trust anyone like that again. And while I do get lonely at times, I have a fulfilling life. I mean, I have you, my friends, and I'm exploring Mars."

Gary tilted his head and spoke with a soft voice. "I know, Jules. But I worry about you. You're such an amazing person. My boys brag to their friends about you all the time."

Julie smiled and blew him a kiss. "You're so sweet." She checked her wall clock. "I'm sorry to make this short. I'm taking Lisa to dinner for cat sitting, and she's waiting downstairs. Talk soon."

***

Julie picked up Lisa in the condo's garage. "Thanks again for taking care of Gizmo."

Lisa waved her words away. "No problem. How'd your trip turn out?"

"Good, at least maybe. I need to go back in a few days."

"If you need me to cat sit again, it's no problem."

She backed out of her parking space and asked, "No, but thanks. I'll be gone less than 24 hours. Where should we eat?"

"I'm in the mood for comfort food. Let's go to Harry's. It's Italian night."

"Cool. I love their vegan meatballs." Julie pulled onto the street. "How was your weekend?"

Lisa's eyes widened. "Let me tell you." She speed-talked about her boyfriend's blowup argument with his sister over Jennings' Climate Initiative during dinner. During the ride, Julie failed to notice a blue Camry, parked across the street, slipped in behind her and tailed them to the restaurant.

Chapter Eight: Turning Point

The White House

Julie followed the security guard through the halls of the West Wing, where she would soon be face-to-face with the President of the United States. Mentally rehearsing the key mission benefits, she failed to notice the priceless portraits and historical artwork lining the famous corridors. When they reached the National Security Council room, a Secret Service agent punched in the keypad code and opened the door. *My future depends on the next twenty minutes,* she thought. She took a deep breath and filed in.

The top-secret room had a low ceiling and felt cramped. Twenty chairs were squeezed around a polished mahogany conference table. Silent monitors lined the walls, and flags of the nation's military branches huddled in the corner. Lush, navy-blue carpet kept the room library-like quiet. Seated at one end of the table were General Scott and a man she didn't know. CJ greeted Julie and introduced her to Phil Locke.

"Nice to meet you," Phil said and shook her hand. "I'll kick off the meeting, and CJ will brief the details. If anything technical comes up, we'll turn to you. If she asks you a question, be direct, honest, and no bullshit. She hates that. Something to drink?"

"Water would be good, thanks." She took a seat across from CJ. "Good to see you again General Scott." He smiled back at her and continued his conversation with Phil.

An attendant brought Julie a glass embossed with the Presidential seal, and she took two big swallows.

CJ noticed the glass trembled in her hand and asked, "You okay, Dr. McCray?"

"Little nervous. Only my career at stake." Julie leaned forward and whispered. "What's she like?"

Then the door sprang open, and President Martha Jennings marched in with her Chief of Staff, Ed Hawkins, trailing behind. Everyone stood. The President made her way to the head of the table. Julie's heart raced up a notch as Jennings' steely blue eyes scanned each of the attendees.

"Morning, everyone. Please sit." She pointed at the CIA Director. "Phil, your meeting. Let's go, my schedule's crammed today."

"Yes, Madame President. With me is Deputy Director Jackson who'll be the point person for the project we're presenting. This is Dr. Julie McCray, Director of Mars Programs at the JPL. I'll start us off."

Jennings waved her hand.

"Several weeks ago, Dr. McCray's rover, Curiosity 2, found evidence of life on Mars."

President Jennings' eyebrows raised, and she gave Julie a quick nod before focusing back on Phil. Over the next several minutes, he and CJ explained the Project Magellan strategy. They finished and waited for the President to respond.

"You want us to go up there, bring the bacteria back, and determine what kind of benefit or threat these bacteria might pose?" Jennings asked.

"Correct," CJ said.

"Who else can go to Mars besides us?"

"No one in the immediate future."

"And we already have the DNA analysis?"

"Yes, with our CRISPR genetic engineering processes, we can replicate the Martian bacteria, but it will only approximate the originals. They're not the same lifeform."

"And you want me to authorize a black box program?"

"Yes, Madam President. We're asking for a presidential order placing Project Magellan under the National Security Act."

"Understood. Thank you, Director Jackson. Take a seat."

Julie perched on the edge of her chair, her eyes fixated on the President, waiting for her fateful decision. Jennings sat up straight and leaned forward. Her determined gaze alternated between the General and Phil Locke.

"The people elected me to solve our climate difficulties. With the volcanoes, the atmospheric CO2 levels have soared past 490 ppm. At this rate, scientists predict, it'll soon be too hot to grow enough food for the world's expanding population. We already have over a million citizens in heat relocation camps.

"If we don't reduce the temperature, the scenarios General Scott has given me all end in chaos. Europe and Asia, same situation. What you're asking me this morning is to divert critical funds needed for the Climate Initiative to what amounts to be a cool science project."

Worry lines creased the President's forehead and she pointed at the General. "What's your assessment?"

"From a military view, the planet's escalating heat is our biggest national threat. However, this discovery shouldn't be ignored. As CJ mentioned, there could be breakthroughs across many industries. My advice is to capture and examine the bacteria as soon as possible."

All eyes returned to the President.

Jennings grimaced. "It could all be for nothing too. Bottom line, since no one can get these Martian lifeforms except us, we can afford to put this mission on hold and go up later." She paused and pointed her finger. "If we don't pull off our Climate Initiative, there might not be a later. Thank you, all."

The President pushed back from the table, ending the meeting. Julie glanced at the others gathering their notes and preparing to leave. *They're giving up!* She cleared her throat.

"Madam President." Three sets of shocked eyes shot over to Julie. "These Martian organisms could be exactly the boost you need."

Jennings' blue eyes drilled into her. "How?"

Julie sat up a little straighter. "Mars is a planet with an atmosphere consisting of 95 percent carbon dioxide. These microbes ingest carbon dioxide to fuel their metabolisms, like we use oxygen. Since carbon dioxide is the primary greenhouse gas causing our planet to overheat, shouldn't we at least determine the extent they could absorb the CO2 out of our atmosphere?"

"Nice try for a save, Doctor." But then Jennings hesitated. She stared up at the ceiling, considering Julie's insight. "There's logic to what you say." She looked over at the General. "Who would do the research?"

"Dr. Emil Grunhart's lined up," Scott said.

"Nobel Prize winner, apolitical." The President thought for a moment. "I'll sign the National Security letter now with the understanding you'll fund Grunhart's study within your current budgets. If he can prove these bacteria will boost our Climate Initiative, I'll fund the Magellan project."

"We'll get the money," said Scott.

"Ed, prepare the document. Let's hope this DNA can help us."

"Yes, Madame President." Then Hawkins pointed to his watch.

"Good luck," she said and strode out of the room.

General Scott shook Julie's hand. "Nice job, Dr. McCray. CJ, keep the project moving. We'll need every minute to hit the launch window."

Phil gave Julie a thumbs-up as he and the General headed out the door.

"You saved it, Dr. McCray," said CJ, smiling.

Julie smiled back. "Thanks." She took another drink of water. "Our environmental crisis is all about planetary science. I simply linked ours to the planetary science of Mars. Seemed logical."

"What's apparent to you isn't always to the rest of us, Doctor. It's why you're on the team. I'll be out the day after tomorrow to read in Dr. Jamison."

***

Next Day

Julie's Office, JPL

With the go-ahead granted by the President, Julie dove in, excited to conduct a comprehensive systems check on C-2 before restarting it. When the analysis from the communications function returned, she gasped, and her hand shot up to her mouth. "Oh, no." She grabbed her phone, her fingers trembling, and sent an emergency message to Layla and CJ.

Moments later, their images popped onto Julie's screen. Layla tapped her fingers on the table while drinking a Red Bull. She wore a neon purple blouse with matching purple horned-rim glasses and had purple streaks running through her red hair. CJ sat in his parked car with a distressed expression on his face.

"What's the problem, Dr. McCray?"

"I'll show you." Julie pressed a button on her keyboard, and an image of two wiggly lines on a graph appeared on everyone's screen.

"These are the transmission frequencies C-2 used to broadcast the DNA analysis to us right before you shut it down."

CJ frowned. "Why two of them?"

"The one on top is from C-2's ultra-high frequency antenna. It handles our transmissions back to Earth because it's fast. This antenna beamed the

DNA data to the Mars Reconnaissance Orbiter. The MRO is our satellite orbiting Mars, which relays data to the Goldstone receiver, part of the Deep Space Network down here."

CJ fidgeted in his seat. "Again, Doctor McCray, why two transmissions?"

Julie shot him a look. "I'm getting there, Director. The second line is from the rover's low-gain antenna. This one is omnidirectional. Its purpose is to receive transmissions directly from the DSN. We don't use this antenna to transmit data back to Earth because it's very slow."

CJ frowned. "Then why use it this time?"

Julie folded her arms across her chest. "That's the problem. We didn't."

CJ's head dropped. His fingers squeezed the steering wheel. "Dammit. Unauthorized access. Why would someone use it?"

"Because no one would track it," Layla said, her voice cutting through the tension. She turned, her fingers flying over her keyboard.

"Correct," said Julie. "The only good thing is the transmission didn't finish because your beam turned C-2 off. The partial DNA sequence took twenty-four hours before it entered our system. We missed it because we were all focused on getting C-2 up and running again."

"I'm tracing it now," Layla said with a determined voice.

"You can? How?" Julie asked.

"I'll explain later," CJ said.

"Got it," Layla said. "The DNA info went into the JPL's Mission Control server before disappearing into the Dark Web. No way to track it."

CJ's jaws clenched. "Now we have to assume..."

"We have a leak," interrupted Layla, her green eyes flashing. "Someone had access to the JPL network and knew when the data would arrive. They grabbed it when everyone was distracted. Easy."

CJ took out his worry stone, rubbing it between his fingers. "It was a perfect plan. Our culprit would've possessed the DNA data, and no one would've known. This person's good."

Julie put her hands on her hips. "No kidding. It's why I'm upset. Look, this type of intrusion doesn't happen at the JPL. It also means this person still has access to our systems and knows how to program my rover. This is a huge threat. You're the security experts, what do we do?"

CJ leaned closer. His face grew larger on the screen. "We find the culprit."

He doesn't get it. Julie bit her lip. "Director, I don't have mission control. This culprit can intercede making about a thousand things go wrong."

"Here's what we'll do" said CJ, his voice determined. "It's likely our thief wanted to sell the DNA profile. Means he or she needs money." He paused, then pointed at the screen. "Layla, probe the personnel files from NASA and JPL. Find out who fits."

"On it." Layla took a sip of her Red Bull and asked, "Dr. McCray, anything you could tell us to narrow the search?"

"Let me think." Julie gazed up at the ceiling. "The last chance to change the program would be right before system lockdown at launch, ten months ago. Anyone hired after that couldn't have done it."

"Good. Who had access?" asked Layla.

"Between our contractors, JPL staff, and NASA, could be a hundred easy."

Layla pushed her glasses tighter against her face. "Not a problem. Our supercomputer can sort them out."

"Okay. What else, Director?" asked Julie, the worry lines still sketched on her forehead.

CJ stared intently into the screen. "First, we need to keep this quiet. If our leak's at the JPL, your scientists might say something to alert the perpetrator and scare him off. Make sense?"

No. Not at all. Julie raised her eyebrows. "No, I don't think making my mission a guinea pig is a great idea."

"It's *our* mission, Director." CJ snapped back at her. He paused a moment then continued, "Since the DNA theft failed, our leak still needs money. If our culprit feels undetected, he or she will need to try to sell something else, but this time, we'll be waiting. Let Layla do her analysis. She'll find out who it is."

Well, she seems on top of things, thought Julie. "I guess I'll have to trust you on this. I don't have time to get sidetracked." She checked her watch. "Anything else for me?"

CJ shook his head. "No, we're done. I'll see you tomorrow to read in Dr. Jamison."

"Okay, bye," and her image vanished from the screen.

"Director, found something while you were talking." Layla's fingers pounded her keyboard. "I used our surveillance program to scan Dr. McCray's security footage."

She took a sip of Red Bull. "This video is when she returned home from your Thanksgiving weekend meeting. You see McCray and her friend leaving. Now watch. See the blue Camry pull out behind them?"

Layla froze the picture, blowing it up to fill the entire screen. "This is the driver. Facial recognition tabbed him a Chinese national working as an agricultural specialist out of the PROC consulate in LA."

CJ pounded his fist on the steering wheel. "Dammit, he's a spy."

"Yep."

"What else, Ms. Burton?"

"The tracking device in her car indicated they went to Harry's restaurant. I got footage from their security cameras. Here it is."

It showed the Chinese spy entering the restaurant about three minutes after Julie. He sat at the bar, but close to Julie's table. Layla froze the video again and moved the pointer on the screen.

"That's a directional mic sticking out the top of his backpack, and it's pointing right at Dr. McCray."

"Dammit." CJ grimaced, staring at the backpack image. "If they're following McCray, it means they're on to us. Any other contact?"

"No. He hasn't returned to her condo, and we have no record of him or the car at the JPL." Layla snugged her glasses up the bridge of her nose again. "I'll keep watching."

"Send me what you have on this guy. We'll keep McCray out of it for now. She needs to stay focused. Good work, Ms. Burton."

Layla waved her hand, and her image disappeared.

CJ gazed out his car window. *Our leak has system access. Makes us vulnerable in about a million different places.* The fear of sabotage knotted his stomach, and his hands quivered, a forewarning of an anxiety attack. He closed his eyes and recited his calming mantra. Minutes later, his body relaxed, releasing its tension.

***

2:12 AM Washington, DC

Mr. Blue: *It will be several weeks before the HAB plans are finalized. I'll need 5 million now and 5 on delivery. Acceptable?*

Mr. Green: *Agreed. I'll send it to your numbered account. I'll have further instructions about the hand-off and will need to know who your proxy will be. We're keeping tabs on the rocket scientist.*

Mr. Blue: *Suggest you back off on her. Makes it harder for me.*

Chapter Nine: The DNA

Stewart Laboratory, Area 51, Groom Lake, Nevada

Dr. Emil Grunhart filed through the last security checkpoint of the Stewart Laboratory, located in the heart of Area 51, and descended three stories underground where the main offices were located. The place was a web of secret activity, and he felt a sense of excitement as he passed several labs on the way to the Director's office to check in. A Swiss émigré who had grown up in the Bay Area, Emil was the director of the Immunology Department at the prestigious UCLA School of Medicine. This was his fourth time conducting top-secret projects at the Stewart Lab.

The energetic scientist approached Major Letitia West's office and knocked on her door.

"Dr. Grunhart, welcome!"

"It's good to see you again, Major." He smiled, went in, and shook her hand. "General Scott said to drop everything and speak with you, so here I am."

"Roger that. NSA sent the Special Access Program file last night. Your instructions are on the computer in Isolation Lab 3. Here's your keypad code to get in. How long are you with us?"

"Yah, thank you. This week for sure." He shrugged. "But I don't even know exactly what I'm supposed to do. It could be longer."

The lab director checked her schedule. "Not a problem. You have priority. When you log in, your lab will officially be off-limits, per SAP protocol. Let me know if you need anything changed. Good luck."

"Thank you, Major."

Emil hustled down the hallway, his rapid footsteps echoed off the sterile walls. The familiar smell of disinfectant crept into his nostrils, dredging up memories of the countless hours of isolation he spent in this tomb of secrecy, cut off from the vibrant life of the University.

He reached the outer section of the lab and tapped in the code on the security keypad. When the titanium bolts snapped open, Emil pushed open the door and entered the lab's buffer zone. It was a carefully engineered space designed as a box within a box to prevent any deadly lifeforms from escaping.

He waited until the negative pressure system activated, and the light clicked green, allowing him to enter the inner lab.

The near-sterile environment buzzed with the low hum of the air filtering equipment. Emil scanned his workspace and confirmed it included the equipment he requested. Stepping over to the computer, he typed in the log-in codes, eager to discover the details of his new assignment. General Scott had only given him a vague description of Project Magellan about a newly discovered DNA strain. He stroked his short white beard as he read the instructions.

Dr. Grunhart, welcome to Project Magellan. In the attachment is a DNA analysis of three types of microbes found in a soil sample by the Curiosity 2 rover in the Gale Crater on Mars. We want you to analyze their properties to determine:

Are any of the three a threat to life on Earth?

Can they be weaponized?

Can they be effective in reducing Earth's temperature and accelerating the success of the President's Climate Initiative?

When your analysis is complete, contact CJ Jackson at the CIA only from this computer. Use the code word 'Magellan.' His information is in the contact list.

Thank you for your service,

General Richard Scott

Staring at the screen, he re-read the instructions again. A chill ran down his spine. "DNA from another planet, Heilige Scheiße"

***

12:15 AM, Reston, VA

Ashton Price peeked into his troubled teenage daughter's bedroom, the soft glow of Katie's nightlight illuminated the peaceful look on her face. One day he hoped she would be released from the torment she felt when awake. But Katie was improving, her therapy gradually taking hold. He crept downstairs and placed his computer on the dining room table. The house had a comfortable quiet; only the muted hum of the air conditioning could be heard.

Ashton stared at the blank screen and made the sign of the cross. "Please, God, send me a job," he whispered.

He logged onto his website, The Friendly Hacker, hidden in the confines of the Dark Web. This side hustle became his desperate lifeline to pay off his daughter's overdue psychiatric bills after his NASA mental health benefits ran out. His heartbeat quickened. A new message waited in his inbox. His quivering finger clicked on it, hoping his prayers were answered.

Mr. Blue: *Friendly Hacker, I am aware of your plight, and I know you work for NASA. I have a special job, but I must remain anonymous. I'll pay you $50k to hand over a copy of the Mars HAB plans to a third party in about one week. 25 now and 25 after delivery. I need to know immediately if you are interested.*

"Holy shit." He stood and circled the table. Questions raced through his mind. Is this a trap? It could be the FBI. Shit. But how does he know my plight?

Sitting back down in front of his computer, Ashton stared at the blinking cursor and began rationalizing. "The HAB is no big secret. There are pictures of it all over NASA's website." He rocked back and forth, gripping his sides. "The money's not for me, and Katie needs her therapy. I have to do this for her."

He bit his lip and typed his reply.

FH: *I'll do it. What are the details, and how do I get the money?*

Mr. Blue: *Glad you're on board. I will send 25k in digital currency now. Send me the account number. Check your site every night for further instructions.*

After Ashton sent the banking information, he sat on the edge of his chair, staring at the screen, praying the money would be deposited. Five minutes later, the confirmation streamed across his screen. Ashton's head fell into his hands as tears streamed down his face.

***

CJ's Visit

Julie's Office, JPL

Marge entered Julie's office carrying her coffee mug and sat at the conference table next to her. "Is he here yet?" she asked.

"Security's bringing him down now."

"Why isn't Franklin joining us?"

Julie shook her head. "Something about compartmentalizing information."

Marge took a sip of her coffee. "I've never met anyone from the CIA. What's your spy guy like, anyway?"

Julie shot her a look. "He's not *my* spy guy."

Marge raised her eyebrows. "Touchy this morning?"

"Sorry, Marge. Not comfortable working with spies. Plus, he's a little stiff." Outside, a courtesy knock came from the door, and the guard brought in CJ.

Julie and Marge stood. "Director Jackson, this is my colleague, Dr. Marge Jamison."

CJ shook her hand. "Pleasure, Doctor. Let's get started. We have a lot to cover." His eyes

darted about the room as he sat down across from the two scientists.

During his explanation of the project and the security protocols to Marge, Julie noticed creased lines on his forehead. He sat ramrod straight, perched on the edge of the chair. His clipped speech came across in a matter-of-fact manner, without much emotion. *He sure seems uptight.*

Marge asked a few questions and signed the documents.

"Can we lighten up a little now?" Marge asked, smiling at CJ.

He stared back, ignoring her comment. "I have some updates," he said "First, Dr. Grunhart started the DNA research. He'll have something for us to review in about a week. Despite the low-gain antenna reprogramming, JPL systems have had no cyber-attacks. But a serious development has occurred." His gaze locked on Julie.

Julie's neck stiffened. "You're looking at me like I'm the problem."

CJ's lips pursed together. "A spy from the Chinese consulate followed you to Harry's restaurant and recorded your conversation the evening after our meeting in DC."

"What? Are you spying on me?"

"You should be more worried about the Chinese, don't you think?"

Julie's hands gripped the side of the table. "Right now, I'm worried about my privacy."

"We've been monitoring you ever since you discovered the bacteria. Had to assess your security risk."

Julie glared at him. "Why haven't you talked to me about this? You can't invade my life."

CJ met her fierce gaze without flinching. "When you signed the national security agreement, the section on personal security clearly states ..."

"Don't give me some fine print bureaucratic crap," she snapped. "What did you do?"

"We installed security cameras outside your building and your condo entrance. We placed devices on your phone and computer to detect any intrusions. Plus we put a tracking monitor on your car."

Julie slapped her palm on the table. "You knew my clothes size in DC, too. How?"

"From your credit card history. But before you get upset, let me explain ..."

"Too late for that."

CJ gazed up at the ceiling and exhaled. He paused and spoke in a softer tone. "Dr. McCray, we had to ensure there were no unstable lovers or any bad habits like gambling or drugs making you a security risk before placing you in front of the President. Make sense?"

"Hmm, what else?"

CJ leaned forward with his palms open. "You're now a crucial person in the nation's security. We need to ensure your safety, especially now with a Chinese spy following you. These methods are for your protection."

Julie took a drink of water, her foot tapping under the table. "Director, we're not off to a good start. First, the C-2 deception, and now I find out you're monitoring me without my knowledge. More deception. How can I trust you?"

He glanced at Marge, then back to Julie. "I realize this is different. Your world is open and collegial. Mine is closed and suspicious. Your definition of deceit is my definition of need to know. The surveillance is intended to shield this project from our enemies."

"Enemies?" asked Marge. She twirled her black curly hair. "I have a child. Are we safe?"

"The physical danger is low. But I'm not taking any chances. The low-gain transmission never finished, but what if it did? What would be the consequences if a terrorist group had bought the DNA on the Dark Web? I'm sorry you feel deceived; it's not my intention. But don't be naïve about who would go a long way to get their hands on your discovery."

Julie pointed her finger at CJ. "If we're not in danger, there's no reason to keep ..."

CJ's face flushed. "Dr. McCray! I'm sorry you're not comfortable. It's not about you. Someone's undermining us, and our surveillance might expose whoever it is." CJ pointed to the wall monitor. "Now, let's proceed with the project review. Where are we?"

Silence hung in the room. Marge's eyes darted back and forth between them. Julie turned sideways toward the wall monitor, her face like a blank slate except her jaws clenched tight. She moved her tablet onto her lap, and with a few keystrokes, the project management software popped onto the big screen.

"Command and control over Curiosity is routed through the NSA network, as you requested," she said, avoiding eye contact with him. "C-2's reactivated, in standby mode. I briefed our personnel on the Magellan project without revealing its real intent.

"The backup Curiosity rover is being prepped, and the MAV assembly is on track. General Avery's chief engineer is scheduled to help us attach the space sail. And Marge is going to the astrobot trials in a few days to monitor progress." Julie clicked off her program and folded her arms, still facing forward. "I've arranged for one of our engineers to brief you on how the rover works. Thought it would make it more real for you." Glancing at CJ, she motioned her head toward the door. "He's outside now."

CJ stood and straightened his jacket. "Thank you, Dr. McCray, Dr. Jamison. Good work." Julie gave him a blank stare and stayed seated. "I'll check in with you next week," he said and strode out the door. Julie said nothing as he exited.

"Holy shit!" Marge blurted out. "We find life on Mars, and now we're in a spy movie, except it's real."

"Uh! I hate this." Julie crossed her arms across her chest again. "Tell me, Marge. Did you buy his protection and 'need to know' stuff?"

Marge tilted her head and faced her. "Well, yeah. Somebody programmed C-2 without us knowing about it. That's alarming. And they're following you. Also alarming."

"How many are watching? Are they listening to me talk to my cat? I feel violated."

"Don't blame you there," said Marge twirling her hair with her index finger. "This CJ, he's an analyst type, right? 'Just the facts' kinda guy. Seemed pretty distant."

"No kidding." Julie reached over and touched her arm. "With what you heard, you still in this with me? I can't do it without you."

Marge grinned. "Like big time. Retrieving our microbes is a once-in-a-lifetime opportunity. It'll be tight, but we can make the launch window, assuming nothing major goes wrong."

Marge paused, giving her a questioning look. "But what about you? You and Jackson got pretty frosty. Can you work with him?"

"Guess I have to," Julie sighed. "But Mr. CIA man sure pissed me off."

Marge fell silent and stared down at the table. Sensing her friend's discomfort, Julie's tone softened. "I agree, this is new for us. I don't know, maybe this surveillance is standard procedure. But this is twice he wasn't upfront with me. My radar's up. Okay?"

Marge managed a weak smile. "Okay, boss."

Julie stood and stepped back behind her desk. "I can't think about this spy stuff anymore. There's too much to do. I'll assign Franklin to configure the space sail. I'd like you to focus on the astrobots. Let's hope they fixed them this time."

Chapter Ten: Making Progress

Manhattan, NYC

Friday Evening

"I'm home," Michael Boxman called out. He slipped off his wet shoes from the rain-soaked Manhattan streets and strolled into their penthouse entrance. Barbara hurried out of the family room and embraced Michael. He kissed and held her tight. "I missed you," he whispered in her ear.

"Missed you too." She looped her arm through his and guided him toward the living room. "Flight okay?"

"Yeah, same as usual."

Barbara looked up and smiled. "I have a surprise. Chef Maitama prepared your favorite sushi."

"Sounds perfect." He tugged her arm closer to his. "When's Emily coming?"

Barbara laughed. "You know, when she gets here."

"Let me make you a drink. I want to hear all about your week."

Michael pulled out the Waterford crystal from the bar and poured a generous measure of scotch into each glass. They settled in the living room. Its two glass walls once offered spectacular views of the city's glittering skyline, now shrouded by the polluted volcanic air. They relaxed in adjacent wine-colored leather chairs, the warmth of their drinks easing the week's tension. Michael slid his hand into hers as they chatted.

Before long, Emily arrived clad a ruby-colored Armani sweater and sleek black leather pants. She stopped at the bar, making herself a tequila on the rocks, and breezed into the living room. Taking a seat across from her mother and stepfather, she flashed a bright smile.

"Cheers." Emily raised her glass to the two of them. "Good to see you, Michael."

Michael smiled and lifted his glass in return. "I love having these Friday night get-togethers. Makes me feel normal. Plans for later, Emily?"

She took a sip and smiled. "Yeah. Meeting up with Jason and Arjun, investment bankers from FNB. They're doing cool stuff with crypto derivatives using some crazy math. Plus, they're fun. Hey, what're we having for appetizers? I'm starved."

"Maitama's sushi. I'll get them," Barbara said. "They're in the fridge."

When she left the room, Michael leaned forward and whispered. "How's Fitz?"

Emily shook her head. "Suffocating. Still has me on a tight leash. Can't wait to go out on my own."

"Yeah, it's your only move. He'll never change, but Barbara will miss you." He paused and took a sip. "How's she doing?"

"Stable. Misses you, of course. Loves managing the bond portfolios." She rolled her eyes. "So boring. But if you're asking if she's ready ..." She stopped and gave him a woeful look. "Sorry," she whispered.

Michael stared into the murky night and drained his drink, the ice cubes rattling to the bottom of the heavy crystal. "When are you planning to exit?"

"Soon, very soon."

***

The Enigma

Same Day, 6 PM

CJ pushed open the door to The Enigma, a sanctioned tavern located across from the Langley campus. Agents could socialize and discuss sensitive topics in a more relaxed atmosphere while adhering to classified rules. He stepped up to the bar and ordered a peaty scotch. Grabbing his drink, he headed to the secure meeting room he had reserved for his project update meeting with Phil. He scanned his ID badge into the reader, and the door snapped open revealing the intrusion-proofed room. CJ slipped into the last booth and waited for Phil to arrive. Minutes later, he walked in holding a beer.

"Thanks for meeting me here," said Phil. "In Congressional hearings all afternoon. I need one of these, maybe two." He took a long pull and said, "How'd your meeting with McCray and Jamison go?"

CJ's eyes darted to the side. "Okay. Dr. Jamison signed on and the security measures are in place. The good news is the mission's on schedule except for some complications with the astrobots. Might need to change engineers."

Phil raised an eyebrow. "Any bad news?"

CJ turned his drink glass in his hand, watching the watery drops slip down the sides onto his fingers. "McCray freaked out when I told her about our surveillance. Got pretty pissed at me."

Phil cupped his beer bottle with both hands. "How'd you handle it?"

He shot a look at Phil. "You micro-managing me?"

"I witnessed Dr. McCray in action. She's a no-bullshit kind of gal. Can't blame her for being pissed, probably felt creeped out. What happened then?"

CJ exhaled and hung his head. "She accused me of being deceitful. So, I explained about the need-to-know and told her there might be other similar circumstances." He paused and sat back in the booth. "Shit, Phil, what else is there to say? Pointless to get into an argument about something I can't change."

Phil's eyes narrowed, but he spoke in a soothing voice. "She needs to trust you, CJ. I know you understand this. She's in unknown territory and only has you as a guide, except she has no idea where you're taking her."

"And?"

"Dr. Lewis says your safe place is to stay detached and distant, but that doesn't help McCray build trust with you." Phil leaned back in the booth, studying CJ. "That sound about right?"

CJ broke eye contact. His thoughts flashed to Nicole, his former fiancée, who said she didn't want to go through life with a damaged man. He took a swallow of his drink.

"These scientists don't understand the risks. I made it clear we're tracking their activities to protect them and the mission from our adversaries."

Phil crossed his arms. "And how'd that work out?"

CJ stared at his glass. "Well, she doesn't trust me much right now."

"Fix it, CJ. We need her."

***

JPL, Pasadena, CA

Marge swiped her ID card through the reader, and she and Julie marched into the massive Mechanical Assembly Building on the grounds of the JPL. In front of them loomed the towering Mars Ascent Vehicle (MAV). It would launch the core samples and the two astrobots from the surface of Mars and dock with the orbiting command module for the return trip to Earth. Its glossy white exterior glistened under the high-intensity lights flooding the space from above.

"They're making good progress," said Marge.

Julie gazed up at the scaffolding surrounding the nose cone compartment. Franklin and another man stood next to it, pointing and gesturing at the capsule.

"That our Space Force engineer?" Julie asked, squinting through the bright lights.

"Yeah, Stu Kaplan. His equipment is by the loading dock." Marge pointed at the massive orange blocks of fabric.

"Those the sails?"

"Yeah. Two of 'em."

They're big," said Julie, her eyes widening. "Let's go meet Stu."

Climbing into the hydraulic lift, they rose to the top of the rocket, joining the two engineers on the platform. Franklin stepped forward and introduced everyone.

Julie extended her hand with a warm smile. "Dr. Kaplan, thank you for coming on such short notice."

"No problem. General Avery explained the situation, and I'm excited to contribute."

Julie slid her hands into her jeans pockets. "How does it work? This is new to us."

"The sail canister will mount on top of the MAV, protected by a canopy. After establishing Low Earth orbit, we'll jettison it, and the sail assembly shoots out, using a mechanism much like a fighter ejection seat, with a titanium tether keeping it attached to the capsule. As the sail unfolds, inflatable booms give it rigidity."

"How big is it?" asked Franklin.

He pointed down at the stack of orange fabric. "Through our testing, we've reduced the diffraction of the laser beam, allowing us to shrink the size of the sail to a hundred meters on each side."

"What do you think, Franklin?" Marge asked.

He stroked his chin with his thumb and index finger before replying. "The modifications shouldn't be difficult, but we won't be able to test the process before launch. We'll have to rely on the Space Force's calculations."

Julie stepped forward. "Not a surprise. Dr. Kaplan, on launch day, could I assign you to synchronize the capsule's orbital trajectory with the lasers?"

"Be glad too." He gave Julie a reassuring smile. "We've done this multiple times, Director. I'm confident we'll be successful."

Julie smiled back and shook his hand. "Much appreciated. It was nice meeting you. We'll let you two get on with it."

On the way down to the assembly floor, Julie turned to Marge. "Impressions?"

"We're moving fast." She raised her eyebrow. "You trust Kaplan's calculations?"

Julie rolled her eyes. "I'm trying not to freak out about it. If he screws up, it's me who has to call the President." Then she sighed. "All this worry could be for nothing, too. If Dr. Grunhart can't prove our Martian DNA will make an impact, the President will cancel us."

"Yeah, we're in limbo. When's the next meeting with Mr. CIA?"

"Next week. It's a video meeting, thank God." They entered the administration section where their offices were located. "Before I go, where are we with the astrobots?"

"Leaving for Advanced Robotics tomorrow. They said they figured out the balance problems. Want to see it for myself."

"Record it for me." Julie hugged Marge. "See you when you get back."

Chapter Eleven: Truce

Burbank Airport, Burbank, CA

Two Days Later

CJ tightened his seat belt as the CIA's plane bounced and jostled through the thick brown smog trapped against the San Gabriel Mountains on its descent into the Burbank airport. It landed and taxied to the General Aviation Terminal. Julie strutted the short distance across the tarmac and climbed up the jet's stairs. Entering the plane, she glared at CJ, her hands on her hips.

"I found out about this trip to who knows where only two hours ago. One of your men came to my office. Told me I had to be here. Mumbled something about a national security situation and used your special code word. Forced me to cancel a very important meeting with Marge regarding the astrobots. What's this all about?"

"Good afternoon, Doctor. Please have a seat." Glancing at his watch, CJ yelled down the aisle to the pilot, "Let's go, Alex! Wheels up as soon as you can."

Julie chose a seat across the aisle, buckling in as far from CJ as possible in the jet's cramped passenger compartment, and looked out the window. CJ observed his peeved partner, recalling the conversation with Phil. He spoke softly.

"We're going to Area 51 in Nevada, Dr. McCray. Things are developing quickly. I used one of our contractors to pick you up in person so as not to leave an electronic signature. Didn't want anyone tailing you."

At least it won't be a long flight, thought Julie but she was worried about Marge's email saying the trials weren't successful. "Whatever you say, Director. But until we get there, I need to review our astrobots' recent test."

Once the plane climbed into the sky, Julie opened her laptop, put in her earbuds, and viewed Marge's video recordings of yesterday's third attempt by the astrobots to carry weighted objects over and around an incline. The rugged terrain of Mars made maintaining their balance over uneven surfaces a priority. Julie pressed the play button. Marge appeared in the trial area next to Jason Ortiz, the project engineer who explained the demonstration.

"In the first trial, Robot One will carry ten kilos up and down a five-degree incline. In the next exercise, Robot Two will carry ten kilos over a five-degree side-hill incline. Let's begin."

Robot One stood six feet tall, its humanoid body encased in a glossy white plastic shell topped with a matching helmet and a reflective gold visor. Julie watched the astrobot totter over and pick up two five-kilo kettlebells, one in each hand. Its fingers methodically wrapped around each handle. It staggered up the thirty-foot incline, pausing briefly at the apex, before descending the other side in a stiff, measured gait. *Still looks unstable,* thought Julie.

Next, Robot Two, identical in design to Robot One, entered the trial area and lifted a similar set of weights. It ambled over to what looked like a giant pitcher's mound, fifty meters long, riddled with uneven lumps. Julie observed the astrobot start with the same stiff walk, then it stumbled over an outcrop. Lurching forward, its feet tangled together, causing Robot Two to topple onto the trial floor.

Julie hit pause and glanced out the window. *This puts us weeks behind. We haven't even started the complex tasks yet.* She pressed play, and Marge's face filled the screen.

"Julie, I'm recording this in the car outside Advanced Robotics. They failed again. They should've had this figured out by now." Julie observed the frustration on her face. "Fred Langford, their best engineer, needs to take over. Mention it to Mr. CIA. This has to happen now."

Julie closed her laptop, agreeing with Marge's assessment. She looked over to CJ, texting on his phone. *I'll ask him on the return trip.*

***

When the plane landed, Julie and CJ hustled into the Stewart Lab Complex. They entered an auditorium designed like a movie theatre with thirty padded chairs facing an elevated stage. Behind the platform loomed a wall-sized monitor with smaller ones on either side of the room to enable remote viewing. Copper mesh lined the walls, and 'electronic noise' emitters were strategically placed in the corners to prevent electronic intrusion.

Dr. Grunhart, in his white lab coat, stood on the stage, waiting for the attendees to arrive. Dr. Mary Williams, head of the President's Climate Initiative, sat in the first row. CJ introduced Julie, and they grabbed seats on either side of her.

"We're waiting for two more attendees," Grunhart said. "They'll be on the screens momentarily."

Julie leaned over and whispered to Mary, "When did you find out about this meeting?"

"Seven this morning, in DC. The General arranged for me to hitch a ride on a military jet out of Andrews." Mary gave her a sheepish smile. "It's what happens when you're bound to the President's schedule, but I wanted to see this in person."

Julie gasped. "What? The President is ..."

The left wall monitor flashed with General Scott's image, and President Jennings, sitting in the Oval Office, came into focus on the other.

It dawned on Julie this meeting would determine whether the Martian bacteria could impact the Climate Initiative and her mission's fate. *Why didn't CJ tell me?* She felt her stomach tighten as Grunhart stepped forward.

The distinguished scientist gave a bow to his audience and smiled. "General Scott tasked me with examining three types of Martian bacteria discovered on Dr. McCray's mission and assess their contribution to the Climate Initiative. We're in luck. One strain absorbs carbon dioxide at an incredible rate. I've recorded an experiment to show you. Let's begin."

The monitor in front of the room flickered to life, revealing Dr. Grunhart standing in a laboratory, behind a countertop with two tall glass cylinders.

"I replicated the Martian DNA into similar Earth bacteria using advanced CRISPR technology. CRISPR stands for Clustered Regularly Interspaced Short Palindromic Repeats, the hallmark of a bacterial defense system that forms the basis for CRISPR-Cas9 genome editing technology. In the field of genome..."

"Dr. Grunhart," interrupted the President. "We trust your expertise. Please get to the results."

"Certainly, Madame President. I'll fast-forward the recording." Grunhart queued the video to the beginning of the experiment.

"I colored the CO2 gas yellow, making it easier to observe the bacteria's absorption. The first cylinder, on my right, mimics the Martian atmosphere and temperature, except we've added light. Watch closely."

Julie inched toward the edge of her seat. She grasped her cross as the colored gas flooded the tube. A timer at the base of the cylinder started counting. The gas vanished in the sealed vessel after twenty-two seconds.

"Wow," Mary whispered. She turned to Julie. "That was impressive."

Grunhart's experiment video continued. "You can see this bacteria strain absorbed five liters of gas in twenty-two seconds. Now for the second cylinder. Again, the temperature is identical to Mars, except it has Earth's atmosphere and light. Oxygen becomes an accelerant."

The three participants in the auditorium stared at the monitor. Julie's heartbeat accelerated, her eyes focused on the timer. As Grunhart flooded the container, the gas disappeared in eleven seconds.

"Amazing," whispered Dr. Williams in Julie's ear. Julie's shoulders dropped. "I hope it's good enough," she said to Mary. Then, the President spoke.

"What are the implications for our Climate Initiative, Doctor Grunhart?"

"Madam President, this strain of bacteria absorbs carbon dioxide out of the air like no other organism on Earth. This, however, is a hybrid organism. I believe the Martian bacteria will be even more effective.

"Therefore, my recommendation is to bring these microbes back to Earth and verify their specific properties. Based on my preliminary studies here, I believe we can enhance their absorption rate even further, making Direct Air Capture a viable mechanism for your efforts."

"Dr. Williams, could this be the answer to our climate issue?" asked General Scott.

Mary turned and faced him. "The absorption rate is impressive. But before we get too excited, my group will be handling an alien lifeform. One thing we need to consider is the danger of introducing an unknown species into our ecosystem." Mary looked up to Grunhart. "Doctor, what happened to the other two DNA strains?"

He put his hands into his lab coat pockets. "They did not survive. But I want to emphasize these were also hybrid organisms. It's another reason to bring back the Martian bacteria. Their impact could even be greater."

"Sounds risky," said Mary. "Dr. Grunhart, can't we use the engineered bacteria? It would save a lot of time."

"Yah, unfortunately, Doctor, after the second generation, the engineered bacteria become sterile. We need the live ones."

Silence enveloped the room as the participants stared at the empty gas cylinders still visible on the monitor. Julie spoke up, breaking the silence.

"Everyone, if we're going to do this, we need to decide now. Our launch window disappears in three and a half months, and we need every day to make it. If we miss it, it'll be over two years before we can go again."

The President removed her glasses and asked, "General, what do you think?"

"While Dr. Williams accurately points out the risk, if we don't bring the temperature down, we'll have hunger riots and massive human and animal migrations. Seems like we have a potential breakthrough. Let's bring the bacteria back and see. We don't have to deploy them if the scientists determine the risk is too high."

Julie stared forward, her face blank, as everyone pivoted to the President's monitor.

She removed her glasses and addressed the group. "Our situation became even more dire this morning. Canada's Prime Minister informed me of a new policy where only Canadian citizens can buy property or rent housing for longer than two weeks. They're afraid of being overrun."

She paused and leaned forward. "I hear your concern, Mary, but we must take every step to reduce our planet's temperature. It seems Dr. McCray's logic was correct and based on Director Jackson's high praise of the JPL, I'm authorizing Project Magellan. Now, what do you need to retrieve those bacteria, Doctor McCray?"

A smile sprang across Julie's face. "Madame President, our robotics program isn't going well. We need Fred Langford of Advanced Robotics to take charge. With him, we could have the bacteria back within a year."

The President pointed at CJ. "Director Jackson, send your budget to Ed. He'll push it through. And General, get this Langford guy to Dr. McCray, like yesterday. The world's citizens are counting on us to fix our badly damaged planet. Get moving." The President's image vanished from the screen.

Julie thought about CJ's actions. *His secrecy about the meeting was weird, but he made sure to include me and didn't interfere with my request to the President. And his last-minute notice wasn't a power move to order me around.* Dr. Williams interrupted her thoughts.

"Dr. McCray? Could these Martian organisms survive on Earth?"

Julie nodded. "We believe so. Earth and Mars formed at similar times in the Solar System and have similar planetary development profiles. They also were bombarded with many of the same types of meteors and asteroids, which deposited organic material, minerals, and water in the form of ice.

"We've also confirmed, over hundreds of millions of years, many asteroid collisions were violent enough to eject material from each of the two planets high into space, where they were exchanged, one planet to another, as they passed through each other's orbital paths."

Mary's eyes widened. "Fascinating."

Julie smiled. "Earth and Mars share similar compounds and minerals, including organic compounds. It's why we believe the Martian bacteria could be compatible here."

"But only three types were found. We have thousands of bacterial species here. Why the difference?"

"From biological research here, it's common for organisms existing in extreme environments to suffer a loss of biodiversity. And Mars is very extreme."

Mary eased back in her seat. "I'm learning a lot from you, Dr. McCray."

"Please call me Julie. But it's time for you to educate me, Dr. Williams. How do you see these bacteria aiding your efforts?"

Mary rubbed her chin. "The Climate Initiative focuses on reducing greenhouse gas emissions. We've nearly eliminated the two biggest emitters, fossil fuel electricity plants, and internal combustion engines. It's the strategy most acceptable to politicians, but takes the longest to be effective because CO2 lingers in the atmosphere for multiple decades. The volcanic eruptions made everything worse.

"What we need now is a greenhouse gas removal strategy. That's where your bacteria fit in. Up until now, Direct Air Capture hasn't been a pragmatic option because it's energy intensive. But your microbes make it feasible. We'll design facilities and deploy them worldwide."

Mary checked her watch. "Sorry to cut this short, Julie. I need to catch my ride back to DC. Good luck with bringing back those bacteria. We're counting on you."

***

Back on the plane, Julie and CJ both grabbed coffees from the galley. They moved to the front and sat across from one another.

Julie took a sip, savoring the caffeine jolt. She scanned CJ and crossed her legs. "Ah, Director, sorry I was a bit snippy with you earlier. Our recent robotic tests failed, and I took it out on you for dragging me away."

The worry lines around CJ's eyes eased as he responded, "I know how squeezed you are for time, but if I ask to see you on the spur of the moment, trust me, I promise it's urgent."

"Trust isn't my strong suit these days, but noted." Her thoughts shifted to the President's decision, and she perked up. "Hey, some meeting. My discovery *can* have a significant impact."

"No question. Glad we got the go-ahead."

Julie flashed her eyes at him. "You sang JPL's praises to the President?"

CJ chuckled. "Don't get too full of yourself, Dr. McCray. I was desperate to keep our project alive. Today we presented a solid team and convinced the President."

Feeling the tension between them ease, Julie relaxed back into her seat. "Any more information about the low-gain antenna transmission? Haven't heard from Ms. Burton."

CJ fidgeted with his paper coffee cup. "She said the person who reprogrammed C-2 had significant computer skills and was familiar with JPL's system. Confirmed what we thought. It's an inside job."

Julie shook her head. "Betrayed by one of our own. Our people are so dedicated to our mission. It's hard to believe."

CJ sat up, placing his coffee cup in the holder. "Unfortunately, it's often how these things unfold." He paused, his expression turning serious. "Your DNA represents a once-in-a-lifetime opportunity. This can drive good-willed people to act in unpredictable ways. It's why secrecy is paramount. We got lucky this time."

He leaned forward, closer to Julie. "Our project is at risk, Doctor, and I don't have a good handle on it." CJ's fingers dug into the armrest. "But right now, I need to know if I can rely on you."

A chill crept up Julie's spine, and her eyes widened. "What are you trying to tell me?"

"Whoever attempted to steal the DNA is lurking inside NASA. You understand the culture. If you sense something's off, tell me, and I'll investigate." CJ paused and glanced out the window. "But for that to happen, we need to be more comfortable with each other, and I think you're pissed at me."

Julie folded her hands in her lap. "When you didn't tell me about the surveillance, I felt violated, and it made me question your intentions. It's why I'm keeping you at arm's length until I can figure out where you're coming from."

"My mistake, sorry." CJ raked his hand through his hair. "I tried to ease you into this clandestine world, especially after we whisked you to DC. Won't happen again. And I'm not a creepy guy."

First time I feel he's being real with me. "Apology accepted," Julie said.

A small smile creased his face. "And will you please call me CJ?"

"Okay, CJ. Let's talk."

CJ eased back in his seat. "Good. Fire away."

"What's your take on the programmer?"

"The most probable scenario is he or she wants to sell the DNA. But what I'm most worried about are the motives of the buyer. Could be another country or a terrorist faction."

"Hmm. I think there's something else going on."

"What?"

"The reprogramming happened around ten months ago, right? It's not an impulsive act. It's part of a well-thought-out plan. Money could be part of it, but maybe it's someone with a grudge of some sort."

"Interesting. Say more."

Julie shifted in her seat. "We're science geeks who love exploring new worlds and uncovering the mysteries of the universe. Each mission takes years out of our lives and time away from family."

"I'm following. Go on."

"Sabotaging a mission is contrary to our values, so why do it? Makes me think our insider might be angry or upset about something like maybe not getting promoted. Make sense?"

The cockpit door opened and the pilot turned and yelled down the aisle. "Five minutes out, Director."

"I'll tell Layla to add it to our criteria." CJ drained the rest of his coffee. "I have one more thing to run by you. When Fred Langford comes to see you, move his operation out to Area 51. I texted the base commander after the President gave us the go-ahead. They're making space as we speak."

Julie looked up to the right. "Hmm. Longhorn Systems is assembling the HAB unit there. Good idea. Co-location will save time programming the astrobots."

"Good, but that's not why. Langford's critical to hitting the launch window. He'll be safe in Area 51. No one can abduct him there."

"Wait, you think he could ..."

CJ leveled her with his gaze. "Until we can zero in on our saboteur, I'm eliminating as many risk factors as I can."

The plane's wheels screeched as they touched down on the Burbank runway. When the plane eased to a stop next to the General Aviation terminal, CJ stood and shook her hand.

"Thank you, Dr. McCray. I'm glad we cleared the air. I'll be in touch soon."

"Thank you, CJ." She walked down the aisle, but when she reached the exit door, she turned and smiled. "And please, call me Julie."

Chapter Twelve: Mixed Bag

NSA Headquarters

Next Day

CJ clicked the 'Join Meeting' tab and entered the urgent video call ordered by Admiral Garza. Julie and Boxman were also in remote attendance. The Admiral and Layla sat at the table across from a man CJ did not recognize. He had a muscular build and was fastidious in his appearance.

"Director Jackson," he said. "I'm Special Agent Jamil Brown, FBI. I'm second in command of our counterterrorism unit here in DC."

"Nice to meet you," said CJ. *Only one reason the Admiral brought in the FBI,* he thought. *Time for the cops to arrest someone.*

"Good afternoon, let's get started," said the Admiral. "Layla combed through NASA's personnel files and found a subject fitting the programmer's profile. Layla, fill them in."

Layla, dressed in a striking velvet navy jacket and lime blouse, adjusted her lime green glasses.

"We scanned for abnormalities in spending, travel, bank accounts, debt, and other factors. In discussing the sabotage with Dr. McCray, we also searched for someone with proficient computer skills, access to the NASA networks, and who was employed over ten months ago. Based on these criteria, one name emerged: Ashton Price, a NASA administrator based in DC."

"Do you know him, Dr. Boxman?" Agent Brown asked.

Boxman cleared his throat. "Yes. He coordinates the HAB and astrobot technologies across all NASA entities, including the JPL."

"Why do you think he's our guy, Ms. Burton?" Brown asked.

Layla folded her arms across her chest. "He's made numerous payments to a drug treatment clinic called One Step Forward. Take a look." On the screen, Price's bank statements appeared with the payments highlighted in yellow.

"Eighteen months ago, his wife died in a car accident. Ashton has one daughter, Katie, fourteen at the time of the incident. The loss of her mother traumatized her, and she began using drugs to compensate. Price hired One Step Forward to treat her condition.

"After his government insurance ran out, he obtained a second mortgage. It cost him twenty grand for four weeks of in-house treatment and two hundred a week thereafter for outpatient therapy. When his daughter suffered a relapse and had to be readmitted four months ago, his funds ran out, making him financially vulnerable. She's back home now."

Layla clicked, and more of his financial records appeared on the screen. "You can see he doesn't have much. But I found something else."

She pulled up two emails on the monitor.

"This first one is a notice from the clinic demanding payment, or they'll suspend treatment." She clicked on the other email. "The second, sent last week, is a receipt for a cash payment of twenty-thousand dollars.

"We've no record of this sudden inflow of cash. My assessment is the Chinese found him from their intrusions into NASA's personnel files and realized his situation. It's reasonable to assume the money came from them." Layla snugged up her glasses and returned to her seat.

"Dr. Boxman, you know him," said CJ. "Does this make sense to you?"

"While Ms. Burton's analysis does make sense, he does not have the personality to do this. He's a very nervous type. Not a risk-taker."

"I agree," said Julie. "He gets frazzled easily, and he didn't need money when the reprogramming happened. That part doesn't fit."

"Yeah, but the cash payment's a red flag. Came from somewhere," Agent Brown said. "It might not be related to your situation, but I need to question him. We have an interrogation site near the Ontario airport."

"Agreed. We can't take the chance," CJ said. "Dr. McCray, could you invite him out to the JPL on some pretext?"

"Wait. Can't you question him here, Agent Brown?" Boxman asked.

"If he's a nervous type like you say, I want to surprise him and put him in unfamiliar surroundings. It'll increase his discomfort. Dr. McCray?"

"This is not my area of expertise. I'll do it if you both think it'll protect our mission."

"Good," said Agent Brown. "Let's shake him and see what falls out."

***

Julie's Conference Room

Next Morning, JPL

Security called, saying they were escorting Fred Langford to Julie's office, where she and Marge waited.

Julie tapped her fingernails on the conference table. "I hope he can fix the balance problems and get on with the HAB and drilling tasks. Have you met him?"

Marge shook her head. "No, but their engineers think he's brilliant. Kind of a folk hero."

Security knocked and opened the door. Fred wore thick, black-framed glasses, a slightly rumpled flannel shirt, and khaki pants. A faux leather phone case was attached to his belt. He took two steps in and stopped; his brown eyes blinked several times as they darted about the room before focusing on his clients.

"Hi, I'm Fred." He reached out and shook Marge and Julie's hands. "Nice to meet you, Dr. Jamison and Dr. McCray. Can we jump right in? Great. I'll sync my laptop to your wall monitor."

As he unpacked his case, he continued talking, "Don't know what happened but somebody on your side read the riot act to my head honchos and, well, here I am. The previous team brought me up to speed. Awesome project. I love it! Here's what I've done. Ready?" Fred brought up the astrobots' schematics on the monitor.

"Here's where your balance problem is. Right here." He sent a beam from his laser pointer to the head area. "See where the cameras are located? Wrong, wrong, wrong. Off by half a degree. They're sending information from the wrong vectors, causing the computer to affix the wrong center of gravity. With me?"

Julie glanced at Marge and nearly burst out laughing. Fred acted like the Energizer Bunny, bouncing around the room and gesturing with his hands as he talked. Over the next twenty minutes, he detailed the root cause factors creating the balance difficulties.

"Don't worry. Already made the changes and fixed the balance. We're back on track, focusing on powering up the HAB and using the core drilling machine. Good idea to move to Nevada. We'll work even faster next to Longhorn. Questions?"

"How soon can you get your team there?" asked Julie.

"They're setting up now. We'll be operational in two more days."

Julie smiled at him. "Good work, Fred."

"Great! Need to get going. Come out in three weeks. We'll have some cool stuff to show you. Nice meeting you. Bye." Then he tucked his computer case under his arm and scurried out the door.

"Wow. Are you kidding?" laughed Marge, no longer able to contain herself.

"Wow, is right." Julie eased back in her chair and crossed her legs. "He's eccentric, but I feel better. I'll go visit and check his progress for myself."

***

Mr. Blue: *The HAB plans are ready.*

Mr. Green: *Good. Who will hand the plans off to our agent?*

Mr. Blue: *You know him. Ashton Price. Very reliable.*

Mr. Green: *How best to contact him?*

Mr. Blue: *Has a site called The Friendly Hacker on the Dark Web. Notify him there.*

Mr. Green: *We'll arrange the meeting logistics the morning of. We'll do it next week.*

Chapter Thirteen: The Leak

FBI Interrogation Site

Ontario, California

The black Escalade hummed down East Guasti Boulevard under the blasting heat of the California sun. When the vehicle passed Sequoia Street, the giant SUV took a hard left and accelerated down a long row of storage facilities. Halfway through, one of the large metal doors clanked open. The big Caddy drove straight in, and Jamil slammed on the brakes, the tires squealing on the smooth concrete floor. The warehouse door rattled down and banged on the pavement. A loud latching sound echoed in the entrance bay as the door locked into place. Silence permeated the interior.

Two heavily armed agents wearing blue FBI jackets flanked each side of the vehicle. The agent closest to Jamil said, "Everything's ready, Agent Brown."

He glanced up at him. "Get this guy into interrogation."

The two agents grabbed the black-hooded Ashton Price by the arms and whisked him away. CJ exited from the passenger side, wearing a blonde wig, blue jeans, and a tan t-shirt with Steve's Landing, Long Beach, printed on the front. Jamil and CJ followed behind the agents.

The interrogation room was small and intimate. Fear and intimidation pervaded its gray concrete floor with beige-colored walls. A one-way observation window faced the suspect, and a bolted-down steel table with three metal chairs rested in the room's center.

Inside, the agents released Ashton's handcuffs from the chain across his waist and transferred them to a large horseshoe metal bar welded to the table. They unlocked the chains around his ankles and removed the blindfold.

Ashton squinted as his eyes fought the ultra-white lights blazing down from the ceiling. His face looked pale and thin. His pants and shirt hung loose on his slight frame. As he acclimated, Ashton's brown eyes darted back and forth between the two men sitting across the table from him.

"Good morning Mr. Price. I'm FBI Special Agent Jamil Brown. The other person here will stay unknown. Now let me––"

"I know my rights," Aston yelled, his face turning red. "You kidnapped me from my hotel. You didn't have a warrant. And, and, ah, it's against the law. I want a lawyer right now."

Agent Brown stared at Ashton and did not respond. As the silence dragged on, Ashton fidgeted in his seat. He looked over to CJ, who gazed at him with a deadpan face. He finally dropped his head and mumbled, "Why am I here?"

Agent Brown leaned across the table, his nose inches from Ashton. "Mr. Price, you're being held under the National Security Act of 2025, and I can guarantee no attorney will be provided. We have overwhelming evidence you've conspired with an unauthorized source, possibly the Chinese government, in exchange for money to pay for your daughter's drug rehabilitation treatment. I have the proof right here." His index finger pressed down on a manila folder. "But first, I want to show you pictures of Fort Leavenworth federal prison."

He shoved a photo at Ashton of an eight-by-twelve-foot cell with walls made of steel-reinforced concrete block. It contained a narrow cot with a stainless-steel toilet and a small sink in the corner.

"This will be your home for at least thirty years, Mr. Price. You understand what's at stake?"

Blood drained from Ashton's face as he stared at the photograph. He looked frozen in place.

"Ashton!" Agent Brown slapped his hand on the table.

His shocked eyes connected with Jamil. "Who'll take care of my daughter?" he choked out. "It's only my sister and me." Tears welled up in his eyes and spilled down his cheeks. He hung his head and sobbed. Brown waited until Ashton calmed down.

"There's a way out," he whispered. "Would you like to hear it?"

Ashton slowly straightened up in the chair. "Yes," he mumbled.

"Tell us how they contacted you and what they want."

He wiped his wet cheeks against his shirt. "You said you had proof. Show me."

Agent Brown revealed how the Chinese Ministry of State Security attacked his personnel file. Then he showed Ashton the emails from the One Step Forward clinic and his bank records. Seeing the incriminating documents, Ashton's shoulders slumped and caved inward, the last of his resistance melting away. His lips quivered.

"I'll do what you want," he mumbled. "As long as my daughter gets the help she needs. She's all I have left."

"Your daughter's fate depends on how much you cooperate with us." Jamil folded his hands on the table and stared into Ashton's eyes. "Now, this twenty thousand. Where'd it come from? The Chinese?"

"I don't know who sent the money," he stammered, dropping eye contact again.

"Did you reprogram the Curiosity rover to use the low-gain antenna?" asked CJ.

Ashton's head popped up, and his eyes flashed wide open. "No. No. I didn't reprogram anything, I, I swear."

"Then how did you get the money?" asked Jamil.

Ashton swallowed and licked his lips. "I have a side job on the Dark Web. They hire me to hack into social media accounts to see if a person's partner is cheating on them, gambling, drugs, and so on. A few weeks ago, a message popped up from a Mr. Blue. He knew I worked at NASA and wanted me to hand off a copy of the HAB schematics to a third party.

"When I agreed, 25k in digital currency went into my account. I used it to pay Katie's bill." Ashton's voice shook, and his eyes teared up again. The handcuffs rattled against the metal bar. "I did it for my daughter. She's so fragile right now."

"What about the handoff?" Jamil continued.

"Someone's supposed to contact me on a burner phone. Next week." He sniffled. "After the exchange, I'll get the other 25k."

Suddenly, Ashton's eyes opened wide. His hands strained against his cuffs. "Oh God, this was an FBI sting. I'm going to be sick," He buried his face in the crook of his elbow, making gagging sounds. The guard in the room quickly unlocked him and rushed him down the hall.

Jamil asked, "What do you think?"

"Well, he's no master spy. Julie was right about him being a nervous type."

"Do you believe him about the money and the exchange?"

CJ tapped his fingers on the table. "Yeah. When we shut down the rover, we anticipated the insider would arrange something else. The HAB sale fits." CJ gestured to Jamil. "The person behind this could be our programmer."

"Regardless, we have someone conspiring to sell unauthorized government documents. Let's hope Ashton can hold up during the exchange. He's shaky, man." Jamil checked his watch. "Let's get some coffees. He might be a while."

When Ashton returned, his face looked gray, and he staggered back to the table. They didn't handcuff him.

"We're almost done," CJ said. "We want you to keep this appointment next week and pass along a HAB blueprint we give you. Can you do it?"

Ashton's drawn face frowned. "What about my daughter? You promised to..."

Agent Brown held up his hand. "The FBI will recommend to the US Attorney a full pardon and you can keep the 50K for your daughter's treatments. This is the best deal you'll ever get."

"If you put it in writing, I'll do it. My daughter's life depends on it."

"You'll have it before we let you go today. Good enough?"

Ashton glanced first to Brown, then CJ, and back to Brown. "Yeah, we have a deal."

"Here's my number." Jamil handed him a card. "After they contact you to arrange the swap, call me right away. I'll send the plans over to you, and when it's done, we'll debrief in your office."

"Okay." Ashton's eyes teared up once more.

Jamil waved his hand, and two agents came in and escorted Ashton out of the room.

CJ leaned over to Jamil. "I know how we can find the source. But I have to convince Julie to go along with it. I'll touch base when I'm back in DC."

***

One Hour Later

JPL Headquarters

The heavy traffic on the I-210 to Pasadena gave CJ time to call Layla and work out a plan to discover who paid for the HAB plans. Then he called

Julie's office, and her assistant scheduled an appointment for the end of the day. He gripped the wheel, his knuckles turning white, thinking through his pitch to Julie. *I hope she'll trust me.*

Arriving at the JPL, security escorted CJ to Julie's office. He knocked.

"CJ? Hey, come in."

"Hi, Julie. Thanks for seeing me. I know it's late."

"No problem. Please let's sit at the table." She took in his outfit. "T-shirt and jeans? CIA going casual?" she said, smiling at his beach dude outfit.

"Jamil Brown's idea." He grinned and sat down across from her. "I'm coming straight from the Ashton Price interrogation, and I, ah, need to confide in you."

Julie's forehead wrinkled, "Okay. What's up?"

"Ashton said an anonymous source contacted him via his Dark Web site to copy the HAB plans and deliver them to an unknown person for 50k. But Ashton's not our programmer."

"Ashton? The HAB plans? I don't understand."

CJ relayed the day's events. Julie listened, shaking her head periodically.

"Yeah, it didn't make sense, it was him," said Julie. "Don't get me wrong, selling our HAB plans is awful, but at least it's understandable given his daughter's relapse. Poor guy."

She tapped her fingernails on the table. "Your prediction was accurate. With the DNA off the table, he or she still needs money. The HAB plans are it. Nice work, CJ."

Pushing back her chair, Julie paced in front of the table. "I know who the buyer is." She pivoted and faced CJ. "Has to be the Chinese."

"Of course, the moon base."

"Right. The Chinese are behind in developing extraterrestrial habitats." Julie's hands gripped the back of the chair. "You should see them at our yearly conferences. They try to copy as much as they can get away with. Pisses us all off."

CJ massaged his worry stone hidden in his jeans pocket. "The exchange is next week. Can you give me a set of the HAB plans without giving away our technology?"

A knowing smile spread across her face. "When people steal space technology, they think it's a shortcut and a leap ahead. But they haven't gone through the learning process themselves. Big mistake."

"I don't understand."

Julie started pacing again. "Space is an unforgiving environment. If the smallest of details goes unnoticed, it can be catastrophic. I know how to give them a setback." She stopped and grinned at CJ.

"Great. How?"

"Pass them the plans for our test HAB."

"Ah, Julie, you're ahead of me again."

"Wait, this'll help." She went over and grabbed her laptop. She typed in a few commands and a picture of the HAB popped onto the wall monitor. She stood next to the image. "One thing we can't replicate on Earth is the damaging radiation of deep space. So our HAB test version doesn't have certain hardened components. It's cheaper." Julie pointed to the test HAB. "The seals on the airlock and around the windows are two such areas."

"Following so far. What's the setback?"

"The test HAB on the moon will be constantly bombarded by galactic cosmic rays and charged particles from solar proton events. This will cause the airlock seals and gaskets to deteriorate, making it impossible to keep the HAB pressurized."

"And they'll have to abandon the base. Brilliant."

"Exactly," said Julie.

CJ bit his lip and tilted his head. "Would you mind giving me the plans?"

"I have 'em right here. I'll put them on an encrypted flash drive." Julie inserted the device, copied the plans, and handed it to CJ.

"Perfect." His shoulders dropped and he sat back in his chair. "Thanks for helping me."

Julie's eyes widened. "Why? Did you think I wouldn't?"

"Well, we had a rocky start, and I thought you might not want to collaborate. I mean this is a deceptive maneuver, and I know that bothers you."

Julie closed the top of her laptop. "I see how people are conspiring against our mission. You can count on me."

"Good." CJ smiled. "Any thoughts on who's behind this?"

Julie bit her lip. "Ah, yeah. I've been thinking about who worked here over ten months ago, who's disgruntled, and who might need the money."

"And?"

Julie rubbed her forehead. "Not comfortable yet. Let me do some more work." She pointed at the thumb drive. "So, what happens next?"

"Well, Ashton will do the delivery. There's more to it, but it's better if I don't say."

"This is the need-to-know part, right?"

"Right. I'm not being deceitful, I'm compartmentalizing."

Julie waved her hand. "It's fine, CJ. When do you go back to DC?"

"I'm on the company jet out of Ontario in the morning. Why?"

"Well, I'm done here for today and could use some dinner. Want to join me?" Julie's hands clenched the bottom of her chair. *I can't believe I did that.*

CJ's eyes shot up, and he smiled. "Yeah. Sounds good. Nice to have company for a change."

***

Next Morning

Julie's Office

Marge strolled into Julie's office for their regular briefing. They gathered at the conference table with fresh cups of coffee. "Morning, boss," said Marge. "You said you have news?"

"Yes. CJ came by yesterday afternoon. He and the FBI questioned Ashton, and he confessed."

Marge's mouth dropped open. "Ashton? He's the programmer?"

"No." And Julie explained the situation.

Marge shook her head. "Parents'll do anything for their children when they're suffering. He must've been desperate. Chinese wanting the HAB plans makes sense."

"I gave CJ the HAB design we're using at the Arizona test site. Ashton will deliver it next week."

Marge blurted out. "Julie, it'll break down in space." Then her palm slapped her forehead. "Of course, duh."

Julie put down her coffee cup and leaned forward. “Our programmer’s still out there, Marge. We need to find him or her soon. Want to play detective with me?”

“Sure. How do we start?”

“Here’s my theory. This person changed the software and had to wait over a year to get the DNA. This person isn’t desperate. I believe he has a grudge.”

“OMG! You suspect someone?”

Julie looked down and frowned. “Franklin fits,” she whispered.

“Franklin?” Marge’s brown eyes widened. “Why?”

“I didn’t recommend him for the promotion at Goddard Space Flight Center. I explained my reasoning to him, but he wasn’t happy about it.” She turned her cup around in her hands. “He has access and the skill set.”

“I don’t know. Seems committed to me, but maybe.” Marge started twisting her black curls. “This whole thing feels creepy. I mean, we’re scientists, not cops. Why not tell CJ and let him handle it?”

“I wanted to run it by you first. You think I should tell him?”

Marge lifted her cup to her lips. “I don’t think it’s him, but it’s better to be sure, I guess.”

“I’ll call CJ and let him know. You’re the only one I can trust about this, Marge. It’ll only be between you and me.”

“Okay. Anything else?”

“Well, yeah.” Julie blushed. “It’s personal.”

Marge reached over and held Julie’s hand. “Oh please, tell me.”

Julie bit her lip and stared back at her friend. “At the end of the meeting, I asked CJ to have dinner with me. I kinda blurted it out.”

“NO! Really? Wow, I didn’t see that one coming.” Marge scootched to the edge of her seat. “How’d it go?”

“We had a nice time. Felt normal.”

“Hold it. You couldn’t stand him a few weeks ago. What changed?”

“I know. You saw how standoffish he was. Cold, distant. Not for me, thanks. But lately, he’s been different, more honest. Even a little vulnerable.”

Marge put her elbows on the table. “Keep going.”

"You know, after Bill, I don't want another person determining the course of my happiness. I'd rather live on my own terms even though I do get lonely sometimes."

"You have some scar tissue for sure. So why ask CJ out?"

"He was staying here until morning by himself, and it's only me and Gizmo most nights, so why not?" Julie twirled a strand of blonde hair and pinned it behind her ear.

"Really?"

"Well, I was a little curious. But I thought it would be more like an interview."

Marge's eyes widened. "But something happened, didn't it?"

"Still processing." Julie smiled and gave Marge a glance. "You know, he wasn't edgy being around an intelligent woman. I mean, I am smarter than him." She raised her eyebrows. "But other than the security stuff at the beginning, he's never talked down to me, and he's kept his cool when I pushed back."

"Sounds like you're rationalizing. Get to it, girl."

Julie swallowed a sip of her coffee. "After we ordered, he passed the bread, and our fingers accidentally touched." Julie paused and gazed out her office window. "I felt a connection, Marge. Only way I can describe it." She looked back at her. "Weird, huh?"

"No, I get it. I mean I'm from Jamaican parents born in LA and I partnered with a Jewish man from Brooklyn. Crossed some boundaries there. But I felt connected to him, and he made me feel complete. I can't imagine being without him."

"I'm glad for you." Julie smiled. "But I'm a long way from that."

"Did you squeeze his story out of him?"

"I started to. He mumbled something about his fiancée leaving, then clammed up. Didn't get the impression it was his idea."

Marge folded her hands. "Can't be easy to live with a guy whose job is keeping secrets."

"Has a wall for sure. Feels like he's carrying something inside he doesn't want anyone to see."

"Are you going to pursue this connection?"

Julie touched her cross. "I'm not sure. I can't afford to lose focus on the mission. I mean the President of the United States is counting on me. No pressure there."

"Okay, so what's next?"

"In a couple of weeks, I'll be at NASA HQ for the technical review with the Chief Science Officer. I'll let him know I'm coming to DC during our next update call and see if he wants to get together."

"Well, you know I'm here for you." She reached over and squeezed Julie's hand. "I'm glad you're stepping out."

Chapter Fourteen: Ashton

NASA HQ

Washington, DC

Ashton Price exited the Metro at the Federal Center SW station. His eyes darted about before slipping on his mask and putting in his earbuds. Last night, Mr. Green left a note on his Friendly Hacker site saying the exchange would be today. Aston swallowed hard and stepped onto Third Street making his way to NASA HQ. Two blocks from his office, his disposable phone chirped. He jerked at the sound, his hands trembled, connecting the call.

"Hello, ah, it's me, I mean, Mr. Blue's friend."

"Do you have the present for Mr. Green?" asked an electronically masked voice.

"Yeah, yeah, I have it."

"Meet me at the Royal Bean on 4th Street. Ten o'clock. I'll be wearing a red Nationals ball cap. Relax and follow my lead." Click and the call ended.

Ashton hurried the rest of the way to NASA headquarters, unaware he was being followed. Climbing up the stairs to his second-floor cubicle, he called Agent Brown.

"Brown here."

"This is Ashton Price." His voice quivered. "I got the call. We're meeting at ten at the coffee shop. He said to follow his lead. What did he mean?"

"Ashton, stay calm. It's a good public place. You'll be safe."

"If you say so."

"The agent will pretend to know you, so play along like you're friends. Follow his instructions and hand him the thumb drive CJ gave you. You ready?"

"I don't know. I mean, after this, won't they want to get rid of me, tie up any loose ends?"

Jamil shook his head. "Just the opposite. They may want to use you again because they know you can be trusted. Besides, you're a federal employee. If you suddenly disappear, they won't want the FBI snooping around. Do what he says, and you'll be fine."

Ashton bit his lip and checked his watch. 8:17.

"One more thing," Brown said. "When you hand off the plans, stay and finish your coffee. Then stroll back to work like you have all the time in the world. Nice and slow. Don't call anyone. They'll be watching. I'll be in your office to debrief. Clear?"

"Okay."

At 9:55, Ashton put on his mask and traipsed off to the Royal Bean, three blocks away. He clutched the thumb drive tucked inside his jacket pocket. When the shop came into view, he stopped and steeled himself. *Get it together. This is for Katie.*

Ashton set his jaw and entered the shop. He spotted an Asian man with a red Nationals cap sitting at a window table, typing on his laptop. He looked about forty and hefty, with a cheeseburger stomach spilling over his belt.

Ashton tottered up to the counter and ordered a regular coffee. After they handed him his cup, he turned and took a step toward the seating area. Ashton felt his stomach roil, so he dashed to the bathroom. Minutes later, he emerged with a pale face, and he took a few tentative steps. A man wearing a National's cap popped up from his seat and waved at Ashton.

"Billy! Over here."

Ashton gave him a nervous smile and staggered over to his table.

"It's been too long since LA!" said the contact. He gave Ashton a big hug, pounding his back with his hands.

"Hey, let's get a picture." After the person at the next table took it, they sat across from one another. The operative launched into small talk about his wife and kids, his move from LA, and his upcoming trip to spring training to watch the Nationals. Everyone around them had returned to their phone calls, internet searches, and emails.

He leaned forward and whispered, "The smartphone camera I used scans for electronic devices. You passed. Glad I can trust you to follow directions. Now, give me the plans."

Ashton retrieved the thumb drive from his jacket pocket and began to hand it across the table. As he reached for it, Ashton interrupted the transfer.

"You'll need to type in an encrypted code. You have until noon, or you won't be able to access the plans. Understand?"

The agent glared at him. "What's the code?"

"ALincoln 349."

The operative plucked the device from Ashton's hand and inserted it into his computer. He input the code, scanned the contents, and began typing. Ashton checked the room, no one seemed to be watching. His knee bounced up and down. *What's taking him so long?*

The man glanced at Ashton. "Relax. Almost done."

After a few more moments, he shut the computer and gave Ashton a quick nod.

"Dude, I got the tickets. We're all set for opening day. Hey, great catching up." The agent stood and put his computer in the case. "Have to run. I'll call you next week." He strolled out the door. When he rounded the corner, he turned back and gave Ashton a friendly wave. No one inside paid attention, each preoccupied with the world on their screens. Ashton sat back and closed his eyes. *I did it. I'll get the money for Katie.* He stayed for another ten minutes then trudged back to NASA headquarters.

When Ashton arrived at his cubicle, he saw a Post-it note stuck on his phone instructing him to go to the third-floor conference room. He lumbered up the stairs and plopped down in a chair across from Agent Brown. Ashton's shirt displayed large wet spots under each arm, creating dark circles on his light blue dress shirt.

"How'd it go?" asked Jamil.

He rocked back and forth in his chair, his arms wrapped around his body. "I'm so glad it's over. I was so nervous. I threw up in the bathroom."

Jamil spoke in a quiet voice. "You did well, Ashton. Now, walk me through every detail from when you entered the shop until your contact left."

Ashton recounted the exchange. When he came to the part where the operative inserted the thumb drive into the computer, Jamil asked, "You *think* he sent the file, or you know he did?"

"He said he got confirmation, so I guess yeah, he sent it."

Brown smiled. "Nice job. Continue using your Dark Web site for work. We don't want to raise anyone's suspicions. They might contact you again for something else. If they do, call me from here." Jamil stood and put on his jacket. "We'll work it out."

"Wait. I get to keep the money, like we agreed, right?"

"Yes. Like we agreed." Agent Brown shook Ashton's hand and left. Outside, he texted CJ as he hiked down to the Metro.

"Package delivered."

***

CJ's Office

When CJ received Jamil's text, he grinned and pumped his fist in the air. A sly smile eased across his face. Julie and Jamil didn't know Layla inserted a sleeper virus inside the faulty HAB document, infecting the culprit's computer network. Soon, they would have an electronic trail leading them to the buyer and the NASA saboteur who tried to steal the Martian DNA.

***

That Night

Dark Web, 2:15 AM, Eastern Time, US

Mr. Blue: *Pleased with the plans?*

Mr. Green: *Yes. Payment is forthcoming. Are you willing to do more?*

Mr. Blue: *We can discuss your ideas once I have the money.*

Mr. Green: *You'll have confirmation of payment within the hour. Talk in two weeks.*

Eighteen minutes later, an encrypted text from his bank confirmed five million dollars had been deposited. When he tapped the confirm button, the bank's server erased the message.

He gazed at the blinking lights illuminating the city from his picture window and poured himself a scotch. His plan worked, and soon he could start his new life.

Chapter Fifteen: Surprise

Advanced Robotics Lab

Area 51, Nevada

Julie stepped out of the military vehicle into the cold desert wind. Grains of sand hit her face like tiny bullets. She hurried to the front of Fred Langford's lab, a one-story building the size of a Walmart. Gripping the handle of the front door, she hoped Fred had the astrobots performing on schedule.

She slipped inside and checked out the brightly lit workspace. To the right was a large section dedicated to training the bots on the analytical equipment. Two technicians with computer tablets were huddled around an astrobot, opening and closing a drawer.

The middle space was a workshop with neatly stacked bins of parts and accessories arranged around two large benches. To the left were office cubicles, a conference room, and a small kitchen.

Julie's athletic shoes squeaked as she moved across the glossy-clean concrete floor. Fred turned at the sound, and he sprang out of his chair to greet her.

"Hey, Julie, glad you're here. Come on, let me introduce you." He grabbed her by the elbow and guided her over to the astrobot. The six-foot-plus human-like machine with its large gold faceplate loomed over her.

"This is astrobot Pat," Fred said. Julie noted several lenses behind its visor, with two small, powerful halogen lights on either side of the helmet and one on top.

Fred spoke to the technician. "Put Pat through the core analysis program, please."

She typed the commands into her tablet. Julie bit her lower lip as she watched the astrobot stride evenly over to a metal cabinet containing several drawers. Pat opened the top one. Its fingers grasped a circle-like drawer pull and turned it clockwise. The robot opened the drawer exactly ten inches and removed a cylindrical blue object the size of a rolling pin.

"It represents a frozen sample," Fred whispered. "Keep watching. The cool part's next."

Pat side-stepped over to a large cabinet and released a compartment door. The updated version of the Alpha-particle X-ray spectrometer slid out on its two tracks and locked into place. The power light turned green, and the sensor indicated 'ready.'

Pat picked up the blue cylinder, placed it in the center of the examination tray, and pressed the start button. The spectrometer drew the sample into the analytical compartment, closing the door behind it. A few moments later, the display read 'finished' and the power light switched to red.

Fred looked at Julie with a broad grin. "Pat's mastered the task of taking a core sample and having it analyzed. Cool, right?"

Relief pulsed up Julie's spine. Her eyes looked heavenward, and she smiled. "Nice job. I feel better."

"Don't worry, Julie. We're on schedule. Being isolated out here, nobody bothers us."

"What about the exterior tasks?"

"Doing those in the Longhorn building, next door. Come on. Let's check it out."

When they arrived, Julie observed the workspace where the HAB was being built and outfitted. Powerful overhead lights illuminated the cavernous workspace and its glistening white walls. A low mechanical humming sound came from the large filtration system, keeping the air inside dust and particle-free. In one corner, an astrobot trained in a HAB mock-up unit. The other section of the building was sealed, providing a cleanroom environment. There, Longhorn workers, dressed in white biosuits, constructed the HAB destined for Mars.

"I have two technicians stationed here full-time. Right now, we're working on getting the solar panels hooked up to the HAB."

Julie and Fred strolled over to the training area.

"This bot's Taylor," Fred said, his hands and arms waving about as he talked. "It's refining the tasks necessary to power up the HAB right after landing. Taylor has to unfold the solar panels, put them in a neat row on the ground, connect them, and plug the array into the power port on the side of the HAB. We're practicing with the solar panels today."

One technician recorded Taylor's movements, and another wrote notes into his electronic tablet. They watched Taylor plug each of the solar panels into one another.

"Another critical mission task," Julie said. "If we can't power up the HAB …"

"Yeah, we're sunk. At night, we link each astrobot to our main computer and transfer what each one's learned to the other. Accelerates the process. We're on track for the desert trials."

Julie smiled. "You and your team have made up for the lost time. Thanks for your hard work. Can we go somewhere with a little privacy? I need to go over a few things."

"Yeah, there's an abandoned office across from the break room. Let's go. I need a cup of coffee anyway."

"The last thing you need is more caffeine," Julie said laughing. Fred wrinkled his forehead. "What?"

"Nothing. I'll have a cup too." Soon they sat around a small plastic table on metal folding chairs.

"What's up, Julie?"

"I want to move up the second launch date by two weeks. What do you need to make it happen?"

"You look worried. Is something wrong?"

"I want as much time on Mars as possible in case we have a technical problem." *Or we get sabotaged.*

"Hmm, two weeks. Let me think." Fred stared up at the ceiling. "Training would need to be completed here in five weeks, dessert trials in four, with three at the Cape to integrate with the command module.

"If we add two more technicians, we can work two shifts. I can make it if Longhorn can finish the HAB."

"Get them in here. Susan Chan at Longhorn said she could do it too."

***

Three hundred miles above where Julie sat, a Chinese Gaofen-13 high-resolution reconnaissance satellite slid into geo-synchronized orbit on orders of Minister Liu Wang.

Chapter Sixteen: Conspiracies

Mechanical Assembly Building

JPL, Two Weeks Later

Julie and Marge watched the large crane hold the space sail bundle in position while the technicians secured it to the launch vehicle. It sat atop the MAV with the backup rover mounted underneath.

"It'll be on the way to the Cape this afternoon," Marge said. She moved a step closer and whispered in Julie's ear. "Any word on Franklin?"

"CJ messaged me this morning. Layla has information and said to stand by for an update. Join us."

"Thanks, but I'm helping Franklin get the payload assembly loaded on the truck for the trip to the Cape. Keeping an eye on him until we get confirmation on his status. See you later."

Julie turned and headed back to her office when a text from CJ came through.

"Meeting with Layla in 15. Urgent. Can you make it?"

She replied with a thumbs-up emoji.

Julie sipped her tea and clicked into the video conference. Layla, Jamil Brown, and CJ were already present. She noticed the background on Layla's screen obscured her location features. Her eyes were red, makeup faded, and her hair hung limp on her shoulders.

"Julie's here. Let's start. Layla, you're up," CJ said.

"The sleeper virus we planted only works during downtime, keeps it undetected but slows discovery. I've been watching it non-stop. The HAB plans ended up in the personal directory of Tien Lee, Director of the Science and Technology Department of China's Ministry of State Security. Not a surprise since he runs their space program. Know anything about him, Dr. McCray?"

"Yeah, he's a brilliant engineer and has moved the agency far ahead since he's been in charge. He's impressive."

"Also makes him unethical and a criminal," Jamil said.

"The Chinese have a different definition of ethical than we do," Julie said.

"Is he capable of bribing someone to steal our technology?" asked Jamil.

Julie smirked. "Most of them would."

"He reports directly to Minister Liu Wang," CJ said. "Wang's under pressure regarding their moon base, so Lee's most likely under orders to obtain a HAB structure and doesn't care how he does it."

"Do we agree Lee's contact is someone from NASA or one of its contractors?" Jamil asked.

"Most likely," said Julie. "Check on the attendees at our conferences. It's where contact with Lee would be the easiest. I have the list from the past three years."

"Okay," Layla said. "Send it to me, and I'll dive in and see who turns up."

"Let us know when you have something," CJ said. "Meeting's over, but Julie could you stay on for a moment?"

"Sure." Her pulse quickened, then she scolded herself. *Why am I getting nervous? Get a grip.*

"I didn't want to mention it in front of the others, but Layla investigated Franklin."

"Please tell me he's not the one."

"He's not; he doesn't need money. Turns out his husband has a significant trust fund, and when Franklin's father passed away last year, he received about a hundred and fifty thousand."

"I'm so relieved. I'll tell Marge."

"I thought you would be." Then CJ spoke in a quiet voice. "Thanks for trusting me."

Julie smiled. "Of course. Say, I have a question about the meeting. Why is Layla and not the FBI doing the investigation?"

"Layla's a special category of analyst. She has top clearances in several categories, giving her access to more sources of intel than the FBI." His eyes suddenly flashed up past his computer, and he held up his index finger to someone off screen. "Sorry Julie, but I have to rush off." And CJ's image vanished from the screen.

Julie clicked on the exit meeting tab. Her reflection on the screen showed a disappointing frown had spread across her face.

***

One Week Later

Launch Prep, Julie's Office, JPL

When Julie's day-long launch review meeting ended with her team, Marge stayed behind for a de-brief.

"What'd you think?" asked Julie.

"We're ready, except I want to run the booster burn calculations again. Need to confirm they included the weight of the space sail correctly."

"Good. We're taking every precaution I can think of."

"How did your media review with Boxman go this morning?" Marge asked.

Julie rolled her eyes. "The usual micromanager. Went over each slide. He even made me change a comma. Drove me nuts."

"He never used to be that bad. What's going on with him?"

"He's getting a lot of political pushback about why we're spending money on Mars when our planet's burning up, so he wants to downplay our launch to the media."

"Yeah, it'd be nice to tell the world saving the planet is exactly what we're trying to do." Marge took a sip of her coffee and eyed Julie. "So, did you meet up with CJ while you were at NASA HQ?"

Julie's lips puckered. "No. I mentioned my trip to him, but he didn't respond."

"Hmm. Why don't you invite him down to the Cape for the launch? We can all have dinner together. Simple. No pressure."

Julie shook her head. "Look, Marge, I can't afford to get distracted. Last thing I need is drama."

"Okay. I'll ask him."

Julie rolled her eyes. "Good lord, this is like high school."

"Sometimes people need a little push. Sounds like he was hurt and feels like you. Besides, it's only dinner. Happens all the time in business."

Julie gazed down at the conference table. "I suppose. You're going to do it anyway. See what he says."

***

That Night

Dark Web, 2:10 AM, Eastern Time, US

Mr. Green: *The boss still wants the Martian DNA. I'm out of it now. Tom Walker will be*

your contact. He'll meet with you in person. Tonight.

Mr. Blue: *No, in person's too risky.*

Mr. Green: *It's not a request. Be at the front of your building at 7:10 sharp. DC Cab 121 will pick you up. You have dinner reservations at Lillette's, 7:30. Remember, he speaks for her.*

Chapter Seventeen: Agent Walker

The Watergate Complex, 7:05 PM

Mr. Blue slipped on his 3-D skin-tight mask and smoothed the material until the edges disappeared. Then he hooked the rotund girdle around his waist, giving him an overweight appearance to any electronic eyes sweeping the area. After finishing, he snuck down to the lobby of the Watergate's private entrance and waited for the taxi to arrive. He accessed the DC Cab Company's app, searching for 121 and found a dozen of their self-driving taxis in the area, but none with his number. He checked his watch. *Is Walker not coming?*

At 7:10, he stepped outside into the sultry evening air. A red Prius EV cab raced up the entrance with its 'Not in Service' light on. The number on the side read 121. *Fake cab. Should have known.* He hitched up his pants and started down the walkway.

When he reached the car, Mr. Blue checked the grounds for any suspicious activity before ducking inside. Staring back at him was Tom Walker, a middle-aged Asian man. He wore a dark blue suit with a yellow tie and had round-shaped glasses in a black frame. The privacy screen blocked the view of the front seat. The low ceiling and dim lighting gave the backseat a cramped feel. He could smell garlic on the man's breath.

"What's with the disguise?" said the Chinese agent in perfect English.

"It's for the cameras. And call me Mr. Blue. Can anyone listen in on our conversation?"

He shook his head. "Don't worry. This car is specially designed with our finest technology; no one can see or eavesdrop on us. We are perfectly secluded."

Mr. Blue stared at him. "Well, I don't trust you."

"Mr. Green said you were nervous about our meeting." He gave him an annoyed look. "Please turn off your phone."

Mr. Blue reached into his coat pocket and complied. The Chinese operative wrapped on the partition, and the car sped forward.

"I'm Special Agent Tom Walker of the Chinese Ministry of State Security. I understand from Mr. Green you were the one who arranged getting us the HAB plans."

He gave him a blank stare and said, "Yes."

"I represent Minister Wang. She requires you to accomplish several additional tasks. I'm here in person to emphasize how important these are to her. The Minister does not accept failure." Walker paused and gazed at his passenger.

Mr. Blue folded his arms across his chest. "Okay, let's hear it."

After Walker gave his demands, Mr. Blue sneered. "My deal with Lee was only to pass information. Not this. I won't do it."

Walker leaned forward, invading Mr. Blue's personal space.

"Your 'deal' as you put it, is now with Minister Wang, and you'll do what she says. If not, I'll let your government know you're a spy, and you can wait for the FBI to show up."

A scowl creased his face. "Exactly how am I supposed to do these things?"

"Don't play dumb," scolded Walker. "With your programming background, make it happen."

Before Mr. Blue could react, Walker pulled a plastic case from his jacket pocket containing a silver disk.

"One more thing. You need to manually reprogram the HAB's mass-spectrometer machine. Here's the program CD. Takes about a minute to download."

Mr. Blue frowned at him. "How do you know it's compatible with our machine?"

"Because we manufacture the components in our factories."

Mr. Blue grabbed the disk and slid it inside his jacket pocket. "Here's the problem—the sabotage of the missions will put me on top of the suspect list. The FBI is already nosing around."

"Then be careful." He waived his hand and leaned back in his seat. "We'll pay you well. The Minister knows money is important to you. Five million now and five more when the tasks are completed. You'll have the first installment in your Swiss account tonight."

His fingers clutched the armrest, his nails digging into the soft fabric. "Fine."

"If you need to reach me, go to your coffee shop and order chai tea. We'll pick you up the following evening like tonight. Same time. Clear?"

"Let's hope it won't be necessary."

He wrapped his knuckles on the privacy partition. "Time to drive you to dinner."

At 7:34, DC Cab 121 deposited Mr. Blue at Lillete's restaurant. Alone in the back seat, Agent Walker peeled off his 3-D, face-conforming mask. "Take me home," he barked to the driver.

Chapter Eighteen: Launch Day

Cape Canaveral Media Center

T -3 hours

Standing behind their podiums, Michael Boxman and Julie prepared to address the small contingent of journalists covering the launch. Mingled in with them were the space groupies dressed in vintage Star Trek and Star Wars costumes. CJ slid into the room wearing fake press credentials.

When the countdown reached T-3 hours, Boxman introduced himself and began his brief. Using a series of graphs and charts, he described the economic benefits of past NASA programs and emphasized the anticipated advantages the expanded Mars mission would bring. When finished, he Boxman gave a brief smile amid polite applause, then introduced Julie.

"Good afternoon," Julie said with a broad smile. "We're so glad you're here to witness the launch of our mission, the first of two going to Mars in this launch window. As depicted on the screen behind me, we'll land our rover in the icy South Polar region to collect samples and study them for signs of life."

"What's especially exciting is we'll be using advanced laser beam propulsion technology. The capsule will execute one orbit, and then the space sail will unfold like the solar panels on our satellites.

"The key innovation is the application of a combined neutral particle beam and laser beam in such a way that neither spreads nor diffracts as the beam propagates. It will originate from our sister lab at the Lawrence Livermore facility. This concentrated beam hits the sail and accelerates the spacecraft to one point five percent of the speed of light. This translates to a forty-eight-day journey to Mars."

Julie dazzled the crowd with graphics and animation mixed with music, visually explaining the mission. *What a difference compared to Boxman,* thought CJ. The energy and pure joy she exuded excited the crowd. After her talk, she received a standing ovation from the audience.

When the time for liftoff neared, CJ took a position along the observation window, looking down at the vast Mission Control room. Below, he saw Michael Boxman and Ashton Price standing together at the far side of the room. Julie stood next to Marge behind the Mission Director's desk.

"Are we ready?" asked Julie, tapping her foot.

"We're in NASA's hands now. They say everything is green for launch."

They donned their headsets and listened to the launch team.

"This is Mission. T minus two minutes. What's your status?" Each department reaffirmed go for launch. Then, the final countdown blared throughout the room. "Ten. Nine. Eight..."

"This is Flight. We have ignition and automatic sequencing."

Julie touched her cross and stared at the image of the Eagle Heavy IV rocket on the control room's main screen. Large plumes of white smoke and fire exploded across the pad. The service access arm swung away as the rocket, riding a tower of flame, soared into the sky.

We're coming, C-2, thought Julie.

When the payload capsule finished its first full orbit, Stu Kaplan, sitting next to Flight Operations, eyed Julie and gave her a nod.

"Mission, this is Flight Ops. Sail has deployed, and we're ready for laser propulsion in three zero seconds."

Julie switched her headset so only Marge could hear her.

"This is it, Marge. Holy shit."

"Yeah, fingers crossed."

An image of the Mars spacecraft appeared on the main screen, taken from the International Space Station. "Great image from the ISS," said Julie. "Looks like a silver bullet surrounded by a giant orange umbrella."

Marge bit her lip. "Countdown's at three."

When the timer hit zero, Julie gasped and put her hand over her mouth.

"Marge. The capsule's gone. I knew it conceptually, but to see it. Wow."

Stu Kaplan's confirming words came through Julie's headset. "Mission, this is Ops. Beam's on target. We're accelerating toward Mars as planned. All systems green."

A big cheer erupted from the mission staff. Engineers and controllers were high-fiving, shaking hands, and slapping each other on the back.

"Dr. McCray, Mission. Handoff confirmed by JPL. It's all yours now, Director."

Julie keyed her headset. "Mission, this is Director McCray. Congratulations to you and your great staff. We had as good a launch as we could've hoped for. Thanks, everyone."

Julie smiled and waved at the crowd of engineers and launch professionals. She saw Boxman standing in the back of the room, next to the exit. He wore a grin and clapped at the successful start of the mission. He caught Julie's eye and gave her a wave.

"Boss seems happy," said Marge.

A rapping noise on the glass from above interrupted them. Julie and Marge turned and looked up. CJ smiled at them, signaling with two thumbs-up.

Marge mumbled out of the side of her mouth. "I reminded him we're meeting for dinner. You're not backing out, are you?"

"Feels a little forced, don't you ..."

"No, it doesn't." Marge smiled and waved at him to come down. "Trust me."

Chapter Nineteen: New Awareness

Spaced Out Restaurant

Julie, Marge, and CJ arrived at Spaced Out, a restaurant full of space memorabilia located a mile from the Cape's front entrance. Tonight, the popular watering hole was crammed with technicians, contractors, and NASA staff celebrating the launch. TVs hung on every wall showing a variety of sporting events, but one screen was dedicated to prominent space missions. John Glenn's Friendship 7 highlights were playing.

"Don't worry, we have a table in the dining section away from the bar noise," said Marge.

"Good idea. I need to chill," Julie said. CJ scanned the room, taking in the activity, allowing Marge to direct them.

Walking to a booth in the corner, Julie and Marge slid in on the same side and faced CJ. A server took their drink order and promptly delivered chardonnays for Marge and Julie and a light beer for CJ.

He raised his bottle and said, "Congratulations, ladies. Great job." They clinked glasses and drank, followed by an awkward silence. Marge jumped in and broke the ice.

"Director, tell us about yourself. You're a mystery to us." Julie stiffened at her bluntness.

"Well, spies are supposed to be that way, don't you think? And call me CJ, please."

Marge laughed out loud. "So, what can you tell us, CJ?"

"I went to college at Notre Dame on an Army ROTC scholarship. Only way I could afford it. Both the Army and ND teach there's an obligation, a duty, to serve something greater than yourself. They assigned me to Army intelligence, and I rose through the ranks to colonel. I ended up as the head of intelligence for Middle East operations."

Marge's forehead wrinkled. "How did you end up in the CIA from the Army?"

CJ paused and glanced down. He started to peel the label off his beer bottle with his thumbnail. Marge gave a questioning glance to Julie.

"Everything okay, CJ?" asked Julie.

He glanced up. "Dr. Lewis says I should talk about it." He let out a big breath. "My last tour was Afghanistan. One day, going to interrogate a prisoner, we rolled over an IED, and it exploded, killing the two soldiers with me. I had severe brain trauma."

Julie's eyes widened. "I'm sorry. I can't imagine how awful that must have been."

He raised his eyebrows and continued, "The Army sent me to Walter Reed to recuperate. Phil Locke recruited me from the hospital. Given my injuries, my Army career would be limited, and he needed more Middle East expertise. He stuck with me through rehab and offered me a job." CJ took a sip of his beer and asked, "What about you, Julie?"

"While finishing my doctorate in astrophysics at Cal Tech, I interned at the JPL on the Mars 2020 project and fell in love with it. Next, I was the assistant project director for the ExoMars 2022, and I've been there ever since. I'm dedicating my career to expanding our knowledge of the universe."

CJ turned to Marge, but she checked her watch and said, "Sorry, but I need to Facetime my husband and two-year-old." She gulped the last of her wine and slid out of the booth. "Hope to see you soon, CJ. Bye, boss."

Julie clenched her hands underneath the table. *Marge, the set-up queen.* "Bye, Marge."

CJ waved, and the server returned with menus. After ordering, CJ asked, "Of all the projects you've done, which one did you like the most?"

The two talked about their past experiences and how they arrived at this point in their careers. The conversation continued well after they finished eating. CJ glanced at his watch.

"Guess it's about time to go."

Hmm. He's ending the evening before I do. "Heading back to DC?" asked Julie as they strolled toward the exit.

"Yeah, tomorrow morning. You're starting the Arizona trials?"

"Yes. Susan and Fred are setting up now."

CJ opened the door for Julie, and they stepped outside.

"Thanks for a nice evening, Julie. Enjoyed it." CJ shook her hand. "And congratulations again on the launch."

"I enjoyed it too. Night, CJ."

He turned and walked toward his rental car. Julie stood and watched the solitary figure recede down the asphalt parking lot. She didn't know anyone who'd been wounded in combat before. *Getting blown up and his men killed. That must take a toll.*

***

Next Day

CJ went straight to the office after his flight from the Cape. He sipped his coffee while his computer booted up. Before he could check his schedule, an emergency message in large red letters flashed across his screen.

"CB. In person. Now. The Admiral."

CJ raced to the Coffee Brew located across the street from the vast NSA complex in Ft. Meade, where hundreds of NSA and government officials procured their daily caffeine. CJ plugged his Porsche EV into an empty charging station and hustled across the expansive lobby to the elevators. He pressed and held his thumb on the basement button, allowing the biometric sensor embedded inside to scan it. The indicator turned green, confirming his appointment for the meeting three stories below.

CJ adjusted his tie and entered the conference room. Admiral Garza sat at the head of the table with an NSA staff person sitting to his left. Layla and FBI Agent Jamil Brown were on the other side.

"CJ, this is Analyst Latrell Smith," said Garza. "He's assisting Layla and uncovered a person of interest." Smith stood and shook hands with CJ.

"Let's start. Latrell?"

"Thank you, sir. First, a quick summary. The computer virus inside the HAB design tracked the plans to the office of Director Tien Lee from the Science and Technology department. With this discovery, Ms. Burton directed me to investigate connections he may have had with NASA personnel or their contractors. Here's what I found.

"Two years ago, Beijing hosted the International Space Agency Conference. Our delegation consisted of seven NASA scientists and five contractors, including Susan Chan from Longhorn Space Systems. Ashton Price and Michael Boxman also attended.

"The next year, it was held in Geneva. Price, Chan, and Boxman were the only repeats. I'm excluding McCray and Jamison. Susan Chan presented at both conferences, discussing the types of structures necessary to support humans in deep space environments.

"Xu Yen, who's the Deputy Director of Science and Technology attended both conferences too. In Geneva, he stayed on the same floor as Boxman and Susan Chan. This morning, we found an email from Minister Wang ordering Yen to redirect one of their satellites to cover Area 51, specifically the buildings housing our HAB and astrobot teams."

CJ's eyes widened. "Hold on. Only a few people have this information."

"Who are they, CJ?" asked Agent Brown.

"Fred Langford's team, Susan Chan's people, Price, Boxman, and JPL's McCray and Jamison."

"We can eliminate some of them," said Layla. "Langford and Chen's teams have been holed up at Area 51, and we've monitored no suspicious communication emanating from them. Nothing from Price or the JPL scientists either, which leaves Chan and Boxman. We're not monitoring them."

"FBI vetted Boxman as part of the Senate confirmation process for his NASA appointment. He's clean," Agent Brown said.

"Let's check out Chan," said CJ.

"You think she's the one?" asked the Admiral.

"Doesn't fit our profile, but she stands out," said Layla. "Too many coincidences. Maybe she's working with another person or group."

"Wang's move doesn't make sense," said CJ. "She already has the HAB plans, so why position the satellite?"

"Think she's sending us a message?" asked Brown.

"Not sure, but I'll send a text to McCray to observe Chan. They're together at the trials."

"I'll get a court order and examine Chan's records," said Brown.

"I'll follow up with Cyber Command," Garza said. "Need to know why they didn't tell us about the Chinese spy bird. And Layla, get that satellite out of there."

Chapter Twenty: The Astrobot Trials

Test Site, Arizona Desert

Julie closed her eyes, letting the warm sun of the Arizona high desert bask her face, one of the few places she didn't need to wear a mask. She opened them and took in the terrain, similar to the rocky surface of the Gale Crater. Julie stood outside the operations trailer while Susan Chan, Vice President of Longhorn Space Systems, organized last-minute details with her technical staff. Fred saddled up next to Julie. She could feel him vibrating as they both drank their coffees.

"Nervous, Fred?"

He blinked and pushed his glasses up the bridge of his nose. "Yeah, but I …"

"Okay, we're ready," said Susan, stepping down the trailer's stairs. "Phase One is the tasks the astrobots are required to complete during the first sixty minutes after touchdown. Questions Dr. McCray, before we begin?"

"How is the equipment and bots handling the high afternoon heat?"

"We've measured no decrease in functionality during the four days we've been here."

"Good. Start whenever you're ready."

Susan pointed to one of her technicians, who announced in a loud voice, "Landing sequence test one."

The hatch of the HAB airlock opened, and the two astrobots ambled out onto the desert terrain. Walking over to an external compartment, Taylor pulled the release lever, and the power cart eased down to the surface. Taylor positioned it ten meters away, connecting its electrical cable to the HAB's portal.

At the same time, Pat unloaded the solar panels arranging them in two neat rows, looking like black dominoes lying on the sandy ground. The bots connected the panels together and plugged the array into the power module. When Pat flipped the on switch, the indicators on the instrument panel blinked green. Then the astrobots marched back to the HAB, securing the hatch behind them.

"Nice job with the bots, Fred." Julie said. "Well done."

"Thanks, Julie," said Fred. "Next, the bots must activate the analytical instruments and mechanical equipment inside. You can watch on your tablet."

The three observed the astrobots energizing the ventilation and pressurization systems. The lights on the indicator panels turned from red to green as each system came online. Taylor stepped methodically in front of each piece of analyzing equipment and switched them on. Then the lead technician announced the end of the exercise.

Julie let out a big sigh. "The astrobots coordinated their tasks perfectly, making the HAB operational. Congratulations, this phase is mission-ready."

Both engineers grinned, and Susan said, "We need a few minutes to set up for the next trial."

When Phase Two began, Julie observed the astrobots drilling a core sample, bringing it into the HAB, and testing it using the analyzing equipment. When the trial ended, they assembled in the trailer and agreed on a few minor improvements. Julie gave a summary.

"We're ready for the final trial, testing the Martian HAB and its systems." A serious look then inched across her face. "Director Jackson informed me the Chinese placed one of their spy satellites over Area 51." Julie studied Susan for her reaction. "They're spying on you."

"What! How'd they even know we're there?" Susan snapped.

"He's working on it. For the final trials, General Scott's going to arrange transportation and send two squads of Marines to cordon off the area. Kinda overdoing it, but that's the plan."

"They're always trying to steal our technology," said Susan, slapping her hand on the table. "It's infuriating."

***

CIA Headquarters

CJ's Office

Opening the FBI's confidential report on Susan Chan, CJ. flipped to the family background section in the report's executive summary.

Susan Chan's father, Bohai Chan, grew up near Shanghai. He detested the Chinese government because they arrested his brother and sent him to a re-education camp, where he soon died. The government gave no information as to the cause of death. Believing he was murdered, Mr. Chan assumed he could be next and escaped through Hong Kong with the help of a cousin who lived in Los Angeles.

Mr. Chan became an American citizen and married Alison Zhao. Susan is their only child. According to Susan's emails and social media accounts, her father is still angry over his brother's death but very proud of his daughter for working with the US space program.

Financial Results

Susan Chan's bank account and credit cards do not show any unusual activity, no deposits out of the ordinary, and no sudden lavish purchases.

Foreign Contacts

Susan's only travel abroad was to the space conventions where she made contact outside of formal convention activities with a Chinese official, Deputy Director Xu Yen of the Science and Technology Section.

Yen and Susan's father went to the same university and became friends. In his official position, Yen couldn't communicate with a close relative of a state criminal, so he used the conferences to connect with Susan about her father. While it appeared suspicious at first, our conclusion is Susan is not involved in any wrongdoing and is no longer a person of interest."

CJ closed the file and went to see Phil.

"CJ, what's on your mind?"

"After my meeting with the Admiral, I sent an alert to all Stations for Susan Chan and any associated names linked to her." He held up the FBI file folder in his hand. "The FBI cleared her, but I have conflicting evidence."

Phil leaned back in his chair. "Go on."

"Geneva Station confronted one of Guardier & Cie's senior partners who's having an affair, and her spouse is not the understanding type. She let the agents view recent active American accounts, and Alison Zhao appeared on the list with a recent five-million-dollar deposit.

"Do you have the printout of the bank record?"

"No. Their privacy laws won't allow it. What do you think?"

"Hmm, doesn't add up. Why use a name so obvious? Leads right back to Chan."

"Yeah, too easy. That's why I'm here. Don't we have a way of getting around these privacy laws so we can track where the money came from and who set up the account?"

Phil stiffened, and his eyebrows scrunched together. "I'll take it from here. Thank you, dismissed."

Odd reaction. Must be classified. Returning to his office, CJ found a text from Julie asking him to call.

"Hey Julie, what's up?"

"I watched Susan like you said. She was surprised and upset about the Chinese satellite. I've worked with her. She's one of those people when they don't tell the truth, they blush and get all flustered. I don't think she's the link to Tien Lee. Anything more from your end?"

"Well, the FBI cleared her."

"You don't sound convinced."

"We uncovered conflicting evidence."

"Okay, what's the next step?"

CJ sighed. "Not sure. Phil shut me down and said he would handle it."

"What does that mean?"

"It means something's seriously not right."

Chapter Twenty-one: Disaster

Next Day, CIA Headquarters

Phil stuck his head in the doorway of CJ's office. "Admiral Garza's going to call you at 0930."

CJ tilted his head. "Okay. Why are you the messenger?"

Phil entered and closed the door.

"He's going to talk with you about a special situation. It's highly protected, and I'm here to emphasize its importance."

"Message received. But why ..."

Phil raised his hand before CJ could continue. "It's good news, but it's a one-shot deal. Don't fuck it up."

***

JPL Mission Control, Mars Landing

Same Time

Boxman and Julie stood behind their podiums in the JPL communication center, ready to address the upcoming rover landing. Julie scanned the sparse crowd. *Not even the groupies are here.* Boxman checked his watch and signaled Julie. "Let's get going."

Julie listened to him go through his canned speech, in a clipped, monotone voice. When he finished, he ignored Julie and marched off the stage. *What's up with him?* She cleared her throat and addressed the crowd.

"Good morning, everyone. This is an exciting and historic day. First, we'll execute the final deceleration burn putting the spacecraft into Mars' orbit. The capsule containing the rover will separate and begin its descent. When it enters the atmosphere, parachutes will deploy, then at five hundred meters, the retrorockets will fire. When the craft reaches twenty meters, the heat shield will jettison.

"The animation on the screen behind me shows the rest. As you can see, eight large cushions, like giant beach balls, inflate surrounding the capsule. They absorb the impact energy as the rover bounces across the surface. When it stops, the bags deflate, and the rover emerges."

After answering the media's questions, Julie said, "Stay here everyone. We'll send our live feed to the screen."

Moments later, Julie joined Marge behind the Mission Control desk so they could monitor the flight status on the main screen. She noticed Boxman by himself, near the exit door, leaning against the wall.

"Went over the deceleration calculations, like, a thousand times," said Marge twisting her black curls with her index finger. "If we're too fast, the capsule will skip right out into the solar system."

Julie put her arm around her colleague. "We've been decelerating for weeks. Your calculations have been spot on. It'll be fine."

The Flight Ops Director's voice came over their headsets. "Mission, this is Flight. We're ready for retro burn."

"Roger, Flight. Go on my command. Three, two, one, engage thirty-second retro burn. I need the reduction rate as soon as you have it."

"Mission, Flight. Rockets fired. We'll know soon."

After twenty long minutes, the Flight Director's relieved voice came through the headsets.

"Our spacecraft is in a sustained high Mars orbit. The rover is ready for atmospheric entry and polar landing."

Julie gave Marge a quick hug. "Nice going."

"Roger Flight, good job," said the Mission Director. Then he turned to Julie, covering his microphone, and whispered. "Are we a go for the MAV, Director?"

Julie bent over and spoke softly. "Proceed but communicate with only Flight Ops and me until the MAV is down."

Twenty minutes later, Flight Operations confirmed the MAV had descended and rested safely in the Gale Crater. Julie clicked on her headset. "Good job, Mission. Continue with the rover landing."

"Flight, this is Mission, begin descent protocol. Prime retro-rockets," he said. Sixty million miles away, the retention bolts exploded, releasing the rover module.

"Mission, Flight. Spacecraft is entering the outer atmosphere at the proper trajectory. The parachutes and heatshield are deployed. All systems green."

But moments later, Flight Ops sent an urgent message. "Mission, this is Flight. The spacecraft passed five hundred meters, but we have no indication the retrorockets fired."

The room fell silent. Julie dropped her head and clutched her cross.

"Could be a sensor failure, Julie," whispered Marge.

"Mission, this is Flight. Rockets fired at fifty meters. Rate of descent is catastrophic."

Julie waited for his next words, anticipating what they would be.

"Mission, we have Loss of Signal. Rover is destroyed."

Julie glanced over to where Boxman stood to gauge his reaction and saw him marching toward her.

"Retros at fifty instead of 500?" he asked. "That's a coding error. Do you have an explanation?"

Julie felt the blood rushing into her face. "We'll investigate, of course."

He glared back at her. "A catastrophic failure is the last thing we needed, Director. The anti-space politicians will hound me over this. Handle the press conference on your own." He spun around and stormed out the door.

***

CJ's Office, Same Time

At 0930, Admiral Garza called. "Good morning, CJ. We've selected the Alison Zhao issue for a special investigation."

"Yes, Admiral, Phil alerted me. What's this about?"

"Right. Since 9/11, banks conducting business in the United States are required to use a special software which can give us access to the bank's operating system."

CJ's eyebrows pinched together. "Doesn't that violate international privacy laws?"

"Not when Proposition Forty-nine is invoked."

"Never heard of this. How does it work?"

"First, we petition a panel of specialized judges, and they decide if our request to invade someone's privacy is justified. It's similar to a search warrant, except the guidelines are stricter."

"How are cases selected?"

"A cross-agency group triages active situations. Phil and I are on it. We agreed the Alison Zhao situation needs investigation since your mission is linked to the President. The hearing's in four days."

CJ grinned and gave a small fist pump. "What do you want me to do?"

"As the lead investigator, you'll present the case. And if it contains are any falsehoods or fake claims, the judges will know who to come after. If they approve your petition, I'll explain how the NSA will abide by the Proposition's guidelines."

"Will Guardier & Cie be notified if we get the go-ahead?"

"No. The banks aren't notified when an investigation is underway. Politicians aren't either."

CJ nodded. "Gives everyone deniability, and all the banks are on equal footing."

"Correct. You are sworn to secrecy about this process. Jail time if you violate it. We have two people who leaked information in Federal prison, and we're the ones who turned them in. This is a very valuable tool for us, and we don't want anyone screwing it up. Clear?"

"Crystal."

Chapter Twenty-two: Aftermath

Julie's Office, JPL

After the staff debrief and grilling press conference, Julie trudged back to her office and collapsed in her chair. She gazed out the window at the depressing gray sky and wilted pine trees with their brittle brown needles. The voicemail light blinked on her phone. CJ left a message asking her to call. She let out a sigh. *I don't need any more criticism.* She phoned him and put him on speaker.

"Hey, Julie. I heard the rover crashed. What happened?"

"The descent rockets fired too late, but we don't know why," said Julie. "Marge is investigating. The MAV's fine and stationed in the Gale Crater."

"Good, but you sound exhausted. You okay?"

Her right hand gripped the arm of her chair. "Not really. They badgered me at the press conference. I felt like I was being cross-examined at a murder trial, and to top it off, Boxman took off and abandoned me."

"Wow. I'm sorry. How are you holding up?"

Julie let out a sigh and gazed up at the ceiling. "At first, I blamed myself. Felt guilty about letting everyone down. But now ..." She paused, looking at the picture of her father on her desk. "CJ, something's not right."

"What do you mean?"

Julie settled back into her chair. "It's like when you shut down C-2. There was no operational reason for it to fail. The same goes for the rover's rockets firing late."

"Explain it to me."

"The majority of our accidents are from equipment failure. The rockets firing at the wrong altitude is a programming issue, not an equipment failure. We're investigating, of course, but we have too many quality control checks in place for this kind of mistake to happen.

"Are you thinking sabotage?"

"Yes, but why? What does the crash prove?" She tapped her fingers on the desk. "Our mission is still a go. Nothing's changed."

"Julie, if this is sabotage, then our programmer is out for more than money. This accident will harm NASA. Maybe even create a political uproar to end our mission. We need to ask who benefits from this crash."

"Right. Marge's analysis will tell me a lot. Then we'll talk. What're you up to?"

"I'm tracking the money. I need to sign off, but I want you to know you're not letting anyone down, especially me. Keep following your instincts. We all believe in you. Bye."

How sweet to say that.

***

Ashton Price's Home

Ashton rolled over in his bed, unable to sleep. The large red digits of his alarm clock showed 2:03 AM. Marge had sent an urgent request late in the day to review the rover software. He plopped his legs over the side of the bed. *Might as well do some work.*

He walked down the hall past Katie's empty room. Ashton's sister invited her to stay for a couple of days for some much-needed female bonding. Grasping the handrail with his laptop tucked under his arm, Ashton lumbered down the stairs and placed his computer on the dining room table. He decided to step into the kitchen for a little Jack D to sip on while he investigated the rover's software.

Ashton put on his headphones, selected his favorite smooth jazz channel, and booted up his computer. A beep sounded, indicating a new message had arrived in his Dark Web account. He ignored it and logged into the JPL system.

***

In the Chinese Embassy, twenty miles away, a priority message came into the State Security section from Minister Wang.

Send this to our NASA informant: Job well done with the rover crash. Next step is vital. Make sure you don't fail. Success will guarantee your New York wife stays safe.

The supervising agent on duty yawned and printed it. He stood, stretched, and stepped out of his office to a row of cubicles where two technicians were on duty, both asleep.

"Feng, wake up." He shook his shoulder.

"Sorry, boss. What's happening?" He sat up, rubbing his eyes.

"Minister Wang wants this message sent to our NASA guy. Do it now and copy me. I'll need to confirm it with Beijing."

The supervisor shuffled back toward his office but decided to make a detour to the break room and brew himself some Oolong tea. He let it steep for a few minutes then carried it back to his desk. He refreshed his computer, and Feng's message appeared in his e-mail queue.

At least the lazy punk did it. Too bad I can't fire a Party official's kid. He took a swallow of his tea, comforted by its soothing flavor. He clicked on Feng's email. He saw the recipient and bolted upright. "Oh shit!"

He sprinted to Feng's cubicle. "You sent this to Ashton Price, you idiot," yelled the supervisor.

"What do you mean? Price is the one who handed off the file to our agent in the coffee shop, right? You mean he's not our informant?"

"No," screamed the supervisor. "Cancel it. Now!"

Feng pounded the keys on his computer, then looked up. "It's too late."

"Never mind, I'll handle it from here." The supervisor ran to his desk and sent Wang's message to the right person. Then he called Agent Walker. His knuckles turned white, gripping the phone.

"We have a problem. Feng sent Minister Wang's message to Ashton Price's Dark Website by mistake. If he opens it, it'll expose our informant. What are your orders?"

"Can you recall the message?" Walker asked.

"If I could, I wouldn't be calling you."

"Dammit. Read it to me."

After hearing the message, Walker said, "If Price goes to the FBI with this before the MAV launches from Mars, the Minister's plan will be ruined. She'll blame us. We need to get to Price if we want to survive."

The supervisor pulled his hand through his hair. "I can rustle a team to get to his house in about an hour."

"Take him out. It's our only option. Make sure you get his computer."

Seventy minutes later, a white paneled van doused its lights and quietly rolled to a stop on a tree-lined street close to Ashton's home. A person dressed in black, wearing night goggles, crept low and snuck around to the back of his house. He inched up the three wooden steps leading to the rear door and peered through the glass into a dark, empty kitchen. A faint light glowed from the next room.

He picked the cheap lock, snuck in, and crouched behind the counter. The agent extended his neck and glimpsed at the flickering light from Ashton's computer screen. He faced forward, his head bobbing to the music from his headphones. The agent took out his small-caliber pistol and screwed the silencer in place.

Meanwhile, Ashton searched the rover's software, starting with separation from the command module. Then he saw the glaring error. Ashton shook his head. *Wonder what idiot did that,* he thought. He wrote his analysis, attached the faulty coding, and sent it to Marge. He took a sip of his whisky and decided to check the new Dark Web message.

Ashton stared at the text on his screen and leaned in closer. Creases deepened across his forehead. *The rover crash? New York wife? Who's Minister...*

The assassin took four long strides into the dining room, placed the barrel inches from the back of Ashton's head, and pulled the trigger. Ashton collapsed forward, face down on the table. His whisky glass tumbled to the floor. The agent moved his computer to the edge of the table and checked with his partner in the van.

"Price is down. Going upstairs to secure the house. Four more minutes," he said to the van driver over his headset.

"Roger that."

When he came back down the stairs to the dining room, he saw the text of Feng's errant message still displayed on the screen. *Might as well erase it,* he thought. The agent dragged the machine to the other end of the table and moved the cursor to the start of the message.

At the same time, a police car pulled onto the street. Its headlights splashed across the van, alerting the driver. In his side mirror, he saw the officer on the passenger side reach for the spotlight. The driver ducked under the steering wheel right before the piercing beam engulfed the van's interior.

He froze in the cramped space, listening to the gravel crunch under the tires as the police car crawled by. When the sound dissipated, the driver peeked over the dashboard. He viewed the vehicle's red taillights bend out of sight. His heart pounded as he keyed his communication device.

"Abort! Abort! The police drove by. Leave now. I'll be out front."

Hearing the panic in his partner's voice, the agent stood and pushed back the chair. He slammed down the computer screen and sprinted out the back door, forgetting to put on his night vision goggles. When he rounded the corner of the house, he tripped over a gnarled tree root and went sprawling to the ground, sending the computer sailing into the front bushes. The agent braced his fall with both hands. He heard his left wrist pop and searing pain shot up his arm. He rolled over, clenching his jaws to avoid screaming.

"Get in the van, now," barked the driver over his headset. "The police might be back any minute. We can't get caught."

The agent, cradling his throbbing wrist, staggered to the street and climbed inside. The driver hit the accelerator and sped out of the neighborhood with Ashton's abandoned computer lodged inside a leafy shrub.

Chapter Twenty-three: Proposition Forty-nine

Washington, DC

Next Morning

A black town car pulled into the main entrance of CIA headquarters. CJ climbed into the backseat. The driver, dressed in a black suit and black shirt, turned around and handed him a blindfold.

"I'm sorry sir, but you must wear this until we're inside our destination."

"Are you serious? Look at where you're at. You think I can't keep a secret?"

"It's our standard procedure, or I don't drive."

After twenty-five minutes, the electric-powered car hummed to a stop. The driver took CJ by the arm and guided him inside to an elevator. He heard the doors close and sensed a downward movement. *This place is underground. Won't be able to see the location*. The driver guided him down a hallway into a conference room where he removed the blindfold. As CJ's eyes adjusted to the light, he heard Admiral Garza's welcoming voice.

"Morning, CJ."

"Morning, Admiral. Interesting journey. Any coffee in here?"

"Over in the closet. They made a fresh pot."

CJ poured a cup and sat down across from the head of the NSA.

"Is the blindfold necessary?"

"Not my call." The Admiral shrugged. "We don't have much time, and I need to brief you on a few things. First, the judges' seats are backlit, obscuring their faces, and their voices will be digitally altered. Inside the chamber, all conversations are recorded, so be careful what you say."

"Understood," CJ said. "Let's review my presentation. I made a few changes, and I'd like your feedback."

A few minutes into CJ's discussion, a security guard interrupted them. "Excuse me, but they're ready for you. This way, please."

They followed the guard down a short hallway until they came to a foyer with a double wooden door. CJ scanned the area. There were no insignias or signage indicating the agency or organization the court represented. The guard opened the door and said, "Please take your seats."

The courtroom felt intimate, about twenty feet by fifteen. Narrow beam lights in the ceiling illuminated a polished oak table with two chairs in the otherwise dimly lit chamber. In front of them were three elevated silhouettes, each in a separate glass box with a faint glow shining from behind.

A red light above the silhouette to the right came on. "Director Jackson, welcome to our special court," the electronic voice said. "You can address me as 'Your Honor' or simply Judge One, next to me is Judge Two, and Judge Three. It's only the five of us, so there's no one here to impress. We only want the facts and the reasons the US government should disregard the privacy of the person or persons you'd like to investigate. We assume you're telling the truth. If you're not, you'll be arrested for contempt and perjury. Clear so far?"

"Yes, your Honor."

The light above Judge Two came on. "Mr. Jackson, you may now present your case." The voice had the same electronic monotone as Judge One.

CJ told the court of the Chinese attacks on the NASA databases, their contact with Ashton Price, the HAB plans, and the rover crash. He further explained Susan Chan's background with the Chinese, her meetings while attending the space conferences, the change in satellite surveillance, and the five million deposited into her mother's account in the Guardier & Cie bank.

The light above Judge Three came on.

"The circumstances of her family background, her father's history of anti-Chinese sentiment, and no unusual spending activity according to the FBI make Dr. Chan a questionable candidate. And while the five million deposit is unusual, you've not proven it's illegal. Could you explain your reasoning?"

"Yes, your Honor. At first, we all agreed. Dr. Chan seems to be a loyal American, and her habits and finances are above suspicion. But someone associated with NASA is guilty of sabotage. The Zhao account is the link between the saboteur and the funder of these acts against the United States government.

"Either Dr. Chan is guilty of espionage, or a guilty party is setting her up for reasons we do not know. If the traitor believes the Swiss privacy laws shield his or her activity, examining this bank account is our best path to identifying the guilty party."

The light above Judge One came back on.

"We'll deliberate now. Have a seat."

A thick black curtain came down from the ceiling, sealing the judges from the rest of the room. CJ whispered to Admiral Garza, "I hope I convinced them."

Minutes later, the curtains ascended and Judge One's light came on. "We've decided to permit the NSA to investigate the account you've identified. Furthermore, if this account is linked to any other specific account, you may investigate it to follow the money. You're only authorized to either prove Dr. Chan's guilt or identify who is placing money into this account. You may also follow any withdrawals or transfers from this account."

Judge Three's light came on.

"Admiral Garza, we need to discuss how your investigation will follow the provisions of Proposition Forty-nine."

"Yes, your honor."

After the judges were finished, the same guard escorted them back to the conference room.

"How do we get started?" CJ asked.

"I'll assign Layla Burton. She'll have to move into our isolation section in Building G. She'll be in touch."

Chapter Twenty-four: Crossroads

JPL, Pasadena, CA

Same Time

Julie closed her computer after sending 'no comment' messages to the dozens of media inquiries asking why money was being spent on a failing space program when Earth was in crisis. She gazed out at the gray sky, feeling frustrated she couldn't reveal the true purpose of her mission when Marge and Franklin rushed in.

"Julie," gasped Marge. "Ashton found the software error. We've been sabotaged." She handed Julie his report.

Julie's hands morphed into fists as she finished reading the executive summary. "Let's sit. How'd it happen, Marge?"

"When the capsule left for the Cape, our master copy had the rockets firing at 500 meters. Someone at the Cape altered the instructions to 50."

Julie's face flushed red. "Let's think this through. We handed the capsule over to NASA two weeks before launch."

"Correct," replied Marge. "Anyone with access to the mission computers could've done it. But get this. The rover's reentry sub-file was accessed at T minus six hours at the Cape."

"Dammit. The saboteur was in the room," said Julie. She pointed her finger at Franklin. "Get me a list of people logged in to the Cape's Mission Control. I'll turn it over to CJ. We'll have to trust him to find whoever did this. I need you two to stay on our mission tasks."

"Okay, boss," said Franklin, and he and Marge exited. Julie made a video call to CJ and his image appeared on her wall monitor.

"Julie, good morning. What's up?"

She stood with her hands on her hips. "We've confirmed the cause of the crash. The descent instructions were altered at the Cape, six hours before launch. The culprit was right there in the room with us!"

"Seems like a desperate move." CJ ran his hand through his hair. "Tell me, Julie, how can someone at the Cape alter a JPL program?"

"Once we transfer our space vehicle to NASA, they have access."

"Why's that?"

"When the payload assembly, in this case, the MAV and the rover, are joined to the launch vehicle, it becomes part of an integrated system with fueling, gantry operations, and so on. During this time, access to the software can only be done through NASA's computers in Mission Control."

"Who had access to them?"

"Certain contractors, launch personnel, and NASA HQ people. Franklin's getting you a list."

CJ frowned. "Why headquarters? I thought you said it happened down at the Cape."

"It did, but someone in HQ could've reviewed the codes ahead of time so they would know exactly where the descent instructions were located."

"Who might that be?"

"Not sure. You see, JPL is technically a contractor, and we're required to turn everything, including our software programs, over to NASA once a project milestone is completed. I go through our contracts department. They do the arrangements, so I don't know the exact process."

"Would the launch personnel know which lines of the rover's code to change?"

"No."

"But people at NASA headquarters would know?"

"Yes, some are authorized. Ashton Price is one of our liaisons, but like I said, I don't know how NASA handles it once we turn it over to them."

"Ashton! I'll follow up with Agent Brown. But before I go, how are you feeling now that you've confirmed the cause? You were pretty down yesterday."

"Better. At least I know we didn't screw up. But it confirms someone, or some group, is out to defeat our mission. You were right about the security concerns. I'm worried about the next launch."

"I'm glad you're feeling better. I'm worried too. Talk soon."

***

Jamil's Office

After CJ's call, Jamil contacted NASA's contract office. They confirmed the rover's software from JPL goes through the program liaison, Ashton

Price, for approval. Jamil jumped in his car, sirens blaring, as he sped over to NASA HQ.

Flashing his badge to NASA security, Agent Brown raced to Ashton's cubicle. It was vacant. After noticing his computer was turned off, he hurried to Boxman's office and spoke with his assistant.

"I need to find Ashton Price. Do you know where he is right now?"

"No. He never showed up today, and he didn't call in," said the assistant. "Unusual for him."

"I'll need his contact information and home address."

"Sure. Is something wrong?"

"That's what I'm going to find out."

Jamil retreated to his car and called Ashton's work and private cell numbers. After being sent to voicemail for both, he sped off to Ashton's home. He screeched into his driveway and hurried to the front entrance, wearing his FBI windbreaker. He pushed the doorbell. No answer. He began pounding on the door and yelling Ashton's name. Silence met his calls.

He stepped off the entrance and squeezed in amongst the shrubs in front of the large picture window to the right of the front door. He noticed a silver object wedged in the last bush by the corner of the house. He sidestepped toward it; his hands pressed against the cedar-shingle siding, with the bushes scraping into the back of his windbreaker. When he saw the blood-smeared laptop, he froze in place, realizing he stood in the middle of a crime scene.

Jamil scootched back to the window and cupped his hands next to his face, peering into the living room. At first, nothing appeared to be amiss. His eyes drifted past the couch into the dining room, where he saw Ashton, slumped over, with a large brownish-red stain covering the white tablecloth.

Jamil hung his head and swore under his breath. Then panic seized him. *Oh, God! Not the daughter!* He ran to the trunk of his car and retrieved an iron battering ram. After splintering the front door, he raced up the stairs.

***

CJ's Office

"Damn it!" said CJ after Jamil informed him of Ashton's murder.

"I called Ashton's sister," Jamil said. "Turns out Katie stayed with her last night. Crime scene techs won't be here for a little while, so I'm heading over to be with them."

"His poor kid. Both parents are now gone," lamented CJ. "How much can one person take?"

"Yeah, no shit. We'll honor our agreement and make sure Katie gets the treatment she needs. Not looking forward to this. I'll touch base later."

Gazing at the brown haze outside his office, CJ rubbed his worry stone. *Why did they kill you, Ashton?* He decided to update Phil and walked down to his office.

When CJ finished, Phil asked, "What do you make of it?"

"They killed him at three in the morning but left a bloody computer in the bushes. Something went wrong. No way anyone would leave it behind. We need Layla to examine it. Can you ask Director Maykuth to release it to her?"

"He'll probably go along with it. What else?

"Ashton wouldn't sabotage the mission software. It would jeopardize his deal with the US Attorney." CJ gazed up, thinking through what they'd learned. "But Ashton was connected to the person who coordinated the HAB deal. The buyer was Tien Lee, who reports to Minister Wang. She's behind this somehow."

"I agree," said Phil. "She's been fucking with NASA from the beginning."

"Yeah, and right now, NASA's a public relations disaster. Makes Jennings look bad, too."

***

Julie's Condo
Same Night

Julie's keys jingled as she opened the door and entered her condo. There, sitting upright was Gizmo, waiting for her. She reached down and gently stroked his head.

"I'm home, buddy, and I'm beat. Been a long day." She dropped her knapsack on the entrance tile. "Come on. I'll feed you."

Julie went to the pantry and put wet cat food in his dish then poured herself a generous glass of wine. Gizmo gulped down his food and hopped up on the counter turning over on his back.

"You're giving me the kitty flop," she laughed, rubbing his stomach. "I know you missed

me. I missed you too. Let's go sit on the couch. I need to take off my shoes and put my feet up."

Gizmo followed her into the living room and curled in beside her. Julie took a sip of wine and sat it on the end table. Tilting her head back into the cushion, she let out a deep sigh as she petted Gizmo between the ears.

"Well, buddy, it's you and me again. I've had a tough couple of days, and tonight, I wish I had someone to talk to. No offense. All I have is work and you. Gary's right, I need to get on with my life."

***

NSA Headquarters, Next Day

The FBI delivered Ashton's computer to Layla in her underground office in Building G. She slipped on her headphones and blasted Black Sabbath's hit song, Paranoia. After taking a big sip of her Red Bull, she broke the red evidence tape and removed the laptop from its protective bag.

When Layla opened the laptop, the screen came to life and asked for the password for a program still running in the background. *Whoever killed him never signed off.* She transferred Ashton's information from his NASA personnel file into the NSA's Password Reveal program. The supercomputer's algorithm took Ashton's information and created thousands of potential passwords per second.

Twenty-four minutes later, Layla unlocked Ashton's Friendly Hacker Website and a partial message flashed up on the screen. It read: *'...safety of your New York wife.'*

Layla's nose scrunched. "What does that mean?" she said out loud.

She texted CJ asking him to give her a call.

***

CJ's Office
Same Time

CJ stared at the phone, massaging his worry stone. He needed to inform Julie about Ashton's demise. But ever since the second dinner after the launch, he wanted to know more about this devoted and highly intelligent woman. *Would she really want to go out with me?* He took a deep breath and started to punch in Julie's number, when Layla's text popped up on his computer screen. He called the analyst back, relieved to have the respite from possible rejection.

"What's up, Layla? Find something?"

"Yep. Examined Ashton's computer and found a partial message. It came in at 2:13 AM. According to the coroner, Ashton died between 3 and 4. Don't think it's a coincidence. Here's the phrase."

'...for the safety of your New York wife.'

"Didn't Ashton do hacker work for people suspecting their loved ones were having affairs?" asked CJ. "Maybe it could be related to that."

"Not sure. Anyway, thought you should know. Oh, the FBI said there were no other fingerprints on the computer, only Ashton's. I'm diving back into our Prop Forty-nine work. Not as easy as I thought."

After she hung up, CJ rubbed his worry stone and called Julie. She answered right away.

"Morning CJ. Something I can do for you?"

Her tone was clipped and sounded official. "Julie, I have terrible news. Ashton Price was found shot to death in his home yesterday morning. I waited to hear confirmation from the FBI before telling you."

He heard Julie gasp. "Oh no. That poor man. What will this do to his daughter?" CJ kept silent, letting her process the information. Moments passed before she continued, "Any reason why he was killed or who did it?"

"We have a clue. The FBI found Ashton's computer outside his house. Layla uncovered a partial email. It said, *'...for the safety of your New York wife.'* Mean anything to you?"

"Not off the top of my...Wait. Boxman goes to New York most weekends. His wife lives there. Takes her company jet."

"Oh, right. I remember. After our Thanksgiving meeting. But Boxman doesn't fit. I mean, he has money, and the FBI vetted him. Anyway, Agent Brown is on the case. What's up with you?"

"You know all the bad press NASA is getting. Well, Deputy Administrator Boyle called and ordered me to Washington to explain the rover crash. I told him the mission is classified. He said he didn't care. He's pissed."

"Sounds like he wants to yell at someone." CJ swallowed and leaned closer to the phone. *What do I have to lose?* "Julie, I'm changing subjects. I enjoyed our dinner after the launch. Maybe after your meeting tomorrow, we could do it again."

Silence came from the other end. CJ bit his lower lip. His shoulders dropped as the quiet dragged on. Then she said, "Yes, I'd like that."

CJ let out a big breath and a wide grin spread across his face.

"My meeting's at four," said Julie. "Pick me up at six-thirty. I'm staying at the National."

"Great. Looking forward to it." CJ hung up, and he pumped his fist over his head. "Yes!"

Chapter Twenty-five: Julie and CJ

Next Day

Washington DC

CJ rolled his shark-blue Porsche EV up to the entrance of the National Hotel at six-thirty sharp. The car's glossy finish sparkled under the bright hotel lights. He sported a worsted wool cream blazer with charcoal gray slacks and Ferragamo loafers. His dark blue shirt was open at the first button.

Julie stepped out without her mask when he pulled up. She wore a slinky black Louis Vuitton dress. Her curled blonde hair hung loose and fell across her left shoulder. Her heartbeat quickened when CJ climbed out and opened the door for her. She smiled as he approached and gave her a quick hug.

"You look fabulous," he said, stepping back.

"Thank you, CJ. You clean up well yourself. Nice car, too. Where are we going?"

"My favorite place, Jaspers. It's quiet, and they have a killer eggplant parmesan. It's only about fifteen minutes away."

"Italian sounds great. I'm starving."

Julie filled him in on her brief meeting with Boyle, where he vented his frustration at taking the heat from Jennings about the crash.

"Yeah, shit flows downhill pretty fast around here."

Julie wrinkled her nose. "It was weird. He was more upset with Boxman. Blamed him for the crash. Still didn't make sense to bring me out here. At least it gave us a chance to have dinner together."

He glanced over and gave her a smile.

When they arrived at the restaurant, the maître d' led them to a booth in back, tucked away from everyone else. Soft halogen lights bathed the table with an intimate warm glow. Julie ordered a lemon drop martini and CJ a peaty scotch with two ice cubes.

CJ gazed at Julie, admiring her, as she ran her finger down the menu pondering her choices.

"I'm glad we're getting together, Julie. It's been a while."

"Oh yeah? Tell me why." Julie gave him an inquisitive smile and sipped her drink.

"You're beautiful, dedicated, and off-the-charts smart. Despite a rough start, it's been fascinating getting to know you." CJ smiled at her and took a sip of scotch.

Wow. That was direct. "How sweet. Thank you, CJ. You said it's been a while?"

CJ glanced up. His right hand throttled his drink glass. "When I came back from Afghanistan, I wasn't myself. My fiancée, Nicole and I struggled, and she decided to end it." CJ raised his eyebrows. "So, what's your story?

Need to find out more about that. "I got married to Bill at the same time I started working at the JPL, my first job post-doc. My boss had me working a lot of late nights. One day, I came home early and saw another woman walking out of our apartment. I stood there, devastated, totally unaware of Bill's affair. I felt like an idiot."

"I'm sorry, Julie. It hurts to be betrayed."

Julie looked up. "Anyway, since the divorce, I've put most of my energy into work."

"Yeah, tell me about that. Why did you become a rocket scientist?"

Julie smiled. "I've always been fascinated with outer space. I gaze at the stars and have all sorts of questions about what's it like on different planets. And the exploration process is technically complex. It involves orbital positioning, gravity, propulsion, navigation, communication; all those things. I love it."

CJ took another sip of his drink. "So is JPL it for you?"

"It's a dream job for sure. An even better one would be the head of all Mars programs for NASA. The position's vacant right now, like a lot of them. Funds've been shifted over to the President's Climate Initiative."

"Why that job?"

"I want to direct all the exploration projects, from colonization, terraforming, astrobiology, and so on. I'm hooked on Mars. It's still a living planet, and it's part of humanity's future."

Julie grabbed a slice of bread from the basket and tore off a small piece. "Last time you said you had a brain injury? What happened?"

CJ hesitated, looking down at the table.

"Is it hard to talk about?"

CJ glanced at her, then looked away. "I'm better about it, but most people don't understand mental problems, so they shy away...more like run for the exits."

"Like Nicole?"

"Yeah."

"Tell me what happened. I won't run."

He stared back down at his glass then spoke in a soft voice.

"Our Humvee rolled by an IED detonated by the Taliban. The shock wave from the blast slammed my head into the roof. I woke up nine days later in Walter Reed. They placed me in an induced coma, and when they brought me out of it, I had amnesia. It's not unusual, but I freaked out."

"What do you mean?"

"The hospital had insignias of military branches and units hung on the walls. They meant nothing to me. The staff addressed me as Colonel, but I had no idea why. Basically, I couldn't place myself in the world. It terrified me that I might never make it back."

"I can't imagine."

"Yeah, but I slowly regained my memories with their help. That's when they informed me about the loss of my two men. It brought on survivor's guilt big time."

Julie took a sip of her drink. "Why did you feel guilty?"

"Because it was my decision to put us on that road, and I'm the only one who made it. Their deaths are on me."

"Why do you think it was your fault?"

CJ gripped his glass, his knuckles turned white. She reached over and held his hand.

"This is kind of intense for a first date. Sure you want to know?"

She smiled at him. "Yeah, if you want to tell me."

He squeezed her hand and took another swallow of scotch.

"We were pulling out of Afghanistan. The regular government took off, making Kabul a chaotic mess. There were rumors the Taliban planned to sabotage the airport and attack our soldiers leaving the country.

"One of our rear-guard patrols captured a guy having information about the airport, and they wanted us to interrogate him. One of my sergeants warned me of high enemy activity on the route to the prisoner. But I decided to take the risk and go. She was right and an IED took us out."

Julie squeezed his hand. "I'm so sorry, CJ."

"I'm better now. I see Dr. Lewis and she gives me techniques to reduce anxiety. I also belong to a support group at the VA, and the job helps too."

"Your job?"

"Yeah, I feel I have a debt to pay. If I serve my country, I can make up for my poor decision."

Julie reached over and placed her hand into his. *I'm glad he opened up to me. Can't be easy.* "CJ, thanks for sharing this."

Two waiters approached with their meals and a basket of freshly baked bread. Julie removed the cloth over the bread, and the warm smells wafted between them. CJ took a piece.

"Any hobbies?" Julie asked.

CJ chuckled. "Nice change of subject. Because of our restrictions, the CIA organizes events and athletic activities. I travel too much for the sports teams, but I go to our wine club dinners. They're a lot of fun. How about you?"

"Work, gym, home, but you already know that from spying on me."

He smiled. "True, very true."

Julie smiled back. "Being born and raised in the Napa area, I'm into wine too. And I'm a pretty good cook when I'm not working."

"Seriously, you're at work a lot."

The accusation came flooding back. Julie winced, reached for her glass, and drank some water.

"I said something wrong there, didn't I?"

"It's not you." She sighed. "I guess it's my turn. Bill used to complain I worked too much, and he didn't like being left alone. He said if I'd been home more, he wouldn't have to be with another woman. He blamed his affair on my job."

CJ shook his head and stroked her hand. "He didn't deserve you, Julie."

"Yeah, that's what my brother, Gary, says."

"Your brother sounds like he cares about you. What else does he say?"

Julie took a bite of her eggplant and looked over at CJ. "He's been pushing me to get back into the dating scene, so I'm dipping my toe in the water."

"Am I your first date since Bill?"

"Yeah."

"What a pair we are. Here's to new starts." The two of them clinked their glasses together. After finishing their dinner, the waiter cleared their plates, and CJ ordered a tiramisu to share. They took turns spooning the Italian dessert.

"This is so good," said Julie, licking the last remnants from her spoon. "Are we going to talk about our project?"

"Yes, but let's do it in the car. This place is too public."

CJ signaled their server to bring the check. He reached out and took Julie's hand. "Tonight flew by, and I'm sorry it's almost over."

Julie smiled. "Thank you for inviting me." She held his hand again until the receipt arrived.

In the car on the way to the hotel, they rode in silence for several minutes before talking about their mission.

"Any information on identifying the saboteur?" asked Julie.

"I'm limited in what I can say, but we have a new lead, and we're finally in a position to follow the money."

"Is it a good one?"

CJ gave her a sideways glance and said nothing.

"Sorry, but I'm nervous. I don't like not being in control. I mean if one thing goes wrong, we won't make the launch window. Mission over."

CJ reached over and squeezed her hand. "I don't like not being in control either. Adds to the stress. But Layla's on it. Among the three of us, we'll get this person."

"Good." Julie gave him a sly grin. "Since I'm officially giving you secret information, don't I need a special code name?"

CJ laughed. "Absolutely. Got the perfect one. How about Space Shot?"

She glared at him. "Not if you want a second date."

"Well, I don't want to mess that up. Anyway, here we are." CJ turned into the hotel's entrance and stopped the car in front. Julie turned and faced CJ. He reached out and touched Julie's arm.

"Before you go, I want you to know I had a nice time tonight. You might not think 'nice' is a great compliment, but for me it's huge. Thank you."

CJ leaned over, gently kissing her on the lips. Julie slowly pulled away, still staring into CJ's eyes. She gave him a lingering look and opened the door. She leaned back in before closing it.

"My turn to ask you out. It won't be long."

CJ watched her walk into the hotel until she disappeared around the corner. *I haven't felt this good in a long time.*

Chapter Twenty-six: Dead End

Building G, NSA

Accessing the Proposition Forty-nine software, Layla quickly located the Alison Zhao account inside the Guardier & Cie bank and clicked the Activity tab. Four entries were listed—two deposits and two transfers—each for five million US dollars. The account also verified the money was transferred out within two hours of each deposit.

Layla clicked on the first payment entry, searching for the sending bank's routing number and account. But the source's firewall blocked her.

"The sending bank's not a part of the Proposition Forty-nine agreement. Gotta be the Chinese or Russians," she mumbled to herself. She decided to check the transfer.

She traced it through a maze of six different banks, all part of the agreement. The Prop Forty-nine software identified the same account holder in each, a Hong Kong citizen named Mi Lang.

Her Google search revealed he was the CEO and primary shareholder of Hong Kong National Bank, with numerous branches and investment brokerages throughout Asia and Europe. He did not have an ownership interest in Guardier & Cie. His net worth exceeded three billion dollars.

Sipping on her Red Bull, Layla checked the last transfer. When the information came on her screen, she jolted upright in her seat. The bank receiving the funds had a G&C routing number.

She entered the G&C account number into the Prop Forty-nine software, but nothing came up. Next, she examined the bank's ledger. Not there either. Layla tracked the second transfer, and it followed the same route as the first. Ten million dollars had been deposited into a Guardier & Cie account and completely disappeared.

How is G&C avoiding Prop Forty-nine? Layla picked up the phone and called CJ. "I'm coming over."

An hour later. Layla zipped into CJ's office and slapped her printed materials on his conference table.

"Afternoon, Ms. Burton."

Layla pounded her index finger on the table. "Prop Forty-nine doesn't work. I can't trace the money."

"Hold on. Not the news I'd hoped for. Walk me through it."

Layla reviewed her investigation and the information about Mi Lang.

"Let me pull his file." CJ retrieved Mi Lang's profile from the CIA's database and skimmed through his political connections.

"Get this. Says here he manages private investment portfolios of senior Chinese Party officials, including members of the Political Standing Committee. How's he mixed up in our Mars project?"

"Some of the transfers flowed through his European banks but not the ones in Asia."

"Shit. You said you assumed the originating bank is Chinese because the software couldn't trace it, right?"

"Yep."

CJ pointed his finger at Layla's printouts. "So, Lang *could* be fronting the money out of Europe for someone in the Chinese government, like Minister Wang."

"Yep."

"See if they're connected. And find out how Guardier & Cie is part of Proposition Forty-nine agreement but can shield the money inside their system."

"I've got a friend who's into banking over at the FDIC. Actually, she's anti-banks but knows a lot. I'll check with her."

"Good. One more thing, Layla. Someone sabotaged the rover software before the second launch. Check who might have had access to the NASA computers in Mission Control at T minus six hours."

"Gotcha. I'll need to talk with the JPL people."

"I'll set it up."

"Gotta go."

After she hurried out, CJ sat back and reached for his sponge basketball and fired shots at the plastic hoop hanging off the back of his door. He thought through the case and, after throwing a few shots, went to his whiteboard and jotted down key points.

- DNA from C-2 sent to Dark Web – insider

- Rover software sabotaged – insider
- Ashton murdered
- Money trail – Chinese – Wang?

CJ stepped back and studied his list. *There's one person we've overlooked.* He went to his computer and pulled up the FBI's Michael Boxman Senate background check as part of his vetting before his confirmation hearing. He scrolled through the executive summary.

He learned Boxman's wife, Barbara Wiley, was a vice president of Wiley & Wiley Investments. It managed two hedge funds. One owned by the family worth an estimated 849 million, and a private hedge fund valued at 1.7 billion. Her yearly income, as reported on her income tax filing, totaled 1.6 million dollars.

Barbara's father, Fitzgerald Wiley, managed the firm. Emily Woodson, Barbara's daughter, was a portfolio manager, and these three were the sole principals. Fitzgerald Wiley contributed to the president's party, donating five million to the Jennings campaign. It outlined their financial holdings, concluding there were no conflicts of interest.

CJ turned to the section summarizing Boxman's employment history. He received a doctorate from Cal Tech and worked for JPL as his first job. Four years later, he enrolled in MIT and received a computer science degree. He married Barbara Wiley, moved to New York, and started work in the family business as an aerospace analyst. He stayed in this position for nine months then returned to the aerospace industry with companies headquartered in McLean, Virginia. He lived there during the week and traveled to New York on weekends using the Wiley jet.

After finishing, CJ leaned back in his chair and picked up his foam basketball. He threw it against his window, catching it and throwing it several times. *There must be someone else.*

Chapter Twenty-seven: Getting to Mars

Launch Day, Cape Canaveral

T-7 hours clicked on the countdown timer. Julie stood in the middle of the bustling Mission Control room, arms folded, foot tapping, waiting for Layla to link her computer to NASA's. CJ and Marge hovered behind Layla at the Flight Ops desk. Then a man dressed in a blue jumpsuit strolled in and stood in front of the main screen. Julie pulled the Mission Director aside and pointed, "Who's the astronaut?"

"That's Bret Emerson. He's been assigned to bring part of your Martian items down from the ISS. You should meet him."

Julie marched over and extended her hand. "Hi, I'm Dr. Julie McCray. This is my mission. Heard you've been assigned to us."

"Yes, ma'am. I'm Bret Emerson. One of the last breeds of spaceship drivers. Don't need us anymore with the robots. This is my last mission."

"Well, I appreciate you bringing down our special package."

"Must be special. Nobody's telling me what it is," he laughed. "Thought I'd come in and watch the launch. Still get goosebumps. Reminds me of when I was a kid. I'd be glued to the TV all day."

"Me too. What's next after this for you?"

"Oh, NASA'll want me to drop by now and then. But my folks have a ranch, dairy cows, out past Lubbock. Promised my dad I'd take it over for him."

Layla's voice came over Julie's headset, saying they were ready.

"Well, good luck, Bret. Glad we're in experienced hands."

Julie hustled over to the Flight Operations desk, where Layla sat next to Director Greg Friesen, waiting to start the software examination.

"Let her in, Greg," Julie said. "Time to find out."

He input his password, and the mission software appeared on his monitor. Layla clicked her mouse, and two million lines of code flooded from NASA into the NSA's supercomputer, comparing the coded instructions finalized at JPL to those in NASA's Flight Ops computer.

Layla's fingers danced over her keyboard. "It's comparing the files now."

The lines of code whizzed by, becoming a white blur on Layla's black computer screen. Minutes later, the screen went blank. Julie bit her lip waiting to hear the results.

"Good news," said Layla, giving a thumbs up to Julie. "The lines match up one to one. You're good to go."

Julie leaned close to CJ and whispered, "I'm so relieved. Now we can focus on the mission. Fred's got the bots primed. They performed great in our final test trials." She glanced up. "Here comes Boxman."

The NASA Administrator strutted down the aisle. His smiling face greeted Julie. "This is the mission we've all been pointing to. Good luck in finding those living microbes, Dr. McCray. Good to see you again, CJ."

He left them and circulated among the members of the launch team.

"Does he always talk with everyone?" CJ asked.

"It's tradition. He knows these people, and they appreciate the boss wishing them well. It's like saying 'break a leg' in showbusiness."

The countdown clock hit T-6 hours, and an announcement rang out asking everyone to gather in front of the room. The staff rose from their consoles and complied.

"Julie, what's going on?" CJ asked.

"It's the weather brief. Standard at T-6."

"How long does it take?"

"Not long. About five minutes, depending."

After the brief, CJ observed many of the staff leaving the room.

He nudged Julie. "Where's everyone going?"

"To the bathroom and getting coffee, probably. The breakroom's across the hall. It's the last time before launch they can ..."

Julie's eyes popped wide open. She grabbed CJ's forearm, her nails pulling his shirt sleeve tight.

"Start your timer now."

CJ pressed the side button on his smartwatch. They watched the staff straggle back to their workstations over the next six to eight minutes.

"What are you seeing?" asked CJ.

"The computers were up and running, including Flight Ops, all during the break. Look over to the right. Boxman's been standing alone the whole time, with no one paying attention to him."

CJ turned his neck to see. "Yeah, okay. So what?"

Julie put her hands on her hips and stared at CJ. "Boxman could've changed the descent code in the Flight Ops computer, *and* he had access to program C-2's additional antenna transmission, *and* he was at the conferences *and* his wife's in New York. These aren't coincidences, CJ. He could be the one."

He shook his head. "The FBI already cleared him, and I checked him too. Didn't find anything odd except he's been living away from his wife for several years. That's not enough ..."

"You're the one who's suspicious about coincidences." Julie's eyes bore into him. "You think there's nothing to this?"

"No. But ..."

"Then do something. This is our last launch window for two years."

CJ stroked his chin with his thumb and index finger. "It's a long shot. I'll get with Phil."

Julie pushed her index finger into his chest. "Good. Go back now. We can't waste a day."

CJ leaned over and whispered in her ear.

"Okay, I'll go. But I'm very disappointed we won't be having dinner tonight. I've been looking forward to it all week."

Julie smiled. "Don't worry. You have a rain check."

Chapter Twenty-eight: Hiding In The Open

Launch Time, Cape Canaveral

The solid rocket boosters ignited. Flames and a large plume of white smoke erupted from the launch pad. Seconds later, the gantry bolts released their hold, and the sleek Mars-bound vessel streaked skyward in a flaming arc carrying the HAB and the astrobots.

Minutes later, the boosters' cameras recorded them separating and landing on their recovery pads. They also documented large swaths of brown polluted air swirling across North America advancing toward Europe.

Here we come C-2, thought Julie as she massaged her cross necklace.

"Great launch," Marge said. "And Stu handled the laser propulsion like last time."

"It's the start we need." Then Julie whispered, "I still can't shake the feeling the mission is in danger."

***

Phil Locke's Office

Late Afternoon

CJ rushed into Phil's office.

"What's going on?" Phil said. "Thought you were at the Cape."

"Came back to follow a lead. It's sensitive."

"Let's hear it."

"We believe Ashton Price accidentally discovered a message exposing our saboteur. Hence his murder."

CJ showed Phil the partial message and explained Julie's reasoning about Boxman.

"The clincher came this morning at the Mars launch. We saw firsthand how Boxman could've accessed the NASA mission computers during the staff's weather briefing and made the fatal software change."

"What about the Alison Zhao account? Lead anywhere?"

"The money's still a mystery, Phil, even with Prop Forty-nine. Layla found two deposits of five million. After each deposit, the money went through several banks, then back to Guardian and Cie, but we couldn't locate the account. Agent Brown said he wouldn't get involved without linking Boxman to the money. It seems unlikely, but Boxman fits. Can you help?"

Phil sat back in his chair and gazed at the ceiling. He said nothing for several moments, then returned his attention to CJ.

"You said he goes to New York on a private plane? They make convenient meeting places. Have Agent Brown check the flight manifests. See if anyone's with him."

CJ shook his head. "He said he'd have to be ordered before he would get involved. Afraid of the politics."

"I'll call Maykuth. The flight manifests shouldn't be a big deal. Hold on." Phil wrote a number on a slip of paper and slid it across to him. "Here's someone who can give you some background."

"Who's this?" asked CJ, picking up the note.

"Hank Labowitz. He's a friend. We went through the Farm together. He's been doing Wiley's business and personal taxes for years and knows the family history. Call him. It'll save you some time."

"Thanks, Phil. Ah, before I go you should know I'm dating Dr. McCray."

"I'll note it in your file," Phil said, smiling back at him. "I'm glad for you. Hope it works out."

***

CJ called the Labowitz number, a 212 area code. A person with a thick New York accent answered the phone, "Rosansky and Rosansky."

"I'd like to speak with Mr. Labowitz."

"Who's callin'?" asked the voice.

"A friend of Phil Locke."

Twenty seconds later, another voice barked at him. "This is Hank Labowitz. You said you know Phil Locke?"

"Yes, Hank. I'm CJ Jackson, Deputy Director, CIA. Phil said you might be able to help answer some questions about the Wiley family."

"I'll call you back in ten minutes."

Ten minutes later, CJ's phone rang. "Jackson here."

"I spoke with Phil and you checked out. My specialty's forensic accounting. I left the CIA ten years ago to work for Rosansky and Rosansky, but Phil and I maintain contact. Now, what do you want?"

"Barbara Wiley and her husband don't spend much time together. Could you enlighten me on their relationship?" CJ heard a loud sigh.

"Long story. The Wiley family dynamics are difficult and centered around Fitz. In high school, a male teacher sexually assaulted Barbara. She received therapy and seemed to be okay at least on the surface."

"But what about Fitz?"

"Fitz was traveling extensively building the business. He felt guilty not being present when the assault happened and blamed Simone, his wife, for not protecting their daughter. This hurt Simone deeply and created an unbridgeable divide. They divorced when Barbara left for college. Fitz's been overprotective and controlling of Barbara ever since."

"How about Boxman?"

"Not yet. Barbara met David Woodson at Harvard. They had one daughter, Emily. However, the marriage ended within a year. Story goes Woodson took his frustration out on Barbara over Fitz's constant meddling in their marriage. The tension among the three became unlivable. Fitz made him an offer to leave, and he did. Hasn't been heard of since, but Barbara blamed Fitz."

"Then what?"

"Not sure exactly, but Barbara meets Boxman in graduate school. She rebels and secretly marries him. Fitz is outraged. He's trying to protect his daughter, but she asserts herself and brings a stranger into the family without his knowledge. The tension starts all over.

"They reached a compromise. With Fitz's connections, he placed Michael in an aerospace company in the McLean, Virginia area, far enough away not to be around during the week, and the company plane picks him up for weekends."

"Sounds like Fitz has some issues."

"No shit. But the marriage arrangement works for Barbara. Fitz is under control, and they run a successful business together during the week. Then she gets to enjoy Michael on the weekends away from Fitz."

"Why did Boxman get the NASA job?"

"Fitz made the five-million-dollar contribution to Jennings' campaign in exchange for appointing Boxman. It's his dream job. Fitz gets Michael out of the way, Michael's happy, and Barbara is appeased. Everyone wins, and peace reigns in the family."

"What a mess. How do you know all this?"

"Emily's my contact at the firm for their taxes. She talks to me. She, Barbara, and Michael have drinks together every Friday evening when Michael comes in and they catch up."

"What about Emily?"

"She's thirty-one. Very smart gal, maybe the smartest of them all. She's ambitious and knows what she wants. Takes after her grandfather."

"Okay, fill me in on this. I've been talking with my NASA contacts. They say Boxman defers to his number two, a guy named Jack Boyle. Know anything about that?"

"Last tax season Emily told me Michael's increasingly unhappy. Seems Jennings gave Michael the job but told him Boyle is the person in charge. Think it happened soon after Michael's swearing-in."

"So the rumors are true. What happened to Fitz's wife?"

"After the divorce, Simone left the country and lives a quiet life in Geneva. She receives a generous monthly payment for life. Emily's close to Simone and visits her several times a year."

"One more question. Since you mentioned Switzerland, know anything about a small Swiss bank called Guardier & Cie?"

Silence sounded from the other side. Seconds passed.

"Where did you get that name?" snapped Hank.

"It came up in another investigation. I thought you might know something about them."

"All I'll say is the Wiley firm has a professional relationship with G&C. The rest you'll have to find out for yourself. I need to go now. Tell Phil he owes me."

***

Later in the day, CJ called to connect with Julie.

"Congratulations on the launch. It looked great on the news."

"Thanks. It's a big relief. Honestly, I'm exhausted. Don't think I would've been good company."

"You've been through a lot. Get some rest."

"When I get back, I'm going to take a day off and decompress. We could both use a break. Want to join me? We could do our project update out here."

CJ's heart rate soared. "Fantastic. I'll be out," he said, grinning.

"Good. I'll make arrangements." She paused. "Did you find out anything about Boxman?"

"Quite a bit, but I'm still working it. I'll have more to say at our meeting."

Chapter Twenty-nine: Building the Case

Reagan National Airport

General Aviation Terminal

Agent Brown wore a chocolate cashmere sweater to ward off the sudden chill enveloping the DC area, a welcome respite from the suffocating heat. He marched into the terminal, approached the customer service counter, and flashed his badge to the attendant.

"I'm Agent Brown, FBI," he announced. "I need to speak with the manager."

When the attendant informed her boss, she rushed out. Jamil began to introduce himself, but she cut him off.

"Please," she whispered, "let's continue this in my office. Right this way."

She took Jamil by the elbow and guided him down the hall.

When they were inside, she closed the door and shook Jamil's hand. "I'm Belinda Ross. Please have a seat. Sorry about rushing you back here but some of our customers jump to conclusions." Belinda shook her head. "If they see the FBI, I'll get calls thinking we're smuggling drugs or transporting terrorists." She settled behind her desk. "Now, what can I do for you?"

"Ms. Ross, we're following up on a security matter involving the Wiley and Wiley aircraft. Here's the registration number. I need to see the flight manifests." He handed her an index card with the plane's tail number.

"Of course. Give me the dates, and I'll pull them off the computer."

"I want the last two years."

"No problem. I'll be right back." Belinda withdrew into another room and soon returned with a thumb drive. She inserted it into her office computer and turned the screen to face Agent Brown.

"Data's organized by the tail number, by owner. Wiley and Wiley own their plane outright. Their flight list is long but routine. The plane goes to New York most Fridays and returns early Monday morning."

"I'll need a copy of this file."

"Of course. Here take this." Belinda handed Jamil the thumb drive.

"Anything else, Agent Brown?"

Jamil leaned over and spoke in a quiet voice, "We're not interested in the Wiley firm, so there's no need to alarm them. Given their connections, it'll come back to me and not in a good way, if you know what I mean. Can we keep this between us?"

"Trust me, I know exactly what you mean. You won't believe the crap I have to deal with around here."

***

FBI Headquarters, Washington, DC

After studying the Wiley manifest data, Jamil sent the information to CJ and called him to relate his findings.

"CJ, here's our analysis. Boxman flies out Friday afternoons to LaGuardia and returns Monday morning, like clockwork, almost every week. Only one other person, Emily Woodson, has been on these flights. And it's only been in the last few months.

"Sometimes she flies down Mondays and goes back Fridays, and sometimes she comes down Fridays and back to New York on the Monday morning flight. Sometimes Boxman is here when she's in town, and sometimes he's not. There isn't a consistent pattern."

"Interesting. I have new information too." CJ told him about the conversation with Labowitz and Julie's observation of Boxman at the Cape. "Come on Jamil. Too many things fit here. We have to do something."

"I'll need to run it up the chain before I can touch Boxman. Just the way it is."

"Can't we at least check out Emily? She won't raise any political concerns."

"Why? Give me a reason."

Damn, what is it with him? "Emily knows about Boxman's unhappiness, and she's flown down here over the past few months at the same time when our mission problems have occurred. Coincidence? Let's find out. If Boxman wasn't an appointee, you'd be all over this. Admit it."

Jamil clenched his jaw. "All right. I'll vet Woodson and see what she's doing down here. But that's as far as I'll go."

"Good. I'm glad you're on board."

"We're only assisting a sister agency in a routine inquiry. There's no formal investigation of Michael Boxman."

He's sure covering his ass.

Chapter Thirty: The Getaway

Julie's Conference Room, JPL

CJ arrived late morning for his update meeting with Julie and Marge. The three of them grabbed coffee and sat around the conference table. Julie and CJ kept glancing at each other and smiling.

Marge rolled her eyes. "There're no secrets here. Can we get started so you two can leave?"

"Good idea," said Julie. "What do you have for us, CJ?"

"After your Boxman observations at the launch, Jamil, Layla, and I've been unofficially investigating him, and we've uncovered some unusual circumstances."

Marge and Julie sat up straighter, their smiles dissolving.

"What are they?" asked Julie.

CJ explained Boxman's appointment to NASA, Jennings inserting Boyle, the family dynamics, and Layla's discovery of the money transfers linked to the Chinese.

"Given this new information, what's your reaction?"

"For me, he fits," said Julie. "What we observed at T-6 sealed it for me."

"It makes sense for me, too," Marge said. "I've been in meetings where Associate Administrator Boyle goes out of his way to make it clear he's making the decisions. All of this can't be a coincidence."

"But what's his end game?" Julie asked. "Boxman doesn't need money. You said his wife's wealthy. So why sell our information to the Chinese?"

"She most likely has a prenup, given the overprotective father. We also found his daughter-in-law, Emily, has been visiting DC over the past few months. Maybe she's helping him finance a new life."

Julie scanned the plaques hanging on her wall commemorating NASA's groundbreaking missions. Her forehead creased with worry lines. "My gut tells me we're not in the clear."

"Why? What are you thinking?" CJ asked.

"Does Boxman have the ten million?" asked Julie.

"I can't be sure. Layla can't track it."

"If he does have access, why stick around? There must be another reason." Julie stood and paced back and forth. "Any ideas, Marge?"

"What's valuable are the living organisms. Maybe instead of the capsule docking to the ISS, it'll rendezvous with the Tiangong space station."

CJ shook his head. "Minister Wang wouldn't go that far. The Chinese government isn't going to inflame relations by seizing a multi-million-dollar asset belonging to the United States."

"You're probably right." Julie turned to Marge. "But let's check everything. Marge, review the navigation instructions on the command module. Let's be sure."

"Okay, boss."

Julie stopped and faced CJ. "Why can't Agent Brown spy on Boxman? He signed the same paperwork as me."

CJ shook his head. "He's afraid any investigation might leak to the press and embarrass the President. Boxman must be linked to the money for him to move."

Julie plopped down in her chair. "Let's hope Layla finds it soon."

"Me too. How's the mission going, anyway?" CJ asked.

"We're on track navigationally," Marge said. "The spacecraft's performing well, and we've avoided being blown up by tiny particles traveling at thousands of kilometers per hour. Soon we'll turn the capsule around and begin decelerating. Meanwhile, we're identifying drilling sites."

"Whatever happened to Dr. Williams?" asked Julie. "Haven't spoken with her in quite some time. Is she working on the Air Cleansing Facilities?"

"All I can say is if you find the bacteria, she'll be ready."

"Need to know?"

"Right."

Marge stood and gestured toward the door. "All right, you two, meeting's over as far as I can tell. I'll follow up with the navigation software. Now get out of here."

***

The Beach

Julie turned the key and opened the door to their weekend cottage. Hazy light reflecting off the ocean blasted through the large picture window. CJ hurried across the whitewashed floorboards and stared at the vast blue Pacific with the waves crashing against the rocks on the beach.

"Look. Patches of blue sky." CJ turned and faced her. "Julie, this is awesome. How'd you find this place?"

"One of our scientists rents it out." She walked over and stood close to CJ. "Growing up, my family rented a place every summer, just down the beach. This part of the coast has wonderful memories of when I was a kid."

"Nice. Listen to those waves. Hey, let's go for a walk. I need to smell the air and take it all in."

"Okay, but we shouldn't stay out too long."

The weathered gray wooden steps creaked under their feet as they stepped onto the beach. They walked close to the edge where the waves washed their bare feet, keeping the sand cool. CJ reached for Julie and intertwined his fingers with hers.

"I love this stretch," Julie said. "You used to be able to see the mountains in the distance."

"I forgot how soothing the ocean sounds. I feel relaxed already. Best part is I get to be here with you."

Julie unlocked her fingers from his and slid her arm around his waist, their hips joined in rhythm with their steps. A few yards more, CJ bent over and gave her a gentle kiss. She lingered, and he kissed her again, longer this time. She drew herself into him, sliding her hand down his back, and she whispered in his ear.

"Let's go back to the house."

Hours later, abandoned dinner plates lay on the dining room table. Julie and CJ nuzzled on the couch, staring out at the ocean, the phosphorous algae lighting the waves. They each cradled a glass full of Julie's favorite Napa cabernet.

"How do you like the wine?" Julie asked, breaking the silence.

CJ smiled. "Love it. Nothing this good at our wine dinners."

"Tonight's a new moon. The sky has some open spots. We'll be able to get a glimpse of the stars. Want to join me?"

They huddled together outside on the wooden steps and sipped their wine. CJ slipped his arm around Julie, and she snuggled against him warding off the brisk ocean breeze.

"I love it here," said Julie. She opened her mouth, then stopped and closed it again.

"Were you going to say something?" he asked taking a sip of wine.

Julie looked out to the sea. "This is a special place for me. I never shared it with Bill. Not sure why that popped into my head." Her fingers squeezed CJ. "Didn't mean to bring him up, sorry."

"Well, I'm glad you're sharing it with me. Why is this place so special?"

"Reminds me of my Dad. He and I would go out every night, right past those boulders, and scan the stars. Easier back then."

Julie stopped talking, tears flooded her eyes. She wiped them with her sleeve.

"I had this funky old white telescope on a shaky metal tripod that Dad gave me for Christmas, not much more than a toy, really. But I loved it. Dragged it down here every year. Then one summer night for my thirteenth birthday, Dad bought me a big Gsyker 80-millimeter astronomical refractor telescope. I screamed all the way down to the beach. Couldn't wait to set it up."

She paused, and CJ let the silence linger.

"He told me if I'm going to be a rocket scientist, I'd better be able to study the planets up close. Giving me the telescope meant he believed in me." Julie fingered her necklace. "I miss him. I wish he could see what I'm doing now."

"He'd be so proud of you." CJ squeezed her tighter. After a long pause, he said, "Maybe this place can be the start of some more great memories. Let's go back inside."

Chapter Thirty-one: Piecemeal Answers

Layla's Office, Five Days Later

CJ wound his way down to Layla's subterranean workplace in Building G, responding to her new discovery. The tomb-like space contained rooms double the size of regular offices, with new furnishings gleaming with their polished wood surfaces. Gray cones protruded from the walls to absorb sound, and a large monitor hung on the long interior wall, the size of a picture window, showing a forest scene. It was designed to give the occupant a feeling of open spaces and in sync with the time of day on the surface.

"Morning, Layla. Takes a while to get down here."

Layla turned in her chair. She wore black leather pants with a purple silk blouse. Matching purple streaks highlighted her vibrant red hair. She pointed her finger at CJ. "I know how the money disappears. My friend explained it to me. It's part of Fintech."

CJ shrugged. "Fintech's been around for a while. How does it explain our situation?"

"The most common Fintech apps allow someone to move money directly from person to person or account to account, but this one is different. The app is called MoneyMove. The funds we've been tracking ended up in a G&C MoneyMove account."

"How do they get around Prop Forty-nine?"

"Wait. What's the most important aspect of a Swiss bank?"

CJ tilted his head. "Secrecy."

"Right. And Prop Forty-nine destroyed it. To get it back, Guardier & Cie bought the startup that created MoneyMove and became G&C's proprietary product. Get this. When Proposition Forty-nine became law in 2013, these sophisticated Fintech applications didn't exist and therefore weren't part of the agreement.

"You mean Congress hasn't updated it in almost twenty years?"

"They have, but MoneyMove was designed to take advantage of one specific loophole they found in the Prop Forty-nine legislation. It still exists. Never been changed."

"You're telling me all I have to do is transfer money from my regular G&C bank account into a G&C MoneyMove account and our Prop Forty-nine software can't track it?"

"Yep. It puts Guardier & Cie back in the secrecy business."

"Find a way to link Boxman to the money, Ms. Burton." CJ gave her a determined stare. "I know he's our guy."

***

The next day, CJ paced back and forth in his office, earbuds securely in place as Agent Brown's voice crackled through with the information he collected on Emily Woodson.

"The flight manifests reveal no particular pattern," reported Jamil in a matter-of-fact tone. "Her credit card reveals no hotel charges, no entertainment expenses, like theatre tickets or restaurants. It's like she stays inside. I'm assuming she's at Boxman's place."

CJ stopped mid-stride. "You said she comes down here at times when Boxman isn't here, right?"

"Yeah."

"What does she do all day?" asked CJ.

"She's on the phone. Before we go there, I found one more thing. Emily travels to Geneva at least twice per year to visit her grandmother. Same thing. No hotel, car rental, or restaurant charges. She stays between four and seven days each trip."

CJ crossed his arms. "What about the phone calls?"

"The numbers match investor relations departments, or they're linked to very high-worth individuals. We're assuming they're investors in their hedge fund."

CJ shook his head. "Doesn't make sense. Why come to Washington to make phone calls? Need to find out what she's doing here. Could you assign an agent to find out?"

"Can't. Staffing's crazy short, and she's doing nothing suspicious. We have too many other priorities we're chasing."

Not a surprise. "Thanks, Jamil." *I'll have Layla do it.*

Chapter Thirty-two: Setting the Trap

Three Days Later

Building G, Layla's Office

CJ hurried down the corridor to Layla's office, his heart racing after reading her urgent text about Emily Woodson's movements. He pushed through her door to find Layla perched on the edge of her worktable, her fingers tapping against the surface as she sipped from a can of Red Bull. The wall monitor illuminated Layla's face, displaying Emily's phone locations from her last six visits.

"Pattern's obvious," she said, pointing to the screen.

CJ leaned in closer, examining the data. "Looks like she goes from Reagan National to this West End condo complex. Is she there the whole time?"

"Assuming she has her phone with her, then yeah."

"Any specifics stand out about that neighborhood?"

Layla took a sip of her drink, her eyes narrowing. "It's a wealthy part of town, filled with high-income people who fit the profile of Emily's clients."

"Which unit is she in?"

"Couldn't tell. Get this," said Layla. "I found significant electronic interference in the vicinity. No camera access either. Very strange. I could only pinpoint her location to a section of the complex. So, I checked the housing records of those units. One of them is owned by Guardier and Cie. They bought it three years ago."

CJ's expression hardened, processing her information. "Guardier & Cie again. The Wileys have a relationship with them, and Emily goes to Geneva where their headquarters are, to visit her grandmother. Another coincidence."

CJ folded his arms across his chest. "She's coming here to be with someone, Layla. She stays inside because being seen in public would be a problem. Since she's single, her lover probably isn't. Nice work. One more thing. The electronic interference suggests someone who needs to be hidden. See if you can find out who."

"Wait. That's not all, Director." A big grin spread across Layla's face as she turned off her monitor. "Found something on Boxman, too."

His eyes widened. "Great. Spill it."

"At first, I checked his bank account, credit card spending, and phone calls, and I found nothing suspicious."

Layla took a hit of her Red Bull, then continued, "Then I switched to his phone movements. Boxman eats at gourmet restaurants two to three times a week. One of his favorites is Lillette's. It's a five to eight-minute drive from his Watergate residence, according to the Uber app. Then, I found an irregularity. It was one week before the first Arizona trials. Here it is."

Layla pulled up Boxman's phone movements on the screen.

"At 7:10, his phone leaves the Watergate Complex. See? It goes around in circles for over twenty minutes. Why? Then it heads directly to the restaurant, arriving at 7:34, but there's no record of payment. Why? At 9:17, he takes a driverless Uber back to his condo. Six minutes. Payment for dinner and the ride home are on his credit card."

A smirk spread across CJ's face. "You have something."

"Yep. I checked the Watergate's security footage. A heavy-set person who doesn't look like Boxman got inside a DC Cab, number 121. But Boxman lives at the Watergate."

"Could be a disguise. Let's assume it's him. Go on."

"Watch." Layla typed on her computer, and an image flooded the screen. "Can't get a total visual, but you can see two legs in the backseat."

"All the driverless cabs have security cameras. What did it show?"

Layla took off her glasses and pointed at the monitor. "Ready? There's no taxi 121 at the DC Cab company. It's a fake."

CJ took a step back, and his mouth dropped open. "Holy shit, Layla. Boxman's having secret meetings."

Layla smiled in agreement. "And who do you think the person in the backseat works for?"

"Tien Lee or Minister Wang."

"Yep, that's my guess," said Layla.

CJ scrutinized the image on the screen. "A cab that's not a cab." Then his eyebrows shot up, and he spun around to face Layla. "And thanks to you, I know how we can link Boxman to the money." He bolted out of the room and yelled back, "I'll be in touch."

***

Four Days Later

Julie's Office, JPL

CJ called for an in-person emergency meeting at the JPL. Layla, Jamil, and Julie convened around the conference table with confused looks on their faces. Finally, General Scott marched in, grabbed a seat, and folded his arms across his chest. His eyes were beet red. He shot CJ a glance and folded his arms.

Jamil's the one we need to convince, thought CJ. He looked at the agent and kicked off the meeting.

"Thank you all for making the trip. Layla and I have uncovered troubling information. After consulting with Julie, we believe our mission is in danger of being sabotaged. We have evidence that Michael Boxman is that person, and we have a plan to prove it."

Jamil's head whipped around, and he scowled. "Him again, CJ? This better be good."

CJ, Layla, and Julie related the information they had collected. When finished, Jamil spoke up. "We've been over this. Without linking him to the money, any investigation is out. It's too political."

Julie's face flushed, glaring at him. "You want to tell that to the President? It's only the planet at stake."

"Tell us what you're thinking, Doctor," ordered the General.

"We've developed a trap to prove he's taking money from the Chinese so the FBI can stop with the excuses and interrogate him to learn what else he might have done to jeopardize our mission."

Jamil stiffened in his chair, but before he could respond, General Scott intervened, "Keep going, Dr. McCray."

"Right. The first step, General, is for you to convene an urgent Magellan meeting. There, Agent Brown will reveal Susan Chan is a person of interest in the rover sabotage. CJ and I will point out her meetings with the Chinese, her access to the software, and the money in her mother's account." Julie took a sip from her water bottle.

"Step two is we reveal how Layla's virus has infiltrated the Chinese moon program. Then, General, you order the NSA to sabotage their upcoming moon mission launch. It's a tit-for-tat thing to get back at them for the rover crash." She nodded for CJ to continue.

"If Boxman is selling intel, then this information will be too good to pass up. It'll prompt a meeting with his Chinese contact, and we'll be waiting to document it."

"That's not going to do it, CJ," Jamil interrupted.

"Hear us out," CJ said. "The timing's perfect. The Chinese mission launches in ten days. Layla scans the restaurants Boxman frequents. If his reservation appears, the FBI stakes out his condo to see if the fake taxi shows up."

Jamil shook his head. "Yes, but we'll need to listen in to confirm he's the one. The Chinese will have electronic interference set up. It'll be a waste of time."

Layla leaned forward and pushed her glasses up the bridge of her nose. "If Boxman carries his phone into the car, I'll be able to record his conversation with our RealTalk app."

Jamil's eyes squinted. "How's that?"

Layla gave Jamil a bored look. "All government phones have a backdoor portal the NSA can use. If he makes a deal, you'll have the evidence."

"Won't the Chinese suspect the phone?" Jamil asked.

"Of course, that's why the app is passive. We won't be able to hear the conversation live, but it'll be stored in the phone's memory. When he turns it back on, I'll download the conversation, and we can listen to what was said."

"How can it work if the phone is turned off?" Jamil said in a dismissive tone.

"Could you be any more resistant, Jamil?" accused CJ. "Are you a member of this team or not?"

"I got this," said Layla. "Many phone functions stay on even when the phone is off, like the time and the phone's location. RealTalk is embedded in the time function."

"Why doesn't Boxman know about the software virus in the HAB plans?" Scott asked.

"We never told him," said CJ. "If you approve our plan, we'll need to move fast. I suggest the day after tomorrow."

"Let's do it," said the General, then he looked at Jamil. "Like Dr. McCray mentioned, it's the President's mission that's threatened. Is the FBI going to stand in the way, Agent Brown?"

The room quieted, and all eyes shifted to Jamil. He looked at Julie. "You sure?"

Julie's neck stiffened. She pointed her finger at him. "Yes, Agent Brown. I *know* he's our saboteur. Now can we please get on with it?"

"All right, I'll set up our van." Then he looked over to CJ. "But you and Layla are coming with me."

***

Fake Magellan Emergency Meeting

Julie paced in her office, clutching her cross, waiting for the video call to start. Then, the video monitor beeped, and General Scott's image filled the screen.

"I've called this meeting because the FBI has new information. Agent Brown, you're on."

"Thank you, General," said Jamil. "The FBI has formally labeled Susan Chan a person of interest for sabotaging the rover."

As Jamil detailed the circumstantial evidence against Chan, Julie's gaze fixated on Boxman, monitoring his reactions. His head twitched slightly, but otherwise, his expression did not change. When Jamil finished, Boxman spoke up.

"I never expected this from her," he said. "I hope you're wrong, if not, it's a shame. Nice work, Agent Brown."

"Ms. Burton, you're next," the General said.

"We've had a major breakthrough." Layla smiled and adjusted her glasses. "The secret computer virus in the HAB documents allowed us to infiltrate the Chinese moon mission software. Admiral Garza has authorized us to alter the second stage coding, preventing their rocket from achieving Earth's escape velocity. Dr. McCray can explain the rest."

Julie focused on Boxman, who stared into the screen, his face a blank.

"Ms. Burton and I have located the line of code controlling the thrust percentage of the rocket stages. After their launch lockdown, we'll program the second stage booster to burn at seventy percent thrust. It's not life-threatening, but the rocket will be trapped in low Earth orbit."

"Wait a minute." Boxman's eyes widened. "I like the retribution, but we need to think about the consequences. This will ruin our relationship with the Chinese for decades."

"Is this the same relationship where the Chinese've been attacking NASA's personnel files?" asked CJ.

Boxman shot him a look. "NASA's congressional directive is one of cooperation amongst all space agencies. Sabotaging their moon mission is a violation of our mandate."

Scott sat up straight. "Don't worry, Dr. Boxman. NSA is officially making the change," he barked. "NASA will be kept out of it. Layla, find the code and change the thrust percentage. Agent Brown, investigate Chan. That's an order. Meeting's over. Scott out."

Julie and CJ stayed on the call after everyone else dropped off.

CJ smiled at Julie. "It's just us. Before we debrief, you look amazing, and I can't wait to see you again."

Julie smiled back. "I'd love to see you too, but I don't think we can squeeze a visit in with our launch so close." Then she gave CJ a serious look. "So what did you think about the meeting?"

CJ glanced away for a moment, rubbing his worry stone where Julie couldn't see. "During our pursuit of Boxman, I thought you and I worked as true partners to convince Jamil. And I, well, haven't felt this good in a long time. Thank you, Julie."

Nicole really messed with him. "That was so sweet, CJ. You and I have come a long way. I'll use your word, it's nice for me, too." Then Julie bit her lip. "Do you think Boxman bought it?"

"Yes. You two were great. We'll know in a couple of days. Are you feeling better about the mission?"

"Sort of. I'm glad the Boxman plan is in motion." She sighed. "But I'm still worried. I mean, what if he doesn't act on it? Then what?"

"If that happens, we'll figure out a plan B. But no matter what, we're all here for you, Julie. Tell us what you need."

Julie leaned into the screen and pointed her finger. "I need you to trap Boxman so we can find out what he did."

Chapter Thirty-three: Making the Case

Next Day, Boxman's Office

Michael Boxman fidgeted in his office chair and gazed at the picture of his swearing-in ceremony. His jaws clenched. Wang threatened Barbara in that email. He pounded his fist on the arm of his chair. *Squeezing a few more million from the Chinese is a way to fight back*, he thought. He smoothed his red silk tie and strode out of the office to The Bean Counter coffee shop across the street.

Standing in line, he scanned the room. Two NASA Directors waved at him from several tables over. He noticed none of the staff behind the counter was Asian. Their network here must be extensive. Then the attendant called to him.

"Dr. Boxman, the usual?"

"No. I'm going to have a chai tea, small. Wife said to give it a try."

"Coming right up."

Moments later, he handed Boxman his drink. "Have a good one, Dr. Boxman."

Two hours later, an alert sounded on Layla's computer. She clicked the notice. A 7:30 reservation had been placed at Lillette's the following night for Dr. Michael Boxman.

***

Next Night

Watergate Complex, 7:00 PM

A blue van labeled Brothers Plumbing slid into the Watergate's visitor parking lot off New Hampshire Avenue. Stationed in the back, CJ, Layla, and Jamil sat glued to the monitor displaying the private entrance where Boxman would exit to meet his ride.

"He's coming down the elevator," said Layla monitoring Boxman's phone. "I'm activating the RealTalk software now."

At 7:09, a DC Cab, number 121, pulled up to the entrance. The technician sitting next to Jamil recorded Michael Boxman leaving the building.

"It doesn't look like him," said CJ. "Are you sure, Layla?"

"Yep. It's Boxman's phone."

"That's some disguise," said CJ. "It would fool our facial recognition software. He's more clever than I thought."

"We have him entering the cab, Agent Brown," the technician said. "Let me know if you want me to make any adjustments."

"Can you identify who's in the backseat?" Jamil asked.

"Negative. Can't penetrate the interference."

"I'd love to know who he or she is," said Jamil.

"When I download the recording," said Layla, "I'll store the voice pattern and have our computers match it against any recorded phone conversations we have."

CJ eased back into his chair. "I hope he makes the deal."

***

After entering, Boxman turned off his phone, and the disguised cab drove out into light DC traffic.

"This meeting's unplanned," snapped Agent Walker. "What's the urgency?"

"I've uncovered vital information that will cause an embarrassing disaster for your space agency and Minister Wang's political career."

"Disaster? What did you find?"

Boxman held up his hand. "Not so fast, Walker. I've delivered on every task you've forced on me. This information is worth a lot. Ten million."

Walker stared at him. "What's the disaster?"

"NSA plans to sabotage your moon rocket. And I know how they are going to do it. It's payback for the rover."

"Give me the details," Walker said in a stern voice.

Boxman shook his head. "Guarantee the funding first."

Walker glared at him but reached inside his jacket and took out his phone. "Hold on. I'll call her."

For several minutes, Walker spoke in Mandarin, then hung up.

"She's authorized five million in good faith upfront. The rest when we find the problem. The usual account?"

"No. Use this new one," said Boxman, handing him a card.

Walker typed in the information and sent it to Wang's office. A few minutes later, the confirmation came back.

"You'll see the deposit when you turn on your phone. Now tell me what you found."

"The NSA penetrated your flight operations system with a virus hidden in the HAB plans. They'll use it to reduce the second stage thrust percentage, preventing it from achieving escape velocity. Have her team look there after lockdown."

Agent Walker leaned close to Boxman. "This better be true, or the consequences will be fatal."

Boxman waved his hand. "Relax, Walker. I've nothing to gain by deceiving you."

Walker snorted and rapped on the privacy partition. "We're done. Go to the restaurant."

***

After the taxi left the Watergate complex, the three agents returned to the FBI's communication center, where Layla could download the RealTalk conversation.

At 8:53, Layla said, "Here we go. Boxman turned on his phone. He's paying the bill." She typed a command on her laptop. "Downloading the conversation now, Director. I'll put it on speaker."

The three of them heard the incriminating discussion.

CJ smiled. "Got him. Julie's plan worked. Nice job, Layla." He turned to Jamil. "We have conclusive evidence of Boxman selling secret information to a foreign government. Agreed?"

He let out a big breath. "Agreed."

"Good. Now can you go and arrest him?"

Jamil folded his arms. "Doesn't work that way. He's a presidential appointee."

"What? Are you saying he won't be arrested for treason and sabotage because it'll give the President a bad hair day?"

"Director Maykuth will inform the President, and her team will get their story lined up. Then we'll select a time and a place that'll be the most discreet."

"Jamil, we need to interrogate him now."

He shrugged. "We're days away from landing on Mars. We have time."

Chapter Thirty-four: Disappointment

Saturday Evening

New York City

The shiny black Town Car pulled up in front of Barbara Wiley's condo building in downtown Manhattan. A random snowflake riding the brisk cold wind slid across the hood. Michael and Barbara strolled through the foyer to the entrance. The doorman rushed to open the door and escorted them to their vehicle. They were off to dinner at Bobby Minh's, their favorite, a French-style Vietnamese restaurant.

After dessert, they relaxed, sipping their wine. Barbara held Michael's hand.

"Michael, you've been quiet tonight. What's on your mind?"

He gazed into her eyes. His lips squeezed together. "Barbara, our weekend arrangements aren't enough for me anymore. I want to wake up every morning and have you next to me."

The anguish in his eyes made Barbara look away. She took a big gulp of wine, the glass trembling in her hand.

"You've been patient with me," she whispered. "But if you're here, there's too much tension with father. Can you please wait a little longer? He's thinking of retiring in a year, maybe two."

Michael shook his head and chuckled. "He'll never give up the firm. It's all he's got." He sighed. "Barbara, my job and my marriage are controlled by others, and I've had enough. I need to live my way, and I want you with me."

She squeezed his hand and looked up at him. "I love you, Michael, but I need my small world and my routines. It's taken a long time, but I feel safe now. My therapist is here too."

He leaned across the table. "I want us to be together."

Barbara hung her head and said nothing. He looked at his wife and stroked her hand. *I knew it would be too much to ask.*

"It's okay. Let's go home." Michael drained his wine in two gulps and said, "I'll pay the bill. Can you have the car brought around?"

When the car pulled in front, Michael held open the door and Barbara ducked inside.

"I'm going to walk back; the cold air will do me good."

"Michael, it's eight blocks. Come inside, please."

"I'll be home soon." He closed the door and put on his mask. *I'll come back for her, but I have to do this now.* He strolled down the sidewalk, taking in the sights and sounds of Manhattan one last time.

***

Sol One, Wednesday

Julie's Office, JPL

Pacing back and forth in front of her conference table, Julie gripped her blue NASA water bottle so firm her knuckles turned white. She checked the time on her watch.

"You're going to crush that thing if you grip it any tighter," CJ said. "Talk to me."

A frown sprouted on her face. "I can't believe the FBI still hasn't arrested Boxman. Until he tells us what he did, I'm on edge."

Then, CJ's text alert beeped. He read it and grinned. "Good news. FBI finalized Boxman's arrest plan. Jamil said he'll send more details later."

"About time." Julie checked the live feed from the command module streaming on her monitor. "Well, it's showtime."

"I'll wait here and be out of your way. Good luck." CJ gave her a quick kiss.

Julie stepped into Mission Control and scanned the room. The staff murmured status updates for the Mars landing into their headsets, creating a low hum throughout the room. Franklin turned and gave her a thumbs-up. The main monitor showed the red-orange planet rotating below the command module. Julie focused on the flight data displayed in the upper right quadrant. *We're in position.* She keyed her headset.

"Looks good, Marge. We ready?"

"Affirmative. Everything's nominal."

Julie and Marge both switched their headphones to the staff channel.

"Director, Mission. Sixty seconds to separation. Are we a go?"

"Mission, you are go."

"Flight, Mission. We are go for separation and landing sequence in thirty seconds."

The command module's camera captured the explosive bolts erupting in a bright yellow flash. The capsule containing the HAB and the astrobots slipped away and began its plunge toward the planet below.

"Mission, Flight. Firing retrorockets in ten seconds."

Julie observed the burst of the rockets as they ignited, the heat shield glowing a fierce red as it entered the thin Martian atmosphere. Both of her hands were clenched tight around the edge of the cubicle. No sabotage yet.

"Mission, Flight. The MAV's transmitting its location. The capsule's tracking it five by five. We're at two thousand meters. Positioning thrusters are firing. We're moving from vertical to horizontal. Chutes are opening. Stand-by."

Julie gripped her cross, her eyes straining at the delayed images of the HAB's descent. "Almost there, Marge."

"It's perfect so far," she replied, her fingers crossed.

"Mission, this is Flight, we're at one hundred meters."

The command module's high-resolution camera captured the bright orange flames of the descent rockets firing, slowing the capsule, and creating a large red cloud of Martian dust, obscuring it from view as it touched down. Julie held her breath. Everyone hushed, waiting for the image to appear, making the room quiet as falling snow.

Slowly the swirling sand and dust dissipated, revealing the glistening white landing craft, standing in stark contrast to the red and black panorama of the Gale Crater. The HAB's legs retracted, lowering it to the granular surface. Explosive bolts flashed, removing the outer skin of the descent vehicle, exposing the HAB's airlock, allowing access to the planet.

"Mission, this is Flight. We are secure in the Gale Crater. All systems green," came the relieved voice over Julie's headset.

A wave of cheers erupted from the engineers and scientists, and they high fived each other. Julie's shoulders dropped. *We made it.* Julie turned to face her jubilant staff, a broad grin replaced the tension lines on her face as she spoke to them.

"Thank you for your expertise and hard work," she called out above the celebratory noise. "Tomorrow, we begin the historic search for life on Mars!"

The staff cheered and yelled even louder. Julie smiled and clicked her headset to Fred Langford.

"Turn your bots loose and get the HAB powered up. Marge and I are taking a quick break. We'll be back in a few minutes."

"Roger that, Julie." Fred signaled her with a thumbs-up. "We're on it."

Strolling down the hallway, Marge put her arm around Julie's shoulders and gave her a quick squeeze. "Nice job, boss. Tomorrow, we extract living bacteria from another planet."

"Thanks. You, too, Marge. If the bots perform like they did in the desert, we'll be done in a few sols." Then she gave her a worried look. "Assuming nothing goes wrong."

"Yeah, Boxman. What's the latest about him?"

"CJ's here, and he's going to brief us. Came out yesterday afternoon."

"Again?" Marge smiled. "Must be going well."

Julie laughed. "Very well."

When they stepped inside, CJ hugged Julie and handed each of them a glass of champagne and gave them a toast. "Marge and Julie, congratulations. Here's to the smartest rocket scientists in the solar system!"

They clinked their glasses and took a collective drink. "Thank you, CJ. This was sweet," said Julie.

"I loved seeing the HAB ease onto the surface," said CJ, smiling. "You two must be feeling great."

Julie's grin was etched on her face. "Yeah, it's as good as it gets." She turned to Marge. "Your deceleration calculations were perfect. It's only the second time we've used the particle beam accelerator, and we made orbit on the nose."

"Thanks, boss. The next couple of days'll be exciting. I only hope we're beyond any sabotage." She looked over to CJ. "Julie says you might have some news about Boxman."

"Yes, finally. Jamil sent me an update this morning. The FBI will be arresting Boxman Friday evening when his plane lands in New York."

"Friday? Why are they waiting?" Julie asked, her hands on her hips. "We only have seven sols to find the bacteria."

CJ scowled. "I agree. Jamil said the President's people think it'll be less harmful to her image to detain him in New York, not DC. Plus, Friday evening is the least-watched news hour all week. Jamil said Boxman's under surveillance. I'm flying back in the morning to take part in the interrogation. Then we'll find out."

"Get him, CJ," Julie said. "We need to know what he's done before the MAV takes off."

"I will," CJ said. "Look, your plan worked, and now we have him dead to rights. So, enjoy this. You deserve it." CJ raised his glass and saluted them. "Tell me, how did the HAB know how to land right next to the MAV from outer space?"

And the two rocket scientists gave CJ a lesson on the basics of solar system navigation.

***

When Julie and Marge returned to Mission Control, they were greeted with the sight of the astrobots walking down the ramp of the HAB with the jagged image of Mt. Sharpe reflecting off their gold visors. Over the next two hours, the bots deployed the solar panels in neat rows, their movements precise and efficient, as they connected them to the HAB's power receptacle.

"Mission, Flight Ops. The HAB is powering up."

"Another big step, Julie," Marge said, her eyes shining with excitement. "Now, C-2 can lead the bots to our primary sites. We'll be drilling tomorrow."

Julie fixated on the bots. They marched single file back through the airlock and began turning on the internal systems. Julie felt relieved as each green light blinked on. When the last system energized, Julie made an announcement.

"Good job, everyone. Sol 2's when we start to dig. Let's go home and get some rest before our big day." She needed them focused, ready for extreme action, with the Boxman threat still looming over the mission.

***

A SecretSessions conversation sprang up between two unequal conspirators.

Mr. V: *Jennings' friends are getting too close. Don't know how but they are tracking the money. Is everything ready for Friday?*

Mr. F: *Yes. I'll need cash this time.*

Mr. V: *A million to your account but only if he makes it out.*

Mr. F: *Fine. What about the Mars mission?*

Mr. V: *Not my problem. Don't let me down.*

Chapter Thirty-five: Conversations

Boxman's Watergate Penthouse

Wednesday Evening

Michael poured Emily a tequila on ice and a scotch for himself. They settled in the plush comfort of his living room, with floor-to-ceiling windows revealing a stunning panorama of the smog-filtered sun setting on the Potomac.

Emily tapped her fingernails on the arm of the chair. "You said it was urgent. What's up?"

"I got the word today." He took a sip. "Friday evening is when we need to leave."

"You sure? Kind of last-minute."

He smirked. "It's how they work. Can you have everything ready?"

"Yeah," her confident voice replied. "I paid extra to have them on standby. We'll go like we planned."

"Good." He said, gripping his glass tight. "What about the pilots?"

Emily snapped at him. "For God's sake, Michael, relax. It's the same flight plan they've been using for years. Nothing will appear suspicious. Are *you* ready?"

Michael's gaze drifted to a lone sculler gliding down the river.

"You know I love your mother. I'm not escaping to be with someone else. I asked her to come with me. She said no." He bit his lip and stared back outside. "I'll miss our Friday nights too."

Emily rolled her eyes. "No offense, but Mom will be fine. Fitz and her therapist create a warm cocoon for her." She crossed her legs. "I'm so fucking tired of being on Fitz's leash. Anytime I don't do something the way he'd do it, he goes ballistic. Time for me to leave, too. Feels liberating."

Michael saw the determination in her eyes. He decided to switch subjects.

"How was your client meeting today?"

Emily gave him a cold stare. "Fine."

Michael wondered why she had been commuting to DC for the past several months. *She's fucking somebody down here, but if I push, she'll bite my head off.*

"Okay, never mind." He gave a dismissive wave of his hand. "I have an investment question."

"Okay, I have a few minutes. Shoot."

"Guardier & Cie's investment arm contacted me. They suggested a portfolio using high-frequency trading. I've heard of it before, but don't know enough about their system. Is it safe?"

He handed Emily the proposal, and she scanned the document.

"High-frequency trading is based on mathematical algorithms where you trade a stock or an option, thousands of times in a short period. Let's say you trade 1000 shares of stock, and with each trade, you make one cent per share. That's ten dollars a trade. Do it a thousand times, and theoretically you have ten thousand dollars."

"Sounds simple. Why doesn't everyone do it?"

"The algorithms need to be constantly adjusted. It takes a team of math wizards to make it work, and they're expensive. G&C has a good program. It's conservative."

He moved to the edge of his seat. "I can't get trapped in a risky program. The money has to last me."

Emily scanned the last two pages of the document.

"This proposal's designed to generate cash flow for monthly living expenses. It's what you need. I recommend the S&P 500. It's a very liquid market, and it's not volatile."

"How does it work?"

"They'll take money from your bank account, transfer it to your investment account, make the trades, then put the money right back into your bank account, every month. All hidden by Swiss privacy laws where no one can track it. You'll be in good hands."

Emily checked her watch and drained the rest of her drink.

"The limo should be downstairs. See you Friday."

Emily hugged Michael and breezed out the door. Boxman poured himself another scotch and watched the sun disappear as darkness slowly consumed the sky. Forty-eight hours to go.

***

Jax's Diner, Pasadena

Thursday Morning (Sol 2)

Marge pushed open the diner's door; the rich aroma of bacon made her stomach growl. Julie texted her at 5 AM saying she had an emergency, pleading to talk with her before work. Marge scanned the half-full restaurant and spotted Julie huddled in a corner booth. Her puffy red eyes highlighted her pale, washed-out complexion. She had a strangled grip on her coffee mug.

Marge rushed to the back and slid into the seat across from her. "My God. What happened?" She reached over and held Julie's hand.

Julie squeezed Marge's fingers, her lips quivering, fighting back tears. "It's CJ. Last night, we had a romantic dinner, we made love, and everything felt perfect. Then around 3 AM, he woke up screaming and yelling, like a horrible nightmare. Then he sat there with his face buried in his hands, weeping and shaking."

Marge's heart sank seeing the pain on her friend's face. "What did he say?"

Julie's eyes glistened with unshed tears. "I've never seen him so broken. I didn't know what to do." She paused and took a drink of her coffee, the cup trembling in her hand.

"I put my arm around him, you know, to comfort him, but he jerked it away. I didn't know if I was safe or what was going on so I slipped out to the couch. Then without another word, he got dressed and left for the airport." A tear seeped out from her eye and trickled down her face. "I've never seen this side of him."

"You did your best to comfort him," she said gently. "But tell me, how are you doing?"

Julie shook her head and looked down at the table. "I'm not sure. This erupted out of nowhere. Did I trigger this somehow?" Julie turned her head and stared out the window. "I don't know what to feel." Marge released Julie's hand and remained quiet. Then Julie faced her again.

"Shit, Marge," her voice tense. "The President of the United States expects me to bring microbes back from Mars to help save the fucking planet. I need to block out CJ for the good of the mission, but I can't turn him off like a light switch. I'm worried about him and confused. I don't think I can stay focused enough, today of all days."

Marge took both of her hands and cupped Julie's into hers. "You can count on us," she said, her eyes steady. "Our team's the best. No way we'll let you down."

Julie eked out a fleeting smile. "Thanks for coming," she whispered. "I knew you'd understand."

"Of course. Now, let's get some food and figure out the best way to manage today's tasks."

***

Julie's heart pounded as she trudged into Mission Control. When the staff saw her, they all rose and gave her a standing ovation. A wave of warmth flowed through her, blushing at the outburst of admiration. *They have no idea how good that makes me feel.* She touched her cross and spoke to her team.

"Thank you so much, everyone." She smiled at them and waited for the noise to dissipate. "This is the day we've all been waiting for. Fred and his team have practiced the search and drill sequence to perfection. Now it's time to retrieve life from another planet. Fred, get them going. I'll check in with you later."

As the team sprang into action, Julie retreated to the solitude of her office, closing the door behind her. Pacing in front of her monitor streaming with the Mars activities, she replayed the images and emotions of the previous night, trying to sort out the implications for their relationship.

Julie shuddered when her phone suddenly vibrated on her conference table, announcing an incoming text. Her back stiffened. It was from CJ, his fifth of the morning. She left it unanswered and jammed the phone in her pocket. *Can't deal with him now.* She decided to make herself a cup of tea and shuffled off to the break room.

When she returned, Taylor and Pat had successfully positioned the core drilling machine at the first set of coordinates. But thoughts of CJ kept invading her. She took out her phone, paused, then clicked on the first text.

"Julie, I'm so sorry this happened at such an important time for your mission. Please let me ..."

Her eyes skipped off the message, landing on the nameplate on her desk. She clenched her jaw and clicked off the phone. Walking to the window, she looked out but only saw her pale reflection in the glass. She froze, and she felt a flicker of determination ignite within her. *Dammit, my place is with my team, not in here feeling sorry for myself.* She refreshed her makeup, brushed her hair, and strode into Mission Control.

Marge came over and gave her a confident look. Julie leaned close to her friend and gave her shoulder a squeeze.

"Thanks, Marge. I'm back. Nice job with the mission."

Marge smiled. "The team's doing great."

"Time for me to join them." She donned her headset and settled into her role.

"Fred, this is Specialist Turner. The sample contains organic compounds. Bring it back to the HAB for analysis."

"Roger that." Fred's voice crackled over the comms.

The Mission Control monitor showed the astrobots making their way back to the HAB. When Taylor placed the sample inside the analyzer, Julie felt a surge of excitement as the indicator light switched from red to amber. The six minutes seemed more like an hour before the results came in.

"Mission, this is Flight. Data's coming in." The staff sitting at their consoles leaned forward, anticipating the results. "We have organics but no live microbes."

Julie winced but saw several of her team toss their headsets with frustration at the disappointing news. Seeing their overreaction, she quickly addressed them.

"Listen up, everyone. While we didn't discover living microbes in our first sample, today was a major success. We demonstrated the bots can accurately position the drill, take the sample, and work the analyzer. This is a great start. All we need to do now is keep digging. Let's go!"

Chapter Thirty-six: Escape

Friday Evening

Washington Reagan National Airport

The Wiley jet arrived on schedule at 4:07 PM and coasted into the private hangar facility at Washington Reagan National Airport. It parked between two other luxury jets waiting for their weekend escapees. Boxman's pilots entered the terminal, checked in, and took seats near the hangar door.

At 4:45, Boxman strolled into the Terminal and approached the service counter. While checking in, he scanned the lounge area, making mental notes of his surroundings. He pocketed his ID and met up with his pilots, chatting briefly before passing through the security door to their plane. Positioned in the corner, an FBI agent texted the command center. *Subject entered the hangar at 1649 hours.*

At 5:02 PM, the Wiley jet taxied onto the tarmac, inching forward as it waited in line for takeoff. The FBI agent remained vigilant, his gaze fixed on the plane as it crawled toward the runway. When the jet finally roared into the darkening sky, he sent another text: *Subject airborne.*

Forty minutes later, the gleaming white Wiley plane landed at LaGuardia and parked in the General Terminal hangar. Three FBI agents stationed themselves near the entrance door, gripping their handcuffs. When the two Wiley pilots came out, the agents stepped closer. Minutes passed, still no Boxman emerged.

Perplexed, one of the agents flashed his badge to the security guard and rushed into the cavernous space. The Wiley jet sat alone, its doorway extended, waiting for the cleaning crew to service the cabin.

He waved to the other two agents. They scrambled inside the plane only to find the compartment empty. One agent hustled out to the security guard posted next to the hangar doors. He confirmed only the pilots exited the plane. The lead agent immediately texted his supervisor.

Boxman never arrived in New York. No passengers were on the plane.

***

General Aviation Terminal, Washington, DC

The FBI agent, stationed at the DC airport, left after the Wiley plane took off and decided to eat dinner at a local Thai restaurant to avoid the rush hour traffic before commuting home. Halfway through his shrimp tempura, his supervisor called using his emergency number.

"Did you see Boxman get on the plane?"

"I saw him walk into the hangar with his pilots," said the agent.

"But did you see him actually board the plane?"

"No. I didn't follow him into the hangar as ordered. Why? There's nowhere to go but the plane."

"Boxman didn't land in New York. Go back and see if any other planes left around the same time. Move it!"

With lights flashing and siren wailing, the agent raced back to the terminal. Sprinting into the building, he flashed his badge, ran down the hallway, and barged into Belinda Ross' office.

"Ms. Ross, I'm Justin Davis, FBI," he panted. "I need your immediate cooperation."

Belinda jerked back in her chair. Her phone tumbled mid-text from her hands onto the desk. "Yes, of course," she stammered. "What can I do for you?"

"At approximately 5 PM, a jet owned by the Wiley company landed here, right?"

"Let me get tonight's flight log and check." Her hands quivered as she located the electronic document. "Yes, like most weeks. It came in at 4:07 and left for New York right after five."

"Was Michael Boxman on it?"

She tapped in a few keystrokes and looked up at the agent. "He signed in as a passenger."

"Did another plane leave here about the same time as the Wiley's?"

She scrolled through the afternoon flights. "Yes, one stopped here for refueling. It left ten minutes after the Wiley flight."

"Was Boxman on that plane?"

"It didn't originate here so the passenger manifest is not in my database. It was only a fuel stop. It would be located where the flight originated."

"Can you find out? It's urgent."

"Yes. I'll check the FAA system. Hang on, it'll take me a moment."

Belinda typed in the tail number into her computer, and the system spat out the results.

"The flight originated in Boston," she reported. "Michael Boxman and Emily Woodson were on the passenger manifest. The final destination's Frankfurt, Germany. Wow, that's different."

***

30 Minutes Later

37,000 Feet Altitude

Walking back into the cabin, the pilot addressed Emily. "We're in international airspace now, Ms. Woodson. We'll arrive in London in about five hours. You'll be deplaning there, correct?"

"Yes, but continue to Frankfurt as scheduled. Thank you."

"Yes, ma'am."

Emily smiled and turned to Michael. "Our new passports will get us into the EU undetected. I made reservations on the bullet train to Paris, then we switch to the express train to Geneva. You'll love it. It's a beautiful ride through the Alps."

"Sounds good." He rubbed the back of his neck. "I may need to contact you while I'm setting up my accounts at Guardier and Cie. How can I reach you without leaving a trace?"

She leaned over and pulled out her phone. "This." She pointed. "It's an app for texting called SecretSessions. They bounce your phone signal all over the world. After you read the message, the app automatically eliminates the text from its servers. There's no way to track it. I use it with my clients for absolute privacy."

"Good. I'll sign up," he said with a sad look on his face.

"Hey, come on, Michael. We did it." Emily popped out of her seat. "I brought something to celebrate."

She strolled back to the galley, where she stashed a bottle of Dom Perignon P3 Plenitude Rose. She filled two glasses and handed one to Boxman.

"A toast, Michael. Here's to our new lives."

Michael raised his glass and gave her a weak smile.

"Why the sad face? Fitz made us miserable and now he's gone." Emily leaned back into the leather seat and crossed her legs. "I've started my own firm, and you have your freedom with enough money you'll never have to worry."

He peered into his glass, the bubbly liquid reflecting the cabin lights, then out into the dark sky over the roiling waves of the Atlantic Ocean. "I thought I had this all figured out," he mumbled. "But being here on the plane, the reality's hitting me. My life feels empty without your mother."

Emily rolled her eyes. "Fitz created this dependent environment to shelter her. You know all that. Your only hope is when Fitz retires, she'll turn to you." *I sure wouldn't wait around.*

Emily stood and went back two rows. She opened her laptop, put in her earbuds, and started to work, her head moving to the music.

Boxman slumped in his seat and stared at the blackness outside. *Fitz is old, eats rich, fatty foods, and is volatile. Here's to a short life you son of a bitch.* He raised his flute and drained the rest of his drink.

Chapter Thirty-seven: Mars

JPL, Same Time

Sol 3 (Friday)

Approaching Sharon Turner's console, Julie observed the astrobiologist's workspace was littered with coffee cups and empty candy wrappers.

"Good afternoon, Sharon. Living on caffeine and sugar, I see. How're we doing?"

She looked up at Julie with bleary red eyes. "We keep finding the organics, but not the live ones. Need to go deeper. The good news is the bots are getting more efficient with the core drilling machine. We're trying to squeeze in three samples this sol."

"I'll tell Fred to increase the depth."

Julie's phone buzzed in her pocket. It was from CJ using her emergency code. She hurried back to her office, anxious to hear the results of Boxman's interrogation.

***

Next Day

Phil Locke's Office

"What happened with Boxman?" asked Phil.

"The FBI lost him." CJ placed his hands on his hips. "He and Emily skipped out on a plane to Frankfurt. Jamil sent two agents over to Rhein-Main, but they weren't there. The pilots said they deplaned in London when they stopped to refuel."

"Didn't they have an agent stationed in the hangar at Reagan?"

"No, just in the lounge," said CJ. "Can't believe it. Shoddy work, if you ask me."

"What's your plan now?"

"Julie's deflated and anxious about potential sabotage. Can't blame her." CJ shifted in his seat. "The only thing I can think of is to grab Layla and go out to the JPL. We'll help brainstorm with Julie's team where Boxman might have disrupted the mission."

"Makes sense to work the ...What?"

CJ lifted his right index finger. "You know, Emily Woodson's been in the picture with Boxman quite a bit over the past few months. Maybe she can lead us to him."

"How?"

CJ pointed at Phil. "Your friend Labowitz seems to know a lot about the Wiley family. Call him."

"You want me to call him?"

"He won't talk to me." CJ ran his hand through his hair. "Look Phil, the Rosansky firm's involved with the Wileys, Boxman's in the wind, and we only have a few more days on Mars. I know it's thin, but it's the only lead we have."

Phil sat back in his desk chair and put his hands behind his head. "All right, I'll put him on speaker."

Hank answered on the second ring.

"Phil, it's not good when you call me, especially on a Saturday."

"Hank, you're on speaker. With me is CJ Jackson."

"Yeah, we had a delightful chat. What do you want?"

"Need information about Emily Woodson."

"She's an American citizen and any of our dealings with her is entirely none of your business. Now, are you going to pull some national security crap on me?"

"You're in business with an accomplice to a known saboteur. We could put a terrorist tag on her which would allow us to subpoena a whole bunch of records from your offices in the US and wherever else we want. Let us ask you a few questions and see where we go."

"This is bullshit, Phil," blustered Hank. "I'm only going to give you public information."

CJ leaned close to the phone and asked, "You said Emily is close to her grandmother. How does she fit in the picture?"

Hank hesitated for a moment, then began. "When Simone and Fitz divorced, she moved back to Geneva to be with her family and resumed her maiden name, Rogers. Fitz sends her a monthly stipend into her account at Guardier & Cie. The divorce settlement also required purchasing a permanent residence. We represented Ms. Rogers in the transaction, which is all part of the public record."

"What's Emily's involvement with her?" CJ asked.

"Emily advises her grandmother on investments, as the sum Fitz sends her is significant. Emily uses the investment arm of Guardier & Cie to execute transactions on her behalf."

"What about Emily and her grandfather, Fitz?"

"Contentious."

CJ cleared his throat. "We know Boxman and Emily left together. Might he end up in Geneva, too?"

Hank paused for a long moment before replying. "Check the real estate transactions in Geneva over the past two months. Are we almost done?"

"Not quite. Are those two romantically involved?" asked CJ.

"Get serious," Hank shot back.

"We'll take that as a no," said Phil, eyeing CJ and moving his finger across his throat.

"How is Guardier & Cie involved with Boxman?" CJ asked.

"I'm not positive, but I believe they're Boxman's bankers and investors like Woodson's. This should wrap it up, don't you think, Phil?"

"Okay, Hank. I can tell when you're done. Thanks for the chat."

After the call ended, Phil looked at CJ. "Reaction?"

CJ leaned back in his chair, processing the information. "Sounds like Guardier & Cie might be managing his money. We'll confirm that. But what about the real estate reference? Boxman wouldn't be stupid enough to have his name on a lease or purchase."

"Find the Geneva transactions involving both Guardier and Rosansky. I'd go back a year. Shouldn't be many."

CJ stood, getting ready to leave. "I'll have Geneva Station do it, but we won't find Boxman in time to protect Magellan. I'll be at the JPL if you need me."

***

Saturday Night
Julie's Condo

Julie sat on the couch talking with Gary when a call from CJ beeped on Julie's phone. She tensed up. *I can't do the relationship talk now.* She started to forward his call to voicemail but stopped, thinking they might've located Boxman.

"Gary, I better take this. Talk soon." Julie clicked the green accept button and placed her phone in speaker mode on the coffee table in front of her.

"Hey, Julie." CJ paused, his voice was soft and low, almost a whisper. "I want to talk about Wednesday night, if that's okay."

It's not. "CJ, this isn't the time, but I am concerned about how you're feeling."

"Terrible." His voice cracked. "I'm embarrassed you saw my flashback. It's been a while, and I'm sorry I upset you."

"You were in such pain. I didn't know what to do."

"There's nothing you could've done."

Julie took a swallow of her wine. "So these flashbacks, do they happen a lot?"

"Dr. Lewis makes me keep track. This was the fourth one this year. The trend is going down but yeah, I've no way of predicting them. It's part of my PTSD, to put a label on it."

Another pause, then CJ continued, "I haven't felt this content in a long time, Julie, and I don't want to lose you." His voice cracked. He took several deep breaths then continued. "I know my issues aren't easy, and if you don't want to deal with them, I'll understand."

"This is all new for me, CJ. I want to talk it out, but right now we're at the most critical part of the mission, and I need to focus, especially with Boxman escaping. Can you give me 'til we're safely on our way home?"

"Of course. It's not the reason I called but when I heard your voice, I ..." CJ cleared his throat and said, "Sorry. This is about Boxman's escape. I'm coming out with Layla tomorrow to brainstorm with your team about how we can protect the mission. I wanted to alert you. Don't want it to be awkward. I'm staying at a hotel."

"It won't be, and I'm glad you're coming. We need to troubleshoot, and Layla will be a big help, too. See you tomorrow."

Julie looked down at Gizmo and stroked his head.

"Well, Giz, what should I do with this guy?" She took a swallow of her chardonnay. "You're right, I need more data. We'll do some research after we're in the clear."

Chapter Thirty-eight: Discovery

Sol 5 (Sunday)

Sharon Turner peeled off another candy wrapper and watched astrobot Pat load the fourth soil sample retrieved from the deeper depths onto the power cart. Taylor pushed the drive button and the cart's wheels ground into the gritty soil on their way to the HAB for analysis while C-2 guided Pat to the next extraction location.

Sharon leaned forward in her chair and decided to monitor Taylor's activities inside the HAB. After the astrobot placed the sample in the mass spectrometer, the machine went through its program. She observed the scan light flip to red, signaling the cycle had concluded. Seven minutes later, the information streamed into Sharon's computer.

Her eyes widened when the confirming figures appeared. She jumped up from her seat and yelled into her headset, "We found them! We found them! Mission, we found the living microbes!"

"Turner, this is Mission. Calm down and congratulations. Nice work."

"Mission, sorry, roger that," Sharon gasped as tears streamed down her cheeks. "Permission to do the DNA analysis."

"Permission granted."

"Team, this is Mission. We're now on official communication lockdown. The only outside communication of this event is through Director McCray. Lock the doors. You know the drill."

The Mission Director leaned over to his assistant. "Go wake up McCray. She's asleep in her office. She needs to see this."

***

The knock on her office door jolted Julie awake. She popped up on the couch, hoping to hear good news.

"Come in," she said.

The door opened a crack and a voice from outside called in. "We found them, Dr. McCray. They want you in Mission Control."

Julie grinned. "Be right there." *Yes!* She gazed at the picture of her dad on the desk and blew him a kiss. Then Julie smoothed the wrinkles on her shirt, gave her hair a few quick brush strokes, and rushed out to be with her team. The mission staff cheered when Julie strolled in. She smiled at them, took a slight bow, and donned her headset.

"Thank you, everyone. This is a great moment, not only for the JPL, but for all of humankind. For the first time in our history, we've captured a living organism not from Earth. Every one of you should be very proud. It's something you can tell your children and grandchildren."

"Director, Mission. We are on lockdown protocol and Specialist Turner requests to see you. It's urgent."

"Roger that, Mission."

Hustling over to Sharon's workstation, Julie saw the worry lines on the astrobiologist's forehead. Sharon looked up at Julie, shaking her head.

"Something's wrong, Director. I have video confirming Taylor placing the sample in the GC-MS. It successfully went through the analysis cycle. See, all the indicators are green. I should've received the results fifteen minutes ago."

A queasy feeling gurgled in Julie's stomach. Her hands balled into fists. *Fucking Boxman.* "The GC-MS could've been programmed to transmit the DNA profile somewhere else." *Dammit, I didn't think to check it.* She talked into her headset. "Mission, this is McCray. Send someone to the hotel and bring Chan in here. I need her now."

Thirty-five minutes later, Susan rushed into Mission Control and approached Julie. "Dr. McCray, what's the problem?"

"I think our GC-MS may be compromised. We've done a system check; it's working to spec but we should've had the DNA analysis forty-five minutes ago. I'm afraid the machine may have sent the data to another location. Can you investigate?"

Susan's hand covered her mouth. "Right away. I'll start with the log." With the time delay due to the millions of miles between Earth and Mars, another half an hour passed before Susan returned with the printout of the signal frequency used by the analyzer machine.

"What did you find?" asked Julie.

"Not good, Director." Susan showed Julie the report. "This is the frequency the analyzer used to send the results. It's not the MRO's. It's one I've never seen before."

***

JPL, Hours Later

CJ and Layla hurried into the conference room where Susan, Fred, Marge, and Julie waited. CJ saw the looks of dejection on their faces. He made eye contact with Julie. Her face flushed, and she pounded her fist on the table.

"Boxman got us, CJ," she snapped.

CJ walked over and settled in across from her. "Tell us what happened."

"We found the live organisms, but when we put the sample into the GC-MS, it sent the DNA results somewhere else. Susan has the frequency; it's not ours." She stared down at her folded hands. "Dammit, I should've checked."

"Give the frequency to me," Layla said, setting up her computer on Julie's desk. "I'll tap into Ft. Meade and track where it went. Won't take long."

The room quieted, waiting for her analysis. The only sound was Layla's fingers hammering the keyboard. Moments later, she faced the group.

"The analyzer transmitted the DNA analysis to the Chinese government via the Mao 3 communication satellite," she announced, pushing her glasses tight up against her nose. "It belongs to the Ministry of State Security."

Stunned expressions spread across the group's faces. "The Chinese government has our DNA?" Julie asked. She gazed up at the ceiling, her jaws clenched. "I hate that guy."

"We did all the work, and they have all the information," Marge said, twirling her black hair between her fingers.

"Susan, how could Boxman have changed the frequency?" CJ asked.

She covered her mouth with her hand and winced. "One of my technicians mentioned Boxman made an unannounced visit. Wasn't there long. Didn't even want a tour."

"Why didn't you tell us?" asked CJ.

"Our customers do it all the time. It's routine for us." She eyed Julie. "I'll bet that's when he did it. Hardly anyone around. Would've been easy."

"Oh, no," said Fred, slapping his hand on the table. "Mandy said he visited, asking questions about the tasking architecture. He must've reprogrammed the bots, too."

During the discussion, Layla pounded her keyboard. "I checked the Area 51 Gate log. Found a date and time when Boxman was there," said Layla. "I'll check the cameras in your building, Susan." Moments later, Layla beamed. "Got it. Sending it to the wall monitor."

The group faced the front, leaning forward in their seats. They observed Boxman, dressed in a clean-room gown, walking toward several tables filled with analytical equipment outside the HAB structure. He paused to survey them before moving in front of a specific machine.

"He's standing next to the GC-MS," said Susan, pointing at the screen.

CJ looked confused. "What's that?"

"It's our gas chromatography-mass spectrometer machine," explained Susan. "It provides us with the specimens' DNA."

On the monitor, Boxman turned around several times, gazing back at the workers inside the HAB. When they stepped out of sight, he reached to the side of the machine and pressed a button with his left hand. An empty disk tray slid open.

"I know what he's doing," shouted Susan, pointing at the screen. "He's reprogramming it. Watch."

Boxman pulled a CD from his pocket, placing it in the tray. He pushed the program button again, and the tray disappeared inside. Then Boxman sauntered down the aisle, bending over and inspecting the other equipment, but he kept glancing at his watch.

"It takes about a minute for the machine to read the CD," said Susan. "See the red light blinking? When it goes green, it's done."

Soon, the light on the tray switched to a steady green. Boxman gave another look at the HAB entrance and pressed the side button again.

"When the tray opens there will be loud ding," said Susan. "Means the new program is installed."

As the disk slid back out, Richard, the technician, suddenly appeared and began to approach Boxman. He moved to the side, blocking Richard's view, and blindly stabbed the programming button causing the CD to retreat inside the machine.

"Stop. Look," remarked Susan. "The disk is still in the analyzer." She turned to Fred. "One of your astrobots needs to remove it. Then I can reprogram the machine from here."

"Make it happen, Fred," ordered Julie.

"I'll get my team to train Pat." Then he asked, "What do you think he did to the bots?"

CJ glanced at Julie, then interrupted. "Let me interject. We need to consider the worst-case scenario here. What could the bots do that would be fatal to our mission?"

"I agree," said Julie. "The MAV is the only way to return the microbes to Earth. The bots could destroy the live bacteria after the MAV leaves the surface. Be the easiest."

"Lay it out for us."

Julie stood and paced around the room. "When our analyzer sent the DNA information to the Chinese satellite, it confirmed we discovered the live organisms. If Boxman programmed the bots to destroy the samples in the MAV or the command module, it would leave us empty-handed. Then the Chinese will have the only accurate DNA sequence of living Martian bacteria, plus the Air Cleansing Facilities need the living bacteria or they won't work."

She pointed at Layla. "Examine the astrobots software. Fast, Ms. Burton."

"On it." She began typing, her fingers banging on the keys.

Fred frowned and said, "Wait, we've already checked the software against the master."

"Not what she meant," said Layla, correcting him from behind the screen of her laptop. "We only compared the tasks to ensure there were no changes from the master. I'm looking for where a new instruction may have been inserted."

"Correct," said Julie, her eyes filled with determination. "Here's what we're going to do. Marge, Fred, and Susan work on changing the analyzer's frequency back to the MRO. Layla, examine the astrobots' programming. Let's reconvene in thirty. We'll make a game plan based on what you find."

While the others dispersed, CJ and Julie sat next to each other at the conference table. CJ slipped his hand into hers. Julie gripped it tight and stared back at him.

"This is my life's work and it's blowing up right in front of my face." Her head and shoulders dropped. "What am I going to tell the President if we can't get this turned around?"

CJ grimaced, seeing Julie's discomfort. "It's our fault, Julie. We let Boxman slip through our fingers, and we let you down. I'm sorry."

Her eyes glowered. "He's been scheming about this for a long time. Dammit, he planned every move perfectly."

Julie let go of CJ's hand, and she paced about the room.

"You know what pisses me off?" She spun to face CJ, her voice rising. "What we do is hard. We *have* to be perfect in our orbital calculations, descent rockets *have* to fire at precisely the right time, rovers *have* to operate and perform highly technical analyses under extreme conditions. All from millions of miles away. We never put sabotage into our mission planning." She put her hands on her hips. "Where did that asshole go anyway?"

"We think Geneva." CJ straightened up in his chair. "Look, your mission is everyone's priority. There's a long line to use those supercomputers, and Layla hopped right to the front. What else can we do for you?"

Julie gave CJ a brief smile. *He's being a good partner.* She sat down across from him again.

"You asked a good question in the meeting. Destroying the bacteria would be fatal to the mission. Easy for the bots to do. So, I'm done taking chances. Once the bots load the organisms in the MAV, I'm leaving them on Mars where Boxman's treachery can't do us any more harm."

***

Thirty Minutes Later

Standing in front of her team, Julie took charge of the meeting. "Okay, let's review." She pointed. "Layla, you start."

She firmed up her white-framed glasses. "I had the supercomputer compare our programmed tasks with the master. As Fred indicated, we found no changes. The bots are coded by task, making it easier to make improvements. Except, it's also a weakness."

She turned to the conference room monitor, displaying the code for everyone to see. "Boxman programmed the bots to turn off the refrigeration system in the bacteria's storage compartment after the MAV obtained Martian orbit, killing them."

Then she faced Fred. "You didn't detect it because the bots were idle during this period. Nothing to test. It's a sophisticated and effective hiding place."

Gasps filled the room as the implications settled in.

Fred stared at the coding, blinking several times. "She's right," he said. "It's diabolical and the task is simple. It's just flipping a switch. I'll remove the instruction right away."

"Nice work, Ms. Burton." *That's one problem solved.* Julie turned her attention to Susan. "How about the analyzer communication problem?"

Susan spoke up. "We have a plan. Fred will program Pat to remove the disk, then I'll reprogram the analyzer back to the original frequency. Marge will send a test message, making sure it goes through the MRO. Then we can resume using the GC-MS."

"How long?" Julie asked.

"About twelve hours, maybe less," said Fred.

"Good." Julie made eye contact with each member of her team. "Nice job. Now let's get our mission back up and running."

Julie saw a renewed resolve on their faces as they hustled out to execute their tasks.

"Nice job, Director," said CJ. He slid his hand in his pocket, grasping his worry stone. "You have it under control, and you don't need me here," he whispered. "Layla and I will go back and focus on finding Boxman." Then he gazed at her. "I hate seeing how he's causing you so much stress."

Julie's emotions flashed back to when they snuggled on the beach steps. She caught the sadness in his eyes. Feeling for him, she came around the table and placed her arms around CJ's neck. Their foreheads touched. They stood in the quiet, taking each other in. Finally, Julie spoke softly to him.

"I do care about you. I need to understand more about what you're going through. I thought if I could speak with Dr. Lewis when this is over, it would help. That okay?"

Hope swelled inside him. "Of course. I'll let her know you'll call."

Chapter Thirty-nine: Good News

CJ's Office, Langley

Next Day

"Thanks for coming out here, Patricia. I know this is a distance from the SEC," CJ said. "Coffee?"

"I'm good. Let's get started," said senior analyst Patricia Alverez.

"What did your analysis find?"

"The Wiley Hedge Fund uses three main investment banks, Hong Kong National, Wall Street Bank in New York, and Guardier and Cie in Geneva. I pored through hundreds of transactions between the Wiley Hedge Fund and these three banks," she said, pointing to the spreadsheet on her laptop.

CJ squinted at the screen, seeing only a wall of numbers. "And?"

Pat smiled at his confusion. "One thing for sure, Emily's a gifted trader. She understands how to leverage options and use the newer exotic investment vehicles."

"Is she trading for herself in addition to the Wiley funds?"

"Could be. If she did want to run a private fund without being detected, she could use the Wiley Hedge Fund as a cover for her transactions."

CJ put his coffee mug down on the table. "How would it work?"

"Emily is authorized, as the portfolio manager, to move funds around from any of these three banks. As long as the audit of all thirty-eight individual accounts added up, no one would detect the transactions, particularly if the amounts were small. I mean in a 1.7-billion-dollar fund, you could move a few million without creating suspicion."

"How could we find out?"

"We can't. If she's trading on her account out of a Swiss bank, we, the SEC, don't have jurisdiction, even though she's an American citizen."

"What if the bank acted as the portfolio manager for an individual?"

"Same thing, off-limits."

But not with Proposition Forty-nine, thought CJ.

"Thanks, Patricia. We'll have to find another way."

After Patricia left, he video-called Layla.

"I have a Prop Forty-nine question. Let's assume Boxman used the MoneyMove app to hide the payments he received from the Chinese. If we could locate these payments in a Guardier & Cie account, could we freeze the account without going back to the court?"

"Yep."

"What if Boxman used Guardier & Cie for his investments too?"

Layla's eyes suddenly sprang wide open.

"That's it!" she shrieked. "Bank accounts and investment accounts are separate entities, even inside the same institution. They have different regulations. I'm on it." The screen went black before CJ could ask why.

CJ decided to follow-up on the real estate lead and called his agent in Geneva Station.

"Good morning, Director," said Nicolas Cernier.

"Agent Cernier, have you verified Michael Boxman's address?"

"Potentially. We have a condominium under surveillance matching the criteria you provided. A Swiss holding company called Estephe Unique purchased the condo. Simone Rogers is the owner and a woman named Emily Woodson has power of attorney to act on her behalf.

"We have a camera pointing at the entrance, but our facial recognition hasn't identified Dr. Boxman yet. We're being careful not to alert the property security staff, who might tip him off."

Boxman's using his mask as a disguise, CJ thought. "Anything else?"

"The court records show in 2021 a similar transaction by Estephe Unique, using the Rosansky firm, to buy the home of Simone Rogers. The funds came from an account at Guardier & Cie. We followed Ms. Rogers, hoping to spot Dr. Boxman but came up empty."

CJ shook his head. "Time's critical, Agent Cernier. Take a more direct approach. Clear?"

"Yes, of course, Director."

***

Mission Control, JPL

Sol 8

The main screen displayed Taylor and Pat maneuvering the power cart toward the MAV, loaded with fourteen core samples of live Martian bacteria. When they reached the return rocket, Pat pressed the access button at the base. The hatch above them hissed open, and an aluminum ladder telescoped down.

"Any word about Boxman?" Marge asked.

Julie scowled. "No, and time has run out. Earth and Mars are starting to move away from each other. If we don't go now..."

Marge put her arm around Julie. "I think we're safe, boss. Layla did an amazing job finding Boxman's dirty work. I mean, what else could he have done? At least we have the DNA profiles now."

"I hope you're right." Julie stared at the bots on the screen and clicked her headset. "Fred, are we loaded yet?"

"Almost. Need a few more minutes."

"Mission, this is McCray. Still green for launch?"

"We are green at T-48, but the wind gusts are right against our upper limit. They've been increasing over the past two hours. We have enough fuel to keep the MAV stable, but I recommend we go ASAP. It's not going to get better."

Julie stared down at the floor and bit her lower lip. *I have no choice.*

"Mission, McCray. As soon as the bots are clear, go to emergency launch."

Chapter Forty: Finding Boxman

Same Time

CJ's Condo, 8 PM

CJ received a text from Layla as he pulled into his condo parking space.

Found Boxman's account. I can capture the money. Call me.

Once inside, CJ grabbed his laptop and sent a video invite to Layla. Soon her face with faded makeup and red bleary eyes splashed on his screen. She sat in her underground office, rock music blaring in the background. Before he could say anything, Layla began speed-talking.

"I figured it out, ready? On the day before the last trading day of the month, twenty million US dollars pops into Boxman's Guardier & Cie regular bank account, then it's transferred into his G&C brokerage account.

"Last month he made almost twenty-seven thousand US dollars. His broker then transferred the money back into his bank account. The funds stayed there for one night then disappeared into his MoneyMove account, where we lose access."

"Whoa, slow down a bit. Why doesn't the money go from his brokerage account straight back to his MoneyMove account?"

"Greed." Layla grabbed her can of Red Bull and took a drink. "You see, the more money on a bank's books, the more it's allowed to lend. By keeping funds across all their accounts, even for one day, the bank raises its lending ability where the banking arm makes its profits. The MoneyMove accounts don't count toward their lending-to-cash ratio."

CJ shrugged. "But how do we seize his funds?"

"Easy. With Prop Forty-nine, I'll freeze the bank account when the money is transferred into his investment account. The brokerage side won't detect this. Then, when the money comes back into the bank account, I'll have it. Frozen accounts can have money come in, but not out."

"But when the funds don't reappear in his MoneyMove account, it'll tip him off."

"Yep, but he'll have no money."

CJ raised his head and stared out the window, processing Layla's idea. "Geneva Station has a lead on Boxman's residence. Once they verify it, we'll go with your plan and arrest him at the same time."

"Give me the word, and I'll be ready."

"Ms. Burton, you're a brilliant agent, and I'm glad you're on our side," CJ said, pointing his finger at her image on the monitor.

Layla blushed and waved her hand dismissively as the screen went dark.

***

Wearing a Swiss Telecom uniform with fake credentials pinned to his collar, Agent Cernier rang the doorbell on the condo purchased in the Estephe Unique transaction.

"Who's there?"

"I'm Josef Heitz from Swiss Telecom, checking on the service we recently installed. Are you satisfied, and can I answer any questions?"

"Everything's fine. I'm quite busy now and can't talk."

"Fine sir, but could you please sign our form? It verifies we performed a follow-up inquiry. It's necessary for the government."

The door opened, and Michael Boxman glanced at Agent Cernier's ID, grabbed the clipboard, and scribbled his falsified name on the form. The camera embedded in the second button on the agent's shirt captured several images of Julie's nemesis.

"Thank you very much for being a new ..."

Boxman closed the door in the agent's face. He heard the bolt sliding into place and the sound of footsteps receding into the residence. Cernier smiled and sent CJ the confirming photos.

***

Gale Crater, Mars

The MAV appeared as a black silhouette against the Martian sunset, ready for liftoff with the astrobots safely inside the HAB.

"Mission, this is Fred. Bots are secure."

"Roger that. Flight, this is Mission. Status check."

"Roger, Mission. The flight computer indicates we need to add thirty-seven seconds to the countdown to maximize the rendezvous window with the command module."

"Flight, you are go for countdown adjustment."

Julie stood behind the Mission Director's desk, massaging the cross on her necklace. *I hope we're safe.* She clicked her communication channel.

"Have to do it, Marge. Launch window is almost closed."

"With you all the way, Julie."

Six years of work and the promise to a president flashed in Julie's mind. With a determined voice, she spoke to Franklin. "Mission, this is Director McCray. You are go for launch."

"Roger that. Go for launch."

When the countdown clock reached zero, Flight Ops relayed the launch instructions. Sixteen minutes later, images of bright orange flames erupted from the MAV's engines. Cameras on the HAB followed the flight path until the rocket became a yellow speck in the Martian sky.

Julie crossed her arms, staring at the floor. Marge twirled her hair.

"Docking in ninety seconds. We are nominal," said Flight Ops over Julie's headset.

Images from the command module camera appeared on JPL's main monitor. Julie saw the small silver image rapidly expanding, filling the screen. Numerous puffs of white exhaust spewed from the MAV's thrusters, aligning it with the command module's docking collar.

"Mission, this is Flight. The MAV is successfully docked. Project Magellan is ready for orbit transposition and return to Earth."

Julie hugged Marge. "We did it. I'm so relieved." *And I can tell the President we have them.*

"Mission, this is McCray. Bring Magellan home."

Chapter Forty-one: Difficult Decisions

Three Days Later

Phil Locke's Office

Clearing his throat, Phil addressed CJ. "Nice work finding Boxman. I understand the FBI made arrangements with the Swiss for you to interrogate and extradite him."

CJ raised his eyebrows. "Yes, with Brown and Layla. That was in my status report. So, tell me, Phil, is there a problem?"

He glanced sideways and grimaced. "I have disturbing news. Director Maykuth discussed the situation with Jennings. They decided not to arrest Boxman."

CJ sat upright and his face flushed. "What? Not arrest him?"

"I don't like it either but arresting a Presidential appointee for treason would embarrass Jennings and hinder her reelection campaign. Makes the FBI's vetting process look bad too."

"They're going to let him go?"

Phil raised his hand. "Hold on, he's not getting a free pass. He's to be confined in an FBI safehouse for two years and divulge his Chinese connections."

Standing, CJ scowled and pointed to the American flag behind Phil's desk. "This is such bullshit. People die protecting this country and our leaders cheapen their sacrifice with selfish decisions like this." Then he stormed out.

***

Jax Diner, Pasadena

Same Day

Julie and Marge found their way to the back of the restaurant and sat in a booth away from the penetrating afternoon sun. Most of the tables were empty. They ordered tea and drank in silence.

"Capsule's on track to the ISS," said Julie. She rotated her empty cup with her hands and cleared her throat. Marge sat still and listened.

"I spoke with CJ. He apologized like every other sentence. He's upset he scared me."

"You feeling better?"

"I guess." Julie paused and stared down at her coffee cup. "Shit, I'm not sure about our relationship, Marge. His issues are more than I thought. I know he loves me, but can I deal with the mental health stuff? Do I even want to deal with them? I mean, his condition interfered with our mission at its most critical time. I know this sounds selfish, but my professional life's important. I have to at least consider it, don't I?"

"Do you love him?"

Julie stared out the window. "I do. It's the commitment part I'm not sure about."

Marge leaned back and waited. In the silence, a worker at the other end of the diner plunged his mop into a bucket and started swabbing the floor.

"With Bill," continued Julie, "I thought I had a clear picture of our future. Got that wrong. Now I'm much less sure what our lives would be like." She stared straight into Marge. "I don't think I could handle another mistake like that again."

"Do you think CJ would cheat on you?"

Julie shook her head. "No. He's the most honorable man I've ever met. It's the uncertainty about his condition. Can I handle it? What if it gets worse? Will it interfere with my professional career?"

"I felt a similar hesitancy, wondering what life would be like with the social challenges."

"How did you and Noah deal with it?"

Marge laughed. "Well, a Jamaican woman from LA marrying a pale Jewish man from Long Island isn't what I ever imagined. I mean, both families reacted. You know, 'you're marrying one of those?' There've been some tough moments for sure, 'cause we don't fit what society expects but I can't imagine life without him. And the assholes aren't going to stop us from following our hearts."

"How'd you figure it out?"

"As a Christian, I didn't know much about his religion. I decided to go to a rabbi in LA who taught me their history and some of their religious customs and practices. Then it didn't feel so foreign or strange. And some parts touched me. If you understood more about CJ's situation, I think it would help make you more comfortable."

***

Two Days Later

Dr. Lewis's Office

"Dr. McCray, I'm glad we could Facetime. Director Jackson indicated you might be calling."

"Thank you, Dr. Lewis. I've prepared some questions and I ..."

"Hold on, please, Dr. McCray. We need to review a few ground rules first. Director Jackson signed the HIPPA waiver, indicating I can share his medical information with you. However, his conversations in our therapy sessions will remain confidential. Now, how can I help you?"

"I understand." Julie bit her lip. "Ah, I'm on unfamiliar ground here, Doctor. I'm not sure where to start."

Dr. Lewis smiled. "There's no wrong place. Begin wherever you want."

Julie ran her finger down the list of questions she prepared for the meeting, then cleared her throat.

"Here goes. CJ and I were asleep when he suddenly woke up screaming with what he said was a flashback from the war. He seemed out of control. I didn't know what was happening or what to do. Do I have to worry about my safety? I mean, what's going on with him?"

"Your reaction is understandable. Here's some background. When he first awoke after sustaining injuries in Afghanistan, he experienced amnesia."

"Yeah, he mentioned that."

"Good. During this time, he feared 'he' wouldn't come back. His flashbacks go to this time of dire distress. Another source of his trauma is the death of his men and the guilt of surviving. The flashbacks bring these emotions to the forefront all over again.

"As for your safety, despite his difficulties, CJ has never acted out or been aggressive to others. At this point in his recovery, I believe any violent behavior, due to his PTSD, is remote."

Julie breathed a sigh of relief. "I've always felt comfortable with him and there were times when I wasn't very pleasant. I'm glad you have data to support that. When these flashbacks happen, what should I do?"

"Be reassuring. Ground him in the present. Tell him where you are, that he's safe, you love him, things like that."

Julie wrote down Dr. Lewis's suggestions, then asked, "How often do these flashbacks happen?"

"Hard to say. We're tracking them, and they're decreasing, but I can't say they will ever go away. But CJ's strong and will get stronger, especially if his support network strengthens."

"Meaning me."

"Only if you want to be. It's entirely up to you."

"Well, how can I be a good support?"

"It's important to talk with CJ about these incidents, the loss of his two soldiers, and his everyday frustrations so his emotions don't build up. It's also a clear sign you accept who he is. Remember, he's not used to having someone present during these flashbacks. I'm sure he didn't want you to see that side of him."

"Yeah, he said having mental issues makes people run for the exits."

"Acceptance of him and his condition is the key part. I'm going to send you a couple of articles explaining PTSD, as it pertains to combat veterans, and how loved ones can support them. Plus a link to the Army website where there's more information."

"I'd appreciate it." Julie paused. "Dr. Lewis, can we have a normal life together?"

"What do you mean?"

"I don't want you to take this the wrong way, but I'm worried his condition will get in the way of my professional life."

"He'll have mood swings and get frustrated at times. There'll be more flashbacks, as I've said. But whether or not you two can work through it is a question only you can answer."

"Anything else I should know?"

"Dr. McCray, this is a wound from the battlefield that lingers and persists. Most of the time, he'll be fine. He has tremendous support here, from the other vets, and Phil Locke. They're critical for him to maintain and improve his coping ability.

"If you do decide to continue the relationship, it's important for you to take care of yourself too. We have several support groups for spouses and loved ones going through the same thing as you. I recommend you participate. They can answer your questions about living with a partner with PTSD better than I can. All sessions are remote. I'll send you a schedule."

"Thank you for speaking with me, Dr. Lewis. You've been very helpful."

Julie stared out the window and processed the discussion. *Those support groups have the answers I need.* When Dr. Lewis's email appeared on her screen, she clicked on the support group schedule and signed up.

Chapter Forty-two: Boxman

NSA Headquarters, Building G

Layla waited until the clock ticked to 6:01 east coast time, a minute past midnight in Geneva, on the last day of the month. She pushed the button on her keyboard, engaging the Prop Forty-nine software and entered Boxman's bank account. His funds had already been allocated to the brokerage side of Guardier and Cie. Layla typed in the proper commands and seconds later, the trap was set to seize his assets.

"Gotcha."

***

Next Day

Geneva, 5:05 AM.

Michael Boxman's eyes snapped open. Someone pounded on his door. He sat up and listened, making sure his ears weren't playing tricks. Then more pounding, only louder. It better be damned important, or the concierge would hear about it. He grabbed his bathrobe and hurried to the front door.

"Who's there?"

"Swiss Intelligence Service, Dr. Boxman. Open up."

His heart raced. *They know who I am.* A queasy feeling surged from inside his stomach. He peered through the peephole. Two giant men held up their badges. He spun around. His panicked eyes searched in vain for a place to escape but there was none. *How did they find me?* Boxman's trembling hand clutched the handle and opened the door.

They rushed in and pinned Boxman against the wall. They searched him for weapons but did not handcuff him.

"What's this all about?" he demanded.

"Using a false identity is against Swiss immigration laws. You'll have to come with us."

Boxman's shoulders relaxed. *Just a bureaucratic issue my lawyer can fix.*

"Take us to your bedroom. We'll watch you change."

Ten minutes later, they motored through the dark, deserted streets, as the lights in the apartment windows began to flicker on. Boxman sat handcuffed in the back seat, stubble-faced, in a blue striped shirt, and gray wool slacks. A brown cashmere coat covered his shoulders.

Entering FIS headquarters, the agents escorted him down a long hallway to an interrogation room. The agents uncuffed him, opened the steel door, and nudged him inside. CJ, Jamil, and Layla sat on one side of the table. A lone chair rested on the other. Boxman stood frozen in place, fixated on Agent Brown.

"Have a seat, Dr. Boxman," said CJ. "We have a few things to discuss."

Inching toward the threesome, he eased into the chair across from them. He put his arms on the table and declared, "I'm not saying anything until my lawyer shows up."

Jamil leered at him. "Under our national security laws, you're not entitled to a lawyer," he snapped. "I can have you flown out right now to one of the CIA's black sites for interrogation with the full permission of the Swiss government. It's in your interest to talk with us now, while we're still willing to tolerate you."

Before Boxman could say anything else, Layla spoke up.

"Dr. Boxman, under a treaty with the United States and Switzerland, there are circumstances upon which we're able to access Swiss bank accounts of individuals who have committed certain types of crimes. As of yesterday, more than twenty million US dollars in your account at Guardier & Cie is under our control. Here's a copy of the order."

Layla slid it over and Boxman read the first few paragraphs. His face turned ashen, and he swallowed hard. *Emily promised G&C would protect my money. How did...*

CJ interrupted his thinking.

"People who are suddenly incarcerated react in a predictable way. You're going through the denial phase right now. You're saying to yourself, 'This can't be happening, I'm too smart, I had the perfect plan.'

"Here's your reality. You're broke. We could give the Chinese your address. They'll want to talk with you about the defective HAB plans when their upcoming moon mission fails, or we can incarcerate you. In short, we have you by the balls."

Boxman stared down at the table, his head dropped; his chin resting on his chest. He whispered, "What's the plan?"

"First, you agree to return to the States under the jurisdiction of the FBI," said Jamil. "We'll protect you against any retaliation from the Chinese. You'll be under house arrest in one of our safe houses. In return, you'll tell us how the Chinese contacted you, their payment methods, and so on. You'll have to sign an NDA as well. After two years, you'll be released, and you can collect the frozen money."

"I'll be free, and all charges dropped? Doesn't seem like the FBI."

"If it were up to me, you'd be going to Leavenworth. But you're President Jennings' appointee and a public arrest would embarrass her." Jamil slid a document across the table. "It's all here in writing. You have one minute to agree, or we send you to a place where no one will ever look."

Boxman balled his hands into fists. They tracked him down and took his money. *I've no way out.* He snatched the pen and scribbled his name.

Boxman folded his arms across his chest. "What is it you want to know?"

"We have you for taking twenty million dollars from the Chinese," CJ said. "Is this the total amount and did you sell information to any other countries?"

"Yes, it's the correct amount, and I gave information only to the Chinese."

CJ continued. "The Magellan space capsule is on its way to the space station. Is it safe?"

"Sending the DNA information to the Chinese and the astrobots turning off the refrigeration in the MAV storage unit after liftoff were the only changes I made."

"What's the relationship between you and Emily Woodson in all of this?" CJ asked.

Boxman sat back and glanced up at the ceiling.

"We both have similar issues with Fitzgerald Wiley. He's controlled our lives for too long, and we both needed a new start. With her financial connections, she helped me set up the accounts at G&C and arrange the purchase of the condo."

"Why did you funnel funds through the Alison Zhao account?" asked Layla.

Boxman kept his eyes locked on Agent Brown. "To monitor your progress. I knew if you were able to get inside G&C to find her account, you were on track to catch me. I used it as a warning sign to get ready to leave."

"Who killed Ashton?" Jamil asked.

Boxman cringed. "I never thought he'd be in danger. Without him knowing it, I told Tien Lee about the situation with his daughter. They attacked the NASA personnel files to provide cover."

"So, you set him up."

"Not the way you mean. His daughter's needs were significant after his wife's sudden death. He used up all his money and credit to pay for her treatments. I gave him money to act as my go-between to hand off the HAB plans. How else could his daughter get the treatment she needed? I mean, no US bank would loan him the money. And it served me as well."

"You still haven't answered my question. Who killed Ashton?"

Boxman gritted his teeth. "Tom Walker was my Chinese contact. He told me the order came from Minister Wang."

"Did you let them know about Area 51?" CJ asked.

"Yeah, it was a credibility check on me."

"How did you know we were on to you at Reagan National?" Jamil asked.

"I paid Belinda Ross to let me know if anyone started asking about me, our flight schedules, that sort of thing. When you came the first time, Belinda called, and I knew you were closing in. But I wanted to get the last payment out of the Chinese. Then we gave you the slip by switching planes."

But how did he know the exact time the FBI was going to arrest him in New York? thought CJ. He gave a sideways glance to Jamil.

Jamil continued, "You said Emily had her own money. Where did it come from? Did she embezzle from their hedge funds?"

Boxman sat back and smiled.

"No, no. She would never do that. Fitz scrutinizes his funds. He'd detect any improper activity. Over the years, she used her own money, and the hedge funds acted as a cover so she could start her own firm without Fitz knowing about it. Now she's on her own."

"Where did her money come from?"

"A chunk of it came from Guardier & Cie. They had a long relationship with Wiley and Wiley, and consequently, they built a close relationship with Emily. She knew G&C invested money into a company called MoneyMove. Emily said it helped G&C guard the secrecy of their clients.

"Fitz assigned Emily to work with Vice President Martin Atkins when he led the House Banking Committee. Emily introduced him to Guardier & Cie. In turn, G&C formed a PAC and donated regularly to his re-election campaigns. I think they still might.

"For that connection, Guardier & Cie gave Emily founders' shares of the MoneyMove company. When they went public, the initial shares went up almost thirty percent. She made over four million. She's very sharp and determined. Has a lot of her grandfather's traits."

Layla and CJ shot each other a glance, instantly knowing the reason why Proposition Forty-nine couldn't follow the money. CJ's face flushed.

"Last question for now," CJ said. "Why did you sell our secrets to the Chinese and sabotage our Magellan Project?"

"Tien Lee said Wang wanted the Martian DNA. But I needed a backup plan after you shut down Curiosity. Lee also needed a HAB structure, so I made a deal for plans. I played them, made off with twice the money to start my new life."

"You're foolish if you think that," CJ said. "Wang's been in this game a long time. She's smart and cunning, and you've given her the Martian DNA, the consequences of which could be disastrous."

Jamil stood and straightened his jacket. "Okay, we're done. Our agents will take you back to your condo to pack some clothes, then to the airport. They're outside now. I'll see you at the safe house in a couple of days."

After Boxman left, CJ looked at Layla and Jamil.

"Did you get what he said about Vice President Atkins?"

"Yeah, that's a surprise," Jamil said. "Atkins must've known not incorporating those new financial technologies would weaken our abilities to subvert criminal activity, especially international terrorist organizations. Shit. No one's going to want to hear about this."

"The good news is the mission is in the clear. I'll text Julie and let her know." CJ paused and drank the last of his lukewarm coffee. "You know, we started with a secret Mars mission to bring back some bacteria. Now look at it. It's way more complicated."

Then CJ turned to Layla.

"You okay? You haven't said much."

"You kidding? The VP? Can't wait to get to the bottom of this."

Brown rolled his eyes. "More likely we're charging into a giant shit storm. Let's go home."

***

Next Day

Mr. V: *Heard about Boxman. Am I safe?*

Mr. F: *Not sure. Boxman talked. Connected you to Prop Forty-nine. You're on the radar. I'll do the best I can.*

Mr. V: *Does he know my plan?*

Mr. F: *No. But the others know about you. The good news is Boxman will be in an FBI safe house for two years.*

Mr. V: *Give me the address of the safe house. Money sent.*

Chapter Forty-three: Changes

CIA Communications Center

One Week Later

Standing shoulder to shoulder in the CIA's Communication Center, CJ and Phil watched the live images of the Long March Five rocket preparing for liftoff courtesy of their KH-14 satellite. On top of the launch vehicle rested the command module holding its two astronauts and a HAB unit built with Julie's terrestrial schematics.

"You talked with Boxman since he's been back?" Phil asked.

"No. FBI's still getting him settled. There's no rush. The Magellan mission's clear and on track to dock at the ISS."

As the rocket's engines ignited and began its climb skyward, Phil said, "They're gonna be pissed."

"They have it coming. They killed Ashton, funded the sabotage of our mission, and stole the Martian DNA. Can't believe how lenient Boxman's being treated. Know anything about that?"

"No. It was between Maykuth and Jennings."

"Still not over it."

Phil pointed at the screen. "When their HAB fails, thanks to you and Julie, it'll be a setback for Wang. Their generals will want accountability. Wang'll know it came from us."

CJ shook his head. "The plans came through Boxman. He's our scapegoat. Wang will think he either stole the wrong plans or double-crossed her. Either way, it's not our fault. That's what Jennings can tell President Junqi."

Phil shook his head. "The Chinese President will never find out about this. Wang'll cover it up. Besides, I never told Jennings. Need to give her deniability so if Junqi brought it up, she'd act naturally surprised. How long before the shit hits the fan?"

"Julie said the HAB seals will decompose in two to four weeks, depending on the amount of radiation exposure. Then they'll have to send the astronauts back up to the command capsule. Mission over."

Phil clasped his hands behind his back. "Good, that's what happens when you take things that don't belong to you."

***

Three Weeks Later

Julie's Office, JPL

Julie returned from the breakroom with the morning's second cup of coffee. As she checked on the status of the command module streaking its way to the International Space Station, a video meeting request from Jack Boyle, Acting NASA Administrator, popped up on her calendar. The topic wasn't mentioned, and it was starting in ten minutes. Sounds urgent. Julie clicked 'accept,' and soon he greeted her.

"Good morning, Dr. McCray. I'm very impressed with your Mars mission, what little I know about it. Thank you for representing NASA so well."

"Good morning, Mr. Boyle. Thank you."

"Dr. McCray, the FBI came over and briefed the management team about Michael Boxman's actions. They confirmed his criminal intent aimed against your mission with minimal details due to its top-secret classification. This type of treachery is unprecedented in NASA. Our people are upset and our morale has taken a hit."

"I know. It goes against everything we stand for."

"To correct this, I need to bring in respected leaders to regain their trust. I've talked with several people in and outside of NASA, and they all speak very highly of you, verifying my own impression."

Where is he going with this, thought Julie. She edged closer to the screen.

"President Jennings also asked me to reestablish our Mars program and suggested you would be a good candidate. Therefore, I'd like you to be our new Associate Administrator in charge of all Mars programming. Will you accept?"

Julie reared back in her chair, her hand covering her mouth, stifling a joyous gasp. She leaned forward and came back into view of the computer's camera.

"This is such a surprise, I mean, honor. Oh, gosh. This is my dream job. Yes, I accept. I'd like a little time to assemble the goals of the Mars program for your review. We can also talk about the logistics and timing of my coming to Washington. Can we speak the day after tomorrow?"

"I look forward to our conversation, Dr. McCray. My assistant will set it up."

Julie sat back in her chair, her mind racing. *One step at a time,* she told herself. She knew the next call she had to make.

***

That Night

Julie's Condominium

Julie perched on the edge of her sofa, clenching a pillow under her left arm. Giz was curled up sleeping beside her. She stared at a selfie of her and CJ when they stayed at the beach cottage. The wind whipped strands of her hair across CJ's face, and the photo captured his laugh. *We were so happy then.*

She touched her cross and tapped CJ's number on her phone.

"CJ, this is Julie."

"Yeah, I know. It's after eleven, everything all right?"

Julie bit her lip. "I need to talk to you about a decision I made today."

"Okay, you sound nervous."

"Jack Boyle offered me the position of Associate Administrator for Mars Programs at NASA. I accepted."

"That's great. You deserve it."

"I'm calling because I'll be relocating to DC, and I want to know how you feel about it."

CJ ran his hand through his hair thinking how to respond to this unanticipated change.

Julie squeezed her pillow tight into her chest. "Don't go silent on me. What are you feeling?"

"Easy, not quite awake yet. Give me a second."

CJ sat up and plopped his legs over the side of his bed.

"We've held many honest talks the last few weeks about what we want our relationship to be. Here's what I'm thinking. The safe play is for you to get your own place in DC, and we ease into it. I say screw it. I love you and want you in my life. Move in with me. I know it's a big step but it's the only way we'll know if it'll work."

Julie teared up. She thought about the conversations she experienced in the veteran's group she'd been attending. They mentioned the challenges, hard at times, but also how they made their love blossom and their commitment to each other stronger.

"You're so sweet. The people in my veteran's support group have figured it out so why can't we? And I'm tired of being lonely. I love you, so let's do it."

Chapter Forty-four: New Arrangements

Hong Kong

Emily Woodson's chartered plane landed on runway Seven R of Hong Kong's International Airport. It taxied to a private hangar where she exited down the jet's stairs and climbed into a waiting Mercedes limousine. The car sped out of the airport complex, bypassing customs and immigration. She pulled the phone from her purse and checked her SecretSessions app. *Still no response from Michael. Hope he's okay.*

When the car arrived at the underground parking area of Hong Kong National Bank, Emily took the private elevator to the executive suite on the top floor of the building. After a quick refresh in the women's restroom, she entered Mi Lang's office.

"Emily, it's good to see you. You look fabulous," he said as he bowed to her.

She smiled. "It's good to see you as well, Chairman Lang."

"Let us sit." He waved his hand, and they stepped into his executive conference room.

Emily glanced at the shadowy outlines of the city's skyscrapers, masked by the thick, polluted air. She took a seat at the end of the long rosewood table. Each of the twenty matching chairs was embossed with a dragon motif and the double prosperity symbol. Emily opened her briefcase and fired up her computer. When Mi Lang sat across from her, she launched into her financial agenda.

"Things are on track. Jennings will approve reinstating China to the WTO if President Junqi agrees to a new proposal regarding the Climate Initiative, something about staffing China's Air Cleansing Facilities. Atkins will let us know when she's ready to go public. We'll make our move before the rumors on the Street are confirmed."

On the table, in front of Emily, rested a formal tea service, a porcelain platter with warm congee, and an assortment of cold fruits. Mi Lang sighed at the cultural slight. He reached over to the tea service and poured them each a cup.

"Since we will be meeting frequently, we Chinese have a custom," he said. "The warm and cold food on the platter represents balance, yin and yang, and suggests hope for a successful meeting." Mi Lang raised his cup.

Emily smiled and took a sip of tea; her foot tapping under the table. "The platter is beautifully presented. I too, hope for a successful meeting."

"Would you like some fruit, Emily?"

"No thanks, Mr. Chairman. Had some on the plane."

He gritted his teeth, ignoring another insult, and drank a few more sips of his tea before continuing. "What investments are you targeting?"

Emily straightened in her chair. "I've chosen three index funds. The China Fifty and the China Three Hundred traded out of Hong Kong National, and the DAX Index, which I'll trade through Guardier & Cie."

Mi Lang rubbed his chin. "Why index funds? We'd make more money with individual companies doing business with China."

"Correct, but for now I'm being risk-averse. We don't want to get caught now when we have much more to gain in the years ahead. The index funds, as you know, aren't as scrutinized by the regulators because there's no insider trading. And our trades will blend in with their high trading volumes. We won't stand out."

"How much?"

"If we go twenty in each, we'll come away with around a hundred million. Here are the trend charts after other similar trade announcements." Emily turned her laptop screen so Mi Lang could see her analysis. "During the upsurge, I'll execute the trades myself."

"Can't we do more?"

"We have to shield Atkins. Remember, we'll have many more opportunities when Jennings terms out after this upcoming election and he becomes President. We don't want to blow it this early. Make sense?"

Mi Lang smiled and chewed a piece of melon. "Agreed. How do you like being a citizen of Hong Kong, Emily?"

***

CJ's Condo

Ten Days Later

After renting her furnished condo in Pasadena, Julie jetted across the country and landed in DC. Ambling through CJ's two-bedroom condo for the first time, she made mental notes of improvements she wanted to make. Gizmo trailed behind her exploring his new space.

"CJ, there is not one living plant in this house," she called from the hallway.

"I travel a lot, so I'd probably kill anything I'd try to grow."

"Drapes, towels, and linens all need an upgrade. I'll handle it." She peeked into the second bedroom. "This one's empty. Do you ever have guests?"

"No. Why don't you use it for your office?"

Julie grinned. "Thanks, honey." She walked back to the front of the hall where CJ waited.

"Ah, you sound critical. Having second thoughts?"

"Sorry. That didn't come out how I wanted it. I'm going to love it here because I'm with you." She kissed him on the cheek. "Just need to make it homey."

"Good. You had me for a minute. Let's go into the kitchen and celebrate." Julie sat at the counter while CJ pulled a bottle of Schramsberg from the refrigerator. He filled two glasses and handed one to Julie. He raised his for a toast.

"Julie, I'm so happy you're here, because you make my life better every moment I'm with you."

They touched glasses and drank. Julie walked around the counter and put her arms around him. "You make my life better too." She gave him a long and passionate kiss. "We'll continue this later. I need to talk with you about logistics."

"Logistics? I thought we might ..."

Julie held up her hand. "Cool it. I need to know a few things like, the best way to get to the office, where's the local dry cleaner, and what's the best gym for women?"

"All right." CJ pulled up Google Maps and oriented his new roommate to the neighborhood. After an hour, Julie had her list.

"I have a few work updates," CJ said. "Once you get the microbes here, Dr. Grunhart will verify the absorption rates at the Area 51 lab, like he did before. If you remember, that's when you were all pissy and didn't talk to me on the flight out?"

She shot him a look. "Careful, you're coming close to asshole-ville, where no one has sex."

"Got it. The plan is to staff Grunhart's lab with scientists from the US Army Medical Research Institute for Infectious Diseases. Colonel Ruiz will be in charge, and Grunhart will oversee the experiments. They'll have two teams. One dedicated to the Climate Initiative and one researching the deadly microbes."

"What are the next steps for the Climate part?"

"Dr. Williams has built a small-scale prototype of her Air Cleansing Facility at Ft. Greely, Alaska. If Grunhart's lab experiments prove effective, they'll grow the Martian bacteria and then plant them in the test ACF."

Julie turned the glass in her hands. "But first, we have to dock with the ISS."

"Why not land it directly?"

"Reentry's the most dangerous part of the mission. What would happen if we experienced a malfunction? All of our microbes would be in one ship, and it'd be at least three years before we could get another set of core samples."

"Makes sense." CJ gave a quick scan around at his cluttered living room where the movers placed Julie's belongings. Gizmo was stretched out on top of one of the cardboard wardrobes. "You have a lot of stuff."

"Don't worry. By tomorrow, it'll all be put away, I promise."

CJ grinned. "Okay. I bought a present for Giz." CJ hopped off the stool and went to the hall closet, pulling out a new kitty bed. "Do you think he'll like it?"

Julie laughed out loud. "That's very thoughtful. But Giz'll be sleeping with us, like in California. You'll get used to it. Oh, and I'm leaving for Houston the day after tomorrow for the re-entry. You'll have to take care of him."

CJ stared back at her. "Me?"

"Come on, honey. Let's go out for dinner. I'm starving. You pick, my treat." She grabbed his arm and hauled him out the door.

Chapter Forty-five: Here Come the Aliens

Johnson Space Center, Houston

Mission Control

"They don't want me to pace around in here," Julie said to Marge. "How can I think standing still?"

"Two more milestones, Julie, docking and reentry. Should all be wrapped up in a couple of hours."

"Magellan is about ten minutes out, Director McCray," said the Flight Ops Director.

"Roger that."

"The move okay?" Marge asked.

"Fine, but I'm still disorganized. Been in DC less than forty-eight hours, and I had to come down here."

"JPL sure feels weird without you."

"It'll be even weirder with you gone. I'll push through your transfer soon as I get back. We're going to do great things together. Think Franklin can take your spot?"

"Yeah, I think he's ..."

Over their headsets, the communication started up again.

"Houston, Nichols. Nav radar is locked on Magellan, systems nominal."

Alison Nichols, commander of the ISS, watched the white blip race toward her on the navigation screen.

"ISS, Houston. Roger that. Proceed with docking."

Nichols entered the observatory to get a clear visual of the spacecraft. In a matter of minutes, it went from a small white dot mixed in with the stars to filling the view window. Puffs of gray exhaust from the capsule's maneuvering jets aligned it to the station's docking port. When the ship eased into the ISS, Alison felt the vibration in her feet when the titanium bolts slammed into the grooves on Magellan's berthing collar.

"Houston, Nichols. We have Magellan. Spacecraft is secured."

"Roger that. Nice job; we're all breathing easier down here. Have Specialist Toolson retrieve the samples and put them in the Orion capsule."

Moments later, he glided to the bay holding the Magellan capsule and removed seven tubes, half the mission's inventory of Martian bacteria. He floated each one down the corridor to the Orion spacecraft. He placed the canisters in the storage module, lined with radiation-blocking material, which kept the organisms at a cold and constant temperature. Toolson secured the canisters in place for the bumpy ride through the atmosphere.

"Houston, ISS. Orion's ready for reentry."

"Nichols, Houston. Descent is in thirty, three zero minutes. Prepare Commander Emerson. The Magellan capsule will follow after two orbits."

"Roger that, Nichols out."

Strapping into the Orion capsule, Commander Bret Emerson went through his pre-flight checklist, preparing for the descent and landing. Then said, "Commander Nichols, Orion is ready for separation."

"Good luck, Bret," Nichols said.

The Texan flashed a wide confident grin.

"Lookin' forward to my last ride. Got cows in my future. Hope the autopilot holds during the plunge."

Emerson stared at the planet rotating two hundred and forty miles beneath him, one last time. Once a vibrant crystal blue, it now featured large gray and brown splotches smeared across several continents. Nichols's voice came through his headset.

"Ten seconds until separation. Godspeed, Bret."

"Thank you, Commander. For all mankind." He gazed up at Nichols watching through the observation portal and saluted her. She saluted back and hit the release of the docking collar.

In Houston's Mission Control, Julie watched the clean separation from the ISS cameras. Another monitor showed the capsule's velocity, angle of atmospheric entry, G forces, and position.

"Orion, Houston. You'll have one orbit to align your trajectory vector then the retro-rockets will fire to begin your descent. It's been uploaded to your flight computer. You're on automatic. Sit back and enjoy the ride, Commander."

"Roger that Houston. See you soon, Emerson, out."

Julie removed her headset and spoke quietly to Marge.

"I'll be glad when the samples are safely in Dr. Grunhart's lab. Then our mission will be finished. It's been stressful."

"And one of the most successful in JPL history. We have a lot to be proud of."

Over the next half hour, the flight computer guided the Orion spacecraft. It descended to a lower orbit, maneuvering for the optimal angle to enter Earth's atmosphere when the alarm blared, and the emergency lights flashed in Mission Control.

"Orion, this is Houston. Two satellites collided and materialized directly in your path. You need to take evasive action to avoid the debris cloud."

"Roger that, Houston," said Emerson. "Disengaging autopilot. What's my vector?"

"Steer ten point eight degrees to starboard. This will put you on a steep trajectory as you enter the thermosphere. You'll need to correct the angle immediately after you clear the debris field. Copy?"

"Roger, Houston. Ready on your mark."

Julie fixated on the Flight Ops monitor. It indicated a sixty-degree angle of entry, seventeen degrees more than the maximum safety level. She flipped her headset control so she could speak to Marge.

"He's coming in too steep."

"Shit, Jules. This debris field is expanding. It's a Kessler syndrome. He'll barely have time to correct his alpha. He's in trouble."

Julie gave Marge a steely look. Kessler was the NASA scientist who predicted as the density of objects in low earth orbit increased, there would be a point where collisions between these objects would cause a cascade of further collisions rendering space activities unfeasible in certain orbital pathways.

"Dr. McCray, this is Mission. He needs to correct his path to over eighty degrees to avoid the debris, but he won't be able to recover in time. What's your direction?"

Julie knew going through the debris field guaranteed destruction and entering the atmosphere at this angle meant the deceleration forces would rip the spacecraft apart. Her stomach twisted into a knot. *He's not going to make it.*

"Mission, connect me to him."

"Orion, this is Dr. McCray."

"Dr. McCray, how bad is it?"

"The debris field's enlarged. To miss it, you must turn another three degrees which will put you at a catastrophic re-entry angle. I want you..."

"Acknowledged. A chunk of debris hit the heat shield. It's not gonna hold. For all mankind, Director. Tell my parents I ..."

The heat and friction of the atmosphere cut off Emerson's transmission. It would be one minute before it could be re-established. The room grew silent. The mission staff stared straight ahead at their screens. Some prayed. Julie grasped her cross, straining to hear Emerson's response or at least the spacecraft's audible beacon over her headset. Seconds ticked by. No one moved. Julie closed her eyes.

At one minute and three seconds, the Comm Director sent his hopeful message, "Orion, this is Houston. Do you copy?"

The Comm Director called into the void six more times.

"Mission, this is Flight. We have debris. Spacecraft is destroyed."

Julie grimaced, and she released her cross. She switched her headset to address the control room team.

"Mission, this is McCray. Lockdown outside communication. Everyone, listen up. We'll grieve for Commander Emerson at the right time and give him the respect his courage deserves. But now, we must bring the bacteria in the Magellan spacecraft safely to Area 51. The world is counting on us."

***

Stationing on the edge of the landing zone in Area 51, Dr. Grunhart and his team waited to retrieve the bacteria from the space capsule. The range finder in their van started to beep. Three red and white parachutes floated downward in the light desert breeze, with the Magellan spacecraft dangling underneath.

Seconds after landing, the van driver raced toward the capsule, pulling up next to the access hatch. Grunhart and his team, dressed in full bio-suits, opened the capsule. The team retrieved the containment strongbox, then transferred it to the van's vault.

***

Julie boarded the NASA jet for the ride home. She plopped down in the last seat, away from the other NASA staff, wanting to be left alone. Flying northward, she gazed out the window at the all too familiar images of parched land, wilted trees, and dried-up river beds. Julie touched her cross. *Your sacrifice, Commander Emerson, is supposed to fix that.*

After landing, a car took Julie home. Walking in the door, CJ rushed to meet her. He held her tight and whispered, "I'm so sorry."

Julie's pent-up emotions of the past days burst out. She cried in his arms, her mascara running down her cheeks onto CJ's shirt as he rubbed her back. Finally, Julie let go. Her voice quivered.

"I'm so glad to be home. I've missed you so much."

CJ held her hand. "Me too. What can I do for you, babe?"

Julie let out a sigh. "I need to peel off these clothes and take a shower. Then I want to be with you."

"Absolutely. I'll open some chardonnay." CJ kissed her again. She turned and trudged down the hall to the bedroom. He watched her go. Her weary shoulders slumped as she disappeared through the doorway.

Twenty minutes later, she shuffled into the living room, her blonde hair tied in a ponytail, wearing a running shirt, and baggy cotton sweatpants. CJ waited on the couch with two glasses of wine, cheese, and crackers. Gizmo curled up in the adjacent armchair, ignoring Julie after being gone.

Julie picked up Giz and gave him a big hug and kiss. He scrambled out of her arms and onto the floor. But as soon as Julie sat down, he bounded up and laid down in her lap, the abandonment all forgiven.

"Well, I see all's well in Giz's world now," Julie said.

"How are you doing?"

"Oh, God. I called his parents and told them. They were so gracious and brave. They knew how he loved being an astronaut. His dad said it's the way he would want to go. Then he started crying. Then we all cried."

Julie reached over and held CJ's hand.

"In the past, when I would pass by the Memorial Grove, I felt a reverence for those astronauts who gave their lives. I appreciate what their sacrifices have taught us about space exploration. But when I went by today, I felt angry and ashamed. He died on my watch. His tree will be a symbol of his courage and my failure."

"When's the ceremony going to be?"

"They said it'll take a couple of weeks to bring in the right people there."

Julie leaned her head on CJ's shoulder, a tear slowly trickling down her cheek. He put his arm around her and tucked her in close, then whispered, "I think about the two men who died in my Humvee every day. They sacrificed themselves for their country. Your astronaut carried microbes to help ensure the safety of our planet. One day, his sacrifice will manifest itself and you'll recognize it. Then, this terrible burden you're feeling will ease a bit, I promise."

CJ kissed her head and squeezed her closer. "For those of us who serve, and I mean you too Julie, it's part of the bond that holds us together."

Julie lifted her head and kissed him on the cheek and then snuggled back down on his shoulder.

"I love you," she muttered and closed her eyes.

Chapter Forty-six: Next Steps

Ten Days Later

Area 51, Stewart Laboratory Facility

Dr. Grunhart, Colonel Ruiz, and Dr. Mary Williams greeted Julie and CJ as they took their seats in the Stewart Laboratory auditorium. General Scott and Layla Burton were present via video.

"Congratulations, Julie," said Dr. Grunhart. "We have exciting news about your discovery."

"We're grateful too," said Mary. "We're sorry about the loss of Commander Emerson."

"Thank you," said Julie. "I hope these microbes deliver what you need, Dr. Williams."

"Ah, everyone," Dr. Grunhart said. "I want to introduce Colonel Ruiz, he's Commander of USAMRIID, and he's been working with us, getting everything going, yah? We've been experimenting round the clock and have made several significant discoveries. Colonel, please start us off."

"The Martian samples contained three types of living organisms. Under the microscope, each has a distinct coloration, blue, orange, and green-orange. We named them by color to keep it simple. I've been working with the orange in a separate lab because we've discovered they're extremely deadly."

"How so?" General Scott asked.

"When they're exposed to oxygen and light, they begin an accelerated propagation process. The next generation turns a brownish color. Somehow their chemical composition changes to accommodate oxygen in combination with carbon dioxide. We do not know how this happens. It's of extreme interest.

"The brown biogen excretes a deadly toxin, in gaseous form, very similar in chemical structure to botulism. In Earth-type botulism, people generally get very sick but normally recover with the proper medication.

"The Martian varietal is different. It causes instant respiratory paralysis. The mice we've tested have died within twenty to forty seconds, often having violent seizures. If we keep the orange bacteria alive, our policies require us to develop a vaccine. If that proves impossible, we'll destroy it."

"What's the security risk, Colonel?"

"Very high, General. It's similar to the Ebola category of viruses. Fortunately, they don't survive in temperatures above freezing."

Scott's forehead wrinkled. "The Chinese have the DNA profile of these bacteria. What are the threat implications, Dr. Grunhart?"

"I can't be conclusive. In our first DNA experiments, the implanted microbes did not survive. But it doesn't mean other combinations would have the same outcome."

"Could you make a bioweapon with certain combinations?"

"I'm afraid the possibility is real, General," Ruiz said. "We'll continue to experiment, but my orders are to prioritize Dr. Williams' project. I'll let her explain."

Mary stood and went to the podium.

"We've prepared a demonstration in the other lab and piped it in here. I wanted you to see it live. Dr. Roberta Needham will explain our findings then Lt. Jennifer LeBlanc will show you in real-time what happens. Dr. Needham, please begin."

"Our experiments with the blue bacteria yielded the most exciting results. When exposed to light, their metabolism increases dramatically. Remember, they've been living underground for millions of years. With light as an additional energy source, they ingest double the carbon dioxide from our first experiments."

"Why's that?" Julie asked.

"The ability to use light comes from a part of the blue's DNA chain which has been dormant until now. This indicates they once lived on the surface of Mars or, as you suggested Dr. McCray, even here on Earth. Could be both.

"When we placed them in an earth-like atmosphere, a dramatic transformation took place. They turned green. In this state, they procreate more rapidly with the next generation being twenty percent larger and they survive at a higher temperature. Oxygen and light make their metabolism more efficient. Here's what we want to show you."

Everyone fixated on the screen as Lt. LeBlanc stepped forward.

"We have two identical 5-liter containers, one with the blue bacteria inside and one with the green. We colored the carbon dioxide gas yellow like last time."

She turned a knob. A yellow cloud invaded the glass columns. The gas in the green biogen container disappeared in less than three seconds while the blue container took eleven seconds.

"What are your conclusions, Dr. Williams?" Julie asked.

"The absorption rate is well above our cost-benefit ratio. For the first time we can build an energy-efficient Direct Air Capture system across the globe capable of extracting millions of tons of CO2. This is the breakthrough we need, and we owe it all to you and your team, Dr. McCray."

The small gathering gave Julie a standing ovation.

Julie blushed. "Thank you. What happens next, Dr. Williams?"

"We have a section of the lab dedicated to growing the green bacteria as fast as we can. We're also leaving in two days to begin field testing our small-scale ACF prototype at Ft. Greely, Alaska."

"Ft. Greely?"

"Yes. It's very isolated and cold. Need to hide it from the media until we understand how the bacteria work in the real world." She finished and took her seat.

"Thank you, Dr. Williams," said Emil. "We'll keep everyone posted. This concludes our presentation."

After CJ and Julie toured the lab facilities, they said their goodbyes and stepped out of the lab complex. An SUV drove them to the airfield where the NASA jet waited. Flying east, Julie watched the barren desert landscape of Nevada slide below.

"You've been quiet," CJ said. "What's going on?"

"Looks like Mars down there. Makes me think about Commander Emerson's last moments. He died alone. I can't imagine what he might have been feeling." She looked at CJ with sad eyes. "When they congratulated us today, I could only think of him."

Chapter Forty-seven: Tangled Web

CJ and Julie's Condo, 10 p.m.

Julie sat in bed reading her budget report with CJ lying awake next to her. When she found herself reading the same page three times, she gave up and closed her computer. She slipped her hand into CJ's.

"You seem deep in thought," said Julie. "How was your visit with Boxman at the safehouse?"

"It was hardly worth the trip. He said Emily set up his money transfers from the Chinese. When I asked him if Emily and Atkins were in a relationship, he said he told us everything in Geneva. Then he stomped back to his room. The whole interview lasted less than two minutes."

"Hmm. Boxman. Can I talk with him?"

"Sure, why?"

"He sold NASA technology and worked with the Chinese to sabotage us. He said he worked with Tien Lee. I'd like to know who his other contacts might be."

"It'd be good intel to identify them."

Julie scrunched up her nose. "That's not it. I mean if the Chinese are using our space conferences for illicit means, then they should be punished, don't you think? I'd prohibit them from coming."

"I like it. I'll set up the interview. You want me to come with you?"

"No. It's better if it's only me. Different relationship. Why are you focused on Woodson?"

"She connected Guardier & Cie with Atkins when he chaired the House Banking Committee. G&C contributed to his re-election campaigns. Atkins, in turn, kept out specific language that allowed G&C to keep certain accounts secret, something other banks can't do." Then he scowled. "I know there's something else, but I can't see it."

CJ slapped the covers with the palm of his hand. Gizmo, lying across CJ's legs, shot up his head and looked back at him with an unflinching glare.

"Frustrated?"

"Yeah. Sorry. What am I missing?"

"A woman as driven as Emily Woodson, would not waste her time coming down here to hang out. She had a purpose. Her high-profile clients meet when it's convenient for them, on weekends, evenings, whenever. Right?"

CJ raised his eyebrows. "Then why wouldn't Boxman say she had business meetings?"

"Maybe Emily's involved with someone."

"Of course." CJ shook his head. "How'd I miss that? Layla tracked her staying at a G&C high-end condo. I'll bet she's romantically involved with Atkins." He leaned over and kissed Julie. "Thank you. I'll dive into it tomorrow."

"You had a session with Dr. Lewis a couple of days ago. How'd it go?"

He smiled. "I talked about you a lot."

"I know it's your private time but I'm here if you want to share anything."

"Well, I do. Last week I went to a meeting. When I returned to my office, my worry stone sat on top of my desk. I never go anywhere without it. I mean, I didn't even know I left it behind. It's because you're in my life."

***

Next Day

CJ's Office

CJ faced his wall-sized whiteboard holding three colored markers. He wrote Emily Woodson, Martin Atkins, and Guardier & Cie and mapped their connections. Woodson connected Atkins with Guardier & Cie. Their political action committee funded Atkins' election campaigns. Guardier & Cie owned the MoneyMove app to ensure client secrecy and Atkins kept out compromising legislation. Finally, Emily received a finder's fee from Guardier & Cie for introducing Atkins to them.

CJ called Layla as his next step. "Ms. Burton, I need to find out if Emily Woodson is romantically involved with the Vice President. Can you do it?"

"This is so totally cool." Layla took a swig of her Red Bull. "People in illicit trysts often use fee-based apps to allow secret communication."

"Can you listen in to these?"

Layla frowned. “It’s a big problem for us. Terrorist groups have latched onto them. We’ve developed tracking software, but have to be logged in to that person’s account to see the messages.”

“Can you find out if Emily’s using this type of communication?”

“Our warrants are still good. These apps have a monthly fee that gets deducted automatically. I’ll check her bank records.

Chapter Forty-eight: Julie's Influence

The ACF Prototype

Ft. Greely, Alaska

Julie and Dr. Emil Grunhart hustled down the ramp of the C-17 military aircraft onto the tarmac. She buried her face in the crook of her arm to fend off the biting, wind-blown snow as the two scientists dashed into the waiting Humvee. Its tires crunched the ice-crusted snow on the way to the ACF prototype. Julie spotted it in the distance and pointed.

"There it is. Looks like a big white tent."

"Yah. Inside is the containment structure. Dr. Williams sent me the preliminary data. Interesting. She said they've had a major change recently but wouldn't elaborate."

Julie turned to the esteemed scientist, "Is a month enough time to have conclusive results?"

"What I'm looking for are the bacteria's propagation rates and the stability of the bacteria population in this type of environment. If they're predictable, we can finalize our calculations with the full-size prototypes."

The Humvee arrived and Dr. Williams came out to greet them.

"Welcome to early spring, Alaska style. Quick, let's get out of this wind."

Emil and Julie entered a double-wide trailer that served as the entrance to the demonstration ACF. They stood in a vestibule behind thickly sealed doors. It reminded Julie of the airlock on the HAB.

"You'll have to put on bio-protective suits," Mary explained. "We have a changing room through these doors. Follow me." After donning the suits, the three entered the experimental tent-like chamber.

"Dr. McCray, in front of you is the containment field filled with your Martian microbes. It's a bowl fifty feet in diameter, five feet deep, and paved with concrete. Throughout the bowl is a labyrinth of sensors designed to detect the density of the biogens, their growth rate, and their location. The basin is filled with soil matching the Gale Crater."

"It's exciting to see this, Dr. Williams," Julie said. "How does it work?"

"At the top are two large vents. The first one draws in polluted air from the outside, compresses it, and then channels it through distribution pipes that spread the air evenly over the field. Once the sensors detect the carbon dioxide is absorbed, the second vent sucks the clean air back outside. Then the intake cycle starts again."

"What are the safety features preventing the bacteria from escaping?" Dr. Grunhart asked.

"There are several," said Mary. "Ringed around the containment bowl are ultraviolet light pods. They switch on when the sensors detect the bacteria near the perimeter, which kills them. Above the bacteria are a series of sprinklers ready to douse ammonia on the entire field. Finally, underneath the soil are a series of heating coils. They can't survive in moderate temperatures if you remember."

"Ah yes, very good."

"Tell me about your experiment," Julie said to Mary.

"It's pretty straightforward. We planted the bacteria in the center of the field. Then we tracked their growth rate, density, spread, and of course, the CO2 absorbed. Then we calibrated the cycle time. Come, the others are excited to share their findings with you."

The three scientists filed inside the staff trailer and sat in the first row of folding chairs. Dr. Needham led the session. "Everyone, quiet down so we can start. Thank you and welcome Dr. Grunhart and Dr. McCray. We're eager to discuss what we've learned. Over the past four weeks, the microbes have expanded from the center of the field to the perimeter." On the monitor, she showed time-lapsed images of how the bacteria spread throughout the containment field.

"They're propagating at a fast rate," said Julie.

"Correct. It's a vital finding because it verifies the bacteria's compatibility with Earth's environment. We'll get to the details in a moment. The next slide is what's most important. As you can see from the graph, after a brief ramp-up period, the density-to-absorption ratio averaged 78.4 percent. This is highly effective. Our conclusion is to move to the next stage and test again in full-scale ACF prototypes."

"Hold on. How do you account for this rapid expansion?" Grunhart asked.

"In the lab setting," said Lt. LeBlanc, "we found oxygen and light amplified their metabolic rate, which accelerated their reproduction rates.

Most of the variation is explained by the fact each successive generation of bacteria absorbs CO2 at a higher rate, and they survive at higher temperatures. Here's the data table."

The scientists dove into the details, scrutinizing the data, day by day. Afterwards, Emil stroked his goatee. "Interesting. The evidence is consistent with our genetic findings." Then he turned to Mary. "Ordinarily, I'd like another experiment to compare the results. But our situation is urgent, yah? Dr. Williams, I support moving to the next phase."

"Me too," said Mary. "China and India have agreed to build two prototypes each in cities with extremely poor air quality. If our ACFs work there, it'll convince the others for full implementation."

***

One Week Later, NASA Headquarters

Julie's Office

Marge knocked on Julie's office door and stuck her head through the opening.

"Hey, boss, I'm here."

Julie rushed to greet her colleague and hugged her.

"Welcome to DC. I'm so glad to see you. Your move okay?"

"Not bad. Noah's parents came down and helped us unpack. They only live an hour away. They can't wait to babysit. It'll give us the break we didn't have in California. Looking forward to that."

"Have a minute?"

"Sure. All I have right now is orientation. What's up?"

"I need to fill you in. Let's sit."

The two adjourned to Julie's worktable. Looking at her colleague across from her, Julie smiled. "I've missed having someone to talk to who knows how I think. Okay, first thing. I'm going out to see Boxman."

"Boxman? I almost forgot about him. Where is he?"

"He's in an FBI safe house. CJ arranged the visit for me."

"What! You mean he's not in jail?"

"Yeah, I know. Disappointing. CJ said he's hands-off because Boxman's a presidential appointee."

She waved her hand. "Anyway, what's your objective?"

"I want him to tell me how he programmed the low-gain antenna without us knowing about it and how he changed the reentry code during the weather briefing. Then we can upgrade our processes so these types of failures can't happen again."

"Good point." She shifted in her seat. "But how are you feeling about him? Will it be awkward?"

Julie paused and thought for a moment. "No. I've appreciated his support, but in hindsight it seemed only to keep the Mars mission going so he could sell our information. Still angry about it. But I'm curious, Marge. He loved NASA. Something turned his passion into sabotage. Probably the Jennings thing but I want to hear it from him."

***

FBI Safehouse

"Welcome, Dr. McCray," Agent Sarnow said. "We have you set up in the living room. I'll be in the kitchen if you need anything. Any questions?"

Julie scanned the modest living area and asked, "How is he?"

Sarnow slipped his hands into his pants pockets. "Edgy."

Julie gave him a questioning look.

"Boredom can eat away at a person in confinement," said Sarnow. "Life is difficult when you're just passing time. You represent his past life when he jetted about, testified before Congress, and the like. Be prepared. There might be some resentment."

"Thank you. Bring him out whenever you're ready."

Moments later, Boxman shuffled out from the hallway. His shirt and pants hung loosely on his frame and unkempt whiskers jutted from his face. He plopped down across from Julie and scoffed. "I imagine this must be a good moment for you, Dr. McCray."

"Dr. Boxman, you supported me and the JPL which I'm grateful for. I'm here to find out how you reprogrammed C-2's antenna so we can fix the process. And why you did it if you're willing to talk about it."

Boxman bent forward, his brow creased, and he stared at Julie. She leaned closer to him and whispered, "I know in your heart you love NASA. Will you help me, Dr. Boxman?"

He sat back in his chair and closed his eyes. He sat motionless for several moments, deep creases emerged on his forehead.

When he opened his eyes, he looked past Julie. "I do love NASA," he muttered. "Growing up, I never missed a launch. Astronauts blasting off into space was the coolest thing. Such a long time ago." His gaze shifted to the floor.

"My father-in-law made a deal with Jennings; a sizeable contribution for appointing me NASA Administrator. Those first few weeks were the best days of my life. I couldn't wait to get into the office."

Then his eyebrows narrowed, and he looked at Julie. "Then Jennings' bulldog Hawkins called. Told me Boyle was their guy, and he'd be making the decisions. She made me a charade, a fake. And everyone knew it. Humiliating."

He slapped his palm on the arm of the chair. "That's when I vowed to get even."

"I didn't know the details. I would've been upset as well."

Boxman eyed Julie. "I'm a rocket scientist too, not some political hack." He dropped his head and stared at the floor again. "They stole my dreams with a 30-second phone call."

Silence permeated the room. After several moments, Julie cleared her throat. "Dr. Boxman, will you tell me how you reprogrammed Curiosity's antenna?"

His head bobbed. "I'd wait for Ashton in the mornings and watch him type in his password while I chatted him up." He paused and pursed his lips. "It's how I learned about his daughter. After Curiosity's software was finalized, I stayed late, logged in to Ashton's computer, and made the change."

"Was he authorized?"

"Yes. Because our contractors often have last-minute changes or revisions. In these circumstances, it's easier to have the coordinator input the fixes. That way, all of our units have the changes at the same time."

Julie tucked a loose strand of hair behind her ear. "What about the software changes to the rover and the GC-MS?"

"The Chinese wanted the DNA and embarrass NASA as well. It would make CNSA look better with their failures. From what Lee shared with me, I think Wang was feeling pressured."

"I meant, how'd you do it? The weather briefing?"

"Yeah. No one logs out like they're supposed to. Easy. And I visited Area 51 while most of you were at the Arizona trials. The astrobot technician explained the software architecture."

"Did you deal with anyone else from their space program besides Tien Lee?"

Boxman shook his head. "No."

Julie crossed her legs. "One more question. Is Emily Woodson romantically involved with Vice President Atkins?"

Boxman stiffened and his jaws clenched. Glaring at Julie, he pushed out of his chair and stomped out of the room.

Chapter Forty-nine: Changing Arrangements

New York Memorial Hospital

Barbara Wiley sat alone, wringing her hands, shaking each time the emergency doors opened into the waiting room. Right before lunch, she found Fitz slumped over at his desk. The ambulance responded within minutes and rushed him to New York Memorial Hospital. Finally, after three hours, a neurosurgeon in green scrubs approached her. He pulled down his mask.

"Ms. Wiley, I'm Doctor Davis. We've had to operate to reduce the pressure on your father's brain caused by the hematoma."

"Hematoma?"

"He suffered a stroke."

She winced then dabbed her eyes with the balled-up tissue she kept in her hand. Her voice quivered, "But he'll be okay, right?"

"It's too early to tell. The next seventy-two hours are the most critical. We'll monitor how he responds. Then we'll be able to better determine the damage his stroke may have caused. He's sedated, but you can visit if you want. Then go home and get some rest. It's been a tough day for you too."

Barbara stared at him with vacant eyes.

"Ms. Wiley, I know this is overwhelming. Once he wakes up, we'll evaluate him and social services will help you decide the best care options for your father."

"Care options? You mean he might need to be in a facility?"

"Don't go there yet. Let's hope the damage is minimal. We'll contact you as soon as we know." Then he turned and walked back through the double doors.

Barbara slumped in her chair. The last few weeks had been unsettling, requiring several additional therapy sessions. First, Michael sent an email from his NASA computer saying he retired and left to start a new life, inviting her to come with him. Then Monday morning, they found Emily's scathing letter to Fitz on his desk, saying she couldn't take his controlling behavior any longer. Emily wrote another note for her saying she'd keep in touch using the SecretSessions app, which she downloaded to Barbara's phone. She'd use it to contact her daughter later tonight.

Then a tear trickled down her cheek. *If you need to be in a facility, Dad, I'll be all alone because you drove everyone away.*

***

Wiley and Wiley Offices

Four Days Later

Barbara trudged to her desk, carrying a heavy heart. The misty raindrops remained beaded on her coat as she hung it on the back of the door. She'd returned from transferring her father to a skilled nursing facility. His stroke damage was severe, and he required twenty-four-hour care. The business was now hers to run. She stepped into his empty office. She could still smell traces of his cologne. She took out her smartphone and selected the Secret Sessions app.

Emily, your grandfather's stroke was severe. He's in a facility and it's permanent. Come back. I need you to run the firm. I miss you. Mom.

She turned in her chair and stared out at the city's smog-covered skyline. Her lips trembled, and her eyes started to tear when her assistant interrupted.

"Excuse me, Ms. Wiley. There's a Mr. Jerry Aldridge on the phone. He's the campaign manager for President Jennings and wishes to speak with you about Mr. Wiley. Are you available?"

Barbara started to say no, then changed her mind. "Yes, send him through, Ellen."

"Ms. Wiley, we haven't met. My name is Jerry Aldridge. I'm sorry to hear about your father. He and I had been in touch about President Jennings's re-election, but I'm calling today to see if we can be of any help during this time."

Barbara leaned back in her father's chair and scanned the many framed pictures he kept on his mahogany desk. But the biggest one, set in a gold gilt frame, was her college graduation picture. She swallowed her tears and focused on the call.

"Yes, you can, Mr. Aldridge. My father believed in contributions where both sides benefitted. My approach is the same. I'm prepared to make a significant donation for a favor in return."

"Of course, we'll do whatever we can, Ms. Wiley. What's the favor?"

"My husband, Michael Boxman, is somewhere in the world. President Jennings knows where he is, or can find out, and I want him to be granted a full Presidential pardon. I need him in my life and be free and clear of any legal problems. Understand?"

"I'll look into it right away. If we could do this favor, what would your donation be?"

"Ten million."

"I'll get back to you."

***

Mid-afternoon, CIA headquarters

CJ picked at a bowl of overcooked chili, the only hot food option the cafeteria offered this late in the day. He scooped down a few halfhearted spoonfuls while contemplating yet another twist in the Magellan mission. Then his phone vibrated on top of the table. A text from Layla popped up. *"Call ASAP."* CJ bussed his dishes and hustled up to his office.

"Got your message. Good news?"

Layla's grinning face appeared on the screen. "Yep. Remember when we tracked Woodson's phone to the West End condo complex?"

"Yeah."

"Get this. When Vice President Atkins was in the House, he lived there. When he moved to the VP quarters in the Navy Yard, Guardier & Cie bought it."

Why didn't the FBI come up with this information? CJ sat up straighter. "Well, we figured Emily stays there because of her relationship with G&C, right?"

"No. Two things. First, on the days Emily flies in on the Wiley jet, Atkins Secret Service detail is stationed at the West End condo."

"That means ..."

"Wait, there's more. Woodson uses a secret communication app, called Secret Sessions. Pays for it automatically from her checking account. The warrant Agent Brown received is still valid. So I got her account number, and we've started intercepting her messages. Ready? I have proof she's romantically involved with Martin Atkins."

CJ slammed his fist on the desk. "Great work, Burton. Show me."

"Here are a few of the recent ones. Sharing them now."

Strings of text appeared on CJ's screen.

> Emily: *I know you're disappointed. I wish I could be there to comfort you.*
>
> Atkins: *When can I see you again?*
>
> Emily: *I can be at our place in two days.*
>
> Atkins: *Send me your flight number and I'll have my detail escort you in. Can't wait to see you.*

"I have more like this. She also communicates with Mi Lang. He's the Chair of Hong Kong National and a few others who aren't related to either Atkins or Lang." Layla took a sip of her Red Bull. "This proves they're linked."

CJ gritted his teeth. "She referred G&C to Atkins, and they contributed to his campaign. That's how the Fintech loophole stayed in any new legislation." CJ shook his head. "Politicians and money. It's so disgusting." CJ ran his hand through his hair. "Let's think. If Emily is connected to Mi Lang, maybe Lang and Atkins are also connected. Find out, Ms. Burton."

Chapter Fifty: Clinching Evidence

Air Force One, Sacramento, CA

One Week Later

President Martha Jennings rushed down the stairs of Marine One into the burnt smell of the Northern California air. The turbulence from the rotor blades whipped her shoulder-length gray hair. Secret Agents encircled her as she strode across the tarmac, her brown boots stained with ash from touring the latest fire disaster. As Jennings passed the throng of media, they erupted, shouting questions all at once. She could distinguish a few of them as she passed, not stopping, wanting to get on the plane as fast as she could.

"What's your administration doing to stop the fires?"

"When's the power grid going to be reliable again?"

"Farmers don't have water. What're you doing about it?"

President Jennings hustled up the stairs of Air Force One. She hoped the meeting regarding the ACF prototype plan, chaired by Dr. Williams, had been approved. As soon as the stairway pulled away, the pilot spooled up the engines for an immediate takeoff.

Jennings hurried to her office in front of the plane and barked at her assistant. "Tell Mary I want to see her."

Mary rushed in and buckled up for takeoff, as the plane rumbled down the runway. "I can smell the smoke on your clothes, Madame President," she said. "Bad?"

"Fucking heartbreaking," said Jennings shaking her head. "Fifteen hundred homes gone; two hundred square miles scorched. People are scared, angry, and desperate for answers." She paused then said, "Okay let's get to it. Tell me about the meeting."

"Lasted over two hours, grappling over every detail."

"Did they agree?"

"Yes." Mary looked at her notes. "The Chinese rep approved two prototype sites, one in Beijing and the other in Tianjin. India settled on Mumbai and Delhi. They insisted we build one, like we anticipated. They were fine with Phoenix. A conference call will be arranged in two days for you to formalize it with the other two Presidents."

The President gave her a worried look. "Will these Martian microbes work?"

"They're performing great in the lab. The prototypes will be the clinchers both scientifically and politically. We're using vacant outdoor sports stadiums. They'll be ready in a couple more months."

Jennings turned in her chair and peered out the plane's window. Passing below, the once productive farmland now showed large swaths of brown empty fields, water no longer available to grow crops. *We denied everything for way too long.* Her fingernails dug into the leather armrest.

"The San Joaquin Valley is down there. Used to produce twenty-five percent of our fruits and vegetables. Now it's only fifteen, and the yields are shrinking. Food shortages are on the horizon. I hope your ACF calculations hold up. It's our last real chance."

***

Julie's Office

NASA Headquarters

"Administrator Boyle," Julie said looking up from her desk. "Please have a seat. What brings you this way?"

He sat across from her desk and crossed his legs. "It's about your Magellan Project research request. Something about examining Martian soil, but the rest was redacted due to its SAP classification."

"Marge and I wondered what happened to it."

"Your request pertains to the parts of the samples Dr. Grunhart and Colonel Ruiz are not examining. Therefore, the legal bureaucrats have determined the samples are not part of the Magellan Project so it must go through a different approval process."

Julie gave him a quizzical look. "Sounds bureaucratic all right."

"No kidding. It's called the Galileo Protocol. It hasn't been used since we brought back the moon rocks. It's sent people scrambling."

"So, what do I have to do?"

"You'll present your case before a five-person committee. It includes representatives from Defense, CDC, USAMRID, FBI, and a federal judge. The hearing room's at the Pentagon. You're the Chief Investigator. If you don't agree with the guidelines the judge sets down, then the research project is denied even though the samples are legally ours."

"Kinda been through this drill before. Do I need to sweat about this?"

"Don't know, it's my first time. They want to talk with you tomorrow, in person. I put the name and number of the contact in an email. Good luck."

***

Layla's Secure Office

Building G, NSA

Layla yawned and stretched out her arms. She popped open another Red Bull. *Time to see what Minister Wang's been up to.* She accessed the shared drive full of thousands of the Ministry's emails, reports, and data downloaded by the sleeper virus before the Chinese removed it.

Her AI program dove into Minister Liu Wang's calendar and scanned the past twelve months. It found Wang traveled to cities in Southeast Asia two to three times per month. Layla put these destinations into her advanced algorithm to detect any trends.

The analysis revealed a consistent pattern of Wang visiting five specific locations in the region where the Chinese had embassies, staying at the same hotels each time. The algorithm flagged a pattern connected to Mi Lang, CEO of Hong Kong National. He had financial centers in the same cities. Layla instructed the program to execute the next level of analysis.

Layla sipped on her Red Bull. Ninety minutes later, her inquiry was complete. Her eyes opened wide, and she gasped at the results. The two's travel dates and locations matched eighty-six percent of the time. *Not a coincidence.*

Layla sat back and contemplated her findings. The money Boxman received from the Chinese flowed through Mi Lang's banks. Lang did business with Woodson, who was romantically involved with the Vice President. Could the Vice President be linked to Lang who was involved with the Chinese Minister of State Security?

Layla called CJ. "Remember when Agent Brown worried about a shit storm? Well, I found it. Be there in sixty."

Layla blew into CJ's office. Her clothes were wrinkled, her makeup gone, and dark circles swelled from under her eyes.

"You look exhausted. When did you last get some sleep?"

"Thirty hours maybe, not sure. Time gets weird underground."

CJ waved his arm indicating she should take a seat. "What did you find?"

Layla sat, her shoulders slumped. She gazed down at the floor. "Don't know where to start. I've never uncovered anything like this. I need your advice before I send this to the Admiral, okay?" She looked up at him with hopeful eyes.

She's rattled. Never seen her like this. "It happens, Layla," he said softly. "Take your time and piece it out for me."

She sat up straight and took a deep breath.

"I uncovered several things. First, more Secret Sessions transcripts between the Vice President and Emily Woodson. Here's the most important one."

CJ's eyes opened wide as he read.

> Atkins: *How did your meeting with Lang go?*
>
> Woodson: *Good. Finalized the plan. We're ready, funds in place, waiting for your signal. When?*
>
> Atkins: *Hard to tell. She's focused on climate. The decision is on hold. I'll push. Did you agree on the amount?*
>
> Woodson: *20 each, yield 100+ Can't wait to see you. XOXO.*

"Could be market manipulation by the VP, but I wasn't positive. I mean, it *is* the Vice President. Next is Minister Wang's calendar."

Layla pulled up her computer analysis.

"See, she's in the same cities at the same time as Mi Lang, month after month. They're linked, maybe lovers." She closed her laptop and faced CJ.

"Here's my summary. Emily's scheming with Lang to manipulate certain securities based on Atkins's inside knowledge of a Jennings' decision. Why does he need the money? Maybe for his future campaign run or to divorce his wife so he can be with Woodson.

"The Vice President is connected to Woodson, who is associating with Lang, who's involved with the Chinese Minister of State Security. By inference, Atkins could be linked to Wang. What should I do now, Director?"

CJ sat quietly for a moment, then said. "It's the WTO."

Layla gave CJ a quizzical look. "How do you know?"

"We've been in briefings. Jennings wants the Chinese President to approve using US personnel to staff all their ACFs. If he does, she'll push to accept China into the World Trade Organization." He pushed his chair back and stood up. "Time to see Phil."

He picked up the phone and called Phil's office. "Margaret, I need to see him. It's Level Five."

"Go to his conference room, Director. He's downstairs. I'm sending the alert now."

"Let's go, Ms. Burton."

Phil rushed in several minutes later and pointed at CJ. "Let's hear it."

Layla walked him through her discoveries, showing him the documents as she went. Phil sat with his hands folded, showing no expression, and listened without interrupting. When she finished, he asked, "Does the Admiral know about this?"

"No sir. I went straight to Director Jackson."

Phil stepped to the front of the room, hands behind his back, and peered down at the barren courtyard. Finally, he turned and faced them.

"If we're wrong, our careers are over, and we might even be prosecuted. Still want to pursue this?"

"It's the right thing to do," said CJ. Layla nodded without hesitation.

"Good, me too. This evidence suggests Vice President Atkins is using his knowledge of the WTO information for personal gain not tied to the official policy of the United States. We need to have ironclad proof in order to move forward."

"Woodson could confirm the plan," said Layla.

"Okay, Layla. Find her," ordered Phil. "CJ, you interrogate her. If she verifies the market manipulation and links Atkins to the money, then I'll bring in the FBI and the Admiral. In the meantime, I'll recommend Jennings delay the WTO decision. Make sense, CJ?"

"We'll conduct the interrogation in Ramstein. But when we do, we'll need to move fast. If Atkins tries to contact Woodson and she fails to answer, he'll know something's wrong."

"Agreed," Phil said. "Since this situation has severe national security implications, I'll contact the DOJ and make sure Woodson's rights are protected. Let's go."

Chapter Fifty-one: Loose Ends

The Pentagon

A young soldier escorted Julie through the maze-like halls of the Pentagon until they arrived at a conference room in the A ring corridor marked with the seal of the State Department. The sentry checked her ID and then opened the door.

The room was barely large enough to accommodate the metal meeting table and six chairs. Its barren walls displayed only a video monitor and emergency evacuation instructions. *Must've thrown this together at the last minute,* thought Julie as she squeezed into her seat. Across from her were two men, one in a blue military uniform with eagles on his shoulders, the other in an expensive black suit holding a remote in his hand. He pointed it at the monitor and the image of Colonel Ruiz and an unknown woman came into focus.

"Dr. McCray, I'm Colonel Wallace representing General Scott, Chair of the Joint Chiefs. This is Judge Eduardo Elum. On the monitor is Colonel Ruiz from USAMRIID and Dr. Debra Mae Martin, from the CDC. Welcome."

"Nice meeting all of you."

"All right, let's get started," Judge Elum said. "A bit of housekeeping. Director Maykuth of the FBI had a last-minute emergency and won't be joining us today.

"We dusted off the Galileo Protocol regarding Dr. McCray's request to research core samples taken from a classified source. The GP exists for two reasons. The first is the safety of the planet. We need to make sure her research won't contaminate our environment, cause a disease we have no medicine for, or start an alien invasion. That's not a joke.

"The other component is to shield the pursuit of knowledge from premature political intervention. It's prohibited to reveal any of the outcomes of your investigation until this committee has approved its release. We, together with Dr. McCray, will determine who in the political system will be the recipient of this knowledge. In the case of the moon rocks, the committee notified the President, but it's entirely up to us.

"Now we'll turn to your request. We've all read it, so I'll open it up to any questions."

Dr. Martin from the CDC started. "It says you want to research portions of soil samples that may contain foreign lifeforms at a secure lab in Area 51. Where did these samples come from?"

"I can't reveal the source. It's classified."

"If I may," Colonel Ruiz said. "Dr. Martin, this is a bit of bureaucratic 'the horse has already left the barn' scenario. I'm aware of the circumstances, and my unit is involved. Dr. McCray has been instrumental in a top-secret government program authorized by the President. This request, however, technically falls outside of this program."

"Correct," said Judge Elum. "To be clear, The Galileo Protocol only has jurisdiction over any new lifeforms found in the samples to be examined. It does not pertain to any lifeforms already discovered."

"Thank you, Your Honor," Julie said. "Our legal team flagged my funding request and Administrator Boyle wanted to make sure we were following the rules."

"General Scott has been involved in Dr. McCray's mission from the beginning," Colonel Wallace said. "I'm satisfied and approve the request."

"I also approve," said Ruiz.

Dr. Martin shook her head. "Only in government does it get this goofy. As usual, the world experts on disease control are left completely out of the loop. I approve. Y'all call us about your other project if the world gets contaminated. Hopefully, it won't be too late." Then her image vanished from the screen.

"Dr. McCray," Judge Elum said. "We have one more step. Since you're the lead investigator, you'll need to sign this document agreeing you'll abide by the Galileo Protocol."

"I take it the people represented here will be the ones I inform in case of any discovery."

"Yes. Their names are noted in the document."

Julie signed it and the meeting adjourned. Colonel Wallace excused himself, and Colonel Ruiz signed off.

"Excuse me, Your Honor, you're from the State Department?"

"I'm on lease to them. I'm long retired, but I put together the Galileo Protocol back then. When your request came through, they called me to officiate."

"Explain the part about shielding knowledge from the politicians."

"Sure. Science and politics historically haven't mixed well. New knowledge, especially surrounding alien lifeforms, creates changes in the assumptions about the world we live in. Politicians in power positions resist change because they're afraid it will upset the current status quo from which they benefit.

"This knowledge, if it's radical enough, also creates new *unclaimed* political territory. Political factions battle it out often making unsubstantiated allegations about the new discovery, like it is against religion, or defying God's will, and so on."

"Hence the Galileo reference."

"Exactly. We want to protect any knowledge your project uncovers. In this way, the agencies on your Galileo Committee will have the benefit of reacting to it before it can be distorted by the politicians and their social media outlets. It's the best we can do to preserve newly acquired scientific knowledge regarding non-Earth lifeforms."

"How did the Galileo Protocol come about anyway? Did NASA promote it?"

"They were supportive, but the military pressed the hardest."

"Thank you, your Honor. It's been an interesting morning."

***

Minister Liu Wang's Office

Ministry of State Security, Beijing

General Cho glared at Minister Liu Wang. His beet-red face looked like a plump tomato about to explode.

"Can I offer you some tea?" she said, trying to diffuse his rage.

The General ignored the question. He leaned forward and pointed his finger at her. "The Moon mission is a total failure because your source gave us faulty plans."

"He's not *my* source," she replied. Then, in a calm voice, she said, "He's Tien Lee's. He verified the technical information and assured me the plans were correct."

"We cannot tolerate such incompetence." His fist pounded on the arm of the chair. "I want accountability," he roared.

"What's your recommendation?"

The tension lines on his faced receded. "Replace Chu. Because he has many close relationships within the Party, arrange a fitting retirement celebration."

"I will see to it."

"But Director Lee is different. He completely failed us. Make it look like an accident." His eyes squinted at her. "That a problem?" he snarled.

"Not if it will satisfy you."

General Cho stood, straightened his jacket, and stomped out of her office.

She immediately grabbed the phone and called Agent Walker.

"Have you found Boxman?"

"No, Minister. Last we knew, he went through London passport control. We can't find any trace of him."

"The Americans must have him stashed someplace. Boxman's not clever enough to stay undetected this long. Find him and then call me immediately. We have to take him out. He'll talk, and it will bring us both down. Top priority, clear?"

"Yes, Minister."

She hung up and went to her window. The polluted air prevented her from seeing the massive Summer Palace only a few hundred yards away. She gritted her teeth. *No one double-crosses me.*

Chapter Fifty-two: Truth Comes Out

Ramstein AFB, Germany

Emily Woodson sat handcuffed in the interrogation room waiting for CJ to appear. She had triggered Layla's facial recognition software when she entered Heathrow using a Chinese passport with an assumed name. Layla alerted CJ who ordered his agents to intercept Emily at the Geneva train station who then flew her the short distance to the U.S. military installation in Ramstein, Germany.

CJ flashed his ID at the prison entrance and hurried through the metal detector. He opened the door holding his captive and glanced at the familiar surroundings. Concrete block walls painted pastel green with an industrial fluorescent light fixture hung overhead, giving the room a pale, washed-out sheen. The small enclosure felt suffocating and smelled stale, caused by human anxiety under intense pressure, coupled with poor ventilation. Besides Woodson, a civilian woman sat at the table and an image of a man in blue suit was on the video monitor.

As he took his seat, CJ evaluated Emily's condition. She wore a faded yellow prisoner's uniform, her hands were cuffed to the table, and her legs chained together. Her eyes darted about the room and her trembling hands caused her shackles to clink against the tabletop.

Emily exhibited the signs of mental shock and confusion due to her sudden and traumatic change of circumstances. Losing her freedom in such a way creates immense cognitive dissonance in a person used to being in control of her life and jetting about the world. *This is the ideal time to interrogate her,* thought CJ.

On the video monitor was Emily's court appointed lawyer, Mr. Stephan Dudeck. The assistant prosecuting attorney, Ms. Shelly Vicars, sat next to CJ.

"Good evening, everyone. I'm CJ Jackson, Deputy Director, CIA. I have several questions for Ms. Woodson regarding a matter of pressing national security."

"Thank you, Director Jackson," said Shelly. "We need to get the ground rules straight for this unusual circumstance. I'm Shelly Vicars from the DOJ's national security unit. I'm here on another case and was assigned to represent the government on an emergency basis. We have an urgent situation which is why the federal judge appointed Mr. Stephan Dudeck to oversee this interrogation session to ensure Ms. Woodson's rights are not violated. Mr. Dudeck?"

"Thank you, counselor. The pending charges against my client are indeed serious. My client is here voluntarily and will speak if I ascertain her case will not be negatively impacted by her answers, and her cooperation in this questioning session will be considered by the court."

"That is correct," said Shelly. "Extradition arrangements will happen over the next few days. We're recording this session for the record. Director Jackson you may begin."

"Has she seen the transcripts, Ms. Vicars?"

"Yes, Director. We've shown them to her."

Emily stared at CJ, her lips trembling. She opened her mouth to speak, but her voice cracked, and she buried her face in her hands, sobbing. After a few moments, she sat up, tear tracks glistening down her cheeks.

"Are you ready, Ms. Woodson?"

"Yes," she mumbled, staring down at her hands.

"We've noticed you have a familiar travel pattern, Hong Kong to Geneva. Could you explain?"

"I visit my grandmother and stay at her guest house." Her voice cracked and she paused before continuing. "I have an apartment in Hong Kong."

Minister Wang gave her citizenship no doubt, thought CJ.

"What's your relationship with Mi Lang?"

"He's a banking client," she said, her voice becoming more stable. "I use his financial products from his brokerage operation to make investments."

"Are these investments for the Wiley and Wiley firm?"

"It used to be. I no longer work there. I have my own clients now."

"What's Mi Lang's relationship with Martin Atkins?"

Emily stiffened. Her eyes darted to her lawyer, and he gestured for her to answer.

"Lang donated to Martin's Political Action Committee when he served in the House."

CJ pulled out the paper transcript between Emily and Atkins, placing it in front of her. "Ms. Woodson, we need to know the meaning of a particular SecretSessions text between you and Vice President Atkins."

"Careful here, Director. We won't admit to any crimes," said Dudeck.

CJ continued, "I'm specifically asking about this one exchange ...*funds in place, waiting for your signal.*" Then he showed Atkins's reply. "*Decision is on hold. I'll push.*"

"I need to know if Vice President Atkins intended to use knowledge of the upcoming decision about China's entry into the WTO for his personal gain. I'm not inquiring what your role might have been, Ms. Woodson. I need you to verify that Vice President Atkins was referring to the WTO decision."

Emily looked at her lawyer. "You can answer," he said. Emily bit her lip and gazed down at the table for several moments. Tears oozed from her eyes, trickling down her cheeks. Only the sound of the struggling ventilation fan cut the silence.

"Martin needed money to fund his presidential campaign," she whispered. "Lang convinced him to use the WTO announcement as a convenient way to do it."

"But his presidential run won't be for several years. Why now?"

"He needed funds for himself too. He intends to divorce his wife. There's a prenup. She's wealthy. He's not."

"What's the meaning of this text ... *20 each yield 100+?*"

She fidgeted in her seat. "It's the investment amounts and projected earnings once Jennings approved the WTO. Martin's cut would fund the initial primaries and the divorce proceedings."

Almost done, thought CJ. "Besides this text, did Vice President Atkins state, in your presence, he's using the advanced knowledge of the WTO decision by the President to financially benefit his political and personal life?

"Yes," she mumbled and another tear leaked from her eye.

"Let's stop it here," said Emily's lawyer. "Satisfied, Director?"

"One more question. Does Michael Boxman have a relationship with Mi Lang?"

She looked up at CJ and shook her head. "No, he doesn't."

"I'm done. Thank you, Ms. Woodson. I'd like a moment with you, Ms. Vicars."

Emily turned to her lawyer on the video monitor. "I've cooperated, and I can go now, right? I mean, I'm not going to jail."

Dudeck glanced at Vicars then at his client.

"Ms. Woodson, you'll be spending the next few days here. I'll go over everything with you tomorrow when you're more rested."

The guard came in an escorted Emily to her cell. After they left, CJ said, "I'll need a copy of the video."

"Of course, Director."

"What's the prosecution's plan?"

"Under the National Security Act, we brought four charges against her. With the cooperation, we're asking four to six years."

"Thank you, Ms. Vicars. Appreciate your help today." CJ stood to leave when she spoke up.

"Director, you've come a long way when you could've asked your questions remotely. Why the personal touch?"

"I needed to get a feel for her, look her in the eyes. Hard to do that through a video camera." CJ paused and pursed his lips. "I'm a retired Army colonel, Captain. An IED hit my Humvee, and the two soldiers with me were killed. I think about their sacrifice every day. Traitors need to pay the price."

Vicars smiled. "I was a captain in the Army JAG Corps. I can assure you, Director, she will. Hurrah!"

"Hurrah, Shelly."

***

Mr. F: *Heard Jennings is going to free Boxman. Can't protect him now. Anything I can do?*

Mr. V: *No. Can't use you for this. Using another source. Cleaner for everyone.*

Chapter Fifty-three: New Developments

Julie's Office

NASA, HQ

Standing at her desk, Julie turned her computer screen around so Marge could see. It was a one-page email. "Here it is, Marge, the approval to start researching the parts of our samples without the bacteria. Finally."

Marge read the memo and looked at Julie. "This is from the State Department? Wait, don't want to know that bit of crazy logic. Says we can only assign one scientist."

"Yeah, most are working on the Climate Initiative. Call Rodriguez and get him out there."

When the committee gave verbal approval, Julie and Marge interviewed several candidates so they could begin the research on the Martian soils as soon as the official go-ahead arrived. They selected Dr. Emilio Rodriguez, hailing from Waco, Texas. He did his undergrad at Texas A&M and his doctorate in astrobiology at Berkeley.

"I'll fill him in," Marge said. "Then I'll let Major West know he's coming."

***

Next Day

Wiley and Wiley

Barbara swiveled around on her desk chair and looked up at the portrait of her father hanging on the wall. She thought of how he would handle the situation to get what he wanted. She spoke into her headset in a confident tone of voice. "Tell me, Mr. Aldridge, do we have a deal?"

"Ms. Wiley, ah, this favor is complicated, as I found out. It presents a difficult situation for the President. However, she has an alternative solution for you to consider."

"Go on."

"We want to delay your husband's release until right before Thanksgiving. The President hopes this will be acceptable."

"Release? You mean he's in prison? Where is he?"

"I'm not permitted to say."

"When specifically?"

"We're suggesting the Wednesday before Thanksgiving in the late afternoon. People will be preoccupied by the holiday. Is this acceptable?"

I'm so relieved. Barbara turned and put her elbows on the desk.

"Send me the wiring instructions. You'll have the money when he walks through my door."

After hanging up the phone, she rested her head on the back of her chair and closed her eyes. *Michael's coming back. Now I'll find Emily. Get her to come back too.*

***

Stewart Laboratory, Area 51

"Major West, I'm Dr. Rodriquez from NASA, here to examine the remainin' core samples from the Magellan Mission," he said in his thick Texas drawl.

"We've been expecting you, Doctor, welcome. I'll have Lt. LeBlanc give you an orientation to our safety protocols, and she'll show you to your lab where the samples are stored."

"Appreciate it, Major. I understand you found three types of livin' Mars microorganisms in the lower parts of the samples. I'd like to check 'em out, if possible. I'm fixin' to see how the soils in the upper and lower portions compare and how it might impact the microorganisms' biology."

"Lt. LeBlanc can arrange it. She's ready for you now."

After the orientation concluded, he and Lt. LeBlanc passed through the UV scanner on the way to the dressing area to put on protective bio-suits. After being scanned a second time, they entered the outer portion of the lab. This sealed-in area maintained negative pressure and was equipped with an overhead chemical spray apparatus capable of killing any lifeform escaping from the inner lab.

"Dr. Rodriguez, here's the security passcode for entry to the inner lab. The computer inside has your mission instructions including changing the passcode. Only you have access. Let's enter. I have a few more things to cover. We're almost done."

LeBlanc entered the code, and Emilio opened the door for her.

"This is the cold storage cabinet where the samples are kept," she said. "Each one is labeled, indicating its extraction location. In the folder on the table is a map of the Gale Crater with the corresponding symbols. It'll give you a visual. If you have any questions, please ask." She turned to exit the lab.

"Say Lieutenant, might you be around later this afternoon? I don't know a soul here and what do people do when their shift's done? I mean is there a place where you kin get a cold beer?" he asked, flashing a smile.

She smiled back. "I'm happy to show you what we have here on base. But don't get your hopes too high for what might be available."

Emilio watched the attractive scientist walk down the hallway then turned and prepared his work area. He checked the safety systems per the lab's protocol, changed his password, and calibrated his sophisticated equipment.

Then he opened the folder Lt. LeBlanc had prepared to decide the order in which he would examine the samples. Her file contained a flash drive and a large paper map of the Gale Crater. His heart raced as he studied the map with the location labels of each sample, including the type of bacteria found in each one. One label had an asterisk with no explanation.

He noticed the samples furthest from the crater's center held a single type of bacteria. Those closest contained all three types. He inserted the flash drive. He stared at the emerging pattern. He wondered if something in the center could be attracting life.

Chapter Fifty-four: Boxman and Atkins

Phil Locke's Office, Early Morning

Admiral Garza and FBI Director Maykuth rushed to Phil's office responding to his Level Five alert. CJ and Layla stood against the wall as the two senior officials filed into the room and took their seats at the conference table. Worry lines creased their faces as Phil kicked off the meeting.

"Gentlemen, we have a serious situation of the highest magnitude. Director Maykuth, CJ came to me with information regarding suspicious activities from the Vice President. At the time, I told him to proceed but tread lightly. He and Ms. Burton found further troubling evidence, and that's why you're here."

Maykuth's face remained stoic, but his voice was terse. "Shit, Phil. You're talking about officially investigating the Vice President."

"That's what we have to decide."

Maykuth crossed his arms. "Alright. Let's see what you have."

Phil signaled to Layla, who stepped to the front of the room. She stood tall, cleared her throat, and spoke directly to the FBI Director.

"The Vice President continues to engage in a long-established pattern of behavior that undermines national security," said Layla, her voice steady and determined. She went on to explain the relationship Atkins cultivated with Guardier and Cie, payments for his reelection, and how he blocked legal updates to specific Fintech-type applications, impairing Prop Forty-nine's effectiveness. She also showed the texts confirming Atkins and Woodson were lovers.

Then CJ took over the presentation.

"On the monitor are texts between Woodson and Atkins, scheming to leverage the WTO decision. The interrogation I did in Germany with Ms. Woodson verifies it. Here's the video."

When the video concluded, CJ noticed Maykuth shook his head and grimaced.

"From our investigation, Director, we believe Lang, Woodson, and Atkins are conspiring to manipulate specific investments for personal gain."

CJ sat down, and Phil said, "Admiral Garza, your thoughts."

He gazed at each of the individuals one by one. The seriousness of the moment enveloped everyone like a heavy blanket. CJ's hands gripped the seat of his chair, waiting to hear the decision.

"It's enough for me," Garza said. "I support bringing charges against the Vice President."

Maykuth first looked at Admiral Garza and then at Phil.

"Yeah, we can't look the other way at this. Atkins' conspiracy is clear. We need to move with urgency because we don't know what other actions he might be planning. Assuming you all agree, it's now a matter of what recommendation we take to the President."

"CJ's shoulders sagged and he mouthed a 'thank you' over to Layla. She smiled back.

"I recommend Atkins resign," Phil said. "We freeze his campaign account, he gets his lifetime pension, and he doesn't give speeches or write any books. He retires quietly in Michigan with his wife."

"And if he doesn't," said Maykuth, "we expose his affair and arrest him for conspiracy to commit campaign fraud and tax evasion, without delving into these other crimes, giving the President political cover."

"When are you going to tell her?" CJ asked.

"This afternoon," Maykuth said. "We can't keep this under wraps."

***

Minister Wang's Office

Same Time

Minister Liu Wang's private phone beeped with an incoming text from Mi Lang.

Boxman will be released from the safe house the day before the American Thanksgiving. Address is 391 Claire Point Dr., Oxen Hill, MD. Source is reliable.

Minister Wang clenched her hand around the phone and smiled. *I'm in the clear.* Then she forwarded the information to Agent Tom Walker.

***

Oval Office

After listening to the evidence against Atkins, President Jennings pushed back her chair and stood behind her desk after reading the incriminating documents in the 'Eyes Only' file.

She put her hands on her hips. "How fucking stupid can this guy be? We made him VP so he wouldn't run against me with the promise he'd be next. If this gets out, we'll all be smeared with it."

She turned, hands behind her back, and faced the barren Rose Garden. Maykuth, Garza, and Phil stood in silence waiting for her orders.

"Keep Woodson in Germany," she directed, still facing the window. "It's one less person to blab to the media. There's consensus with your agencies he should resign?"

The three looked at each other and murmured their agreement. Jennings spun around glaring at them.

"Good, because I don't want any grousing later. Each of you will resoundingly support my decision as best for the country. Let's confront him the day after tomorrow, 4:15, after the markets close. Get everything ready. Don't fuck it up."

Chapter Fifty-five: The Galileo Protocol

That Night

CJ and Julie's Condo

CJ and Julie relaxed on their living room couch, the soft glow of the lamps casting a warm light around them. They each held a drink, their feet propped up on the ottoman, while smooth jazz filled the air. Gizmo stretched out beside Julie, who glided her fingers through his shiny fur.

"Any more news on the ACFs?" asked CJ.

"Yes, very exciting. Mary held a Zoom meeting with the contractors and local officials to review the prototype blueprints before they start construction." Julie took a sip of her Chardonnay. "She said everything is secretive. That your idea?"

CJ dipped a piece of apple in the hummus. "Yeah. We recommended not to get everyone's hopes up in case they don't work. Afraid of riots. Plus, it's an election year."

"Makes sense, I guess. Everyone's on edge, for sure." Julie glanced at CJ. "You look like you're on edge too. What's up?"

"Had a big day today. We presented our case to the NSA and FBI. Then they went to see the President. Going to be some changes happening."

"How do you feel about it?"

"Good, mostly. Phil gave me the headlines, and the guilty party is going to be held accountable. You'll hear about it." CJ took a drink and then frowned.

"And?"

"Shit, Jules. If you or I were caught doing the same thing, we'd be sent to Leavenworth for twenty years. Politicians, on the other hand, get their full pensions and go home."

CJ gulped down another large swallow. "How about you? What are you up to now?"

"We're investigating the parts of the Martian samples that don't contain the microbes. And tomorrow we start our budget process, yawn-city. But boring is good compared to the tension of the Magellan mission. Gives me a chance to settle in and get to know my people. Anything about Boxman?"

"No. Haven't heard a word. You?"

"Nothing. Let's feed Gizmo and cook up dinner."

***

Next Day

Stewart Lab, Area 51

Dr. Rodriquez, dressed in his bulky bio-suit, carefully extracted the third core sample of the morning from the storage freezer. The first two he examined were from the crater's edge, furthest from the center. They contained similar minerals and soil compositions, including organic remnants. He decided to investigate closer to the center of the crater, where the highest density of living biogens was found.

With a steady hand, he loaded the round sample onto his laser cutting machine, like a meat slicer in a grocery store's deli department. After the red laser hummed to life, Emilio aligned the frozen sample and cut a thin slice off the end. He viewed it under the microscope, finding it comparable to the other samples, then ran it through his mass spectrometer.

His shoulder slumped at the results. The sample had no significant differentiation from those at the crater's edge. He took a picture of the sample slice and saved it to his project file. He repeated this process through several more cycles.

A rapping sound from the lab's outer glass wall broke his concentration. He looked up to see Lt. LeBlanc gesturing for him to come out and take a break. A smile spread across his face and he returned a thumbs-up.

They made their way to the cafeteria outside the lab complex. It resembled a large urban Starbucks with large glass windows letting in views of the desert landscape. However, by mid-morning, the heavy see-through shades were drawn to diminish the sun's searing heat. The smell of fresh scones wafted through the space.

Emilio bought her a latte, and they sat at a table far from the other occupants. He reached over and held her hand. "Hey, Jenn, I started to examine them samples from the middle of the crater where the microbes are highly concentrated. Do you have an explanation?"

She shook her head. "No. It seems odd to me, given the soil has similar composition throughout this section of the crater. Distribution should be even. What're you finding?"

"Nothing conclusive yet, but I'm startin' to look at the center. I'll let you know if I find the answer." Then his face lit up, and a broad smile crossed his face. "Hey, there's a football game on tonight. Wanna come over and watch it with me? I'll make you some real Texas chili."

Her eyebrows shot up. "Chili in the desert?"

He laughed. "Okay, I'll turn the air conditionin' up high."

She squeezed his hand. "All right, cowboy. I have to get back. See you tonight."

Emilio executed the lab's reentry safety protocols, ensured his suit was secured, and resumed his investigation of the crater's center-most samples. When he peered through the microscope at the next slice, a small shiny dot emerged in the middle of his specimen. He increased the magnification to get a better look and put the image up on the monitor. It appeared metallic, not mineral. He decided to take another sample.

In the next slice, the dot became larger. Same with the next two. With the fourth one, another dot emerged right next to the first.

Emilio's heart rate picked up. "There's somthin' buried in here." He went to the sample and used his portable laser saw to excise the object. With a surgeon's skill, he exposed a silver metallic structure, having three long digits and an opposing one, looking like a human hand, about 20 centimeters long. The hand was severed at the wrist. Wires and conduit material hung outside its jagged metal edge.

His pulse raced as Emilio took a series of pictures and uploaded them into a special project file. His hands trembled, scrolling through the computer's files until he reached the one labeled Galileo. He entered his password and scanned his biometrics. The file opened, revealing a single urgent directive:

"Immediately contact Dr. Julie McCray. Codeword: Galileo Protocol. Contact no one else. She will give you instructions."

A chill ran down Emilio's spine, the enormity of his discovery now sinking in. The metal alloy was not one NASA used in its robots, and NASA was the only agency on the surface of Mars. The three-fingered hand could only have come from another solar system. He swallowed hard and sent the message.

***

Julie and her team were an hour into their budget review process when her assistant barged into the room and handed Julie the message from Rodriguez. Staring at the words, she gasped, then looked up at her team. "I, um, have to go." She stood and put on her suit jacket.

"Dr. McCray, you all right?" Marge asked. "Is it CJ?"

"No, but I can't say. Carry on. Marge, you're in charge until I get back. I'll be gone for a couple of days."

She hurried out of the room and turned to her assistant.

"Call the commander at Andrews. Tell him Galileo Protocol and to scramble a jet to take me to Area 51. I'll meet him in forty minutes. Then get me on our chopper. I'll leave in ten."

"But Dr. McCray, Administrator Boyle has it reserved."

"Not anymore he doesn't."

Chapter Fifty-six: The Committee

Area 51, Six Hours Later

Julie paced around the table in Area 51's secure conference room, waiting for the Galileo Protocol team members to sign into her video call. Director Maykuth's office texted saying he'd be delayed. She checked her smartphone for messages. She found several news alerts announcing the Vice President's resignation for personal reasons, and General Scott had been nominated to take his place. *That's what CJ meant last night*. Dr. Rodriquez interrupted her thoughts.

"Dr. McCray, while we're waitin', I don't know much about the Galileo Protocol. Could you fill me in?"

"Sure. Let's get coffee and have a seat. We'll be a few minutes."

They settled across from each other at the conference table.

"Since you were the one to discover the advanced lifeform, you're automatically involved in the next part, the examination phase. We'll ask you to help us determine where it came from, its composition, and how it might impact Earth."

"Why is it called Galileo?"

Julie leaned back in her chair. "It's named after him because, in 1616, this renowned scientist proved the Earth revolved around the sun, not fixed in the sky, as stated in the Bible. The Pope, the dominant political figure at the time, warned him not to promote his discovery. But when Galileo persisted, he was tried before the Inquisition and then imprisoned for heresy."

Emilio looked perplexed. "Is this about religion and science?"

"Not religion. It's designed to temporarily protect national security information from political distortion and funnel crucial information to key decision-makers. Not until a process for guaranteeing national security and scientific investigation is in place are others informed."

The five-second warning beep sounded, interrupting their conversation. Julie stood, straightened her suit jacket, and faced the wall-sized monitor. She smiled at the team about to initiate research on an intelligent artifact from outside Earth.

"Good afternoon, everyone. For the record, I'm Dr. Julie McCray, NASA Associate Administrator, and I initiated the Galileo Protocol. I'm sitting here with Dr. Emilio Rodriquez, our NASA astrobiologist, who made the astonishing discovery prompting me to bring us together. We're in the Stewart Laboratory located in Area 51 where the extra-terrestrial object is located. It's under military guard as we speak. This group hasn't worked together before so let's introduce ourselves."

"I'm General Joe Remus, United States Air Force, Acting Chair of the Joint Chiefs."

As each person spoke, their face became larger on the screen.

"I'm Dr. Debra Mae Martin, Director of the Center for Disease Control. Good to be here."

"I guess I'm next. I'm Edward Maykuth, FBI Director. Sorry, I'm late. Busy day."

"I'm Colonel Ruiz, Commander of the Medical Research Institute for Infectious Diseases. Glad you're here, Debra."

"Thanks, everyone," Julie said. "Several weeks ago, a classified mission to Mars brought back several core samples, the contents of which are top secret."

"We're here because of dirt samples?" interrupted Remus.

Julie's lips drew thin across her face. She crossed her arms and stared at him through the video camera. She said nothing for several moments.

"General, to have an intelligent discussion, which we will have, it's important not to interrupt before the data is fully presented. I'm in charge here. This is how we'll conduct ourselves concerning one of the most important discoveries in the history of our planet."

The General's face flushed. He sat back in his chair in a huff. *At least he's quiet now,* thought Julie.

"NASA asked Dr. Rodriguez to examine the sample portions not involved in our classified project. Doctor, show us what you've found."

"Thank you, Dr. McCray. Hello, y'all. I've prepared a little slide show, thinkin' it'll be faster that way."

The faces on the monitor rescinded to the upper right side and the slide show flooded everyone's screens.

"We examine these core samples by takin' thin frozen slices. The first slice revealed a small gray dot right in the middle. After the second slice, I figured there was an object inside the sample. I excised it. Here it is."

The picture of the hand, three digits and thumb appeared. All the members moved closer to their screens as if to get a better look.

"What is that, Dr. Rodriquez?" Maykuth asked.

"It's part of a highly intelligent biological bein' or somethin' created by one. It's metallic, but I haven't researched it. Once I realized the hand came from a complex form of life, I immediately called Dr. McCray, per the Protocol's instructions."

The group stared at the image proving intelligent life existed on another world. Julie took over, interrupting their trance-like attention.

"Thank you, Dr. Rodriquez. The protocol is quite definitive about this. It requires notification immediately upon discovery. The research to answer the questions on everyone's mind right now hasn't started. So, what's the best way to proceed? Opinions?"

"I suggest we continue to use the Stewart Lab," Colonel Ruiz said. "It's Level Three which seems appropriate for the circumstances, and NASA can continue to do the research under military security. Seems ideal, at least for now."

"Dr. Rodriquez, any idea how old this sample is?" Dr. Martin asked.

"I can't tell by visual examination. But I found it five centimeters from the top of the core sample, meaning it hasn't been buried for long. Less than six months is my educated guess."

"Part of our process is focused on national security," General Remus said. "Unless you found a squadron of alien spaceships up there, I think we can cross off an invasion."

"This isn't a living biologic so it can't infect anyone," Dr. Martin said. "I agree to keep it there.

Julie stood with her arms crossed. "I'd like to add a key variable to our thinking."

"What's that, Doctor?" asked Maykuth.

"In all of NASA's research, there's no scientific evidence Mars evolved to the point where it could produce this level of biological complexity. It is scientifically impossible this artifact originated on Mars. It originated from outside our solar system."

***

Over the next hour, the Galileo team engaged in an animated discussion and arrived at a series of next steps. Julie summed up their decisions.

"We've agreed on three action items. First, we search for any signs of an alien spacecraft or materials on Mars. This lifeform came from somewhere and needed a vehicle to get there."

General Remus raised an eyebrow. "How would you go about finding it, Dr. McCray?"

"We have several satellites orbiting Mars. We can reconfigure their sensors to the same composition as the hand and conduct a planetary sweep."

"The Protocol required me to keep a billion dollars set aside to fund whatever we agree to do. It's officially available now."

"Thank you, General," said Julie. "Let's proceed this way. I'd like my Deputy, Dr. Marge Jamison, to program our satellites and search for further evidence of this material. She's been an integral part of their development and knows their software and technical capabilities."

The group gave their consent.

"The second agreement is to have one of the FBI's forensic experts come here and assist Dr. Rodriguez in researching the hand and the remaining samples. The third item is another Mars mission. Comments?"

"You're the expert here, Dr. McCray," Remus said. "Since the robots are already on Mars, it seems we can use them to uncover the rest of the object. Could you bring a mission plan for our next meeting?"

All agreed.

Can't wait to get started. Julie smiled, containing her excitement. "Thanks, everyone. We'll meet in two weeks to get a status update. McCray out."

Chapter Fifty-seven: New Challenges

CIA Director's Office

Three Days Later

Phil Locke called CJ to his office. He stood in front of his monitor, watching the political news regarding the Atkins resignation and the ascendance of General Scott.

"Check this out, CJ."

The familiar voice of Scott Schirack filled the room.

"This is Scott Schirack reporting from the Capitol. Only four days after Martin Atkins's sudden and mysterious resignation, the Senate, in one of the fastest nomination processes ever, confirmed by acclamation General Richard Scott, former Chair of the Joint Chiefs, as the next Vice President of the United States. The swearing-in ceremony will be this Saturday at the White House. He'll be on our Sunday morning show, Today's Politics. We'll have a close and revealing interview with this intriguing public figure. You won't want to miss it."

"Feel better with him in the second seat," Phil said, as he clicked off the TV.

"Me too. He's a good man," CJ replied, slipping his hands into his pockets. He raised his eyebrows. "Usually when you call me in here, it's to give me news. What is it?"

Phil grimaced, the lines on his forehead deepening. "Yeah, shit. Maykuth called this morning. Jennings granted Boxman a Presidential Pardon. The FBI's releasing him Wednesday, and he'll have full access to his Chinese money."

CJ's mouth dropped, a stunned look sprang onto his face. "You've got to be fucking kidding. After all he did and he gets to walk? Why did Jennings do it?"

Phil dug his hands into his hips. "The Wiley firm pledged ten million to Jennings' reelection campaign upon his release."

CJ fixated on the flag behind Phil's desk. His face turned red. "We risk our lives to capture traitors and protect our country, and we're betrayed by simple greed."

"This is a hard one for me to swallow, too. Go see him before he leaves. Get some closure."

A smirk spread on CJ's face. "I'll think about it."

"If you go, give him one for me."

***

Wednesday Before Thanksgiving

FBI Safe House

CJ pulled into the driveway of Boxman's safe house. Waiting on the front steps was Agent Sarnow. He approached CJ and shook his hand. "Agent Brown said to fill you in, but it's better to talk out here. Can't record us."

CJ tilted his head. "What's up?"

Sarnow turned up the collar of his shirt to shield against the stiff breeze. He spoke through his mask. "Boxman's pardon has put us in a bit of a gray area. I have orders to find out where he's going and how he's getting there, but not to interfere in any way. Boxman's been on the phone for days working on an exit plan. He even asked my advice."

"He's afraid of the Chinese or should be."

"No shit. He's using a law firm, Rosansky in NYC, to make the arrangements."

At least Labovitz is a pro. Might give him a chance, thought CJ. "I know them."

"Yeah well, they chartered a private jet. Going to fly him out of Washington Executive Airpark. Car service should be here to take him pretty soon."

"Where's he going?"

"Long Island, MacArthur airport. Someone from Rosansky's firm will pick him up and take him to the Waldorf using a reservation under an assumed name."

"What? New York?" CJ shook his head. "They'll be waiting."

Sarno rolled his eyes. "I told him it was dangerous, but he said his wife has travel issues. Anyway, get this, a few days ago, an Amazon package arrived. We searched it. He bought a 3-D mask. Thinks it'll protect him from the cameras. He's using his Swiss identity papers as ID."

CJ scoffed. "Whatever. Still can't believe he's getting off. Anyway, you must be glad to get out of here."

"Got that right. Can't wait. Sent in the final report this morning. Soon as he's out the door, I'm right behind him. Let's go inside. I'll get him."

Boxman marched out, and the two sat in the living room like before.

"Surprised to see you, Jackson," he said with a self-assured smile. "What do you want?"

CJ leveled a stare at him. "I came out here to tell you if it were up to me, you'd be in jail for treason. Ashton was murdered to protect you. Have you even spoken to his daughter?"

Boxman shot him a look back. "Whoa. Hold it, CIA man. Those HAB plans derailed their military moon program for years. They blamed Tien Lee for it, killed him, setting back the Chinese Space Agency." He pointed his finger at CJ. "It's better than any plan you had." He sat back in the chair with a smug look on his face.

CJ felt the blood rush to his face. "You tried to destroy the bacteria intended to save our overheated planet and sent the DNA information to the Chinese. Call that being on our side?"

"According to Grunhart, the DNA information is useless to the Chinese without the living microbes." He waved his hand dismissively. "As far as the bots, I programmed them to give me leverage against you in case I needed something to negotiate with."

CJ glared at him.

Boxman leaned forward and continued, "I know how this looks to you. What I did was risky and my motives were for myself. But none of this would've happened if Jennings didn't rip NASA away from me and made me look like a fool. I had to get out."

CJ's jaws clenched. "You selfish bastard. You sold out your country and tried to sell out the world."

Boxman laughed. "Me, a sellout? Look at Jennings. What a joke. When Barbara waved the money in front of her, all that honor and patriotism evaporated like a snowball in Phoenix. Now I'm free as if nothing happened."

"Minister Wang will come after you over the faulty HAB plans. You'll be looking over your shoulder the rest of your life."

Boxman twitched at the insult. "They blamed Tien Lee for the plans, so maybe I'm off the hook. Anyway, like I said, I have a plan to slip into New York. And no one knows I'm leaving except you and the FBI." Boxman stood up from his chair. "Nice chat, Jackson. Have a good life. I will."

CJ flashed to his two fallen soldiers and felt the rage flare through him. *Gotta leave before I do something stupid.* He turned and hurried out of the house. He flung open the door of his Porsche and raced down the road, passing a disabled truck parked off to the side.

***

Mr. V: *You betrayed Emily and me.*

Mr. F: *NSA tracked you down not us. Should've kept your dick in your pants. They traced your love notes and your Secret Service detail. She ratted you out by the way.*

Mr. V: *I paid you to protect me. Don't think you're going to get away with it.*

Mr. F: *Don't threaten me. You're nobody now. I'm the one who brought the formal charges to Jennings. Remember, because of me, you're not in jail. I can change that.*

Chapter Fifty-eight: Bad Justice

FBI Safe House, Five Minutes Later

A man holding a clip board and dressed in a crisp white shirt exited the large Escalade. He walked up to the front door and rang the doorbell. Agent Sarnow answered.

The driver checked his papers and said, "I'm here for a Dr. Michael Boxman. Is he ready?"

"Hang on. I'll get him." He scanned the limo's logo on the side of the vehicle. It matched his information, but the ride was early. *Told me not to interfere.* He shrugged and yelled down the hallway. "Hey, Boxman, your ride's here."

Boxman pulled his carry-on into the living room and bustled through the front door without saying a word.

"Please sir, let me take your suitcase," said the driver. "Follow me."

They went to the passenger side of the SUV. The driver dropped the suitcase and opened the backseat passenger door. Boxman put one foot in and began to duck inside, then froze. *It can't be. How did they know?*

Boxman tried to pivot but the chauffeur nudged the off-balanced scientist in the rest of the way and locked the door. Boxman's heart raced and his mouth opened but no words came out.

Agent Tom Walker smiled. "Hello, Dr. Boxman."

He felt the prick on his neck and then everything went black. The driver hustled into the front seat.

"Let's get out of here," Walker said.

"Yes, sir. The truck's ready. One minute out."

The big Caddy raced down the road. The disabled box truck CJ observed moments before, now deployed a steel ramp. The truck driver signaled the SUV, and it rolled into the cavernous cargo area. The driver pulled down the rear metal door and latched it shut. Then he pushed a button on the side of the truck, and the hydraulics hummed, folding up the ramp mechanism.

Inside the SUV, the driver turned and faced Walker. "Our cargo plane is fueled and ready. GPS says thirty-one minutes."

Walker pulled out his phone and typed a text.

Minister, mission complete.

***

Monday Evening After Thanksgiving

CJ and Julie's Condo

Julie and CJ settled into the comfort of their couch, drinks in hand, while Gizmo stretched out up next to Julie.

"Nice to get out of town and meet your family, especially your brother," said CJ. "Good guy. But next time, let's not travel on Thanksgiving. What a zoo."

"Fine by me." Julie bit her lip. "Thanksgiving at my mom's brings up a terrible time in my life. I couldn't have done it without you."

"Glad I could help." CJ leaned over and kissed her cheek. "Been meaning to ask you. How are you liking DC?"

Julie sighed. "Okay, sort of."

CJ turned to her. "You're not happy with me?"

Julie patted him on the thigh and shook her head. "I love being with you. You've let me decorate and make changes here, allowing me to make this my home, too. But everything is new. My office, my colleagues, commuting on the Metro, no ocean or mountains," she paused. "I'm still adjusting, takes a lot of energy."

"What can I do to help?"

"Keep doing what you're doing in there." She tilted her head toward the bedroom and smiled. "And let's do trips into the city. Help me familiarize the area. It gives me a sense of place and grounds me."

"It's a deal." He took a sip of his drink. "Anything going on at work?"

"Nothing new. Everyone's getting back into the flow. How about you?"

CJ turned his glass around in his hand. "Jamil called me. Get this. Boxman's car service pulled up to take him to the airport on Wednesday. Twenty minutes later, another car service pulls up for him. Boxman never showed up at the airport, and no one knows where he is."

Julie turned and faced CJ. "Oh, no. Is the FBI looking for him?"

"Nope. Once he received the pardon everyone was ordered hands off."

"You think the Chinese nabbed him?"

"No question." CJ took a sip of his scotch. "I'm sure Wang ordered it. No surprise. Anyway, the FBI checked the cameras on the main roads to the airport. Couldn't find the limo."

"Think he's dead?"

"Yes. Boxman was Wang's source for the faulty HAB plans. If anyone found out, it'd be over for her."

Julie shook her head and took a sip of her wine. "You don't seem too upset an American citizen was abducted by foreigners right under our noses. Usually, that sort of thing bothers you."

"Yeah. Don't get me wrong, I'm not an advocate of what Wang did."

"But?"

CJ gripped his glass. "Boxman betrayed us, and he's partially to blame for the death of Ashton Price. In my view, justice prevailed, but not in a fair or legal way."

"It brings you back to Afghanistan, doesn't it?"

"Yes, it does."

Julie reached out and held his hand. "Anything else bothering you?"

"Yeah, Jennings." CJ paused and looked out the window. "I can't believe she gave Boxman the pardon. It's such a betrayal. Destroys my trust."

CJ grabbed his drink and took a big gulp.

"You okay, baby?" she asked.

"I am because of you. These last few months have been the best in my life. You mean so much to me. I planned something more romantic, but I don't want to wait. Be right back."

CJ hustled back to their bedroom. Moments later, he emerged and knelt in front of Julie. He opened his hand and showed her a small black box. He opened it. The diamond ring glistened in the light.

"Julie, will you spend the rest of your life with me?"

"Yes!" she gasped, tears flooding her eyes. Then she threw her arms around his neck.

Chapter Fifty-nine: Wrap Up

Three Days Later

Phil's office, CIA Headquarters

Marine Two turned into the wind, its rotors creating a dust whirlwind as it landed on the CIA's helipad. Vice President Richard Scott stepped out carrying a small parcel under his arm. Dr. Mary Williams followed behind. Secret Service agents flanked them as they entered the facility.

They marched down the polished hall to Phil Locke's office, where the remaining members of the Magellan Team waited. Julie, Layla, Phil, CJ, and Jamil stood and applauded when Scott entered the room.

The Vice President smiled and raised his hand. "Please sit. I brought some refreshments to celebrate. Director, could you break out the glasses?"

He opened his small case and pulled out a fine California chardonnay and a bottle of twenty-five-year-old scotch from the White House stash. They passed them around and the team filled their glasses. The VP cleared his throat. His voice resonated throughout the room.

"The Magellan team came together and performed brilliantly in the service of our country. No one will ever know the vigilance and determination this group demonstrated, giving the world's elected officials a fighting chance to save our planet. We owe it all to you, Dr. McCray."

Everyone raised their glasses and drank. Julie smiled and blushed.

"As Dr. Williams will remind us," continued the Vice President, "we still have much to do. But the five prototypes are under construction, and they'll be operational in a few months."

Vice President Scott took another sip of his drink and sat down. The room became quiet as the team followed his lead, except for Julie. She opened her computer and everyone at the table turned toward her. She smiled at the group, her eyes gleaming.

"Thank you, Mr. Vice President. I have an official announcement to make. I invoked the Galileo Protocol two weeks ago and the committee has made several decisions. One of them involves us, the Magellan team."

"What's the Galileo Protocol?" Mary asked.

Julie projected the purpose and procedures on the monitor and explained the process.

"Intelligent life, Dr. McCray?" the Vice President asked.

"Yes. We found a metallic hand in one of the core samples from the Gale Crater. I have a picture to show you."

Julie took in the shocked expressions on the team's faces. They leaned forward, staring at the image of the three-fingered hand on the screen, then started asking questions all at once. Julie raised her hands.

"Hold on, everyone. The hand is not biological. It is, however, a product of an advanced lifeform. We can also confirm it did not originate on Mars."

"This is totally cool," Layla said.

"Then where's it from, Dr. McCray?" Mary asked.

"We don't know, and it's why I'm sharing this with you. The Galileo Committee has authorized me to involve you in planning another Mars mission to the Gale Crater. Its goals are to determine how the hand got there, find any remaining pieces, and discover where it came from. Here's our starting point."

Julie typed and brought a picture of the Gale Crater onto the screen.

"During the mission, the MRO swept the Gale Crater searching for chlorates and we uncovered a blank spot. We didn't investigate because we were focused on finding the bacteria."

"What does the blank spot indicate?" Mary asked.

"Means we detected something our satellite wasn't programmed for. We sent C-2 to investigate. Turns out this blank area is a big pile of rocks, the remnants of a landslide. We reprogrammed our satellite to detect the hand's metal and here's what we found."

Julie sent a different picture to the monitor.

"You can see a reflected image approximately ten meters long and three meters wide. We think it's a space capsule. Unearthing it is part of our next mission."

"Amazing," Scott said. "Contact with another intelligent species. We truly are at a pivot point in human history. You have my full support for the mission." He checked his watch. "I must return to the White House. Dr. McCray, brief me as your mission progresses. Congratulations again, and good night."

As the Vice President left, Julie grabbed a chair and sat. She reached for a glass of water, and her hand began to shake as she brought it to her mouth. She glanced over to CJ and tilted her head.

CJ stood and walked behind Julie, helping her out of her chair. "We need to be going too. Thanks, everyone."

On the way to the car, CJ said, "How are you feeling? You look wiped."

"I'm exhausted. The last few weeks just hit me." Julie put her arm around CJ and leaned into him. "Thanks for getting me out of there."

CJ gave her a squeeze. "Hey, your Mars announcement created quite a stir. Big surprise."

"Oh, don't take it personally. I'm only compartmentalizing information. Strictly a need-to-know situation."

CJ smiled. "Touché, smart guy."

***

Once they arrived home, Julie and CJ sat on the couch, having a nightcap with Gizmo stretched out on the arm, licking his paws.

Julie exhaled and stretched her neck back against the cushion. "The Magellan mission's officially over. Thank goodness." She closed her eyes. "It was so intense."

"True, but the one great thing about it was I met you." He leaned over and gave her a gentle kiss. She smiled and snuggled onto his shoulder.

"I thought you deserved more recognition tonight," said Julie. "You guided us rookies through an unknown minefield and had to contend with a troublesome, headstrong woman."

"Well, she better not change."

"Thanks, honey. There is one thing bothering me. The Chinese have the Martian DNA. What are the implications?" Julie sat up. "Do you know anything?"

A stoic look crept onto CJ's face. "No. The President is focusing everyone on the Climate Initiative, including Grunhart. He's growing Martian bacteria as fast as he can to fill the ACFs, so the Chinese situation is backburnered."

"Seems like one of your loose ends. Does it bother you?"

CJ sat up. "That's not the only one. Tell me, how did Boxman know the exact day to escape from DC? The FBI waited for him in New York, but he knew not to go there. Coincidence? And how did the Chinese get the address of the FBI's safe house and the logistics of the car service?"

Julie felt CJ's intensity. "You think the FBI leaked it?"

"How else?" CJ took a sip of his scotch. "Minister Wang had help from our side. It had to be them." CJ looked down at his glass. "But Maykuth didn't hesitate to go after Atkins when we laid out the evidence." His knuckles turned white, gripping his drink. "So maybe I'm wrong."

"I can feel you tensing up. I don't want you having an attack over this. Big picture, things worked out, right?"

"Yeah, at least for now." Then CJ slid back into the cushions and intertwined his fingers with hers. "But you have one more mission step left."

Julie sighed. "Emerson's memorial service. That'll be hard. Come with me?"

"Of course."

***

Four Days Later

Johnson Space Center, Houston

Julie remained in the back of the theater, away from the other NASA dignitaries, during the remembrance ceremony for Commander Bret Emerson. After several heartfelt speeches from fellow astronauts, friends, and loved ones, the mourners streamed out, heading to the peaceful and reflective landscape of the Astronaut Memorial Grove, positioned in front of the Johnson Space Center.

The throng of seventy plus stood quietly at the place where Bret's live oak tree, symbolizing strength and endurance, had been planted. A gentle breeze wafted between the leaves, casting dappled shadows throughout the grounds. Administrator Boyle stood next to the newly rooted tree, looking skyward. He spotted the four Navy jets with red, white, and blue streaming colors, about to perform their commemorative flyover. In a few swift moments their roaring engines disrupted the tranquil grounds, contributing their respects with the rest of the attendees. Only then was his plaque revealed.

CJ held Julie's hand. She waited patiently until the last of the mourners filed by, many laying flowers and whispering prayers in memory of their fallen colleague and loved one. Julie released CJ's hand and approached Bret's memorial alone. She gazed down at the plaque, remembering his last words before his spaceship disintegrated upon reentry. A tear trickled down her cheek. Then she slowly removed her mask and cleared her throat.

"Well Commander, you saved us, all of us. If it wasn't for you, the Magellan capsule would have left the ISS the same time you did, and the debris field would have destroyed it. Now, because of your sacrifice, our Martian bacteria will be placed in five prototype facilities and will start absorbing the greenhouse gases suffocating our planet.

But here's the big news. In those samples, we found an artifact of intelligent life from another star system. We're going back up to check it out. When we find out who they are, I'll be back to tell you the rest of the story."

The End